1635
A Parcel
of Rogues

1635

A Parcel
of Rogues

Eric Flint
Andrew Dennis

1635: A Parcel of Rogues

Copyright © 2016 by Eric Flint & Andrew Dennis

A Baen Books Original

Baen Publishing Enterprises
P.O. Box 1403
Riverdale, NY 10471
www.baen.com

ISBN: 978-1-4767-8109-9

Cover art by Thomas Kidd
Map by Michael Knopp

First printing, January 2016

Distributed by Simon & Schuster
1230 Avenue of the Americas
New York, NY 10020

Library of Congress Cataloging-in-Publication Data

Flint, Eric.
  1635 : a parcel of rogues / Eric Flint and Andrew Dennis.
     pages cm. — (The ring of fire ; 20)
  Summary: "When the diplomatic embassy from the United States of Europe was freed from the Tower of London, most of i
ISBN 978-1-4767-8109-9 (hardback)
1. Alternative histories (Fiction) I. Dennis, Andrew, 1971– II. Title. III. Title: Parcel of rogues.
  PS3556.L548A6185 2016
  813'.54—dc23

                              2015030723

10 9 8 7 6 5 4 3 2 1

Pages by Joy Freeman (www.pagesbyjoy.com)
Printed in the United States of America

To Linda May

Contents

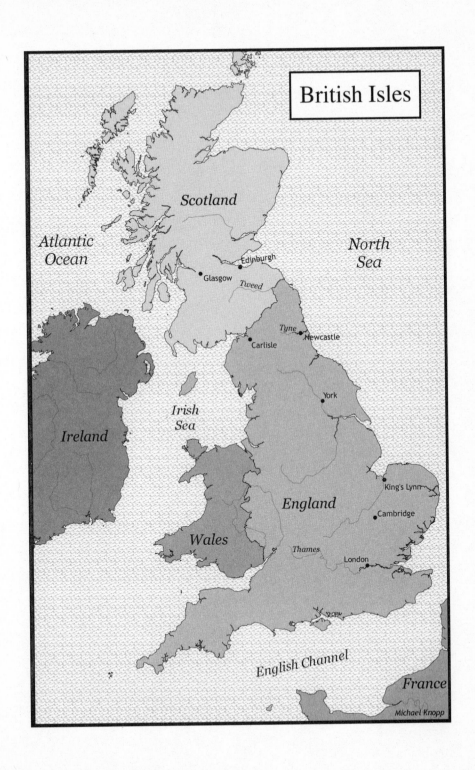

British Isles

Atlantic
Ocean

Scotland

North
Sea

Edinburgh
Glasgow
Tweed

Tyne
Newcastle
Carlisle

York

*Irish
Sea*

Ireland

King's Lynn

England

Cambridge

Wales

Thames

London

English Channel

France

Michael Knopp

Part One

May 1634

Fareweel to a' our Scottish fame,

Fareweel our ancient glory;

Fareweel ev'n to the Scottish name,

Sae fam'd in martial story.

Chapter 1

"All right, let's put our backs to it," said Stephen Hamilton, as the barge carrying the rest of the escapees from the Tower of London began to pull away downriver, Harry Lefferts waving over the stern.

Hamilton waved back, then turned to look north, toward the left bank of the Thames. "We've some rowing to do," he carried on, "and upriver, what's more. Unlike those lucky sods."

Darryl McCarthy grabbed one of the oars racked down the center of the boat and swung it overhead to drop into a rowlock. As the boat turned gently in the current, it brought the receding barge into view. "Hallelujah," he said softly, "I'm finally rid of the Schoolmarm From Hell."

He heard a mild cough and turned to see Cromwell frowning at him from the other end of the thwart he was sitting on. "What?" he asked.

"Young fellow, if you propose to be my recording angel as I go up and down in the world," Cromwell said, "I would ask that you not blaspheme like the devil you make me out to be."

Darryl's jaw dropped.

"He's got a point, Darryl," Gayle Mason called over. She was getting settled by the tiller while Stephen Hamilton was organizing himself on the rearmost thwart alongside Paddy Welch. "You got a potty-mouth on you."

Darryl bit down on the first retort that came to mind. And the second. Because, he realized, both of them had been pretty ripe. Not four-letter stuff, but then that wasn't nearly so big a deal nowadays. His mom hadn't stood for Taking The Name In Vain, and hadn't stood for it in capital letters with quite a lot of volume. Most folks nowadays set the bar on blasphemy even lower than she did. Some set it even lower still. Lowest of all for, let's face it, Puritans. Like, for instance, one Oliver Cromwell.

Not so long ago, while maybe being a bit shamefaced if a lady'd called him on it, Darryl wouldn't have cared two cents what Oliver Cromwell thought. Not Oliver get-you-to-hell-or-to-Connaught Cromwell. Not Oliver butcher-of-Drogheda Cromwell. He could have cared less what the man—demon, rather!—thought of the way a McCarthy spoke.

Now, though . . .

"All right, sorry. I'll watch my mouth." *Goodbye, Schoolmarm From Hell. Hello, Puritan Watchdog.* All the more ironic—a word he'd learned well from that very schoolmarm, who'd been amused by his detestation of the man turning into wary respect—that he'd insisted on following Cromwell to make sure he didn't get up to the atrocities he'd committed in a future history that was now never to be.

"Backs to it, lads," Hamilton called. "Mister Lefferts has left us transport at Stratford. Only a couple of miles up the Lee. Mistress Mason knows the way. Master and Mistress Mackay, Vicky, watch forward if you would. Now, ready oars and—stroke!"

The tide was running with them, fortunately, and the day was shaping up to be a cool morning. Darryl dug his oar in and pulled, watching Hamilton for the right way to do it. Damned if he was going to admit not really knowing what he was doing. Besides, how hard could it be? He'd paddled canoes back up-time, once or twice. There were six men rowing—Hamilton and Welch on the thwart astern of him, and Captain Leebrick and Dick Towson at the front. Alex, Julie and Vicky were perched in the bows on top of the load of baggage up there, with Gayle Mason perched on the crate holding her radio at the back.

Gayle certainly looked like she was enjoying the ride, the sea breeze up the Thames ruffling her hair as she scanned the river ahead. Darryl, for his part, began to find that rowing got old very fast. Like, five minutes fast.

"So, Stratford," he said, timing his words between strokes of the oar, "that the place Shakespeare's from?"

"Different Stratford," Towson said from behind him. "Master Will, God rest him, was a Wiltshire lad. My da knew him. I can sort of remember him, a bit, but I was only a nipper when he went home to die."

"There are a lot of Stratfords," Cromwell remarked, leaning into his oar. "Three in Buckinghamshire that I can think of." *Stroke.* "I used to go fishing at Fenny Stratford, when I was a lad." *Stroke.* "We had cousins there. I remember—" *Stroke.* "It was a long day's ride with my father."

"Two in London," Hamilton remarked. "We're going to the one on the Lea. Bit of a hole on the Colchester road. Marsh country."

"Making good time," Darryl said, after a few minutes, thinking the while that maybe the unit of rowing travel wasn't the mile, it was the backache. Or maybe that was why they called it knots, on boats. Because you got knots in your damned spine. Not that he could say anything with Vicky right behind him. Admitting pain in front of the ladies was bad enough, but a guy's intended? He'd laugh while they sawed his leg off, if it came to that.

"Still downriver," Hamilton said. "We'll be turning up the Lea in a little while."

"Get harder then," Cromwell observed.

"We're catching up to the barge," Julie called back. "I reckon you guys should take a breather. Besides, the testosterone is crinkling the paint on this thing."

"Up oars," Hamilton called, and swivelled on his thwart. "The what is doing what?"

"Oh, come on," Julie said, grinning back as all six rowers glared at her, Darryl hardest of all since he'd known what she was talking about. "Nobody wants to be the sissy who doesn't row as hard as everyone else. Give it up, we're not being followed and not likely to be for hours."

"Well, I wasn't rowing any harder than I learned as a lad," Towson said, "and Master Hamilton set the stroke. How about you fellows?"

"Me neither," Hamilton said. "And of course we're going faster than the barge, they've got fifty souls aboard and there's but the nine of us in this cutter."

"Isn't this a wherry?" Welch asked. He was a little flushed in the face, Darryl was pleased to note.

"No, a wherry's smaller, they're those little boats the watermen use upriver," Towson said. "They have to be of a size set by statute to be licensed. This is bigger, I think Master Lefferts bought this one off a ship. Or stole it, if he didn't like the ship's master. I reckon it was a ship's pulling cutter, the kind they use for towing them out of a lee harbor."

"I didn't know you knew so much about ships, Richard," Leebrick remarked.

"Well, I grew up in the busiest port in England, so I picked up a thing or two. Enough to know I was never going to sea for a living. Did enough rowing as a lad to be sick of the sight of water."

"'Bout quarter-hour, for me," Darryl said, which provoked a round of chuckles.

"We need some forward motion, or we're just going to drift on the current," Gayle called. "Stephen, if you call a slow stroke or something, you boys can save your sweat for going up the Lea."

"Suits," Hamilton said, "although we'll get there slower, I suppose it's as well to get there with some wind left for trouble. Watch me for a slow stroke, lads, and..."

That made things a little easier, Darryl found. With all six rowers pulling, even not making any great effort, the boat felt like it was traveling along at a good pace. After maybe an hour, and the Thames making no less than three near-hairpin turns, Gayle swung the boat hard left—or was it port? Darryl had no idea and cared less—and called out "River Lea, upstream from here, boys!"

"Not so hard, though," Hamilton answered. "The Lea's a marsh river, very slow. We're not going far, just another mile or so. Less, as the crow flies, but there's nowhere to tie up the boat this far down."

Darryl bit down on a groan. And then, on a stream of riper observations. The unit of rowing distance wasn't the backache, that had settled down once he got warmed up. It was the blister. And he couldn't say a damn thing. Boat full of hardasses. Even one of the chicks was a hardass, nobody ever said Julie Mackay was soft. Come right to it, Gayle was made of pretty strong stuff and if Vicky was a little less steely, it was only by comparison with the two lady shooters. If Darryl was going to hold up the West Virginia hillbilly end of hardassdom in this boat, he'd have to keep his mouth shut. Even leaving out of account that there were women present, no matter how salty.

"Things are closing in somewhat, too," Alex Mackay called back from where he was spotting for his wife. "Sharp eyes all round, if you please, we're in range of even muskets now."

Made sense, Darryl thought. The banks of the Lea might consist of low green growth that wouldn't hide a man with a musket, unless he was willing to dig right in, but they were maybe twenty, thirty yards away each side. A musketeer willing to wade—and somehow armored against a boat full of hardasses with up-time weapons, granted—could probably get to ten yards' range without getting his nuts wet.

"If one of you could stand?" Hamilton suggested. "We're in flatter water now, it should be less tiring. And it makes sense we should be watching for river-rats and the like. An alert watch will deter them, if there are any about."

"More a winter thing," Towson said, easing into the faster, stronger stroke Hamilton had started setting. "This time of year they're taking laboring work in the fields. Easier than robbing passing boats."

"Easier'n rowing them, too," Darryl added. "You know, this is the first time I ever rowed a boat? Paddled a canoe a couple times, but never rowed." Apart from the sore hands, it was actually getting easier. And he was definitely better warmed up now. It helped that he had Hamilton ahead of him, who seemed to know what he was doing, and he was picking up little tricks as he went along.

"You're doing fine for a first-timer, then," Towson said. "The basics are easy enough. Most of the rest is working at it enough to be able to do it all day and every day without killing yourself, such as the watermen do."

As he spoke, Gayle was putting the tiller hard over to the right, which nearly had Darryl clashing oars with Hamilton—on the inside of the turn, Hamilton was instinctively shortening his stroke and he'd nearly missed the change in rhythm.

"Of course there are some little things to pick up still," Towson said, chuckling, "which is why you're on this side between me and Stephen, and Master Cromwell is by you between Patrick and Anthony. Our two worst rowers where they can take stroke first and have a better rower behind them to pick up their mistakes."

"Aye," Cromwell added, "it was rowing that convinced me to stay a farmer. Did I run away to sea, I might have to do this more often. For all of me, I think rowing ought be a punishment for a blaspheming tongue."

"All right, I got the message," Darryl said, quite amused despite himself at the quiet and dry wit.

"Hard left coming up," Gayle called.

"That means you take a longer stroke," Towson said. "Watch Stephen for the right length and pressure."

Darryl just grunted. All this effort and blisters and he had to think about what he was doing? Yeah, the guys who'd decided to stay on land were as right as right could be. Not a whit of argument from him, no sir.

"Just leave the boat," said Anthony Leebrick. "But make sure you tie it up properly, Richard. Adrift, it's likely to draw attention."

Towson gave him a look that was not filled with admiration. "Indeed. And what other sage advice do you have, O my Captain? Make sure that I don't drive the wagon stark naked, shouting in every village we pass through that we're the ones who just carried out the biggest escape from the Tower of London in English history?"

Leebrick gave him a grin that was somewhat sheepish. "Well... point taken."

Gayle Mason, meanwhile, had been giving the wagon that Patrick Welch had brought out of the nearby village's stable a look that was even less admiring. "I thought Harry's coffers were the envy of Midas. He couldn't afford anything better than this?"

"Which is exactly why I'm riding one of the horses," Julie said. "No way I'm trusting my spine to that thing."

"Swell." Gayle gave the horses in question an equally sceptical examination. "But as I believe you know, 'Gayle Mason' and 'horseback' go together about as well as ham and ... and ... and ... whatever. Not eggs. Maybe tofu. Or rutabagas."

Spotting the smile on Oliver Cromwell's face, Gayle asked him, "And what's so funny?" The expression on her face, however, removed the crossness of the words themselves. Now that she and Oliver had been able to spend a little time together in person, the very peculiar quasi-romance that had developed over months of nothing but conversations on walkie-talkies seemed to be ...

Coming along quite nicely, she thought. Still very early days, of course.

"Actually, I think your Harry Lefferts is something of a genius at this work." Cromwell nodded toward the beat-up old wagon and the four nags that drew it. "This won't draw any attention at all. Not anywhere in the English countryside, and certainly not in the Fens."

Alex Mackay swung into the saddle of one of the other horses. Gayle thought there was something vaguely comical about the motion. He went into the saddle with all the ease and grace you'd expect from an experienced cavalry officer. Much the way a champion motocross racer might climb onto a tricycle.

Those other horses weren't quite nags. But she hoped they didn't pass a glue factory along the way, or the horses would head for it unerringly.

"All right, all right. Oliver—you too, Darryl—give me a hand loading the radio gear into this heap, will you?"

To Gayle's gratification, "give me a hand" meant that Oliver took one end of the heavy damn thing and Darryl took the other. To her was left the proper chore of giving orders.

"But be careful putting it into the wagon. Be very careful."

Cromwell grunted as he helped lift the thing up to the wagon's bed. "Fragile, is it? You wouldn't think so."

"I'm not worried about the radio."

Cromwell smiled. Darryl kept his mouth shut. The blisters had faded to a dull ache over the last half hour of rowing that had brought them to this little village by the ford, but lifting the radio crate up into the wagon had popped everything open. He wandered off, fishing quietly in his pockets for a handkerchief to clean off the gunk. It didn't look like it'd be worth unpacking everything to get the aid kit out just yet. He could wait until they got to wherever they were stopping for the night. Get some boiled water, too.

"Darryl McCarthy, you are an idiot," Vicky said.

He turned round and saw she was watching him. "Isn't much," he said, shrugging. "Just some blisters. It can wait until we stop."

"Infection? Does that up-time word not ring any bells? You spent long enough locked up with the Simpsons. Did Rita not teach you anything?" If Vicky had a fault, it was that she had the native Londoner's love of sarcasm in double measures. Heaping helpings, in fact. She grabbed Darryl by the collar. "Come on, they'll have salt and hot water and clean rags at the inn here.

You'll sit still while I clean those hands before we ride, it shan't take a quarter hour. And you'll not ride well with sore hands. The reins will hurt you and you'll hurt the poor horse most likely."

Darryl grinned, trying to put as good a face as possible on getting mother-henned. "Wouldn't want to hurt those poor horses. They're very poor horses. So poor they're like to keel over dead if we're not real careful."

"Quite," she said, steering him into the back door of the inn.

Vicky worked quickly, as she'd promised. A penny had got them all the boiled water and rags and salt they needed, and more than Darryl had wanted on account of that stuff *stung*, dammit. They were out and Hamilton and Cromwell were conferring.

"Back into town would be a poor move, I think," Hamilton was saying. "If the hue and cry has gone up, we'll be heading right into it."

Cromwell made a face. "I know the way on the North Road, and the Cambridge road. I've never been far into Essex. If you can be sure of taking us to Cambridge, I know the way from there."

Hamilton shrugged. "I've been as far as Colchester a couple of times, and I think there's a road to Cambridge from Romford, which we'll pass through on the way. Just a lot of simple travelers, heading out to the fens."

Cromwell chuckled. "Aye, such simple folk. Five plain soldiers, three up-timers, as the word seems to be, and one gentleman farmer who's not seen his farm these eighteen months past. If Romford is a town of any size, we should skirt it, not be seen there. As we change our road, best we not be seen, eh?"

"I think you've the right of it. Your wounds all bound up, Darryl?"

Darryl grinned back. So much for hoping nobody noticed. "Not a job I'd ever done, so I got blisters, and Vicky wouldn't take no for an answer." He shrugged. "Probably as well. I was going to leave it until we stopped, but maybe I'd've picked up an infection."

"Aye, cuts on your hands, they give you lockjaw. Especially in the web of your thumb. So my mother told me, and I never had cause to doubt it. Perhaps it's the dirt in the cuts, did I understand that right?" Cromwell was looking over at Gayle.

"Sure. It's tetanus, and that lives in the soil pretty much everywhere. A cut on your hands will let it get into your system if you're working with the soil, which is where the superstition comes from." She caught sight of the look on Cromwell's face. "Not superstition in that sense, silly. Just something that people believe that isn't so."

"Ah." They'd all noticed, in contact with the man during their stay in the Tower, that he could be a little touchy on theological matters. Gayle had learned that he'd come to the Puritan faith, and even to serious religious belief, late in life—only a few years previously, as it happened—and he still had all of the recent convert's zeal. Getting captured and thrown in the Tower for something that he hadn't done yet and never would hadn't helped steady him down any, either. The associations he'd picked up for the word *superstition* tended toward fervent denunciations of the Catholic church.

"This is science, as you call it?" he asked.

"Yup." Gayle nodded.

"Had a tetanus shot before the Ring of Fire," Darryl added, "on account of if you're out hunting a cut can get you lockjaw, and a miner always has a few scrapes and cuts. So I figured the few dollars a vaccine'd cost was worth it."

"How do these vaccines work, then?" Cromwell asked as he mounted his horse, "I think that might make a pleasant conversation as we ride."

Chapter 2

The Tower of London
London, England

"Well, they certainly made a mess."

"My lord, those responsible—" Captain Holderness said, visibly sweating despite the cool of the spring morning.

Richard Boyle, first earl of Cork, made a chopping gesture. For silence, certainly, but a nervous man who had just had the biggest breakout from Europe's supposedly most secure prison happen on his watch, well, he could see the stroke of a headsman's axe in the gesture. "Those responsible are already making their way to whatever refuge they have chosen. This was long in the planning and I don't doubt Strafford—Wentworth, we must now call him, since his impeachment—laid his plans deeply enough that he ensured he was ready to break out of this place if he was ever put there. The weasel always has a back entrance to his burrow, mark you well, the weasel always has a back entrance."

"My lord, the Americans, Cromwell—"

"Are Wentworth's bargaining counters. Do not let me learn you have said otherwise in the matter, sir. Do not let me learn it. We have our traitor, and he has compounded his treason with misprision and flight. That is the truth of the matter, whatever else you may have heard or inferred from a too-hasty consideration of the evidence before you."

Of course, the earl himself had been here only minutes,

himself, and now stood before the wholly-slighted St. Thomas' Tower looking at the havoc wrought on the medieval structure by the explosions. If he was condemning other interpretations as "hasty" it was for form's sake.

"As you say, m'lord," Holderness agreed, hastily.

"Cromwell will have been taken as a weapon to use against the rightful power in England. The man would have been Wentworth's competition in the other history, so for certain sure that was why he was locked up so readily. Now that Wentworth is exposed and scotched, well, the devil will use what tools come to hand. The Americans, there to gain him entree at the Swede's court, no doubt. Or possibly as hostages to win him favor with Richelieu. We shall see where he appears next." Boyle sighed. "Nevertheless, the stable door is open, the horse is bolted, we should at least try and chase the beast."

The next day, Boyle greeted James Graham, fifth earl of Montrose, at his London town house. Like so many such meetings since the Ring of Fire, they exchanged a look. Any man of notability in these times had something of a record of what he would have done in the future that never was, and whether a man believed in the truth of those histories that had poured out of Thuringia over the past three years, they were always present in mind.

Montrose had tried, in the civil war that would have been, to fight at first for royal power against the Scots churches, episcopal and presbyterian alike, and for all his military successes, had made no progress in getting the divines to stick to spiritual matters. He'd fought for the covenanters against the bishops to break their power, and switched sides to the royalists to keep the presbyters from securing more political power. He'd led highland regiments to great effect, during the times when he could keep the prospect of plunder in front of them, and led disciplined Irish mercenaries when the highlanders failed him.

Here and now, he was a handsome man in his early twenties, hereditary chief of Clan Graham and, after a shaky start—acceding to the earldom at the age of fourteen was hardly an auspicious start—now a serious figure in Scots politics. And, if he'd read his own future biography, he had his mind concentrated wonderfully by the knowledge that his eventual fate had been to be hung, drawn and quartered by the king's enemies, his head on a spike for ten years.

If that weighed heavily on his mind on this bright afternoon in London, however, he gave no sign. "Things have changed mightily since I received your invitation to visit, my lord Cork," he said. The faintest hint of a smile was about his lips as he spoke.

"If all this were happening to some other nation, my lord Montrose, I'd laugh heartily at their misfortune. And I take no pleasure in having the king's confidence in times like these, I assure you."

There was a bitter truth. Charles's own folly had put him firmly in Boyle's hands, given England an *eminence grise* to match the one that had been an easy target for the pamphleteers of France's enemies for so long, and Boyle found himself frantically working to keep a fracturing nation together rather than advancing his own wealth and power. It would take all the cunning at his disposal not to end up with his own head on a spike. Even with Cromwell in the Tower, there had been more than enough discontented gentry to foment rebellion. With Cromwell now out and given the cause for a grudge that would awe even Boyle's own feud-happy Irishmen, it was time to try attacking the problem from the other end.

Boyle had seen that in the beginning of the civil wars that would have ravaged England, Scotland and Ireland had been plagued by enough factions that none could convincingly end the conflict and secure a settlement by force in the beginning. It took twenty years for enough blood to be let to exhaust them all to the point that reason and the settlement of the restoration could prevail. If there was anything left to the royal power at this time, Boyle was resolved to use it to nip that in the bud before it bloomed into civil strife.

"Nor would any man with more wit than a rabbit, my lord," Montrose said, "and I've no truck with those that say you press your own advantage on the king's misfortune."

"Nor should you. And I'm not surprised that plenty are saying that. I'm not ashamed to say I've always striven to do well by myself, ever since I went to Dublin with the wealth I could carry and my sword and dagger to keep it with, but what price mere baubles and rich lands if the nation is crumbling about them?"

"Quite, quite," Montrose said, "but how can I be of service to

His Majesty in the matter? I'll confess I was surprised to receive his summons from my estates. It's said I was destined to take against the king for some of that future, and it has gone passing hard for such as me lately."

"Results matter, my lord, results. His Majesty, and I can't say for sure as I had not his confidence at the time, was likely of the hope that a man who'd died for the king in one time might be inclined to measure his loyalty better in another. And I'm of like mind, my lord Montrose, for a strong king can guard his subjects better than a weak one."

"That's right enough. How, then, to make a strong king of a weak one?"

Boyle smiled. The question itself could be counted treasonous, assuming as it did that Charles Stuart was a weak king. But then, there were village idiots who could see that not all was well with His Majesty's rule. Only able to stay in power through foreign subsidy and foreign troops on the streets of London, he was now bedridden with his injuries, unlikely to ever be more than a halting cripple. It was taking all Boyle's political skill not to look like the very epitome of the evil counselor. He'd read of the famous dictum a future Cromwell would utter, of putting a sword in the tenth man's hand when nine in ten subjects would disagree with his policy, but Boyle had seen armed men swarmed under by sufficiently angry mobs at odds less than that. The trick was getting the nine to think the tenth man's sword was there for their protection and benefit, and if they could be brought to think that the unpopular policy was imposed by someone who had their best interests at heart, so much the better.

"My lord, we are faced with factions and parties within and foreign conspiracy without. Wentworth, rot him, cozened the king into taking French gold in return for provoking Gustav Adolf and his Americans. Offered them further insult by imprisoning their embassy. Failed to keep them secure once imprisoned, so now their agents are loose within the realm. Factions within, conspiracy without. The foreign troubles, His Majesty may, with good advice, attend to himself. The factions within, we must repair ourselves so the kingdoms seem strong behind the king."

Montrose gave Boyle a level, measuring stare. As an assessment of the situation, that mixed truth with bare-faced lies in about equal measure to offer a compromise everyone could accept without taking a portion of blame down with the bitter medicine. Good politics, in other words.

"His Majesty will have to make some concessions on episcopal power, if only to make the presbyterians less strident. Power outside the kirk, mind you. If we can stop the presbyters' and bishops' power at the walls of their churchyards, I think something can be done. And there's precedent for it, now, with half of Europe crying freedom of religion. Do we only stop the mouths of the divines in politics, three parts of our factions become nothing."

Boyle rocked a hand. "My learning on the estates of the Scots Parliament is a mean thing at best, but I recall one of the estates is the bishops?"

"Aye, but if we get them to maintain the fiction that they're there as larger landowners as much as lords spiritual, and promise not to try and impose overmuch on the presbyterians for the time being, I know at least some of them will shut up."

"If I can secure that from His Majesty?" Boyle was pretty certain of that. Charles Stuart was no longer quite so melancholy as to sign and seal anything in front of him so as not to be troubled in his grief and pain, but he would still give way to any sufficiently persistent attempt at persuasion. Boyle would have found the experience a heady one, wielding the power of the king without trammels, were he not mindful of what tended to happen to men in that position.

"If you can, then there is much I might do to get Scotland united behind His Majesty. Argyll's the rub, though, I'll warn you. The man's only still at liberty by being the most powerful man in Scotland and he'll not consent to anything that makes him a second-rate power in a united kingdom. Not easily, at any rate."

"Argyll's the man I want you to work on, then. We can promise him much if we can only keep the kingdoms together, united or not. If we fall to squabbling now, with the USE looking greedily across the North Sea, he'll be but a pilchard in that ocean, warn him of that. We can discuss the details later, but now I know your mind I can seek to persuade His Majesty on the subject of the bishops."

Montrose wished him luck he'd not need, and took his leave.

Chapter 3

Romford
Northeast of London

"That's Romford?" Darryl stood up in the wagon bed for a better look, and then wished he hadn't. There was the usual haze that hung over every town in these pre-clean-air-act days, perhaps a little thicker than the ordinary, and the wind had backed easterly. A gust brought a billow of the small town's haze and even at most of a mile it made his eyes water. "What're they doin' there, burnin' turds?" He sat down again, trying manfully not to retch. Even in an age when the concept of below-ground sewerage drew blank looks from most, the place reeked.

"Famous for leatherworking," Towson said, "and the tanner's trade uses stuff to make a man puke. Nightsoil's the least of it, and you don't want to know what the scrapings bins smell like when they're near full. Be thankful it ain't high summer, mate."

"We'll be upwind soon enough," Hamilton added. He'd sampled the wagon's suspension briefly and announced he'd rather walk, and wasn't horseman enough nor light enough to inflict himself on any of their elderly nags. He'd set a stoical pace that he looked like he could keep up around the clock for a week, and given the impression he really wasn't much more than idling. Darryl himself had no idea what his endurance for a long walk might be like, and announced he wasn't going to test it until they either had to or he could do it without risking anything.

19

Oddly, that had got him more of an admiring look from Vicky than anything he'd ever done in the way of more traditional showing off. *Okay, turns out she likes smart.* He'd spent some uneasy time mulling that before he decided he'd just have to do the best he could and hope.

"There's a left just here," Alex Mackay called back. He was standing in his stirrups and using his spotting scope to check the country away to the left. "Looks like it might could take us to the Cambridge road, too."

"Take it, then," Darryl said, "If we get lost, the king's guys won't be able to find us either, right?"

That earned a round of chuckles.

"I like your thinking, Darryl," Leebrick said, "and comes to worst we can always just use farm tracks and cut across fields. I've slogged enough military carts through the shite to know how it's done, and Mister Cromwell's a farmer so he'll know better than any of us the tricks of it. After that it's just compass work to find our way. And your up-time compasses are excellent pieces. The trick you have of making such good ones so cheaply is a fine one."

He pulled the instrument Harry Lefferts had given him out of his pocket and flipped the cover open. It was down-time made. There had been some guys in Magdeburg making small quantities of Bakelite for things like this when Darryl left, and doubtless there were more guys at it now with the coal gasworks there turning out coal tar by the bargeload. Getting a compact, durable compass of that size and accuracy down-time meant paying an instrument maker for the results of a lot of hard, skilled work. Harry had been able to bring enough for his whole crew to have a spare and a few to give as presents. They were, after all, not just useful for traveling. Leebrick was inordinately pleased with his—liquid compasses were unknown in the seventeenth century, even as simple a thing as a notch-and-wire sight was the province of expensive surveyors' instruments, and getting a compass that didn't have a sundial gnomon getting in the way of using it for navigation was a lost cause. On some level he knew it was a lot cheaper than it had any right to be, and a perfectly reasonable small, practical present from someone he had helped. Mostly, he kept taking bearings with it because the novelty had yet to quite wear off. Darryl suspected that, up-time, he'd have been one of those guys who had to have the new gadget the minute it came out. What he was going to be like when he got to the USE where things like that were increasingly common and getting cheaper all the time was anyone's guess, but Darryl could see, somewhere in Leebrick's future, a headline like *Englishman Found Dead Under Huge Pile Of Gadgets: Starved Self To Buy More Toys.*

Two hours later and Darryl was wishing Harry's presents had included a lot more rope—on principle, they didn't have enough, too much was just plain impossible—and some decent winching gear. Hell, a tracked bridge-laying tank would've been ideal, there was bound to be some clever guy working on something like that back in Magdeburg. As it was, the river that Romford stood on was still in their way even after skirting the place; they needed to get across to cut over to the road that led north to Cambridge. It wasn't a big river—they had the horses walked over, laden with most of the wagon's freight, in fifteen minutes, and penned up in a nearby field alongside some cows that nobody seemed to be minding for the moment. While the horses goofed off in best equine style—ambling about, taking a moment to roll, sampling the local weeds—it was left to the humans to figure out getting the wagon over without wrecking the thing. The horses could always be brought back when there was heavy pulling to do. And, of course, there was a late lunch to have.

"This," Cromwell said, "is going to be a right pig."

"It's the steep banks that do it," Leebrick said. "We could do with fascines for this, but that'd leave too much trace."

Hamilton emerged from under the wagon. "We should be able to get the axles off and then it's just britches' arse power to get it over the stream."

"I was afraid of that," Darryl put in. "I ain't afraid of hard work, I'm a miner. Don't mean I have to like it."

"The man that does is a bloody fool," Towson said, "but standing about griping about the business won't get anything done. Who's going under to get the axles off?"

"Best be Darryl, I think," Hamilton said, "I think Captain Lefferts has done some fettling under here, nothing you can see from above, but the ironmongery's...odd-looking."

"Yeah?" That was definitely worth a look. When he got under the wagon, he had a low whistle to let out. You could certainly not see any difference from up above, but under the cart the usual blacksmiths' work—ranging from nearly as good as a twentieth-century machine shop to brutal and slapdash, but usually massively overbuilt—had been replaced with machined parts. Bearings, bolts, axle bushings, all were distinctly modern with thin timbers screwed in place to hide anything that wasn't immediately obvious. The suspension was seventeenth-century design—not much more than some metal hanging straps, and those only enough to give a bit of flex over rough ground—but the steel was machined, up-time style. Whether Harry had brought a kit of parts on the off chance or a small set of portable machine shop tools, Darryl had no idea, but it was a hell of a feat of forward planning. It looked like a seventeenth-century English common carrier's wagon, standard issue, but it was a hell of a lot lighter and more reliable.

"You coulda told me, Harry," he complained under his breath, and then, louder, "gonna need some light under here, and the small red toolbox, the one with my socket set in it. I'll yell out when I need stuff lifted." If Harry hadn't had his guys alter this thing to be taken apart easily, Darryl was going to have a quiet word with that boy about tricks and the missing of same.

It turned out to be even easier than his first guess. The bed came off in one piece and was an easy, if cumbersome, lift between four guys. The frame and tongue came off in three parts after a few seconds of swearing at each lock-nut, and the wheels turned out to have metal bushings around the axle and be suspiciously heavy for plain wood. If there weren't steel reinforcing rods in there somewhere, Darryl would be very surprised. And the axles were split, the split cunningly hidden in a turned wooden sleeve that kind of looked like a repair to the axle-tree from a distance. Each side could rotate independently on, yes, sturdy roller bearings rather than the standard-issue bit-of-wood-between-two-pegs-with-a-ladle-of-tallow. There was even a block of wood fitted in each, bearing on a discreet metal sleeve, that provided an authentic squealing noise to hide the fact that the axles had proper bearings. Darryl had just assumed that one of Harry's guys had thrown some extra grease in there to make sure the thing wasn't quite as bad as it looked. Turned out Harry'd had a whole bunch extra done, out of sight.

"Harry's getting to be a real sneaky son of a bitch, ain't he?" Darryl remarked to Gayle as he was loading his tools on the wagon when they were over. "You'd never know but that weren't a perfectly ordinary wagon."

Gayle grinned. "She might not look like much, but she's got it where it counts?"

"Something like that. We get time, and if it looks like we're going a long way in that thing, I can think of a few improvements. I think Harry tried too hard to be sneaky. He missed a few places he could've got away with some more things. We find a good carpenter's shop, maybe get some parts from a blacksmith, we can put some four-bar suspension links in there, which wouldn't look much different to what the frame's made like already. Some leaf springs, we could get a real smooth ride, even better wheel wear than we're getting, and a lot more speed if we could just find some better horses. Be pretty obvious if we had to take off fast—it'll go faster and smoother than any wagon got any right to, but by that time we're not gonna be worryin' about sneaky."

"And if the complicated mechanism breaks at speed?" Leebrick might have the first stirrings of gadget-happiness, but he knew what a coach crash could do, having seen the king he was supposed to be guarding nearly die in one. His queen actually did die in it. And come right to it, he was a career soldier, a man who knew exactly what excessive complication did under pressure.

"I'll have to check it carefully, but I think I can arrange it so the axle fails back into the mountings it's in now. Won't be perfect, but it'll stay driveable, and still have all the advantages of the stuff Harry did. If we're going a long way, we'll have a chance to test it."

Gayle nudged Vicky. "Cute, when he talks dirty, ain't he?"

Vicky grinned. "Very." She'd made her way over and hugged his arm.

Darryl decided he could take a lot of mockery for the sake of that. "Keep it up, ladies, I'm on the way to a sensitive artistic disposition as it is."

"Keep it up by all means," Cromwell butted in. "The humility will do him good, but let us keep it up on the journey. Fifty miles at least to Cambridge, and we need to find shelter before dark."

"Now *that* is the Cromwell I learned about at my momma's knee. Malicious." Darryl grinned. He genuinely couldn't take it amiss. He'd got his girl on his arm, he'd just done an interesting nearly-an-auto-and-as-close-as-it-got-hereabouts job, and there was a possibility of tinkering with a vehicle to make it go faster in the near future. There were ways for life to get better, but mostly they involved huge amounts of cash, unlimited free beer, and Vicky turning out to have a frisky twin sister.

That night, they stopped at a barn they'd paid a small handful of farthings for the use of, along with some firewood and a basket of what the farmhouse had to spare by way of food. Darryl took an early watch since he wanted the last of the daylight to make sure he was up to speed on maintaining his guns. It was hardly comfortable working on a spread of cloth while he sat cross-legged on his coat, but an armful of hay helped. He hadn't fired anything since the last time he'd cleaned them, but a long ride in a wooden box in a grubby wagon would probably have gunked up the oil some. And care was more important now than ever. Replacing these was getting more and more possible as down-time metalwork caught up to twentieth-century standards, but it'd be decades before it ever got as cheap as it'd been. He'd stripped his collection down to a basic rifle, shotgun and pistol when the call went out for stuff for the army. Back up-time they'd been his old reliables, all stuff he could keep and maintain on a young miner's pay and for a pretty long time if he ever got laid off. Cheap, plain-vanilla stuff but in the seventeenth century, this was high-end work for a skilled gunsmith who'd charge a premium to cover the loans on the modern tooling he'd've bought to do this kind of work.

Set against that, oil and pull-throughs and a little time and effort were pretty damned cheap.

"I do like to see you working with your hands like that," Vicky said, sitting beside him and resting her chin on his shoulder so she could watch him work.

"I noticed you seem to like that kinda stuff," Darryl said, feeling no more than a mild moment of panic. He'd almost started to appreciate Hamilton's approval at a gut level, and anyway they were out in the evening sun in full view of everyone. Whatever the down-timers might say about approving of a betrothed "coming through the window" to get in ahead of the wedding, up-time that sort of thing was a big deal. And, well, scratch a hillbilly and you'll find a bred-in-the-bone conservative-with-a-small-c.

"I talked with Miz Melissa about that," Vicky said, "and she said it was probably growing up surrounded by Yeomen Warders that did it. All of the decent men I've ever known have been men of their hands, both ways a body can mean that. So when I took a shine to you, it was so nice to see you could use your hands too. Proper manly, it is."

As she spoke, she was using her own hands, running one up the back of his shirt and rubbing his spine. "Heh," he said, "keep doing that and I'm gonna start purring like a cat, see how manly that is. And didn't Miz Mailey have somethin' to say about liking what's manly?"

"A little. We talked about it a lot, actually. I quite like doing a lot of the woman's work stuff, and don't mind it so long as the man's doing the man's work. Fair, you see? She said she could see that, so long as it was me doing the choosing. And she said I'd been spoilt, what with most of the men in my family being hard workers, plenty of women didn't get the choice, and to see how they'd like it if I'd wanted to follow a man's trade. Well, I told her about my second cousin, Annabel, she's quite a bit older than me, and she's a journeyman wheelwright over by Cripplegate, and nobody much minds. Pays her livery dues and everything."

"That so? Well, whatever suits, long as its fair, I'm fine with it. You ever do any shooting?" He picked up his deer rifle and slipped the bolt he'd got nicely clean back into place. "Couldn't rightly practice now while we're guests and I reckon those kids in the farmhouse'll be going to bed soon, but we could go over the care and feeding of these here."

"Maybe another time. I've fired muskets a time or two, and I've been along fowling with my dad on Hackney Marsh. For now, can we just sit and watch the sun go down? We've been scheming for weeks, running since the morning, and we're probably going to be doing some hard traveling for a while yet, finding Master Cromwell's children, poor man, and getting to Scotland. This might be the last comfy time we get, hey?"

"Might at that," Darryl said, putting the rifle back down, and packing away the oil bottles and tools into the wooden box he transported them in. "I guess there's a time to relax, and if this ain't it I don't know when is."

Vicky answered with another nuzzle against his shoulder. "Until we can get a room of our own at some inn, hey?"

Darryl chuckled. "Hope you looked around for Stephen before you said that, honey."

She scratched between his shoulder blades. "He likes you, silly. And it's not like we can't marry whenever we please. We don't even have to do it in secret unless you've got people who'd object."

"Don't we have to stop somewhere, marriage banns or something?" Darryl had a vague memory of hearing, probably in some old movie watched through the deadening fug of a hangover, about couples from England running away to Scotland to get married. A town just over the border, something Green, but he'd never taken the trouble to remember it. Girl stuff, basically.

"Rita thought that too, when she had a little chat with me about you. Me and Mum set her straight. Don't need a church at all, there's some as says marriage isn't even a sacrament. Of course, if we was to marry with just Stephen as a witness for the family I'd never hear the end of it. Although Mum did say if we couldn't wait until everyone was together for the celebration, she'd understand. Not that I'm going to take her word for it, she's got a mouth on her if she's annoyed."

Darryl called up his mental file on Vicky's mother Isabel and decided that he, too, would verge on the side of caution. The scary thing was, the woman didn't look or act like a ravening monster most of the time, but Darryl had watched from the Tower's inner walls one time while she took a couple of mercenary privates to task for disregarding the hygiene regulations Rita Simpson had drawn up. None of the Yeoman Warders had missed on them by so much as a thousandth of an inch—professionals all, with good reason to take Rita's word for medical matters—but the mercenaries King Charles had dumped on them toward the end of their stay in the Tower had been a different story.

The resulting explosion—no, detonation! brisance!—of furious denunciation had had more than one sergeant within earshot taking notes. Yeah, pissing off Vicky's mum was a bad idea. Especially since it was such a reasonable request. He'd spent time taking his ease with those folks, seen them with cause to celebrate, and there was every reason to think that Vicky's nuptials would be the kind of party that could be seen from space.

"Yeah. I'd love to just marry you quiet-like." Darryl noted that the internal critic that'd recoiled in horror at the thought of marriage now just sat in the corner muttering *fine, not like I care whether you listen to me anyway.* "But it'd be a shame to disappoint your folks."

She gave his arm a squeeze. "That's why I want a private room at an inn. One with a window for you to come in through. Tradition's important, y'see."

Darryl squeezed back. "Tradition be damned," he growled, "if there ain't no window, I got dynamite that'll tend to that little detail right quick."

"I love it when you talk dirty, Darryl."

Chapter 4

The Tower of London

"Is Finnegan here yet?" the earl of Cork asked Captain Holderness, the moment he entered the still-half-destroyed ruins of what had once been St. Thomas Tower.

Startled, the captain looked up from his examination of the hole in the wall. What he hoped to find there, this many days after the explosion that had blown the hole, was a mystery.

The captain glanced from Boyle to the corner behind him.

"Here, y'lordship," came a voice from that corner. "And a fine mess you have for me."

Boyle whirled round and addressed the man. "Behind me, by stealth, Finnegan—not lost your touch coming over the water?"

Finnegan grinned, a world of villainy in the broad, charming smile. "Not hardly, not hardly at all, y'lordship."

Boyle grinned back. There was more than a little mockery in the title Finnegan gave him, but there was no cause for offense, if you knew him. The ruffian respected nobody who couldn't get a knife to his throat to compel it. His father had been cut from the same cloth, albeit with less of a veneer of good taste and manners. Boyle had been driven out of his estates by the aftermath of the O'Neil rebellion, and when he got back in he'd made sure, through judicious use of such men as the Finnegans, that none of the seeds of rebellion lay dormant in his lands. It had the happy side-effect of keeping them busy away from stealing other mens'

29

horses and cattle, both popular pastimes in the wilder parts of Ireland. Paying for a little education and training for such men in their youth reaped dividends. Paying for a lot more education for their sons in turn, and hold out the prospect of an income for those lads that didn't come from brute farming or thievery, and they'd rob the teeth out of the devil's head for you. It was the kind of long-term thinking that Boyle liked, and excelled at.

Rapid improvisation in response to events was not his strongest suit, he knew, but if a fellow had laid the groundwork and ensured he had a ready supply of the Finnegans of this world at hand, then surprises could be handled.

"A fine mess, indeed, Finnegan. And knowing that such were about to be made, why, who could I send for across the water but you?" Boyle rubbed his hands against the briskness of the morning. "Have you not made some fine messes in your time? I'm sure you'll be the right fellow to clear this one up."

"Ah, well, if that turns out the right thing, yer earlness, sure and I'll see it done. If not, well, who could yez have sent for over the water but me? By the by, and sure it's only idle curiosity, but who's the langer, here? And what's his part in this mess?"

Finnegan tilted his head at Holderness as he spoke, and Boyle could see a look of concern on the man's face as he tried to work out what he'd been called. Deciding that he didn't need Finnegan killing a man in a duel to add to the day's tomfoolery, Boyle waved him off. "You've plenty to be about, Holderness. And since it's plain you've no Irish, Mister Finnegan addressed you with a title of the respect he feels you're due. I know him of old as a man keen to show all proper respect."

With Holderness safely away, Finnegan returned his attention to his master after a thoughtful-looking inspection of the damage to the Tower. In truth, not as bad as it looked, but plenty to cover a mass escape. "Almost like they were really only trying to make it look good, y'earlship. How many of the regular garrison are missing? With their families?"

"Sharp, Finnegan, yes, there are some Yeomen missing. I don't know about the families yet, but Holderness, the useless streak of piss, will have that report for me tomorrow. And speaking of sharp, you're going to get yourself cut with it one day, Finnegan. Supposing he'd known what that meant?" Boyle knew Finnegan didn't care a bit, but the man's education had been expensive and seeing it wasted in some pointless duel, or more likely in hiding the man away until the trouble over a killing died down, would offend his sense of parsimony.

"About as likely, my chief, as him realizing just exactly how much respect he's due, so. Which I'll remind you I gave him every bit of. He was in charge here, yes?"

"Yes, though to be fair His Majesty dumped the poor man into an impossible situation, watching over the Americans after they'd had months to work their subversion on the Warders. You'd have done better, but I doubt many would." Boyle wasn't quite that sure; he'd had his own spies inside the Tower and from what he'd heard it'd be a hard man and a cunning man both who got ahead of them with their suborning. Finnegan was both, but enough to outbid or outfox people who could see a child live who would have died?

That was the Americans' signal advantage: paying in considerably more than coin. Boyle was sure there were some things he could learn from them and use back in County Cork to buy even more of the peoples' loyalty. And there was every chance the Americans would provide the knowledge to do much of it just for the asking. It was a frustration his own youngest boy wasn't older; from the future histories he'd have a name to make in the natural philosophies, and having the family's own famous scientist—the new word still sounded odd to him—there to bring the new marvels to the people would be a nice touch. As it was, one of the older boys would have to serve. Either Richard, to cement him into the minds of the people as their future earl, or Roger, to give him something besides his martial ambitions to think on.

"I'm sure your lordship sees no harm in having the man sweat a while. So, who am I to catch for you?"

"The missing so far are Wentworth, Cromwell, and all the Americans we had here. I'll see you get a list before you've got your boys ready to ride. Picked up anything by yourself, yet?" Part of what made Finnegan so bloody useful was the fact that outside County Waterford, everyone assumed he was just another bog-trotting paddy, if English, or a ruffian *torai*, if Irish. Behind the brutish facade, that he could turn up and down like a lamp-wick, was a keen mind that could get ahead of his master's orders in gratifyingly useful ways. Never an excess of zeal, no, but frequently armed with just the right information or preparations to get at the task in ways that left other servants standing. Boyle had more than one bright man in his service, but Finnegan was definitely one of the best. Top three, at least.

"Nothing yet, apart from a quiet word with folk as we strolled in. Boats went downriver, two of them, maybe three, maybe just the one. Your earlness knows what a lot of half-stories come out of a mess like this. I've given Mulligan and O'Hare a bag of pennies to buy drinks down by the water to get some tales told. Sure and they're nothin' but ignorant culchie paddies, that anybody'll tell the tale to in their shit-shovellin' britches. Them boys'd make friends with the cat I haven't got and have him telling every grand tale he knows in half an hour."

Boyle laughed. "Aye, and they'd have the cat's daughters pregnant in half an hour more. I've heard the tales."

"Sure they've the vices of their virtues, now." Finnegan grinned. With a little easy-going charm it was possible to make even his crew of monsters seem like loveable rogues. Mulligan and O'Hare had rarely turned up as a team before Finnegan collared them, but then tricksters and cheats seldom worked together. And it would surprise Boyle not a whit to find that one or two of those heartbroken maids hadn't quite said yes first. As long as he kept them in coin, though, they'd confine themselves to whores or it'd not be a trial for rape they got but a quiet dagger where it'd teach them not to embarrass their master. And Finnegan would wipe his conscience clean at the same time he did his blade. Nor would Boyle lose any sleep, come to it. He'd hold the leashes of monsters while they were useful, but only a fool would shed tears when it came time to put them down. Finnegan's own guise of virtue came, Boyle knew, from cold calculation—he got more and more reliably through looking like a faithful, if grim, earl's man. If he knew he faced no repercussion he'd wallow in blood and take a pleasure in it that was all the more chilling for how mild it was.

"Be that as it may. Downriver's likely. Don't trouble yourself with where they've taken ship from, I've sent word to Chatham to get a sea-search in hand. I've no more idea than you whether such a thing is even possible, so I've asked for word of what success is likely by return of messenger. I'm more worried by what they might manage that stay behind, and I heard about two boats too. If one of those was some second mission, we've a rat loose in the pantry. I want it, them, whoever, caught."

Finnegan touched a forelock. "Am I not your earlness's terrier, to rat at command?"

"That you are. Stay on the trail, have messages back to me as often as may be. Run them to ground if you can, frustrate whatever knavery they're about. I've a fine lot of politics to play here in London, and you know how I am with surprises on that score. Keep Cromwell, Wentworth and the Americans from pissing in my gravy while I work on the king. You know me for a generous master, and if I can take this trick, Finnegan, I'll have much to be generous with."

"Now that I can warm my heart with, my lord."

"See that you do. See to your boys and what you can learn here. I've a clerk going hot-foot back to my house for a pouch of all I have on Cromwell and Wentworth, copied against need. You'll carry it with you and learn what you need as you go. See it's burnt before it falls into anyone's hands but yours or mine. More than one of the little birds that told me what's in those papers would pay with his life for telling me what he knew, and where would I be without their songs to delight me?"

"I've not to kill any birds while I chase your rats for you. Right you are, your earlnessship."

"Be off, before your jests make me forget how useful you are."

Chapter 5

"It comes to something that a man may easier read shite than take one," Robert Mackay muttered. Getting from the commode back to the bed was no joke, but when a man broke his back, that was what he'd to put up with. There was probably a bloody theologian somewhere blethering something about God's plan out his arse, and be damned to the prating pederast. All the pain and indignity of being helped to the pot, all the indignity and pain of being helped back, and then the *fucking paperwork* was still waiting.

"Will ye haud ye're noise, ye auld fool? If you'd bided on that bluidy mare ye'd no be led theer greetin' yer wame in ma lugs, forbye. And will ye bide readin' an' no mither me? F'puir auld Meg? So's I can clean, here?"

Mackay sighed. She'd a sharp tongue on her, but she spoke sense. Of the nurses he'd hired to mind him while he was waiting to be measured for his last overcoat, this one was the only one who'd not gotten on his nerves beyond all enduring. Largely by trying her damnedest to get on his nerves, as far as he could tell, which made a change from irritating servility or slovenly dullard idleness. And she'd a half-sister who was a grand nurse for the wee girl, and a fair portion of her family had served here in the Edinburgh house over the years. Her closest relative was one of the hostlers down in the mews, if Mackay recalled aright. Of course, it'd been years since he'd been anywhere near the stables. A carriage for long trips, a litter for short ones. And so much arse and elbow he tried to avoid it if he could.

35

Which meant he was sat here, a fowl on the water for crap like his chief had sent him. Clan loyalties cut through Scots politics like fault lines, which was to say they only really mattered during quakes. Or if you were mining for something, which Reay definitely was. Oh, he could dress it up all he pleased, but he was after something that Charles Stuart would not like. Of course, what Charles Stuart did not like and what he could do anything about were two different things. The man hadn't called a parliament in years. Mackay couldn't recall precisely how long, but it couldn't be much less than ten years. Without taxes and levies, the House of Stuart was governing from its prerogatives. For a certainty, something had come in from the deal with the French, but how much of that remained in the Stuart's coffers was a vexed question. Not much, if the reports on his spending on all those mercenaries were right. And there was replacing the navy ships the French had gotten shot to pieces. That had to cost right enough, and a necessity since Stuart seemed dead set on offending the United States of Europe.

"Something's no' so much shite, I reckon."

"Aye? And what'd ye ken, fishwifie?"

"Och, fishwifie, is it, y'aud de'il? I ken ye're grinnin' like ye've been thievin' frae bairns."

"Aye, just that that idiot Stuart—"

"Papist—" Meg put in, as though she didn't even notice she was doing it.

"—who *may* have *some* papist sympathies or at least be willing to tolerate them—is fire and flame for making himself a nuisance to the USE—"

"Papists."

"Aye? And wha' wad oor wee fishwifie ken?"

"They'll get a cardinal soon, bound to. Papists ha' cardinals. This is aye weel known."

Mackay looked at her. He could tell when she was quoting the blithering idiot of a preacher at her dementedly independent kirk, because she lost her own accent and used his. And the blithering eejit claimed to be a good Scots presbyterian, like he knew any more of scripture than a hungry dog that'd ate a testament. "I'll remind ye, Meg, that yon bampot ye set store by disnae ken good sense fra' a pint o' pish on the subject o' European politics or any religion he cannae get fra' the bottom o' a bottle."

"Och, you tak' that back, ye auld thief! The reverend is a pious man—"

"Haud yer tongue!" Mackay bellowed. He'd had to learn to put up with a lot since he'd broken his back, compensations like the granddaughter his bastard son had presented him with notwithstanding. But he wasn't listening to some rabble of a half-educated excuse for a minister described as a pious man when the nearest he got to piety was sobering up on Sundays, the better to rant a meager collection-plate out of an ignorant congregation of waiting-women and idlers. After hearing one too many quotes from the man, Mackay had made inquiries. The man was technically no more than a deacon putting on airs as a curate, for all he insisted he was a lecturer after the Puritan style. Even the rest of the congregationalist mutton-heads in the kirk he preached at knew better than to let him make himself out an elder. He was permitted to preach before the main services to a mostly empty room. Mackay had been amused to discover that there were waiting-women there anyway, there being idiots willing to pay a penny to show that they were pious enough to make sure of their place at worship and rich enough to pay for it done. Which was how the place was on Meg's regular Sunday-morning round of services, finishing up at St. Giles's for a Leith warehouse-owner who never turned up anyway. Apparently he thought paying Meg to sit in for him on her creepie-stool and listen to the Word on his behalf would be enough to get him in to heaven. Whatever, the idiot at the independent kirk could spout all the shite he liked but Mackay wasn't going to listen to it quietly.

He glared at Meg, who'd adopted the dropped-jaw, shocked stare of the rarely-contradicted. "The USE is not papist. It's not Calvinist. It's not Lutheran, for a' that Gustavus Adolphus is a Lutheran and a pious one from what I hear. And there's nothing so much wrong with Lutherans, not at all. The worst ye can say is they're wrong in the matter of religion. And they're folk for a' that, ye daft hen. As for the papists, aye, they've a cardinal for the USE. Because there's papists in the USE. And they're let be as they should be, to be wrong in their ain way. Or would ye seek tae save 'em against their will? Do mair than witness? Get yersel' tae heaven through good works, will ye? Like these blethering meddlers in the kirk that want tae rule as well as minister?"

He kept up his glare. Meg sat down heavily on a chair. Mackay was secretly gratified. He'd had a stare that could quell the unruliest private soldier in his day, and it was pleasing to see that being crippled hadn't taken the edge off it.

"Didnae think o' that, did ye? No? Now take yon pot o' shite oot o' here, and mind it'll do ye more good than anything ye hear from a whole regiment o' divines if ye don't mind the truth o' religion, which is to save yer ain soul, no' rule the world. Out!"

Meg left in a hurry. Mackay sighed. He'd either got her to shut up with the constant refrain of *no popery* that was the only bit of her goading he didn't find refreshing, or he'd lost the first nurse he'd been able to stand at any price.

Still, yelling at her had given him a few thoughts to reply to Reay with. His chief had been careful to couch his letter in terms praising the merits of the freedom of religion the USE was now practicing, and how harmful enforcement of *cuius regio, eius religio* had proven in the Germanies. It was surely, purely a coincidence that the packet had included some information on the course of the wars of religion from future scholars, and that the pages concerning the Bishops' Wars were right at the front.

And then all the material on how Scotland ought, in the future when her soldiers came home from the wars, be best served by a united government that settled secular affairs securely and left the divines alone. That he was entirely silent on how the divines would be involved in secular affairs was surely just an oversight, a matter he had chosen not to deal with at that time. The fact that he had said nothing about whom the government of Scotland might be united *under,* well, only a fool would see that he was not taking it entirely as read that that meant a United Kingdom under the House of Stuart. To suggest otherwise, well, that would be to accuse Reay of rankest treason. Only the rankest traitor would compass his words in that way, surely?

Mackay smiled. Donald Mackay, Lord Reay and chief of Clan Mackay might act the bluff soldier, but he was chief of one of Scotland's greater clans—even in numbers; in quality there was none finer than Clan Mackay—and as such bore a heavy weight of political responsibility. Under such a weight, a man grew cunning or failed, and Reay hadn't failed yet. He and several of his sons were now senior commanders under Gustavus Adolphus, their estates in Caithness and Sutherland doing well by all accounts and, in the event of clan strife, able to be defended by several thousand veteran soldiers with the latest in modern arms and tactics.

The Ring of Fire had been an opportunity that the Mackays had been well placed to grasp—not least because it was a Mackay who was the first of Gustav Adolf's soldiers who'd encountered the Americans. Robert Mackay's own son Alex, in fact. Who'd found himself a bride into the bargain, now a baroness of Sweden, which was a weight off Robert's mind. It would not do for a man to leave his legitimate issue short to support his bastard, so seeing young Alex make his own way in the world with great success was a fine thing. And it meant that the fast friendship between Alex and his other sons would never be troubled by vexatious disputes over property. The boy even had his own retainers, when those lads finished their terms of service with the USE. He'd be a credit and an asset to the clan, and none would give him grief over his bastard birth. Not lightly, anyway. Julie's rifle was a thing of legend from one end of Europe to another, and a man who could treat your death as so minor a matter as to leave it to his wife was nobody's whipping-boy. As he'd pointed out to several idiots who'd made snide remarks.

How the Mackays would have fared if their patron had died at Lutzen was a detail Grantville hadn't brought back, although Donald had backed the losing side in the civil war that would have happened. It looked as though he was minded not to make that mistake again. Or the first time, if a fellow wanted to be particular about it. So, Reay was sending oblique communications. Assuming that your opponent had the intelligence to read your mail was a good one, so you'd to couch it in terms you'd both understand that could be explained away as innocent. Using a cipher was a dead giveaway, of course. There'd be room and time to clear up misunderstandings later, at need. Unless Mackay missed his guess, this fellow Lennox, who'd be coming over to Scotland soon, was one of his son's hard crew of borderer cavalry. A reliable fellow, to hear Alex speak of it.

Lennox would no doubt have been been briefed in full by Lord Reay. Though he was not a Mackay clansman by birth, but a border reiver who'd decided to take up respectable soldiering, Lennox had come to enjoy the security of a clan loyalty.

For the time being, though, Lord Reay wrote of curbing the

secular power of the divines and uniting Scotland's leadership. So. Who was most likely the target, here? The trick with Scots politics, of course, was to stand back and squint a little, to get the broad strokes of the picture. Once you started in on the details of clan and family feuding, litigation and lesser disputes, you'd never be stopping. You had two main lots, though: the presbyterians who disagreed with James VI's dictum *no bishop, no king*—they were quite happy to do without bishops and treated monarchy as a separate matter—and the episcopalians, who supported bishops in order to support the king. There weren't many in Scotland, other than the bishops themselves, who regarded episcopacy as a good idea in and of itself. Of course, there were plenty of smaller factions looking for more independence for the various independents, but mostly it was the adherents of the covenant of 1580 against the episcopalians. Call it covenant against royalist, but it was more shaded than that.

And then you had the highland-lowland rivalry, what with the highlanders still counting plenty of papists among their number. The chances of actually extirpating the old religion in the wilder places were remote at best, whatever the Covenant might say on the matter. And when you got right to it, more than a few of the greater lords of the Scots peerage, Reay of the Mackays included, counted thousands of highlanders among their people, and if put to it could raise fine private armies of savage light troops more than willing to wreak plentiful havoc for the promise of plunder. Of course, that'd have the lowlanders taking up arms against the prospect of thieving, drunken highland savages let loose in their midst.

Mackay shook his head ruefully. He was letting himself get drawn in. Covenant and Episcopal parties. Stick with that. It was a matter on which everyone had a mind which side he was on, and there were real political consequences to it. Not quite Crown against Parliament the way the English did it, but close enough. Lord Reay—and who else? A question for another time, that—was looking to add a third faction to the mix. Taking over one or another of the first two or recruiting from both to get bigger than either? From the hints Reay had scattered through his letter, he was looking to unite a new faction behind the idea of loyalty to Scotland first and only. Which was interesting, but any fool could see there was a reason Scotland had ended up the subordinate kingdom after the Union of the Crowns in the person of James the Sixth and First. It wasn't simply the inability of Scotsmen in the mass to agree on anything no matter how trivial, although that had certainly contributed heavily. It was the plain fact that Scotland, as a country, had no resources save the flower of her manhood with which to make her way in the world. Three quarters of the country was good for hard-scrabble herding and little else. There were mines here and there, but precious few of those, no great ports, no towns with long traditions of manufacture. If you couldn't butcher it or sell its wool, Scotland produced very little of it.

There *might* be a hint in the shape of the digression Reay had made about the value of the Wietze oil-fields, where they were mining the oil that made the fuel for the wonderful machines Grantville designed and Magdeburg built. Was there a source of that under Scotland? If so, there was something reduced the matter to the irreducible. Or irreducible when it came to Scotland, say. The factions. Who to talk to about that? Mackay decided it was time to make some notes, and rang for his secretary.

Chapter 6

Montrose had come heartily to the conclusion that he'd no time for his lordship the earl of Cork nor His Majesty Charles Stuart, at least on a personal level. Politically, he'd a lot more time for Cork than his king. Cork was a chancer and a businessman, and for him power was a means to very easily assessed ends. Even his well-known talent for grudge-bearing and vengeance-taking was a tool; a warning not to cross him. As plain as a bull's stamping and snorting.

Whatever they'd come up with between them, Montrose sincerely hoped it came more from earl than king. The king's father, God rest him, had been a pure bloody fool for episcopacy, having the fool notion that without bishops there'd be no king. So Scotland had to have bishops her kirk neither wanted nor needed and had done perfectly well without for the best part of fifty years. James VI had wanted his bishops, though, and forced them into the kirk in a series of steps, bit by bit. There were plenty of Scots who were still grumbling about that, and the least whiff of popery would have them rioting at the very least. More than one man of letters was ruminating aloud about the prospect of freedom of religion in a general spirit of anarchy, for if once the State did not control the most important aspect of a man's life, his faith, control over the smaller parts must surely wither away.

Of course, to a man in Montrose's position, with only the loosest leash on the kirk within his dominions, there was a certain attraction in getting the king out of religion. There were, after all, a lot more ways to control a preacher than with the force of law, and a laird in his dominions was a lot closer than a General Assembly of the kirk that might or might not be in session a long way away.

And yet here he was, cordially summoned to appear before His Majesty along with the earl of Cork. There was only a short wait to be summoned into the royal presence, with its attendant stink of the sickroom barely covered with rosewater and pomanders. The king was laid in his bed, the sheets raised over him on some sort of frame. Whatever the king's physicians were doing to help him heal of his injuries looked to have made little progress in the weeks since the coaching accident that had robbed him of his power to walk; the man had gone from the rude health he'd always been known to enjoy to a wasted, skeletal look.

"Your Majesty," Montrose offered, making the proper bow.

"My dear Montrose," Charles Stuart said, "you are already acquainted with Our most trusted counselor, Cork." The king paid no mind to the small flock of attendant courtiers and physicians. Not a one of them seemed inclined to be more than mere cyphers, at that, so Montrose respected their effacement. Cork, meanwhile, looked more than a little apprehensive. From a man that sure of his face in all surroundings, the look said much. Most of it on the subject of not having persuaded his king to a proper course of action. Charles must be recovering his health after all!

"I hope I find Your Majesty improving?" Montrose marveled at his own ability to get the barbed comment out with a straight face. It wasn't as if Cork wouldn't have mocked another, and that savagely.

"By the Grace of God, a little better as each day passes," Charles said, "although Our patience is often taxed, and that right heavily." A significant look at Cork, with that one.

"His lordship the earl of Cork has explained to me that the matter of Your Majesty's rule of Scotland is proving vexing, and that I might be of assistance. Is it, perhaps, that Your Majesty has summoned me to vouchsafe the manner of that assistance?"

A palpable wince from Cork. Montrose wasn't sure whether to be amused or appalled; while Cork was a scheming, unprincipled bastard he was at least a clever scheming, unprincipled bastard whose plans weren't entirely likely to result in disaster. As witness the fact that His Majesty was now abed with an assortment of broken bones healing and rumors abroad that he'd never walk again, if he even lived the year out. The bedridden tended to have short lives, and unhappy ones. This, with young Charles barely five years old. Regencies tended not to go well, in England or Scotland both.

His Majesty let the silence drag on a moment. "My lord Montrose, We are minded to appoint you Lord Lieutenant of Scotland entire. Your loyalty to Us is well known and evidenced both now and in the other time."

Montrose bowed again. "Your Majesty honors me beyond my humble worth," he said—and thought but did not say: *and ignores that I would have stood against him, at the start, and in the matter of prelacy and the Book of Common Prayer.*

His Majesty waved the formal modesty aside. "Letters patent are being prepared in the matter. We are minded to give you broad discretion in the governance of Scotland. Our directions are these: keep the peace, silence dissent, and give no concessions in the matter of unrestrained presbyterianism to the Church of Scotland. We are determined that they will obey."

Montrose nodded. Not quite what Cork had said he would urge on the king, not hardly at all. "Does Your Majesty have any mind to advance the part of the prelates from where it stands at present? Or to further uniformity of worship with the Church of England?" Montrose braced himself for the answer. He'd just been made the clear aiming-mark for every gripe and grumble at the king's rule in Scotland; it remained to be seen whether Charles Stuart had heated the thing to a red glow before tossing it to his ungloved hands.

"For the time being, no. Our most trusted Cork has urged on us a Fabian strategy. Little by little, we shall edge them away from error and misfeasance. Let it be clear to those who would defy Our rule that we are patient, yet unyielding. We are confident that we can endure beyond troublesome presbyters, and in time discredit them one by one. They will assuredly hang separately if given no cause to hang together."

Just hot enough to burn, then, Your Majesty. Montrose suppressed a smile at recognizing the quotation. He'd been told it wasn't original to Stearns, but the sentiment lost nothing for its lack of originality. "I shall need a broad power to act where those outside the Kirk seek to use it as excuse for their own particular schemes, Your Majesty."

"You shall have it. Mind that We hope to hear only silence from north of the Tweed, in all things sacred and secular."

"I shall give my utmost to oblige Your Majesty in that regard," Montrose said, wondering how in the name of God he was expected to keep Campbell of Argyll quiet. The man was no staunch presbyterian, but anything that brought royal power closer to Scotland, where he was far and away the most powerful man for all he wasn't technically the earl yet, was going to have the man causing trouble on general principles. And he'd surely have read the future history in which he was executed for treason for doing just that, for almost exactly those reasons. The only reason the man hadn't spent the last few years in the Tower was the aforementioned power. Montrose had the sinking feeling that if he couldn't get Campbell on his side quickly, he'd have to get working on the highlanders and just go straight to war. It would undoubtedly be a great saving of time if nothing else. And throughout he'd be sticking up for the blasted prelates, whom he'd no time for.

"We have the uttermost confidence in your lordship," Charles Stuart said. "My lord Cork, you have some matters to bring to Our dear friend Montrose's attention?"

Cork harrumphed, and beckoned to one of the small cloud of clerks and attendants lurking in the shadowy side of the room, away from the window. "That I have."

He took a leather portfolio from the clerk who'd stepped forward, and waved the man back to his spot. He opened the papers, licked a thumb and took a deep breath. "First and foremost, His Majesty is concerned regarding the various peers of Scotland and other, lesser notables currently serving overseas. They were given leave to take up arms in the Protestant cause in the Germanies, under Denmark, and, largely through want of objection on His Majesty's part, under Sweden. It now appears that they are serving, whether formally or not, the armed forces of the new United States of Europe. His Majesty is concerned that in so doing they serve the anarchistic principle of freedom of religion, in peril of their souls and to the prejudice of the good order of His Majesty's realm in the event of their return. His Majesty desires that you be in communication with all such of the rank of knight or greater to secure from them sureties that their services are purely in the Protestant cause, failing which they are to return to their home estates on penalty of fines in the first instance with the prospect of forfeiture for those persisting in their default."

Montrose nodded. There was always going to be a problem with the returning veterans of the wars in Europe, one that would require careful handling to ensure that such men saw nothing that got in the way of them returning to a warrior's repose on their own lands. It would be distressingly easy for men accustomed to serving together abroad to band together at home if they felt that there was aught to remedy by force of arms to secure a retirement they felt was quiet enough. How like Charles Stuart to look for a source of fines in their return if it was in any way tardy. And, of course, to pick a method of doing so that would antagonize the USE. Gustavus Adolphus would more than likely welcome a pledge of service to the Protestant cause, but he was not even close to being the only political power in the Germanies these days. Montrose had more than a few friends and relations doing handsomely by themselves in the USE's armed service these days, and there had better be some way of obeying the letter of His Majesty's command while pissing on the spirit of it or there'd be a fine lot of trouble. Or—and it was a spur-of-the-moment thought, perhaps some of the more serious dissenters could be brought back in direct service? There was a plentiful supply of mercenary veterans of the German wars in service with His Majesty south of the Tweed. Surely a few could be found to deter rebellion north of it—and so much the better if they were native Scotsmen seeking to have peace in their homeland by making rebellion a fearful prospect for the would-be rebels? He'd have to weigh up the likelihood of the returners choosing the presbyterian faction instead. The numbers would be interesting to account.

"Your Majesty echoes many of my own concerns," he said aloud, "and I have a good many friends and relations among such men whom I would urge to come home regardless, since the USE is so well found for armies in these times. If they can be persuaded to return to lend their strength to the common weal of Scotland regardless of the matters of faith, I feel much good may be done."

"As you say, my lord," King Charles put in, "but see to it they are warned to leave the notion of religious liberty on the far side of the water. Our late father averred that with no bishops, there would be no king. We are minded to add that without an established church, there is no king worth the name."

"As Your Majesty says," Montrose murmured. Gustavus Adolphus seemed to manage, and the USE did without royal power and established church both. Charles Stuart would call it an illegitimate state, but if illegitimate it was, it was a big, powerful bastard that no cautious man would trifle with.

Cork cleared his throat and began reading again. "His Majesty desires that every presbyter who seeks to oppose the Crown and the Established Episcopalian Church should be most closely watched. The least evidence of wrongdoing, no matter how arising, is to be seized on to bring all such before properly constituted consistory courts charged to ensure that all errors of clerics are suitably chastised."

Montrose mentally translated that to *harry the dissenters through the courts, and see that the courts are suitably stacked with prelates' and king's men; deprive them of their livings through the forms of law with a figleaf of criminal prosecution rather than by prerogative fiat. Failing that, ruin them with the costs of defending themselves.*

It was, at least, an improvement over what would be Charles' likely first response, which would be naked prerogative and a riot or two provoked at the very least. When it came to remedies for the abuses of Rome, Scotland vastly preferred Calvin's to Luther's, and would certainly see monarchical government of the Church as popery by the backstairs. Especially if it came to naked repression. On this one, he felt he could get away with simply making much of a few token prosecutions. It should not be beyond a smart clerk or two to find a small but steady stream of presbyters with their hands in the wrong pockets or their britches unbuttoned in the wrong bedchamber. Aloud, he said "Your Majesty will not find me wanting in the proper punishment of all wrongdoing."

A sharp look from Cork led Montrose to think he might have laid overmuch stress on the word *proper* but schooled his own face against any exchange of speaking glances with the man.

Cork read on. "Further, His Majesty desires that the work begun under his father to bring the Erse away from the popish errors they are prey to and the barbarisms and cruelties they use. Efforts to educate them must be redoubled, both among the great and small of them. Such of them as are willing to recant their popish errors and confess the proper and episcopalian creed of the Church of Scotland may be found profitable service with His Majesty; there is much tumult throughout the kingdoms of Great Britain and Ireland and the suppression of same is greatly to be desired."

Despite himself, Montrose felt his jaw clench. The highlanders were, he'd be the first to allow, a fractious, quarrelsome, inconvenient lot of nuisances; the same people who'd turned back Rome's legions at the Wall. But they were, in large part, *his* nuisances.

His Majesty's father had been content with an outward obedience to the law, and provided you didn't insist on that meaning not stealing cattle and feuding, the highlanders carried on as they had since time out of mind. They would cheerfully confess themselves good Protestants to your face and hear Mass every Sunday when your back was turned. For a certainty, they'd rally to any cause of plundering the presbyterian lowlanders who set such store by suppressing their language and religion and scorned them as illiterate savages. But whether they'd take mercenary service in England to allow Charles Stuart to continue to rule with French gold and without Parliament was another question.

And, of course, there were all the thousands of them that were Campbell's—which way would they go? *Not red-hot, Your Majesty, but another hot enough to burn.* There was already a great fear that the king meant to use Irish mercenaries to enforce his will, again with French gold—and wasn't that a beautiful thing, after half of Scotland's Reformation had been to get French influence out that country, that two reigns later the king should bring it back into England? They were already calling Cork the *premier ministre* in scurrilous pamphlets, Richelieu's principal secular title being a byword for unprincipled tyranny throughout England.

"Your Majesty, the work of civilizing the Erse of the highlands continues today as it did in Your father's time and before that. Whatever my poor efforts may do to hasten it along will be done." Again, not a direct lie. Civilizing the wretches would do them direct and measurable good, no matter the religion they followed. The papists of Spain, France and Italy were, after all, civilized and seemed to do well by it. If the divines wanted them converted to the uncorrupted faith of Calvinism, they could get about the work themselves. Perchance it would keep them out of mischief.

The remainder of the king's charges to his new Lord Lieutenant were considerably less disheartening. What *was* disheartening to

Montrose was that he had been given the greatest office short of the crown itself in Scotland, and the charges laid on him with it were, indeed, disheartening him.

Later, awaiting their mounts to be brought from the stables to go to their respective London houses, Cork gave Montrose a wry smile. "I trust you're seeing how I feel about great power in these times."

"A burden, aye," Montrose said. "I trust that should I choose to do more of the spirit of His Majesty's charges than the letter, he'll not hear any contradiction from you? I'm of a mind that that first charge, silence north of the Tweed, is the one that counts?"

Cork's grin was twisted and rueful. "That's about the size of it. Between Wentworth and Laud, we've a merry mess on our hands in England. Between Spain, France, and the USE, it's our task to keep our feet and not end up provinces of one or the other. And I'm fucked if I know where Spain's going to fall out on this now the queen's dead—nor can I see any prospect of a new marriage for him to settle anything with anyone on Europe. Marriages of state are often cynical matters, but they have to be marriages for all that, and short of a miracle His Majesty can't contract a valid one and keep it valid, if you take my meaning?"

Montrose felt a lurch in his guts. In his heart of hearts he didn't think Charles Stuart the man was worth as much as a pot of piss, but there were some things not to be wished on anyone. He swallowed the lump in his throat and manfully suppressed the urge to grasp his own jewels. He tried to make a joke of it. "So it's you and me the king's only working cods now, is it?"

Cork's laugh was a single, harsh bark. "Bollocks any way you look at it, my lord. Bollocks."

Part Two

June 1634

Now Sark rins over Solway sands,

An' Tweed rins to the ocean,

To mark where England's province stands—

Such a parcel of rogues in a nation!

Chapter 7

Finnegan peeled off the second boot and let his feet wave in the breeze. He'd had the innkeeper's wife bring him a footstool for just this purpose. She'd also fetched beer, bread and cheese, and his lads were behaving themselves. Which was to the good, since he was minded to question the lady further in a short while. She'd been quite forthcoming with the news about the party that'd arrived by boat and left by cart, but there was always some other small detail one could catch in conversation.

"D'ye have t' do that, Finnegan?" Tully'd snagged a small barrel to sit on while he munched on a couple of apples. The inn was doing quite well out of travelers this day, it seemed. Everyone had arrived with a hunger and a thirst on him.

"What?"

"Have yer sweaty feet in the face of a man about his food, so?"

"You can always sit elsewhere. Besides, it's not good for a man to be constantly shod, nor is it. The day's been a warm one, and what poor oul' bog paddy likes to wear boots nor shoes?"

"I can feckin' *tell* it's been a warm day, with the stink of you. Hold on while I move upwind, ye smelly *gaimbín*." Tully matched deed to word and dragged his barrel around. "Now I've the sun in my eyes instead of warming my back, and all with the feet of you. I hope yer mother's proud of the son she raised, Finnegan."

"Oh, hold your noise. The boyos are all fed and watered, if you've time to complain like an Englishman?" Finnegan relied on Tully for details like that. You'd never describe the man as scholar nor saint, but he could see to the beasts and the men alike for their comforts. "Apart from the few that're still abroad, that is?"

"O'Hare caught up with us a quarter-hour past. They've all found bedding above the stables, there's rooms for the gentry of us in the inn, yer woman there promises a rich stirabout and dumplings for our supper at a good price for these parts, and the beer's passable. So until Mulligan and Welch get back from Romford and we're all together again, things are as settled as they can be."

Finnegan raised an eyebrow. "O'Hare's back from Tilbury and not a word for his chieftain?"

Tully sneered as he spat a pip across the inn's yard. "Chieftain my puckered and sweaty ring, Finnegan. He says there was but the one boat at Tilbury, just as you said, and don't ask him for a civil word until the aching arse of him has had a night's rest to recover. A hard ride you sent him on, sure, and a long one. He did well to be on us this much before sundown."

Finnegan took a pull on his beer. "He did, at that, and I'll excuse much for a sore arse got by hard riding. If you catch the eye of one of the family here before I do, have them tell you what's a good spirit hereabouts and to send a half-pint of it to O'Hare, he can soothe his bruised behind at my expense. Did we find out what the craic was with whores hereabouts?"

"Nothing to mention. I didn't ask if there was an arrangement to be had with any of the serving girls yet, I told the boyos to get themselves and their horses fed and bedded before they unbuttoned their britches. They know the rules. Leave 'em smiling in unfamiliar country, so, or don't leave 'em at all where they'll be found. And we're too busy to be hiding anything, with what we're about."

"Aye. Let it be known I'll find some pretty ones out of the earl's pocket to amuse them when we catch these birds. Until then, nothing that's not quick and paid for. There's a trail to pick up, and quarry to get ahead of, romance can wait."

There'd been a couple of incidents before Finnegan made the rules. Only one after. He didn't take much pleasure in disembowelling a castrated, crucified man, but he'd put his hand to the task again at need. You didn't need to be a savage yourself to lead a crew like his, so long as they had the clear and constant notion that it was something you could do better and more imaginatively than they could if they drove you to it. Like most *torai,* their instinct about rules was that they were for the sheep, not the wolves. They required education in the matter, and if that took an instructive lecture over the expiring corpse of a gutted rapist, so be it. They'd take *that* lesson to heart where no amount of holy words would do a bit of good.

Tully nodded. After a decent interval to separate the subjects of whoring and duty, he went on, "Will ye have a wager on where this Cromwell fellow went to?"

Finnegan flipped a morsel of cheese—good cheese hereabouts, too—into the air and caught it in his teeth. A moment to chew and organize the thoughts that came so much better with his feet able to breathe. "I will not. For one thing, we don't know that it was Cromwell came on this boat, for all the king's got his arse in an uproar over the man. For another, if it is Cromwell, he's heading for his children."

"You're that sure?"

"Would you not?" Finnegan shot Tully a sharp look. The man had a few bastards by an assortment of women, and as time and work allowed he saw most of them and cared for them in a rather negligent here's-a-present-now-leave-your-mammy-and-me-be sort of way. He'd probably be quite irate if someone hurt one of them, even if he hardly did a thing toward their general welfare. It was something Finnegan really disapproved of, inasmuch as he could bring himself to care much about anything.

His own da had been as foul a scoundrel as you could turn up in a camp of cattle thieves anywhere, but he'd actually been attentive in his rough sort of way. He'd sold his loyalty to Boyle— scraped up enough to sell to *anyone,* was miracle enough—to buy an education for Finnegan himself, for starters.

A few years paid for at the Cathedral Grammar School in Dublin had helped him enormously. Finnegan's own sons, for the moment, were too young to need much beyond what the local hedge-school master could provide, and Finnegan made sure the man had a dry room to teach in and enough books to teach from. By happy accident it made him the big man in his home village, with a lot of respect that came in useful in seeing his own family was looked after. He sometimes wondered what it was like for everyone else, to *feel* that sort of thing was good, rather than just weighing it up and taking a decision. It generally ended with a little mental shrug and the conclusion that what a man never had, he never missed. He cared nothing but for getting on as far and as fast in the world as ruthlessness and a sharp blade would take him.

Tully busied himself with a tricky bit of apple peel for a moment. "Sure, and I think I would, at that. I'm none of the best of fathers, but there'd be a reckoning if someone hurt my little ones. And God love them, they think the world of me and they'd be sad to see me put away in some castle somewhere, I'd want to let them know daddy'd got out. I'm after thinking you're right, so. Do we know where his children are?"

"Ely, but that was last year, when he got caught. They weren't taken, but what happened after that the king's men didn't bother their arses over. We'll have to find out, I think. If it's Cromwell." Finnegan picked up the tankard—the innkeeper had given him the good pewter, as fit the chief man of his day's customers. "And I don't know why he'd have headed out on the road to Chelmsford, nor do I. Wrong direction altogether."

"A conundrum and a mystery, so it is," Tully said. "Unless it's as simple as this was where the wagon they wanted was left and it was the Chelmsford road or back to London and capture."

"Well, when we know more, we'll know how simple it is or isn't. For now, I've the sun on me, the wind in my toes, and beer to drink. I'll take the simple pleasures when I can, Tully, and so should you."

"I'll keep to taking them from upwind of the feet of you, Finnegan, whatever else may befall."

"As you please, Tully. Now unless Mulligan comes riding in with great news enough to not mind his sore arse, see O'Hare gets his drink and leave me be." Finnegan reclined against the wall and let his hat tilt forward to shade his eyes.

He'd spent the days before mostly sat in a public house in Southwark while his boyos went up and down in the world of London's docks. They'd found plenty, just by being cheerfully ignorant paddies and micks, chatting to people, buying drinks and keeping their ears open. Most Londoners assumed that because they'd been born in the big city, and it certainly was that and smelled like it, they were three times the men and ten times the scholars that anyone from the rest of England could be, and double that for Irishmen, who were well known to all be illiterate thieving vagabond papists. To be fair, that was about two-thirds of Finnegan's men to the life, but that didn't mean stupid, it didn't mean deaf, and didn't mean not reporting to someone who was smart and well educated and thinking ferociously about how he'd do what had been done that morning. The facts that came to light were simple enough. There'd been shots, explosions within the Tower and on the wall, and an explosion on London bridge. Two boats had been seen heading downriver and around the bend past Rotherhithe. After that, picking out the right boats from the general river traffic was impossible, and only a few had watched the boats all the way out of sight. Nobody around the bend in Rotherhithe had paid enough attention to pick one or two boats out of dozens.

A look at the site of the explosion on London Bridge showed that a lot of smoke and noise had happened, but no real damage. On the one hand, it was a bomb to discourage pursuit south of the river. On the other hand, did it make sense that people clever enough to put everything else together would make a bollocks of such a vital part of the escape? Lots of possibilities. Two escaping parties, one in the boats and one not, the land party's diversion having failed. Or, two escape routes prepared, and they all went in the boats so the bomb on the bridge had its fuse burn down to cover nothing. Or, the bomb on the bridge was the purest of misdirections, a wild gesture at an escape to the south to get the hounds running that way. The earl had sent men away on all the roads to the south, he had enough to cover everything. Finnegan's job was to get ahead of the quarry and wait—it was a poor hunter who just chased, after all. All of those king's men riding the roads into dusty exhaustion were, as far as Finnegan cared, just beaters.

What decided the matter was collecting enough accounts from enough people. Nobody had really paid full attention to all of it—quite a lot of London Bridge was busy enough that people really hadn't noticed a bomb going off four hundred yards away, or at least not enough to realize that it was important at the time. But, adding half-story to half-story, Finnegan had pieced together that whoever had placed the charge on the bridge had done it to go off barely a few minutes after the one on the outside of the Tower. If it had been intended to stop pursuit after they went past, it had gone off too early and too weak. And nobody had seen any large movement of people between the Tower and the bridge at the right time. It was nearly a quarter mile; someone should have seen *something* if there'd been a flight that way.

And, indeed, nobody had seen anyone leave the Tower other than by boat by any other route, either. If they had, they'd done it without leaving a trace that could be followed, and Finnegan had reported as much to the earl as soon as he was sure in his own mind, sending a runner with a brief in hand. He had got men far enough down the south bank to have it clear that at some point two boats had indeed become one, and that one had gone all the way down to Chatham and taken ship there. Said ship being one of the USE's steamships that Finnegan didn't remotely understand, despite the best efforts of a sailor with a beer in him to explain. Big ship, very powerful. Enough understanding for Finnegan's purposes. So, the escapers had got some or all of themselves away over the water. The "some" was the important bit, and Finnegan felt his earlship would want an answer on the point. So, nothing landed on the south bank as far as he could find by sending eyes and ears as much as ten miles down, perhaps four as the crow flew, what with the river being so bendy.

And this was why he'd spent the day at an inn table, enjoying the fine air and good ale while he read the documents the earl had given him. Wentworth would be one candidate to stay, looking to get to his political base in Yorkshire. The Mackays—and some of the shooting said Baroness Mackay had come down from Scotland—would be another, since the king's agents knew that she'd been in Edinburgh visiting the in-laws. If she'd left, word hadn't come down yet and reached the earl of Cork's spymaster, but it wouldn't be the first time spies delivered the necessary news late or not at all.

Cromwell. There was the one to watch. If any man had a grievance against King Charles of England and Scotland, it was he. And, as it happened, a record of looking after the people of his own home. Lord of the Fens, they called him, for his speaking, and his litigation against the king's project to drain the marshes of that country. Well, it wasn't like any of his boys were unused to the wet and wild places of the earth. Waterford had no bog country to speak of, except on the mountains here and there, but, well, if you were tired of rain you were tired of Ireland and the bits that weren't bog were hard to tell from the bits that were, if you came at them in the right season. So, if anyone had split off from the party on the boats, they were going north. As witness the boat left tied up with nobody to say they'd been the owner of it longer than a day. Finnegan slightly wished he'd had the forethought to get more of a description of the boats that left the Tower, but it was only a slight wish. Not a one of his boyos had more than a bull's notion of boats or boating, so any description would have been mangled by lack of understanding. Finnegan himself had seen one or two around Dublin when he'd been there as a boy, but that was about the limit of it. It'd taken them all day to find the thing, and the word they'd had from O'Hare's ride to Tilbury and back confirmed that this was where the smaller boat had come. Not certain, but certain enough and it fit with everything Finnegan had puzzled out already. In the morning, they'd have word back from Romford, the next town of any note along this road, and he'd decide which way to go.

It was Welch who arrived first, come the morning, apparently having started back before dawn. After he'd had a bite of bread and a chance to duck his head in the rain-butt, he presented himself to report. "Nothing past Romford, Chief, Mulligan's casting about for sign around there. I've come back early to check for any good turn to another road that might be the one they took, but."

"Sign of them before Romford?" Finnegan realized he'd be buying another tot of spirits before the day was out, Mulligan having done more than was asked of him. That said, Mulligan was one of the smart ones, who could see that anything Richard Boyle dispatched them on personally was likely to see the earl being more openhanded even than his normal generous self if there was a quick end to the matter. Either way being seen to give a reward would be the right thing to do.

"Sure and a couple of field lads saw a wagon go by. Four horses, so it stood out. Did I hear that that was the wagon that left here?"

"You did. Get a change of mount, that screw's had ten miles at the trot and we're well found for remounts, and we'll be off in the quarter-hour, so."

The conclusion was pretty obvious. They'd set out for Romford and Chelmsford as a feint, probably on the spur of the moment rather than stay near the pursuit in London. Finnegan liked that, it said he was chasing men unused to pursuing or being pursued. A sensible bandit would've cut straight away from the main pursuit, rather than running ahead of it. Changed for faster horses—whatever was in the wagon was surely not worth capture—and changed direction again. Split and regrouped several times, anything to confuse the trail of witnesses. Just as hunting was done best by getting ahead of the quarry and waiting, flight was best achieved by not going where the hunters would be waiting. Of course, if both hunter and hunted knew that game it got very confusing very quickly and the hunter would have to fall back on hoping he had enough men to cover every possible avenue of flight.

Not so today. The escaping party—Finnegan was still very carefully not thinking of them as Cromwell's party—had sought to feint to the east and turned either north or south. There would be a limited number of places to do so between the last sighting Welch had reported and Romford. Which it might be was the vexed question. All of the possible motivations Finnegan could think of for a party remaining in the country instead of flying by sea said they would go north. South suggested they had a second ship and some errand had delayed them on land, to make a quieter getaway than the main party.

Or, and this occurred to him as he mused, just as it must have to Mulligan at Romford, they'd skirted that town to carry on east with a broken trail that simply *looked* like a feint-and-turn. Finnegan grinned. You could never truly think your way through a tangled haystack of needles such as this, but it was fun to try and you could take bets on the outcome. "Somebody open a book!" he shouted. "I've got sixpence says they turned north, last road before Romford. Any takers?"

They found Mulligan an hour later at a turning just before the town. "This way, I found a spot where someone took a heavy load over the river. If I'm any judge, they were after not being seen, and whatever they need that wagon for, they're not done with it."

"And here's me with no takers for the bet I made that they'd do just this very thing," Finnegan said. "It fair to makes a man weep that he leads not a single idiot."

That got a round of chuckles. Now and then he'd lose a bet like that one, but not often enough that anyone cared to take the wager without serious long-shot odds. A few of the smarter boyos had caught on to it being a polite, pleasant, method of suggesting the boss was wrong, and Finnegan was careful to listen. After all, an opinion a man was willing to put money on was an opinion he'd thought about. Finnegan liked thought, it paid well. And more than once he'd put a man where he could get a feather in his cap for "checking to see if his fool's wager would pay," and the good-natured codding was worth it for the credit he could take when reporting to the earl.

"The sign on the riverbank says yesterday afternoon, if there wasn't rain overnight, so I fancy they're after moving as quick as they can with that wagon. Will we go straight after them?"

Finnegan thought about it. In their boots he'd have kept moving into the night and looked for a change of horses somewhere, which would cost them given the cheap nags they'd had, and that in turn would leave a trace. Also in their boots he'd have taken a few roads off the line they wanted and come at their intended target—either Ely, for Cromwell's kin and children, or a cut west at some convenient road to get back to the Great North Road and the way to Scotland. It'd be slow work picking up some sense of where they were going, and at this point a wrong guess would be disastrous. Whatever else might befall, a company of stout lads with plenty of cash and remounts could be halfway to Scotland by this time on the morrow, so as soon as their quarry—only *probably* Cromwell, remember—settled on a destination then a short, hard ride would see them in a proper ambush position. Making that ride too soon would cost them the chase entirely.

"We will not. Find us a farrier in your town, there, and we'll see the horses' feet are good while I talk to whoever knows the roads here. We'll have a plan, so, and not go at the thing like a bull at a gate. Tully, see to it while Mulligan here shows me the tracks on this riverbank."

Chapter 8

"Top of the morning!" Finnegan knew as well as any man how to come the cheery Irishman. It certainly did better than what most of the folk here across the water thought about his countrymen. In a lot of cases, of course, they were right, but letting that get in the way while he was about his chief's business was not to be borne. "And how might you be this fine morning?"

"Right enough," said the thatcher whom they were overtaking. The fellow had a cart full of rushes, which apparently was the thing for roofs hereabouts. To Finnegan they looked odd; he was used to seeing straw, both at home and in the parts of England he'd seen so far. English roofs looked a little different without the layer of turf scraw he was used to seeing, but that was about the limit of it. The reed roofs were somehow less bulky and looked like they'd not be as warm in bad weather. It was a measure of how tedious the last week of riding up and down every bastard road in eastern England had been that he was thinking about roofs, of all things.

"Can ye say what town is that, up ahead?" Finnegan asked the man.

"Bishop's Stortford, but there's no market there today, if it's horses you're after. Some good inns, though."

"That'll do," Finnegan said. "We're well found for horses. Do you know how much further Ely is from there?"

"Ely? Can't rightly say. It's over past Cambridge, if I do recall rightly, but Cambridge is as far as I've been that way, and that

63

when I were but a boy. Ask in town for Cambridge, and ask in Cambridge for Ely, would be my advice to you, sir. Have you room to pass, there?"

"Sure we've enough, and it's a fine day for a slow ride. One more thing, mind. Have you seen a lot of travelers, maybe a dozen, perhaps less, traveling with a four-horse wagon?"

"No, sir. If I had I'd ask you for a penny for the tale, but I don't even know anyone who owns such a wagon that'd be about with it at this time of year. Not a lot going even to the small markets about now, let alone up to London such as you'd take a wagon for. Now, I know a squire over by Much Hadham, he'd a fancy to go to Parliament and nothing would do but he got a two-horse coach to go in." The thatcher laughed uproariously. "Bless the poor fellow, the year after he came back down from Parliament, there's never been another one since, and he's never used his coach again but to go to church of a Sunday."

"Ah, but there's no rare ould fool like a fool with land and money to his name, I'm thinking," Finnegan said, horribly aware that he'd shortly be faced with choice between more of this or stabbing the culchie in the cart. The stabbing was looking awful attractive, at that. But, no.

"Well, I've business of my master's to be about, so I'll bid ye good day." With that, he urged his horse out of the walk.

A half mile down the road, Tully nudged his mount up alongside as Finnegan let his own come back to the walk, safely out of reach of further rural anecdote. "No use, then?"

"But that we've reached our final marker, no." Finnegan let that hang a moment, and then, "Is it me or is this country full of fucking amiable *amadáin*? Back home they'd have been just as cheerful, but we'd've been lied clear out of the fucking county, worse if we'd offered money."

Tully shrugged, "They don't see trouble, nor do they. Such as us could do well in country this soft, had we a mind. Or if his lordship ever falls on hard times and we have to shift for ourselves."

"That we could, but for now we've a purse and a task. And I think it's time to go to the next part of it. We've missed them, do you not think?"

"They've made a turn we missed. With twenty men, there's

much we've not seen. Or we missed the one fellow who saw which way they went. Do you still think Ely?"

"I do, at that. We got nothing to the west, not at all. That says they don't want the North Road, and that means not Yorkshire and not Scotland, not for their first. They've kept the wagon, too, and God love them for it. Everyone that saw it remembered it."

Tully tossed his head. "Whoever planned this wasn't a country boy, that's for sure. I don't think I saw a wagon before I was ten, at all. It says they're after a long trip, though, or a heavy load."

"I think a long trip, before they're done. That wagon's been mithering of me, while I think on who it is we're after. Does it not seem to you that there's nothing to say it's just Cromwell, or just Wentworth, or just the Mackays?"

Tully gave that some thought, taking a moment to get his hat off and the wind through his thin and sandy hair. "Now that you say it out loud, nothing at all. All three? Or which two? And are we to open a book for this?"

Finnegan laughed. "It could be that we should. See what odds the boyos give, maybe one of them has thought of something we haven't?"

"Wouldn't be the first time, rare though it is. I'll pass the word when we get bedded down. We wait at this Bishop's Stortford, then?" The two of them were speaking Irish between themselves, there being no English ears around to mark them as foreigners. They'd long since discovered that most people assumed their accents were simply from a distant part of England. One fellow in London had been sure they were all from Lancashire. Finnegan had been there, briefly, having come over from Ireland via Liverpool, and been forced to conclude that the fellow had never met a Lancastrian or some other Irishman had told him the lie to avoid being damned for a papist savage. The English place names sounded funny in the stream of Irish, to Finnegan's ear, especially the way Tully tended to mangle them; there were lads who could switch from one tongue to the other easily, but not Tully. He needed a pause between one language and another, as if his brain had to change horses, stopping for a piss the while.

Finnegan nodded, and then added: "Until all the boys are back in, and then we'll send a few to York to cover the Great North road, I think O'Hare, while the rest of us head for Ely and try and track down Cromwell's wee ones. And there should be letters from his earlship waiting for us in town, he should have a man there waiting for us. Unless someone's been lucky and caught sight of our prey, that is."

"Okay, let's see how she goes." Darryl was laid under the wagon, watching the suspension bars he'd made and fitted over the last day. He'd put a couple of tracks of broken bricks, small branches, and general trash in the way of the wheels to see how they handled it, and Cromwell, as it turned out far and away the best wagon-driver among them, as befit a farmer, urged the horses on.

Some minutes later, Cromwell came back to find Darryl still on the ground, beaming happily. "Totally worked. Let's go back and show off to the ladies."

Cromwell reached down to give him a hand up. "The ride is much smoother, and I fancy the nags found it less effort. Will we tell Colonel Mackay that it was a Scotsman's invention?" Cromwell's grin was impish. Hard-core fundamentalist Puritan he might be, but he had a barbed, dry wit. And truthfully, it seemed the closer they got to Scotland, the prouder Alex became of his homeland.

"He'll claim it for them anyway, I reckon," Darryl answered, deadpan for deadpan, "so it's not like we'd be sparing him any effort. Besides, having the Scotsman's invention in there meant I really couldn't put Ackerman steering in there, and that's an Austrian or a German invention, I think. Sounds like it, anyway. Or an American with folks in that part of the world, I guess. There's definitely a way to do both at the same time, most automobiles have both, but without one to copy, I don't know enough geometry to just make one up. Suspension linkages just have to be strong enough and have enough springs in 'em."

"Aye, once I saw the model you made, the principle was clear enough. I've no great mechanical learning, but the geometry is easy enough with what my schoolmaster beat into me."

"Yep. One of those ideas, when you see it, you kick yourself you didn't think of it first. Took a genius like Watt to think of it at all. I'm glad, now, I spent all that time listening to the steam nuts right after the Ring of Fire, they're a goldmine of useful stuff like this. I thought I understood autos before, from tinkering and such, but those guys, they could blow a guy away with the theory. Thing was, he didn't invent that for suspension, it just turned out useful that way. Father Mazzare told me all the things you could find it in once, he musta gone on a quarter hour with it all. The only one I recognized was the suspension arms, which I could take apart and put back together before, but now I understand 'em well enough I can build a simple one like this."

"It is, as you say, 'cool,'" Cromwell said, "and so easy to hide."

"Yep. She still don't look like much, but she's got it where it counts, now."

"Right enough," Cromwell said. "God be praised." He took himself off a ways to kneel and say a prayer to, Darryl assumed, that effect.

Darryl himself didn't bother much with praying, being at most a Christmas, Easter, weddings-and-funerals kind of guy when it came to church, and Cromwell didn't seem to be pushing it on him. Gayle took that moment to wander into the empty ground out the back of the inn that they were using to test the repaired wagon.

"So, is he praying thanks for a successful test?" she asked quietly.

"That, and James Watt in general, I think. It works just fine. And we went back to plain wooden axles. Sticking a reinforcing rod down 'em is what broke the one we lost. There's bearings in the wheels, and a lot more wood in there now, so I don't think we need worry so much. And I got that old geezer to cut us a spare set of everything."

Their first weeks on the road had been utterly frantic. Every sight of horsemen on their back trail had sent them picking random turns off the course they wanted. Alex and Julie had taken turns with their scopes and binoculars, staying behind to watch for pursuit and galloping forward whenever they saw horsemen. Four days of that and they'd made sure they were unobserved as they manhandled the wagon and load up a narrow track to camp in a small coppice. They'd run into an old bodger there, damned near incomprehensible over his treadle-lathe, but surprisingly hospitable with his campsite that he shared with a small crew of charcoal burners, whose smoke was fine cover. Cromwell had spoken quietly but urgently with the men when the horsemen—they'd long passed the stage of suspicion by then and *knew* they were being tracked—appeared nearby. Whoever they were, though, they'd taken one look at the narrow track from the main road and assumed that no wagon was going up *that*. Of course, it damned near hadn't, and Towson was still nursing bruises from where they'd accidentally rammed him into a hedge with the wagon bed while lugging it between four up to the campsite. They'd been more careful coming down, two days after the horsemen had left, and being at that point thoroughly lost, aimed for "generally north."

Both Darryl and Gayle had privately agreed that what England really needed was someone to completely rebuild its road network, someone who actually understood the concept of straight lines and right angles. Roads that maintained the same direction for more than fifty yards at a time, and preferably aligned neatly with the cardinal points of the compass. And, as the roadside vegetation grew apparently by the hour as spring hit its peak and summer made its presence felt, Darryl quietly thought a few planeloads of Agent Orange would be right handy. The natives—Alex and Patrick assured him that the roads in Scotland and Ireland were, if anything, even twistier—didn't mind the lack of straight lines so much, but the fact that even standing up in the wagon bed visibility was half a mile at best across the rapidly greening countryside was getting to them. The occasional milestone would have helped if they'd had a map that even showed these tiny hamlets and villages; knowing that you were half a mile from Creeting St. Mary did you not a damned bit of good if, when you got there, it turned out even the *inhabitants* didn't have a clue where they were.

For the best part of ten days they'd wandered lost in the wilderness of Hertfordshire, Suffolk and, later, Norfolk. As near as Darryl could figure it, Hertfordshire was reasonably dry and comprehensible, Suffolk was wetter and a bit less comprehensible, and Norfolk averaged ankle-deep in fen with an option on bottomless and if it wasn't for Cromwell translating the local accent and dialect, they'd not have had a chance. Gayle had remarked that it sounded like they'd been taxed their every last consonant by the king.

They'd managed to replace the horses, one by one, depleting their money in the process as they went; they'd proven beasts of stamina and absolutely damn all else. They had one pace, dead slow, but they could keep it up more or less forever. Eventually they had everyone mounted and the wagon pulled by somewhat more decent draught animals that could maybe be ridden in a pinch, and were making progress, having finally picked up the Ipswich-Norwich road. Wildly off course, but at least they had a grasp of where they were and Cromwell was now within forty miles of his home country. Darryl now clearly understood why that counted as a long way hereabouts.

Of course, that'd been too much for the Demon Murphy to tolerate, and they'd broken down about a mile short of Diss, when the clever reinforcement of the axles turned out to be too clever, and the front offside had decided to separate into wood and iron. That meant a pair of new axles, but it seemed Diss was a town of some note hereabouts, possibly having a population of as many as a whole thousand. It even had a market square, proudly named as such despite being triangular, although by this time Darryl was past being surprised by the wild disregard for geometry the English countryfolk seemed to have. There was also a really big lake the townsfolk were quite proud of, a carpenter's shop, a farrier, and, the Friday after they arrived, a market where they could pick up a healthy supply of what was in season to pack for the road. Mostly greens and the last of the over-wintered roots among the things that would keep, but there were plenty of eggs, a few assorted poultry they could keep caged on the wagon for eggs until they got barbecued, and a flitch of bacon that was nearly as big as Vicky. Darryl figured he'd investigate the greens right after the bacon and eggs ran out; for the time being they were doing all right eating at the inn. It was variations on stew and dumplings, mostly, since none of the really fresh crops were in yet, but it filled a hole.

"So," Gayle said, "are we good to go tomorrow?"

"Pretty much. Any word from back home?" Part of the torment of being lost in Norfolk had been, whenever they found the privacy and the right conditions to radio back in, was the mockery that the radio-room geeks engaged in. Turned out you could get a lot of sarcasm into sixty seconds of Morse, and Gayle used it all in every return volley. There wasn't much she could report except to confirm they weren't dead yet, but she never failed to point out that there was damn all Magdeburg could do to help or advise, so they could stuff it.

"Nothing significant. Word from Amsterdam is that the

Warders and their folks have gotten settled in with Becky and Mike as more or less their private security, so that's nice to see."

Darryl nodded. That had been a bit of a concern for him. Stephen Hamilton, the patriarch of the group of Yeoman Warders who'd helped them escape from the Tower, had come along as being up for one last adventure before he had to retire, and to watch over his niece-by-courtesy Vicky, who wasn't going to let Darryl out of her sight if she could help it. But the rest of them had had to up stakes and leave their homeland. Darryl knew their monarch had betrayed them first, but there was no way any king of England was ever going to see it that way, so they'd never be able to come home. And the position of a royal military elite, which was what the Yeoman Warders really were at this time, was always going to be a ticklish one after they defected. Mike had solved it.

"Good. Have you told Stephen and Vicky yet?"

"They were right there with me when the messages came in. Vicky's getting pretty good at helping out, and Stephen doesn't mind pedaling as it gets him out of spending all day down by the mere fishing with the other boys."

Darryl chuckled. "They catch anything yet?"

"Nope."

"Guess that fuss was over nothing, then."

"Guess so. Although I figure they'd do better if they had bait on them lines."

Darryl snorted again. Towson, Leebrick and Welch had decided that, lacking any better way to occupy their time, they'd enjoy the fresh air of what was shaping up to be a fine English summer down by the mere, relaxing. A few lunchtime ales, and they decided to cut ash poles, hunt up some string and hooks, and go fishing. Their reaction to being told they couldn't had involved big smiles and cocked pistols, which they assured everyone they were carrying because the pike in some of these village ponds could grow to monstrous sizes. There'd been grumbling over that until one of the sharper-eyed locals had spotted the lack of bait, and Darryl, to whom the three mercenaries had been a bit of an unknown quantity, had let out the breath he'd been bating. Slightly loopy behavior due to mild boredom he could well understand. Hell, cooped up in the Tower of London all those months, he'd *agreed to get married*, for Christ's sake.

Getting those boys on the road before they started on the practical jokes would be a fine thing. And here came Cromwell, his prayers done for the moment. "Oliver," Darryl said, "any advance on Thetford as our next stop?"

"Nay. I know the way from there, and from here 'tis but fifteen miles of high road: a peddler who came from there was here this morning and firmed it in my mind. We shall be there on Wednesday, if we start early morning. Thereafter, three, perhaps four days to Ely, for there is no straight road."

"I'm kinda looking forward to what counts as not straight in roads hereabouts," Gayle remarked, earning a grin from Cromwell.

"Aye, the roads are crooked, Gayle, but the hearts are straight enough."

"Aaaand I'll leave you guys to it," Darryl said, heading over to where the horses were awaiting attention. "I'll get one of the stable guys to give me a hand with the horses. You go take a walk in the sunset."

"Darryl?" Gayle called after him, "What's it worth to keep that nice streak you got quiet?"

He blew a raspberry and flipped her off, which didn't offend anyone hereabouts. Doing it with two fingers, now, that could get you in trouble. One finger was catching on as a friendly get-outta-town-you gesture, since nobody hereabouts had ever seen it except as between friends. Some liberal-arts professor in about a hundred years' time was going to come through here documenting folk gestures and get really, really weirded out.

Of course, the nice streak came with a price, but what the hell, he'd already earned his beers today. Be good to earn a couple more. And the inn had a nice little nook next to the fireplace where the innkeeper's wife figured he and Vicky looked so sweet, she'd bring them a little jug of mulled sack as a nightcap. And, yes, they had a room to themselves. Darryl was, all things considered, very well disposed to notions of romance right at the minute.

And would remain so as long as the rubbers held out.

Chapter 9

"Fuck, fuck, fuck, *fuck*!" Mulligan was busily kicking in the wattle walls of the tiny house, bellowing his rage at the innocent timber and daub.

Finnegan had to admit that, crude as the sentiment was, he could see the point of it. They'd come on the place just before dawn, barely a murmur in the morning dew. Every man in Finnegan's band had got his start as a livestock thief in country far better guarded than this. Or at least, far better guarded than they thought this was.

They'd taken their time around Huntingdon, split up, tried not to act like an organized search party, watched carefully until they got the right place—old hand off Cromwell's farm, right part of the world, right ages of children, answering the meager descriptions they had. Questions, innocent enough, were asked and answered wherever folk grew expansive over their beer.

Finnegan himself had found and talked to a man who'd worked for Cromwell on the farm he rented out toward St. Ives a way, and visited the place. New tenants now, it seemed, and they'd been perfectly happy to talk with him about the famous fellow who'd been hauled away the year before.

More questions, more patient watching, more careful hiding of the attachment of one group of men to another. Finnegan had made sure, or so he thought, that no one lot of them looked like they were getting close. It would take a cunning fellow to add up all that was being seen and learned and deduce that they were getting closer day by day to whoever had given Cromwell's children shelter.

He'd even let two groups of the lads blow off steam in a tavern brawl one night, trying to make a show of them being rival groups of mercenaries after the same bounty. If it looked like they were working across each other, they might not scare away their prey. Finnegan and Tully had laughed together at how over-careful he was being as he finally narrowed the search step by step to a fensman's cabin seven or eight miles out of town down the local river, the Great Ouse it was called, and into the edges of the real fens.

Slipping by night through the fringes of the fen country, boggy as it was, proved no great hardship. The height of the growth, even this early in the summer, would have covered regiments.

Finnegan had been sure he'd had the place properly surrounded, and blown his whistle as soon as he could be sure of enough light to rush the house properly. With the door kicked in and the place surrounded, five men in, and seven to stand watch around would be enough to make sure nobody showed fight. The last thing he wanted was dead children; corpses were poor hostages and wonderful for provoking a man to revenge, so every man had gone in with bata in hand in place of sword or pistol. A cracked head would put the fight out of a man or woman and wouldn't kill a child, and he'd sent in the five best stick-fighters in the band.

Except it had turned out that whoever had been left inside that hut had had a gun, a dubious-looking old matchlock, probably a fowling piece older than its owner. The ambush-party-of-one had let drive with a load of bent nails, chips of gravel and cheap, sulphurous powder and then run in the confusion. It was a miracle that nobody had lost an eye to the thing; O'Halloran was missing a tooth and a piece of moustache where one of the bits of stone had taken him in the top lip.

That had been the signal for slingers—slingers! in this day and age!—to rise from the undergrowth and start pelting Finnegan's men with rocks. Even the smaller ones had been enough to raise painful welts through buffcoats. There were a couple of broken fingers and Tully wouldn't be seeing much out of his left eye nor standing up without an attack of dizziness for a week or two. A volley of stones, and the slingers had vanished altogether. How they'd done that in very near plain sight was between them and the devil, that was for sure.

Finnegan had had his lads out into the smallholding that surrounded the cabin, and beyond into the fens all morning and half the afternoon, but caught sight of nobody. From time to time a stone would hurtle out of nowhere and knock one of them arse-over-end into the muck. No smoke, no noise, just sudden pain. Occasionally they'd catch sight of some ragged figure whirling his sling. Of course, they'd be vanished by the time anyone reached the spot. Finnegan had, eventually, fallen them back on the cabin.

"Sure and we were spotted coming," Tully said, holding a wet kerchief to the side of his head, the linen slightly pink where the cut was still oozing. "And we should've brought helmets and breastplates."

"Spotted before that," Finnegan growled. "They're not as soft nor as foolish as we fooled ourselves they were. Burn this. We lay up and wait for Cromwell back near town. He's to come here to start finding his children, we'll have him then."

Finnegan wasn't one who gloried in the wreck and destruction of war, but there was a satisfaction in watching the cabin go up, the thatch tinder-dry in the warm breezes of summer. It might've been a little more fun to do it at night, but you took your entertainment where you found it.

"Mulligan!" Finnegan called the man over. With O'Hare up at York, and no word from him yet, Mulligan was his best for sending off for independent action. "Take six fellows and get over to Cromwell's old farm and put that to the torch as well. Turn out the people before you burn it, it's them that led me here, so it must be them that warned of us. See Cromwell's friends suffer for aiding him. I want that man with no safe place when he comes here."

Mulligan frowned. "We've to leave witnesses alive? Arson, that they hang a fellow for?"

Finnegan waved it aside. "I'm away to find a justice of the peace. I've a letter of commission from the king, given me by the earl. He'll not have constables after us for what's done at the command of the king, not without us being able to go before a court, at least. I've money for lawyers and the king has more, to attend that matter for us. Even if they can find a judge who'll hear it quickly, we can be gone before it comes to gaols and rope. Just see there's no dead, a hue and cry for murder we don't need at all."

"I'll be about it. Consider the place burnt before sundown." Mulligan turned to pick his usual cronies for such things, and Finnegan left him to it. Now he thought on the matter, there were other things a king could commission besides a manhunt. Was it the king who appointed constables, or the justices? Or, and here was a simple next step for you, get himself appointed justice of the peace for this locality and the boyos—or at least the smarter of them—as constables and he could go about his manhunt with no need for lawyers at all. For, when all was said and done, prison-breaking, escape and rescue were all felonies, and all of the concealment that was going on was misprision. If he got a commission as justice of the peace he could arrest, and sentence for that himself. The fines would help cover his expenses, and the threat of a whipping, branding or the pillory might loosen a few tongues. The earl would like that as a solution, since he'd complained bitterly about the lawyers and the courts hampering things he wanted to do. Finnegan could turn that on its head and make them regret all their careful precedent and argument while it served the king's need.

"You look like you're thinking," Tully said, still with the cloth clamped to his head. "And not about anything pleasant, either."

"Nor am I," Finnegan replied. "I think some of you boyos are going to have to be constables for a time."

Tully laughed, a bark before he stopped, wincing. "Don't make jokes, man, my head's fit to murther me. This lot, constables?"

"Constables. There's a lot of blather in this land about tyranny, Tully, and I think it's time they learned the meaning of the word from Irishmen, that know it." Finnegan stamped his soggy boots to try and fit them a little better. "I'll pay a call on a squire or two this evening after I've sent to the earl for the commission I'll need. We'll see how badly the king wants this Cromwell brought to justice for his prison-breaking, when the earl asks him to commission a lot of *torai* as constables and their chief as a justice of the peace."

Tully barked again and winced, and the other boyos around laughed too. "Jesus, Mary and Joseph, Finnegan, have mercy on a wounded man. It's like a spike in my head to laugh right now. You, a fuckin' justice of the peace?"

Finnegan grinned. "Let's be back to that fleapit we're staying in, I've letters to write."

He spent the afternoon in the taproom of the Falcon in Huntingdon composing his letter to the earl. He didn't think he'd have to argue too hard to get himself appointed as a justice; the mere fact that it would jam sideways in the throat of every one of the country gentlemen who got in the way of the king's plans for the nation would be argument enough. Still and all, he'd learned proper rhetoric in the grammar school and it wasn't in him to make less than the best case he could.

Mulligan returned just about as he was done, smelling faintly of smoke and grinning. "Sure and it felt good to do that, fair put me in mind of us getting evicted when I was a little boy. I ran the family off from town a ways, since I thought you'd want to get to the justices before they did."

"You thought right, Mulligan, and before you sit down to your supper after a good day's work, you get to pick who rides back to London with my letters to the earl. Charge him to bring back an answer as quick as he can."

Mulligan nodded and took the packet, and Finnegan set out to see the local justice.

"Mister Pedley, Esquire, I presume," Finnegan said, when he was let in to the man's house.

"I am," said the old fellow who'd risen from his seat by the fire to greet his visitor, "and who might you be?"

"William Finnegan, of County Waterford, in service to the earl of Cork and His Majesty the king, squire. I've fetched my letter of commission for you to see. I'm after the man that broke out of the Tower of London last month, and I've cause to believe he'll come here within the next few days."

"I'd heard talk of questions being asked. You're in charge of that lot of Irishmen about town, then?"

"They are indeed my sworn men, sir, and in the course of executing my commission this morning two of them were wounded. By the grace of God and His providence, sir, not grievously, but I'm after laying information before you all the same as soon as I have names to give. There's also the matter of me and my men being given false information regarding the fugitive, sir, and so soon as I can find time to furnish full particulars there's information to be laid in that matter too. In furtherance of my commission"—he paused to lay the document on the side table beside Pedley's chair, noting the while that he'd not been invited to sit at all—"I exacted punitive measures on those most directly responsible for the misprision, sir."

Pedley regarded him levelly. "Am I to understand that this commission, sir, is like to the French *carte blanche*?"

Finnegan reached the obvious conclusion that here was a man who'd have been for Parliament in the future that never was. "I'd know nothing of the French, sir," he said. "It is a plain commission from the king to take a felon and a traitor in flight wheresoever he may be found. And if you care to tell me, sir, that when he was arrested he was no felon, by his prison-break he became one."

Pedley harrumphed. "I dare say there's a lawyer who'd make a pretty mess of that case, and likely another who'd make a pretty present of it. My duty, sir, is to keep the peace, and since I hear not a quarter hour since that your brigands have burnt a farmhouse and barn, showing mercy only to the lives of the family therein, I have to wonder what best to do for that duty. And now you tell me the king commands it? That's a color for your actions, sir, but not the color of law."

Finnegan smiled gently. "I am in pursuit of a felon and a traitor, sir. Hot pursuit, if you will, for all I've got ahead of my man. And while it may be that there's a bench somewhere that might convict me for my actions, I'm told His Majesty is much fond of exercising his prerogatives, one of which is the prerogative of pardon. Things would have to change greatly in London before I'll face gallows or gaol for anything I might do short of murder in my commission, sir."

"I suppose, in these times, a man should be grateful for fair warning before the royal tyranny buggers him again?" Pedley's tone was acid, sour and sharp. Finnegan had to give him credit; he had an armed man in his home explaining that he'd been given license to do all short of killing and he wasn't acting the craven.

"Ah, now tyranny I understand, sir, and tyranny this is not. Rough and ready justice for a traitor and a felon, and all those who aid him, but not tyranny." He was careful to keep his tone soft. He knew what had happened to his country under the plantations, and had some idea of what *would* have happened to it over the next few years. For his own part, he cared nothing for it, so long as he and his suffered little or nothing. But it struck him as monstrous that this fat old fool in his fine warm house with, yes, his bottle of sack, could complain of tyranny. "I'll take my leave of you, sir, and ask you to expect my information laid within the week. In the meantime I await further commands from the king."

"As you say. See yourself out, commissioner," Pedley said, handing the king's letter back to Finnegan unread. "I'm sure I'll be hearing more from and about you."

"Just until I have my man in hand, squire Pedley, just until I have my man in hand."

Tully was waiting outside, minding the horses. There might be a surprising lack of thievery hereabouts, but old habits died hard. "From the face of you I take it that went as poorly as could be expected?"

Finnegan shrugged. "We knew the Cromwells were a big family hereabouts, and before he was arrested our man was making himself popular with the bog folk. Something about drainage schemes, as I recall. Seems he was a known man with the gentry as well, because that man wouldn't have given me the steam off his turds without I had the king's letter in my hand. Which he troubled not to read, mark you."

Tully snorted. He'd stopped groaning hours before, so Finnegan supposed the buffet to his head wasn't so bad as all that. "The talk of you after you've spoken to gentry is always such a delight to hear, so."

Finnegan rolled his eyes. "I had the learning of it at school, it never leaves a man. And it pays to talk to the bastards the way they expect or you're just another fucking bog-trotter they can safely ignore, king's letter or no king's letter. Well, we've been handed a fine opportunity to shove the bog firmly up their arses, one way or another, doubled if the earl persuades the king. More than one of the boyos will welcome the chance to have at the Saxons, *torai* though they be. It's one thing to have your countrymen to chase you for the sake of stolen cattle, quite another to be run off your land by foreign soldiers for the sake of other foreigners."

Memories of the confiscations and plantations of colonists after the Nine Years' War were still raw. Boys who'd grown up dirt poor, paying hard rent on good land their grandfathers had owned—in some cases were still around to complain bitterly about—could and did turn to thieving to keep body and soul together. Caught, and offered a pardon by the earl, they carried on as the enforcers of the order that had broken their families. It put money in a man's pocket, but in the small hours of the night he could be excused a certain amount of resentment. Oh, indeed, there'd be some relish in getting the whip hand over the Saxons. Tully, for example, was from around Kinsale. His grandfather had died the year after the siege there was broken, driven off his land entirely for plantation as punishment for a rebellion he'd had no part in, or so he insisted. Tully's father had fought through the courts for years to recover the land, only to have the title he'd recovered called into question because he was a Catholic. He'd gotten something of a price for it from the earl, who'd been plain Richard Boyle back then, and probably more than he'd have had from any other buyer. The poor old fool had been pathetically grateful.

The younger Tully had been less impressed with the deal, but he could at least see that Boyle was the best of a bad lot among plantationers—he'd got his first stake in Ireland by marrying an Irish lady, or at least one of the Old English, who'd come over in peace and settled. The fact that he'd been imprisoned several times on suspicion of aiding the rebel side in the Nine Years' War helped, too.

That had never impressed Finnegan overmuch. Any man on the rise as Boyle had been would make enemies, and collusion with rebels and foreigners was a useful handful of mud to throw at such.

Still, Tully was grinning in the last light of the day. "That will be a true nightmare for the Saxons, to be sure. An Irishman with a constable's warrant set over them? We'll have to hold their reins tight, so we will."

Chapter 10

"Praise be for a real bed," said Gayle Mason. Examining the item of furniture in question and then her two companions, she added: "It'll be a tight fit, though. That's *without* adding any extraneous males, you understand."

Julie Mackay and Vicky Short both grinned, albeit for different reasons. The down-timer's grin was cheerful, recalling instances in which her bed had been shared with a male whom she did not consider extraneous at all, one Darryl McCarthy. She wouldn't be enjoying his company this night, though, because the town they were staying at—say better, village; better yet, hamlet—lacked an inn and the only cottage they'd found with an extra room the inhabitants were willing to rent had nothing more than a bed any American would have called a single bed.

The bed was normally shared by two young daughters—neither more than ten years old—who would contribute to the family's finances tonight by sleeping on the floor of the main room. The men in their party got to sleep in the barn. Which was at least a lot roomier.

The up-timer, Julie, whose enjoyment of marital privileges had now lasted long enough that she took them for granted, had a grin on her face that was more resigned than anything else.

"Praise be," she muttered, remembering less seventeenth-century times when she and Gayle, dyed-in-the-wool Americans, would have said *Thank God* without even thinking about it. But both of them were now romantically linked to Calvinists, who took the third commandment dead seriously.

Vicky left the room to bring in the few supplies they'd want for the night. Julie and Gayle exchanged a rueful smile.

"Look on the bright side," said Julie. "Most of what we grew up hearing about up-tight fun-hating straight-laced Puritans turned out to be bullshit."

Gayle chuckled. "Complete bullshit, at that. But"—she glanced around quickly, to make sure they were still alone—"dear God, they take their theology seriously, don't they?"

Julie sat down on the bed and bounced up and down on it a couple of times. "Well, at least it isn't too soft. With three of us in it, a soft bed would leave the middle one buried beneath the other two. Ain't it the truth about the theology? But I will say this: it works mostly in our favor, when it comes to dealing with the menfolk. At least of the husband variety. The Calvinists are so bound and determined to pick a fight with the Catholic church that if the pope frowns on sex, they approve of it, and if the bishops and priests yap about the virtues of celibacy your good Calvinist—sure as hell my husband—is bound and determined to prove the papist bastids is full of crap."

The smile that came to her face this time wasn't rueful in the least. "Which is fine by me."

She then bestowed upon Gayle a look that might be called speculative.

Gayle shook her head. "I can't say from personal experience one way or the other. Oliver's no prude, that's for sure, but he is...what's the word?"

"Serious?"

"Yeah, that's it. When it comes to some things, anyway. And it's not as if opportunity is knocking. It's one thing for married couples like you and Alex—even Darryl and Vicky, for that matter—to figure out ways to squeeze in a little nookie here and there. But when you've got two people like me and Oliver who are groping around trying to figure out..."

Gayle shrugged. "Everything. How we feel about each other. What he's going to do with his life now—and do I want to fit myself into that? Because whatever he does you can be sure and certain it's going to involve a grim determination to shorten one Charles Stuart by about eight inches—and let's kick over the whole damn rotten applecart while we're at it. Not to mention that he's got a bunch of kids to deal with if and when we can find them."

She took a deep breath and sighed it out. "Like I said. Everything. And while we're doing so there is no way that Mr. Serious Cromwell is going to dally with my affections. As they say. Which… I have to admit, just makes him that much more attractive to me. The more time I spend in his company, the more time I want to spend in it. Which my hardheaded grandma once told me is the only definition of 'falling in love' that'll stand the test of time. I think she was probably right."

She went to the room's one tiny window and peered out. As bad as the glass was, she couldn't see much. In the seventeenth century, except for palaces and the homes of the wealthy, *through a glass, darkly* was a simple statement of fact.

"The truth is," Gayle said quietly, "if Oliver and I do get married—and that's all that man would ever settle for—the only big problem I see is that Puritans seem to find a theological justification for the wife being subordinate to the husband. And that's sure not something I agree with. I'm no feminist, but—"

Julie laughed. Gayle turned to give her an inquisitive look. "What's so funny?"

"You." She waved at herself. "I guess I should say, us. I once said that very same thing to Melissa Mailey. 'I'm no feminist, *but—*'"

Gayle smiled. "She must have reamed you a new one."

"No, actually, what she did was worse. She just made fun of me. Ridiculed me, dammit. What she said was that every working-class American woman—girls, too—said exactly the same thing. 'I'm no feminist, *but.*' And then we proceed to follow the 'but' with the entire litany of feminist demands that we're in favor of. Each and every one."

Julie raised her hand and began counting off her fingers. "Lessee, now. Right to vote. *Check.* Right to hold property. *Check.* Right to get paid the same for the same work. *Check.* Right to divorce the bum when he turns out to be a bum. *Check.* Right to make contracts in your own name. *Check.*"

She dropped her hands. "Melissa challenged me to come up with a single feminist demand I *didn't* agree with. Best I could come up with was that I thought burning bras was stupid."

Gayle chuckled. "Same thing I would have said."

"Yeah—and then Melissa explained to me that that was a bunch of bullshit invented by assholes. Turns out no feminist ever burned a bra."

"Really?"

"Nope. Melissa told me the myth got started when a group of women protested the Miss America contest in Atlantic City—that was in 1968, if I remember right—by tossing bras along with girdles, cosmetics and high-heeled shoes into a big trash can. They also crowned a sheep. But they never actually set fire to the can."

"Ha!" said Gayle, shaking her head again. "You learn something new every day."

She looked back through the window. "I wish I could see the future better than I can see through this thing. I have no idea—well, okay, that's not true; I have an *idea,* you bet I do—what'll happen between me and Oliver. But..."

"Don't sweat the wifely obedience business too much, Gayle," Julie said. "Alex will swear by the same silly crap." Her voice got a little sing-songy and picked up a Scottish burr: "It says right here in the Good Book that—prattle, prattle, prattle. But in the real world? He never pushes it. Men who are sure of themselves—which is part of what makes them attractive to us, let's face it—just don't seem to feel the need to keep proving who's wearing the pants in the family."

She and Gayle both looked at Gayle's clothing. Which consisted of a bodice, ankle-length skirt and a bonnet—the same thing Julie was wearing herself.

"I sure do miss blue jeans," said Gayle. "Although I admit this stuff isn't as uncomfortable as I would have thought seeing it in movies. By now, I'm used to linen instead of cotton. Don't even notice the difference anymore."

Julie nodded. "That's pretty much how it is being married to a seventeenth-century fella, too—as long as you pick the right one. There are some differences, even a few big ones, but after a while you hardly notice anymore. But I emphasize the part about picking the right one."

Gayle turned away from the window and cocked her head slightly. "So what do *you* think about Oliver? Think he'd be a right one for me?"

Julie pursed her lips. "Well...He's a little...Well. Scary, I guess."

Gayle snorted softly. "We *are* talking about Oliver Cromwell, girl. *The* Oliver Cromwell. Cut off a king's head, ruled England like a dictator for years. Not to mention, if you listen to Darryl, slaughtered half the Irish."

"Darryl hasn't said that in a long time. I don't think he even still believes it. The truth is—he won't admit, at least not yet—but he likes Oliver. A *lot,* if I don't miss my guess."

"No, I don't think you do," said Gayle. "Darryl's a real hillbilly and when you get down to it, for all the obvious differences there's something very hillbillyish about Oliver Cromwell too. If nothing else, they're both bloody-minded in that scary-as-all-hell practical way they have about them."

There was silence in the room, for a moment. Then Julie said: "But I'm not trying to duck the question. He's a little scary, but the truth is I like Oliver myself. A lot, by now. And, yeah, I think he'd do okay by you, Gayle."

A grin came back to her. "Keeping in mind that some people—whole lot of people, being honest about it—would say that you and me are pretty hillbillyish ourselves."

Vicky came back into the room, carrying a bundle in her hands. She studied the bed for a moment.

"How'll we do it?" she asked. "Decide which of us has to sleep in the middle, I mean. Draw straws? Flip a coin—assuming either of you has one, because I don't."

Gayle and Julie looked at each other.

"We could fight for it," said Gayle.

Vicky sneered. "Me—against a couple of hillbillies? Do I look mad? I'd as soon wrestle a bull. No, we'll do it civilized."

In the end, they settled on rock-scissors-paper, after they explained the rules to Vicky.

Vicky won right off and picked the side away from the wall. Julie lost the runoff to Gayle.

"I'm fucked," she grumbled.

"Not tonight," said Vicky. "There'd be no room even if you weren't in the middle."

Part Three

August 1634

What force or guile could not subdue,

Thro' many warlike ages,

Is wrought now by a coward few,

For hireling traitor's wages.

Chapter 11

"I hope my lord Montrose will forgive me not rising," Mackay said, indicating with a gesture the uselessness of the legs under the blanket. He'd had a couple of footmen, with Meg fussing, lift him and move him into a chair. Sitting up for any length of time hurt damnably, and he could all but feel it wearing his life away like a blade on a grindstone, but he was determined that the last of him to go would be his manners with guests. Besides, the pain made him sharp in his mind, and he'd need that.

Montrose, polite himself, waved it aside as of no matter. "A broken back's excuse enough for any man," he said, "and if it would serve you better to lay down, I'll not hear it said I made a man suffer for formality."

"I have comfort enough as I am, my lord," Mackay lied. It would not do to admit any more weakness than he absolutely had to until he knew which part Montrose had taken. He'd known of the Graham clan chief's summons to London, and word of his elevation to the Lord Lieutenancy had preceded him back. Was he talking to Charles Stuart's bought-and-paid-for man, or simply the nearest the king could find? Scotland's peerage was stacked to the rafters with men no more constant than the nation's weather. "Will you have a drink? I find a brandy at this hour helps."

"Wine, if it's to hand," Montrose said. "I've mair folk to see the day, I'll save the brandy for when I'm done. Don't let me stop you with the brandy, though, I'd want one myself were I afflicted as you are."

That was a common reaction. A fall from a horse could happen to any man, and it was a rare and skilled horseman who never had so much as a bruise, and not many more who hadn't at least broken a bone or two. A broken back, well, anyone could look on a man damaged as Mackay was and shudder that there but for the grace of God went he.

Mackay let Meg put the brandy in reach of his hand and a decanter of good wine by Montrose and leave them. The afternoon was a pleasant one, the rain outside soft on the streets of Edinburgh but otherwise it was warm. The faint smell of wet wool was about the place, not strong as the showers were stopping and starting, and there was promise of a fine fresh day in the later afternoon.

"I'll be blunt, my lord," he said after they'd taken a moment to have a small drink, glasses raised to each other in a polite, if silent health. "I'm more than a little mithered as to what His Majesty's about with yon earl of Cork, who I've long thought an equivocator of the worst kind, which is to say the kind that comes out on the winning side every time. Did he not spend time imprisoned over the Irish business all those years ago? I was but a young boy myself and not minding matters in the plantations overmuch, but I recall he was a rebel for a time with his people in Munster."

Montrose shrugged. "He stood acquitted of all the charges and Her Majesty of England granted him high office, after. That much I have from some of my older people; it was before I was born. If it's between us two here and now, I'll not gainsay you on the man being devious, unprincipled and after naught but his own advancement." He held up a hand. "If you think that's the beginning of me saying he's an evil counselor, as the saying has it, think again. The sense I have of the man is he has a wildcat by the tail and dare not let go. If anything, the man regrets his move against Strafford, who's in all likelihood Wentworth again now. They were drawing up attainder and impeachment when I left London. But Cork? If he's a lying, back-stabbing, unprincipled snake of a man, and I do rich insult to snakes with that, he's exactly the man His Majesty needs in England these days. And now, without His Majesty on a secure throne, Cork is, and pardon my crudeness, fucked."

As such things went, that was as good a dissection of the cadaver of English politics as Mackay expected to hear from anyone. And it came from this sharp young man, of an age to be his own son, who'd met all concerned, and that recently. He nodded. "A sorry state for the state of England, I'd say," he said.

Montrose's expression was distasteful. "No more would I want the like here in Scotland, if I can help it."

"Aye, I'll raise my glass to that notion," Mackay said, doing so.

Montrose answered him likewise. "His Majesty has charged me to secure silence north of the Tweed, among other things," he said, after taking a sip. "I'm to ensure that there's no reversal for the episcopal party, although, and here I sense Cork's hand, there's no charge on me to advance the swine either."

Mackay raised an eyebrow. "The king's ain party in the kirk? Swine?"

Montrose chuckled. "I'll swear any oath you care to name I said no such word. Concerning those swine nor any other lot. I've no time for prelates, we had well rid of them in my grandfather's time, but added to that I've not much patience with presbyters neither. Their place is in the pulpit, not in the governance of the realm."

"That would sound awfully like the separation of church and state, my lord, and I should be much obliged if you could explain to me the reason it is not so?"

"Well, as His Majesty is the head of the Kirk in Scotland, is it not the case that he may command the presbyters thereof to leave off the secular governance? As he guarantees their establishment, is it not reasonable that they—" Montrose gestured vaguely, looking for a phrase.

"Render unto Caesar?" Mackay suggested, suddenly taken by the imp of the perverse.

Montrose grinned. "Aye, or words to like effect. I shall have to remember that one."

"The presbyters will call it a short step from freedom of religion," Mackay said, sure they'd call it worse than that if given the least liberty.

"If it's a lack of freedom they desire, I'm empowered, and on one reading charged, to administer it them, and that right harshly. I've charges from His Majesty, but as long as they hear nothing south of the border, how I undertake them is a matter for me."

"Aye? I'd heard you were made Lord Lieutenant over us, but from the sounds, you've all but been made viceroy."

Montrose rocked a hand back and forth. "Ye might call it that, ye might not. Certain sure I am that I could govern as one right up until the rebellion it created."

"There's always that," Mackay answered. He'd felt a mounting sense of unease, and not simply from the pain he was in. He himself was none of the movers and shakers of Clan Mackay, still less now he was a cripple. He was personally acquainted with Lord Reay, was a cousin four times removed or something on the close order of that, and had a number of closer kin in the Mackay regiment in the Germanies. So *why* was his lordship the earl of Montrose, Chief of Clan Graham, whom he had met perhaps twice before, treating him with such friendly familiarity?

"Aye, that," Montrose sighed. "And ye needn't fear for me on that score. I've no intention of creating mair trouble than the nation truly needs. We've had and signed the National Covenant in my grandfather's time and the less said about that the better. England's misfortunes will be to Scotland's benefit in at least that much. His Majesty won't be trying to press the matter of the liturgy or the power of the prelates any further, he having larger matters to occupy him. There's a smaller matter he's paid mind to, though, and it's the reason I came first to you, for on it hangs much else."

"Aye? I can do little but advise, crippled as I am."

Montrose fixed him with a stare. "There's a lot more you can do, Mackay of the Mackays. Father-in-law of a Swedish baroness. Cousin to Lord Reay, however distant. Old drinking companion of Robert Leslie. And others I might list, but choose not to for the moment."

"You mean those gone for soldiers in the Germanies, of course. I take it His Majesty means for them to come home peacefully or not at all?"

"Somewhat more, in which regard I want your help in the persuading of those men. You among others, of course, you're not the only man with kin and companions currently serving the king of Sweden. His Majesty Charles has already made shift to see that some of those who stood against him on the other history cannot do it in this. Cromwell, for one, some others in England the names of which I can't recall. There would have been more in Scotland, save that Leslie was in Germany, and others it was not...practical to take captive."

Mackay laughed at that. "You mean Argyll let it be known, beyond any manner o' doubt, that if any man north of the border was so much as touched for his part in that other history, he being at the top of the list, the Bishops' War would start ten years early and wouldn't stop at Newcastle? You know he already has a fine body of men about him that would answer such a call, beyond even the usual clans he can call on at need?"

Mackay had only learned the full extent of that particular correspondence days before. At the time it actually happened, he'd missed much of the detail. When he'd heard the full story he'd pissed the bed laughing and not regretted a drop. He knew Argyll was a peppery wee bastard, but the likely reaction of Strafford and His Majesty to such a naked defiance, however privately expressed, would have been a sight to see. It was Mackay's guess, supported by a few other fellows he'd written to, that the only thing that was stopping him for now was that he wasn't yet earl of Argyll in his own right, at least until his father died in his self-imposed exile in London. For every worthwhile purpose, though, he was Chief of the Campbells and his Lordship of Lorne sufficed to give him lawful authority in that matter.

"If I was to put my hand on my heart, I'd agree with him," Montrose said, "and it's exactly that manner of thing I mean not to have with the German veterans. Ye ken Leslie would have been arrested if he'd been in the country, and Argyll had not spoken as he did? I was a mite troubled my name was on the list when I heard, too, though it seems His Majesty cares for the end result rather than the first thoughts. As matters stand, I've been given the Lord Lieutenancy only after Strafford, Laud and the like have heated it to a red glow for me, and I mean to have the matter of the veterans be the least of my troubles. I can delay and delay and delay the sending of letters patent to those men demanding their return, allegiance and good behavior on pain of forfeiture, but there'll come a day when His Majesty must take notice of my doing nothing in the matter. I mean by then to have a solution all, or at least most, are content with, that they may return home or have their affairs in order for exile. I'll chafe as I may at some of His Majesty's charges, Mister Mackay, but he and I are of one mind that Scotland is to be peaceful. There'll be no lamentations of Scotland to match the same in Germany, if at all it can be helped. Heaping up a pan of fresh embers from the smouldering of Germany to tip them into the bedding of Scotland strikes me as no help at all in that regard."

"I have every warmest sentiment toward your aims, my lord," Mackay said, temporising while he thought. How much had Reay been in communication with Montrose? Argyll? How much were the Scots officers in Gustavus Adolphus' service in agreement on the matter? Nothing suggested itself as a way forward. "What would His Majesty have, precisely, of the Scots abroad?" he asked, hoping to buy time to think.

Montrose's face brightened a little. Perhaps he had been expecting an immediate refusal. Mackay had a clear idea of what perhaps a dozen of those lords and gentlemen thought, and some of their followers besides, what the king's spies might have told him was a closed book. There was also the possibility that Charles Stuart, being Charles Stuart, had got hold of some other notion of his own about what the veterans abroad thought.

Montrose took a deep breath and began reciting. "His Majesty is principally concerned that his subjects granted leave to fight abroad remain in the service of the king of Sweden, not the United States of Europe, with which there exists a state of hostility, short of outright war but nevertheless unfriendly. He is further concerned that inasmuch as they bear arms in Sweden's cause, Sweden is closely aligned with the United States of Europe and as such His Majesty's subjects are bearing arms in support of a nation that espouses the heretical and anarchical doctrine of freedom of religion. In so doing they are in peril of their souls and he is much exercised as head of the church to which they are properly adherent that they remove themselves from the said peril as soon as may be. He requires, in the first instance, that they give undertaking and surety that they serve the king of Sweden only and that only in conflict with avowedly Catholic arms in the Germanies. He also requires that all of the rank of major and above resign their commissions and return to their estates in Scotland to the great benefit of that nation."

He took another breath. "My charge continues in the same vein for some time, with many places and means whereby delay and obfuscation may occur, but the essence of it is that they should be at home and at peace lest His Majesty take to the notion that they are preparing to levy war against him either here or abroad."

"Put thus, it seems like a fair command, as commands go," Mackay said, "although I've no means of knowing how any man to whom it may come will see it. His Majesty says as he will of the notion of freedom of religion, but how is it seen by those living with it? There was a time when the reformed religion was declared by kings to be heretical and anarchical, after all, but it was found good in Geneva."

Montrose answered that with a level stare. "I'm not minded to debate that matter at all, neither with His Majesty nor any of his subjects. I want peace, but when all's said and done, if His Majesty's subjects wish to reside in His Majesty's realm under His Majesty's peace, the price is obedience to His Majesty. North of the Tweed, through me. I believe it was His Majesty's father who said all he desired was an outward obedience to the law, and that I am content with also. Those that can't obey, well, they may sell their lands and settle where obedience is easier, and I mean to make that easy. But those are the choices. You, among others, I ask to present those choices to the men that must make them so they may mull them before anything is said *ex officio*, and persuade them that, by command of His Majesty I cannot be moved beyond tolerance of mere delay."

"I'll send to those I know, my lord. It's not for me to dictate their answers."

Montrose nodded acknowledgement of the point. "Nor do I ask it. I merely wish to be sure that I only give the command to those that will obey it, and ensure that those whose conscience bids them remain abroad not find themselves ruined thereby. Conveyed privately, by friends, I hope that that will be clearer than it might be by official letter."

Mackay nodded. "In this much, then, I am my lord's servant."

"Aye, and in perhaps one other thing. You've a son out of wed-lock who's been back in the country, do I understand correctly?"

Mackay noted the wording. He had his own suspicions about what Alex and Julie had been up to in London, dark suspicions indeed. But he was sure they'd not left Edinburgh with any prov-able intent to take part in that, and if their part in it, if any, had been witnessed the Montrose would not be half so cordial today. Indeed, there'd be warrants, summonses and questions to answer, and likely he'd be accused of being an accessory to felony rescue. How a bench of Scots judges would try that Mackay had no idea, but there was plenty of precedent for them taking on such matters whether or not there was strictly any law covering it.

"Aye, for all he's from the wrong side of the blanket, he's a fine boy who's done well for himself."

"His wife, too." Montrose was giving nothing away with that remark, but Mackay felt he was justified in assuming the worst.

"A bonny wee lass, and a fair hand with a rifle," Mackay said. All true facts, not open to debate.

"Aye, and possessed of a barony of Sweden," Montrose added, also a fact not open to debate. "I've no notion of where your boy is, Mackay, but if it turns out he or his wife had anything to do with the prison-breaking at the Tower of London, and you've any influence with him, see he doesn't show his face where I might have to turn my attention to him. I can wink at much, but when a man takes open warlike actions against one of the king's own fortresses, well, that strikes me as a bit much. What's more, I don't want it coming to anybody's attention that you're in communication with him if such turns out to be the case. I need your services as intermediary with the veterans abroad far more than I need to hang a crippled man as accessory to treason and felony."

Mackay glared. "If my lord cares to accuse me publicly of misprision of treason, he is welcome to do that, and be damned to him."

Montrose growled back. "That's not what I want, and you know it, man. Strafford did the stupidest thing a man could do by those arrests in England, and while I've little use for Campbell the man, Argyll the politician did righter than he knew when he made it known he'd take it ill if there were proscriptions of that kind in Scotland. His Majesty's father did ill enough proscribing the Mac-Gregor, broken men and outlaw brutes though they were. To have that against decent folk would be more than could be borne. Now, if your boy took a hand in correcting that stupid mistake, I for one care not a whit for it. So long as I don't have to take official notice of it as Lord Lieutenant of Scotland, and none of the consequences come within this kingdom, I'll carry on not caring. It is to my benefit, your benefit, your son's benefit, and *Scotland's* benefit if I can keep to not caring. See to it, as well as you may."

With that, and the most perfunctory of pleasantries to contrive that he did not wish to be unfriendly but had been put out of sorts by their conversation, Montrose took his leave.

Chapter 12

"No, totally burnt to the ground," Towson confirmed. "Not too long ago, by the looks, there's still a lot of ash and charcoal about the place, but we couldn't go too close to be sure. Not a lot we could see from the road, but every building in and around the farmhouse is burnt back to a shell. And, just in case we thought this was a coincidence, a couple of smiling lads happened to be around the place for us to ask what had happened as we ambled along, nothing but a couple of idle old soldiers home from the Germanies, off to visit an old friend up the road a ways. Well, they didn't have a lot to tell us, but they're not local boys. Irishmen, the pair of them."

"And since your humble servant here kept his mouth firmly shut," Welch added, "they had the fool notion of thinking talking in Irish would be private to them. They're watching the place and decided that their chief ought to know as soon as Mulligan, whoever that was, came round in a short while. So that's why we're late, we'd to find another way back since they'd certain sure be waiting for us."

Darryl could see the pain on Cromwell's face. He'd only been a tenant on that farm, slowly and carefully working his fortunes back up from what sounded like near-bankruptcy, but it had been his home for more than three years. And whoever was tenant there now might have been able to tell him where his children had ended up. "Did they say aught of the children that once lived there?"

"Nothing," Welch said. "They had a little to say of the family that was there most recently, though. Two, very little. Run off with their ma and da and two farmhands, they said, when the farm was burnt."

"Did they say why?" Darryl asked, beginning to feel a cold, hollow feeling he wasn't sure would be warmed other than by administering some righteous hillbilly justice. He'd been along with the scouting parties that'd gone out right after the Ring of Fire and seen some of the shit guys down-time could and did pull on ordinary folks in their own homes, and the fury'd never really left him. Seems like some of it got out in his voice, since both Cromwell and Hamilton were giving him funny looks.

"Order of the justice of the peace, under commission from the king, they said. Sounds like lies to me, though. Even across the water the justices can't just have someone's home burnt, especially if it's tenanted and not freehold. They've punished the landlord as much as anyone." Welch shrugged. "I think we'd need more than the word of those two ruffians to get to the bottom of it."

"True enough," Cromwell said. "I never completed my studies for the bar, but I can tell you that much. Fines and seizures can be compassed by a justice of the peace, but burning a farm and driving the tenant off? I never heard the like before and never thought to."

Darryl felt a moment of grim humor come over him. "You know, Oliver, with all the grief I gave you over what you would've done in Ireland, I never stopped to think about the bit where you rebelled against the king. And if this is the kind of thing you have to put up with from His Royal Assholeness, I can't say it wasn't purely the right thing to do."

"If it was not before, it is now," Cromwell said, and there didn't seem to be a trace of jest in his words. "It remains that we should find them. Robert and Oliver will have come back from school by now, if they had not already. I cannot recall where I stood with the school in the matter of fees. I can only hope that God's grace guided them to find the little ones and the friends I have in this county."

"Robert's your oldest, yes?" Hamilton said, "Fourteen now?"

"But a month past. He and Oliver were away at school when I was captured, or they might have been shot. Oliver will be thirteen come November. Bridget, Henry and Elizabeth are the little ones. Bridget will be eleven years old soon."

They'd all heard Cromwell speak of his children, the hope in his voice a thin veneer over a chasm of worry. On the one hand, the Cromwells were a rich and influential family in Huntingdonshire, and there would have been no shortage of relatives to take them in. On the other hand, it would have taken time to get word to any of those relatives, and much could have happened to them in the meantime. And between Cromwell's children and his relatives there were all the enemies he'd made only a couple of years before in Huntingdon itself, speaking his mind clearly and vociferously against the terms of the town's charter of 1630.

To Darryl's amusement, the man had had no idea of the name "Lord of the Fens" and still less of any plan to drain the Fens that he might have helped anyone with. He'd certainly made himself popular among the poor of Huntingdon by what he'd publicly called the mayor of that town over the terms of the new charter, which more-or-less allowed the mayor and aldermen to help themselves to town property intended for poor relief. He'd had to apologize in privy council for his language, but the council itself had sustained his objections to the terms of the new charter and amended it. It probably hadn't helped that he'd accepted a post as justice of the peace under the new charter to get himself a public platform to say those things. Darryl was, quietly, looking forward to twitting Miz Mailey over that one, to be sure. And learning that Cromwell had deliberately gotten inside City Hall to fight City Hall, and won, took him up a notch or two in Darryl's estimation. That shit was *tactical*.

If the absolute worst hadn't happened, and Cromwell had enough trust in his neighbors that it hadn't—with plenty of credit given to Divine Providence along the way, of course—the next possibility was that through sheer carelessness they'd fallen on the tender mercies of the poor-law system for the parish of St. Ives. That had the potential for real disaster: a poorhouse orphanage was a chancy proposition at best. Bridget might have been old enough to go out maintained as a needleworker in some gentry home, but little Henry and Elizabeth, who'd be six and five by now, might or might not have survived in an orphanage. Farm children in the here and now, even offspring of a gentleman farmer, had no easy life, but from there into a parish orphanage would be a terrible blow for them.

And, while Cromwell didn't think any of the enemies he'd made hereabouts were that petty, there was every possibility that they'd have gotten one of the less pleasant deals that the already-savage English poor law could hand out purely out of ignorance. There was even the possibility that someone, meaning well enough, would have split them up and moved them on to other parishes, or fostered them somewhere in secret, seeking to preserve their lives from a capricious monarch apparently bent on slaughtering his subjects at random. Who was to say he'd stop at the parents and one of the elder brothers? Cromwell had spent enough time as a justice of the peace, part of the administration of these things, to know that even with the best of intentions it was entirely possible to make some shockingly harsh decisions even in respect of the impotent and deserving poor. Under pressure of the need to preserve the lives of children? It would be all too easy for a man to find it in himself to do the children a little injustice now to preserve them from murder later.

"I suppose there's some good reason why we can't go back, grab those two boyos and beat a bit more than a half-story out of them?"

Welch plainly shared some, if not all, of Darryl McCarthy's concerns in the matter. Darryl had talked to him plenty over the last couple of weeks and discovered that whatever Strafford and Cromwell might've done in the future, it would've been little more than a garnish on what was the ordinary lot of the Catholic Irish, and a fair number of the Protestant Irish who'd gone native enough to count, in this day and age. And, under the hardened and cynical mercenary exterior, there was a firebrand who'd only been dampened by recognizing there wasn't anything he could do by himself. Presented with a couple of hired thugs at the sharp end of repressing the people? They could probably tie those two goons to a chair apiece and let them listen to him and Darryl argue over who got to work them over. They'd sing like canaries out of fear.

Stephen Hamilton had plainly figured out what was making the grin spread across Darryl's face. "No, and don't tell me you weren't thinking it. It speaks well of you that it's your first thought, Darryl, but just thundering in with your kicking boots on ain't the right move, not yet."

"Oh, I figured that," Darryl said. "I was just taking a moment to enjoy the thought."

"Well enough," Hamilton said. "Mister Cromwell, who should we talk to first? While I'm with Lieutenant Welch here on the subject of beatings, I want to make sure we're breaking the right heads."

Cromwell sighed. "I also. There wasn't a lad could stand against me in singlestick at Cambridge, and the thought of giving in to the deadly sin of wrath is a sore temptation now. We must speak with Esquire Pedley. My first thought was one of the Montagus, but they'll be taking the king's part in all this if I'm not mistaken. Even if I am, why take the chance when there are other choices? If he has knowledge of my family's whereabouts, then we may talk to them. I have better and closer friends, it must be said, but none so local or more likely to know what has happened here."

In the end, Cromwell surprised Darryl by asking him to come along to Squire Pedley's house. "Save only this, young Mister McCarthy, hold your tongue and listen, and think on what might be said and, more importantly, not said. I know you have no love for me, so let not my distress distract you, but think on the fate of my little girls. The boys might manage for themselves, in time and by God's grace, but this is no world for a girl-child to be alone in." Darryl had been touched by that much trust, and had wondered aloud whether or not he'd rather have Gayle along for that.

Cromwell had smiled ruefully. "If we are seen and ambushed, Mister McCarthy, that fine set of pistols you carry will serve well, and I shall not worry for your survival. God has granted you a strong hand, if I am any judge of such matters, and my mind will be clear to cut my own way free, sure you shall give a good account of yourself. Gayle? I should worry too much that I might lose one of whom I have become fond. I cannot bring myself to believe in my heart she would survive a scrimmage. And you don't carry yourself like a soldier, so if we're seen near Squire Pedley's house you'll not attract notice the way Leebrick or Hamilton or the others will."

Darryl'd nodded at the implied compliment. "Ain't gonna argue, but I reckon Gayle'd fool you on that score."

They'd left it at that. They'd found a barn that a tenant farmer

Cromwell only vaguely knew was willing to rent out. The wagon was there, with Gayle to make the reports in the evening's radio window, with Leebrick, Towson, Welch and Hamilton to stand guard. Hamilton had to stay behind to make sure Vicky did, of course. Alex and Julie had ridden along part of the way and set up an ambush point just off the road to Pedley's house. If they were attacked, that would be where they fell back to, with Julie to ensure that the assailants got the shock of their suddenly-very-brief lives. The summer evening had the sun low in the western sky, so if Darryl and Cromwell rode hell-for-leather along the road back to St. Ives their pursuers would be beautifully illuminated from Julie's vantage. No need for signals; if they were at the gallop, whoever was chasing them was fair game.

The precautions seemed to have been unnecessary, though. Darryl wasn't ever going to be the horseman Cromwell plainly was, but he was comfortable enough to look around plenty. Since his role for today seemed to be "younger guy along for the ride" he felt he could get away with gawking, and played his role to the hilt. If they were being followed or watched, whoever was doing it was being subtler than he knew how to spot.

Pedley himself turned out to be exactly what Darryl would've assumed if you'd said *English Country Squire* to him, right down to the glass of what smelled like sherry in his hand—not a small glass, either—and the buttons down his front straining to contain a truly impressive gut. "Oliver," the man had said, without a note of exclamation in his voice, "I knew you were at large again, but it does me good to see you safe."

"Nicholas," Cromwell said, "permit me to name Mister Darryl McCarthy to you, who was most solicitous of my health during my captivity and helped me to my liberty after."

"Pleased to meet you," Darryl said, remembering to have his glove off before offering his hand.

"A friend to Oliver is a friend to me," Pedley said, shaking his hand and waving to his manservant. "Peter will have chairs and drink for you momentarily, I'm sure. Not that I think you'll be staying long, Oliver. If that scoundrel Finnegan hasn't eyes on this place one way or another you may call me the most startled man in Christendom. Best you be away as soon as I've satisfied you as to your childrens' fate."

"You know?"

"Aye, I know, and Finnegan can bloody choke on it, him with his justice's commission with the ink wet on it and all his talk of misprision. Prison-break's no felony if you weren't in there lawfully in the first place, and His Royal Majesty can buy all the bench and their dogs too for all I care, it won't change the law of the land in the matter. Be that as it may, Sir Henry saw a roof over the three little ones before that day was out, and Elizabeth and poor young Richard decently buried at St. Ives. The headstone says Bourchier, after Elizabeth's people. They paid for the stone, once they'd heard, and thought it best not to have your name on it in case the king decided they be disinterred for ignominious burial."

"He'd *do* that?" Darryl couldn't contain himself.

"Why take the chance?" Pedley answered. "We knew he was all set to carry on like some French tyrant once poor Oliver here was taken. Perhaps we should have seen it coming with the refusal of parliament and all these novel imposts he kept making, but how would we know that he'd take French gold and hire foreign troops? We'll not be caught unawares twice."

Darryl was getting a serious case of mental whiplash, here. He shouldn't have, of course. Portly old Squire Nicholas, here, was exactly the kind of guy who, a few years from now, would saddle up and go to war against his own king over royal misdeeds not nearly so bad as what had actually been done. He might *look* like a genial old soak with his drink and a warm fire and a comfortable chair, but like Gayle, he'd fool you. Sat right there in that easy chair with his boots off, looking the very picture of Rural Conservative Gentleman, was a no-kidding revolutionary in the making. And, of course, accustomed to leadership, long- and short-term planning, the logistics of farming—not too different, in the seventeenth century, from the logistics of a military campaign—and with a keen understanding of life on the wrong side of the tracks on account of it being dragged before him for judgement on a regular basis. Darryl began to realize that there were damned good *reasons* why Parliament won the civil war.

"Where are they now, Nicholas?" Cromwell was plainly having trouble keeping himself in check. "I saw that the farm I rented from Sir Henry was burnt."

"A bad business, that, and no mistake. Your Robert and Oliver were there, earning their keep and something for their sisters. They weren't recognized, praise God for that mercy, but the ruffians they'd sent out to have their heads broke by some breedlings took offense at that little jape. They came back and burnt the place down. Sir Henry's fit to be tied over it, you may count on him for all the help you might need—that farm is sixty pound a year to him, tenanted, and now he has to find for the family driven off it. He has no objection to Christian charity, but the necessity of it he blames firmly on Finnegan."

"So, this Finnegan?" Cromwell said, in a voice that said that he, too, was coming round to Darryl's views on heads and the breaking thereof.

"King's man, by commission, but the earl of Cork's creature in every way that counts. Set after you when you escaped, I gather, and came here to get ahead of you. He was seen and marked for what he was, and your Robert seems to be made much of by the breedlings for your sake, so he arranged with them to set up an ambuscade out in the fens. He and Oliver the Younger were already working for the Sewsters on your old farm at St. Ives—"

"Sewster?" Cromwell asked.

"Yes, the same Sewsters your brother married into," Pedley said, and launched into a rapid summary of how they'd been related, by marriage and various obscure bits of ancestry that Darryl didn't follow, not knowing any of the names. Of course, he'd probably have been able to give a fair account in the same vein of a lot of his neighbors in Grantville and neither of these two English squires would've been able to follow it. Even if he never felt right at home in this part of the world, Darryl figured, he'd probably just found a bit of its culture he could understand. If it turned out they liked shooting and could keep a feud alive for generations, he'd be back as soon as he could with a truck-load of gimme caps that these people plainly needed to complete their evolution into proper hillbillies.

With the explanation finished, Pedley finished up by explaining that Finnegan had had a justice's commission sent from London, sworn his gang of cutthroats in as constables, and begun throwing his weight about. "And you may depend on it that every worthless half-vagrant and rogue from St. Ives to Godmanchester is getting money from them. Our real constables are hearing of far less in the way of casual theft and public drunkenness. What happens when that scoundrel finally leaves them enough time to return to their former mischief I dread to think. For the time being, Robert and young Oliver are making themselves useful for Sir Henry. Good lads that they are, they'll not take charity while they've strength in them. They've been kind enough not to burden me with knowledge of where the little ones are, and they're all Finnegan's asked after thus far. You know me for an incompetent in the art of lying, so I do like to be telling the truth when I deny knowing anything."

"I'll have some mischief of my own to work, Nicholas," Cromwell said, after a little smile at Pedley's disclaimer. "I fancy you may impress on your regular constables that there are some matters they may find strike them temporarily blind?"

"You fancy correctly, Oliver. It might be we can drag a fish or two across your trail in any event. Finnegan's not the only one who can pay for informants, you know, and my coin spends a lot better in these parts than his. You're not the only fugitives we have in the parish. Some fellows wanted in connection with the attempt on the king have been seen; one of Finnegan's ruffians recognized him, a mercenary named Towson. There's three on that warrant, him and two other soldiers returned from foreign service, and I fancy—"

"No, Sir Nicholas. Those men are with me. Innocent of any wrongdoing in the matter of the king, the earl of Cork sought to use them as scapegoats. It may be that they can be used to confuse the trail, but I beg of you consult with me first—if I have need of their arms to spirit my children to safety, that need will come first."

"Ah. I had given no orders in the matter, and you may depend on me, Oliver, depend on me entirely. Now, finish up your drinks!" Pedley rapped on his chair arm for his manservant, "Peter! Our guests' horses to the back door, if you please, and see if any of the little birds perched in the trees are singing of unfriendly eyes about our garden."

It turned out there weren't, and they took the ride back to Julie and Alex at the trot. Darryl found watching Cromwell's smile on the way educational. It had started relieved, turned joyous, and by the time they were out of sight of Squire Nicholas's house, positively predatory.

He wondered what Cromwell would be praying about before bed tonight. Thanks for his childrens' safety? Or forgiveness for his bloodthirsty thoughts? Probably both. Darryl couldn't see where any decent god wouldn't forgive a man in Cromwell's position a few happy daydreams of carnage, but Cromwell felt the Almighty hewed to a higher standard of conduct in thought and deed.

Chapter 13

"Daddy!" Young Robert Cromwell might have been a mature thirteen years of age, and Darryl could remember how much he'd cared about not being a little kid at that age, but the sight of his father had turned him back to about eight. His younger brother, at only twelve, hadn't even been that restrained, and had simply leapt wordlessly into his father's arms.

It was, truth to tell, a heartwarming sight—and Darryl decided it was one he was going to turn his back on for a while. As a family, the Cromwells had been through some major grief over the last year or so, and if they needed some time for hugs and, quite possibly, tears, it wasn't for him to intrude. He wandered over to the other side of the room, where a nice leaded window gave a view of a garden that was being wet by a faint drizzle. Vicky had picked a spot there, doing her best to make polite conversation with Sir Henry, who seemed to Darryl to be a gloomy old geezer.

He'd reason to be gloomy, of course, what with the burnings and the political situation, but the stern and Puritan religion probably wasn't helping. He was of an age with Cromwell, to whom he was a distant relative—there'd been another of those complicated explanations—and the pair of them had been at college at the same time. They'd been pretty different characters, from the look of things. Cromwell had talked of his time at university mostly in terms of riding and singlestick and football—from the sounds of it, a completely different game from English soccer and a lot more like the football Darryl knew.

Except, possibly, more violent, played without padding or helmets, with only the sketchiest of rules and occasionally resulting in fatalities. Oh, and the ball was made out of a bull's scrotum, just to make sure it was as manly as possible. He'd also taken part in Camp-ball, that they sometimes called Camping. And that was, from the sounds of it, nothing but a straight-out fight with a ball in there somewhere, with rules that sounded *exactly* like they'd been come up with by guys who got kicked in the head a lot.

In short, Cromwell had been a college jock. And he'd only been there a year before his father's death meant he had to go home to support his family.

Sir Henry, on the other hand, was working on a book of theology—a table where the window would light it was covered in papers and a large pot of quills—had finished his first degree and gone back for another, and didn't have even a quarter of the brawn Cromwell was carrying around. About the only thing they had in common was their local accent and that revolutionary streak that seemed to go so well with being Puritan country gentlemen. They'd be mannerly and polite about it, but they'd throw Molotov cocktails all the same, if push came to shove.

"Young Mistress Short tells me you and she are to be married," Sir Henry said, by way of including Darryl in the talk. "From all she tells me, you will be very well together, very well indeed. Now you are here, perhaps I might show you somewhat from the future." He reached over to the table full of theological notes, and picked up a small book that, Darryl could see, showed every sign of being bound in Grantville. "There is a minister in Grantville, the Reverend Green, who has been publishing the writings of the godly, quietly and without great circumstance. He says the spur to it came from Ussher, in Ireland, who is unsound on some details but a good scholar for all that. I have been much exercised lately by the proper and godly business of family, and this came to my attention. From a man who has not been born yet, but seems to have been moved by a spirit of such charity and love he cannot but have been a godly man."

Darryl had managed to grasp that the Puritans, while they acknowledged the name, preferred to refer to themselves as the godly. "Puritan" had started out as an insulting nickname for them, and a lot of them weren't comfortable with it for that reason, even though quite a few reveled in it as an in-your-face defiance of the pressure to conform. It sounded like Sir Henry was one of the first lot.

He was flicking through the book. "Here it is!" he said, with the nearest Darryl had seen to pleasure on his face so far. He read aloud, "'The woman was made of a rib out of the side of Adam; not out of his feet to be trampled upon by him, but out of his side to be equal with him, under his arm to be protected, and near his heart to be loved.'—I hope my own wife has as much from me. And it is good advice, and an excellent reading of that part of scripture. Do you talk to Oliver about his own dear Elizabeth, you will hear the like. They had, by God's grace, a great affection between them."

Darryl nodded. "He's told me about her. It's been . . . moving." Fortunately, the only other up-timer here was Gayle, so the chances of him getting mocked for that level of seriousness were slim. And it looked like Vicky approved entirely, as well. He figured she'd probably not mentioned the use they'd been putting inn rooms to over the last few weeks to Sir Henry, who'd probably Not Approve. Although Darryl was learning, fast, not to jump to conclusions about that sort of thing.

For the moment, Oliver and himself and Vicky and Gayle were visiting with Sir Henry, while everyone else was scattered about the country watching the approaches to Slepe Hall, the Lawrence family residence. They'd been careful about it, as the farmhouse Cromwell had rented was literally just along the road, and they knew that was under watch. They'd come out before dawn and done their best to look inconspicuous. The horses left with a livery in St. Ives proper, a couple of miles to the north, they'd walked here to arrive just as the staff of the manor house were running up to speed on the day. Fortunately, part of that involved getting hearty coal fires lit, which was a great relief after walking through precisely the kind of rain that wet a man most efficiently.

"Father tells me you're an up-timer," Oliver Junior said, having broken away from where his older brother and father had sat down to discuss something in low, urgent-sounding tones. Darryl was vaguely aware that there had been a brief session of kneeling in prayer, and now that was over they seemed to be attending to business.

"That I am, kid," Darryl said, "West Virginia born and raised, right up to the year two thousand. Now I'm back here for a spell. Hear you sent some bad guys off to an ambush?"

The kid seemed like a good one, to Darryl, and it was purely a damned shame that he'd had to grow up so fast. His biggest causes for complaint ought to be schoolwork and chores, not the fact that he was on the lam after his dad had been thrown in the Tower and his mom and little brother shot dead.

"That was Robert," Oliver said, "he's been talking to the Committees of Correspondence!"

Darryl grinned. "That sounds like a fine idea he had," he said, and meant every word. If the CoCs had started in England, between them and the Puritans he figured His Majesty King Charles was in for a hot time of it. And if the revolution wasn't *just* the Puritans, there was every reason to think that there wouldn't be quite the same amount of nastiness happening to Ireland. The Plantations had been about shitting on the Catholic Irish, after all, and if the Committees were involved and making damned sure their freedom of religion platform was part of the new government, things would turn out at least that much for the better.

"It might be, and it might not," Cromwell senior said, joining the conversation along with Robert and, now, Gayle. "I know little of these men, and much of the kind of mischief young men get up to without proper governance." There was a rumble of suspicion in his voice that reminded all present, Darryl included, that whatever Cromwell's own revolutionary sentiments, he was still Dad around here, and don't forget it.

Darryl shrugged. "I can tell you about Grantville and Magdeburg Committees," he said, "on account of I know a lot of the guys involved. Gayle, too," he added, waiting for the nod from her, "but the thing is, what kind of Committee you get in any place depends on who's doing the organizing. There was something getting going in Italy, last I heard, and that was different again from what the guys in Magdeburg were up to. There's sort of a rumor there's some undercover ones in France and the Spanish Netherlands, and they'll be different again. Robert, why don't you tell us what you know?"

Robert did that right well, too, stepping up and explaining about the dock workers in the Hanseatic yards at King's Lynn, the main seaport for the east of England which was about fifty miles down the Great Ouse from Huntingdon. They'd got the word about the Committees via sailors from Hamburg, and organized. There were the beginnings of a union movement among the dockers there, seeking better pay and conditions. While they'd yet to call a strike of any kind, they'd made a little progress in one way or another, mostly by furnishing the port's bosses with excuses for being behind with their Ship Money payments to the king. Of course, that wasn't the limit of their activism, and the fact that the Great Ouse was navigable as far as St. Neots, a good fifteen miles upstream from where they were now in St. Ives, meant they had plenty of reach.

Robert had connections with King's Lynn through school; one of his friends was from there and had been full of news of the new politics during term-time. They had even formed a "Young Committee" before the schoolmasters had shut it down with beatings all round, at which time they went underground.

When the king's tyranny had come to Robert's own home—his exact words, and Darryl fought *hard* to keep his face straight, because for this little kid it was serious, damn it—he'd prevailed on the friend, who he was careful not to name, for an introduction. He and Robert had made sure their younger brother and sisters were safe with relatives and then gone downriver. On the way, they'd made more Committee connections, this time among the bargees and breedlings, who liked the Committee for the work they were doing organizing against the undertakers who were messing with the downstream navigation of the Ouse for profit.

In the end, Robert had ended up getting more help from the bargees and wherrymen that navigated the Great Ouse. They had more reason to know the name of Cromwell than the dockers of King's Lynn to start with, and a few requests sent back via the North Sea trade to Hamburg had brought histories that mentioned the Lord of the Fens. They had relatives among the breedlings of the fens, and there were plenty of places for a family to hide among them when the king's men came looking. Which, two weeks ago, they had done.

"It's so good you've come back, Father," Robert said, when he felt he'd given all the information he could, "because I don't know what to do next. Everyone has helped so much, but if this scoundrel Finnegan begins to burn more houses, we shall have to give ourselves up or bring more destruction on one and all."

"That is how he means you to feel," Cromwell said, the growl in his voice growing deeper and fierier.

"Seems to me there ought to be a reckoning with this Finnegan," Darryl said. "I don't think much of a man that'll take orders from the likes of King Charles anyway, but chasing after kids to get a man to turn himself in? I ain't having that, not on my watch."

"We are, then, of one mind," Lawrence put in. "His commission as a justice is valid on the face of it, but with him thwarted, he'll get no help from the real justices of this parish, or any other surrounding."

"It might be that Leebrick and his fellows would do to distract him?" Cromwell suggested. They'd all talked it over the night before, and the three mercenaries had said they'd be happy to oblige Finnegan with a first-class wild-goose chase, if there was a ship waiting somewhere to take them off at the last minute. It was on the list to raise in the next radio window.

"Father, if I might counsel my elders, it seems to me that the end we must seek is getting Bridget, Henry and Libby away to safety." Robert Cromwell sounded a lot older than his years, now, decades older than the boy who'd been delighted to see his father only minutes before. "It seems to me that keeping them safe puts good friends at hazard, and the work of it is work that does not serve to bring down the king."

"Does it come to that?" Steward said, sharply. "His tyranny falls lightly on most, even among the godly. Is there not still sanctuary in Holland for such as we?"

"All of us?" Cromwell asked. "You might flee, with your wealth, Sir Henry. Once I might have, but all my goods and money are gone from me. Even now I might, with help from the United States."

"Pretty sure you'd get asylum," Gayle put in, "and the fact you'd be coming in with me would seal the deal."

"True enough," Darryl said, "and even if it weren't official-like, things are still pretty wild and woolly even in Magdeburg. Long as you didn't make trouble or look like you were a spy or anything, folk would leave you alone. Lots of work to be had for a guy that wants to live quiet-like." It would solve Darryl's problem entirely, of course, if *this* Oliver Cromwell was simply, say a USE Army officer. He was supposed to be pretty useful in command of cavalry, and what harm could he do then?

Cromwell held up a hand. "Aye, well enough for me and Sir Henry here. But what of the Sewsters, their home and all their goods burnt for taking over the farm after I was gone and giving employ to my sons? What of them? And lower than them, without the ranks of the gentry? Sir Henry, you know I speak my mind on behalf of the poor. Spoke it, indeed, before the privy council. I might have spake uncouthly, and said my sorries for the words of passion, but I took back not a word of the substance."

Sir Henry sighed. "There's that much, Oliver, I'll give you. And, yes, as gentry we have in charge the common weal of the poor folk of our parishes, as best we may. But such a step—?"

The man's face was pleading, but resigned. He'd surely be horrified if anyone were to quote scripture about letting cups pass from him, shocked that his own agonizing be compared even jokingly to that of Jesus, but there was the same sense about the man that, if he must, he'd drain it to the bitter dregs. And Darryl knew there was really not a lot that smart guys like that wouldn't stop at, if you convinced them to fight.

"Such a step, Sir Henry. We must take it. God's providence has placed it before us, will we or no. You think that man would stop at foisting a false justice on just one parish?" Cromwell spat the words *false justice* with a venom. You could say this for the man, Darryl thought, once he had hold of what was right and wrong, he didn't hold anything back. Even, as he'd taken to, referring to King Charles only as *that man* didn't carry the same glow of scorn.

"Well, let us take it, then. Will we raise rebellion here, or take time to prepare?"

"If the thing's to be done, Sir Henry, let it be done properly. You're the man of letters here, I pray you will write many letters. Let the whole country know what is being done in the king's name. Aye, and not by evil counselors, by the king. We'll not give him even that figleaf to hide his shame."

"And when he orders the justices of the peace to put me in the stocks for seditious libel?"

"May God grant that by then others are repeating your words. And if there is an ounce of persuasion in me, there'll be stout lads around you in the stocks to ensure your stay in them is comfortable."

"Hang on," Gayle said, "if they're going to prosecute you for libel doesn't it have to be false?"

"Not in matters of sedition, Mistress Mason," Sir Henry said. "Sedition's a criminal libel, and for that, the greater the truth, the greater the libel."

"That's nuts!" Darryl blurted out.

"If you mean madness of the rankest sort, I heartily agree, Mister McCarthy. I can only hope there are enough holy fools in England to raise a more wholesome lunacy against it." Sir Henry smiled as he said it, plainly pleased with the turn of phrase.

At that moment, the sound of gunfire rattled the leaded windows.

"What the *hell*?" Darryl snarled, grabbing Vicky and roughly shoving her down out of sight. He leaned against the jamb, keeping as much cover as he could while rummaging down the back of his jacket for the pistol he kept in its belt holster back there. "Sounded like muskets," he said.

"Muskets, aye," Cromwell said, taking the other side of the window with his own revolver already out. He'd had a small amount of practice with the thing, but was far more likely to do any mayhem that happened with the heavy straight sword, of a kind he called a back-sword, that he'd bought just before they left Diss.

Whoever had fired first, the answering shots were sharp and rapid. Two harsh, flat, quick cracks, like the whip of a goddess of pain. Whoever it was, Julie Mackay was firing back.

Chapter 14

"Leebrick, do you see them?" Alex Mackay murmured into the walkie-talkie.

"I do. They're coming right toward me and Stephen. We'll have them in full view when they get to the bend." Leebrick's voice had the calm-but-tense air that all professional soldiers got with action in view. "Have I mentioned how much I love these things?" he added.

"Repeatedly, and no more than I do," Alex said, grinning. Being able to communicate instantly, undetectably and reliably across hundreds of yards with no line of sight? Professional soldier heaven, as far as he was concerned. The Ring of Fire could have brought nothing else back at all and he'd have been satisfied with the matter of radio alone. Of course, for him to be *happy* it had to bring him a wife—

"Tell him to marry the thing," Julie said, fussing at her scope with a cloth. "Gonna have to go to iron sights, I think, this drizzle's not agreeing with the scope. Wind's shifted into our faces and we don't got enough shelter to keep the lens dry."

"I've the case for it here," Alex said, passing it over and elbowing up on the tarp they'd spread to peer out from under the hedge they were using for a hide. Waterproof, lightweight tarps. Och, you could *keep* your internal combustion engines for another day, dry above and below in this weather? Marvelous. Of course, they had to poke their faces out at the enemy and that meant a little cool, refreshing rain on those faces. Quite pleasant, actually. But even the superb optics Julie had brought back from the twentieth century had their limits, and shooting in the wet was one of them. A proper hide would have solved that handily, but they had neither time nor reason to build one, and it would have had to be deep to keep out the swirling drizzle of this otherwise-mild English summer morning. It would be glorious sunshine by eleven, but right now it was two hundred yards, if that, of swirling gray shite. His binoculars and spotting scope were handling it fine, but he didn't need to pick up precise detail with those. Didn't need them at all for the ranges he could actually bloody *see*, come to that.

Naturally, whoever this was coming down the road from St. Ives had picked this moment to show up. Julie, who was working rapidly but carefully to get all of the screws on her scope rings loosened—and re-zeroing the thing was going to be a tedious bastard of a job—muttered "the enemy shows up at one of two times..."

"When he's ready and when you're not," Alex capped the quotation. "It's like you read ma' mind, love." One of his old regimental lads, one of the ones who'd studied for his literacy certificate, the one they all called their ticket of letters, had come across "Murphy's Laws of Combat" that someone in Grantville had saved from the internet of mystery and legend. Not a single professional soldier who'd heard the thing hadn't laughed himself puking over the thing, and Alex could quote the bloody lot. He'd seen at least half of them happen with his own eyes, and knew some old sweats who'd let on that the whole thing was nothing but flowery optimism.

Mirth didn't distract him, though, and he kept watching. "Leebrick, is that someone coming oot frae the Hall?"

"Yes," came the response, "And he's armed."

"Shite," Alex murmured. "I'll no' hurry ye, love, but I think someone's about t'be very, very stupid up at the hall." There were four of the presumed enemy moving up the lane; they'd passed Alex and Julie's position entirely oblivious. Towson and Welch had spotted them first, from the spot they'd taken in a couple of trees, with the other two pair of binoculars they had. They were the two who'd actually met their presumed enemy. At least one of the mounted foursome they could see looked familiar. They'd been spotted coming up the lane, it seemed, and someone from the Hall had wandered out to the road. Slepe Hall wasn't one of those manor houses with a long drive, but stood about twenty yards back from the road. It wouldn't take much of a watch to be kept to see someone coming. Some oldish fellow, probably one of the house servants, had wandered out, with what looked like a middling-length fowling-piece under his rain-cape, the lock tucked away dry and a plug of rags keeping the charge at least in the barrel if it slipped out from where it was wadded. Not, when all was said and done, a particularly unusual thing to do, and in fact with a river full of ducks less than half a mile away, there was every possibility he'd picked just that moment to go out and administer a hearty dose of birdshot to today's lunch. From the size of the thing, probably a couple of meals over the next couple of days while he was about it. The fact that he had a dog with him, plainly pleased to be off out with master, might have suggested as much. Of course, with four out-and-out scunners coming up the lane, doubtless armed to the teeth and expecting trouble, carrying a fowling-gun was not going to help.

"Working as fast as I can here, honey," Julie said, through gritted teeth.

"I ken richt enow, love," Alex said, easing his .45 up to where he could grab it for the fifty-yard charge he'd need to get amongst the bastards. "It's only that circumstances are conspirin' good an' quick, here."

"One word and we're at 'em," Leebrick's voice came from the radio speaker. Leebrick and Hamilton were closer. Alex was where he could cut them off. Towson and Welch were out of the fight—by the time they got out of those trees, it'd all be over one way or the other.

"Wait until you see me close enough," Alex replied to Leebrick. "I've more experience with a modern pistol than either of you two. Charge the back o' 'em when I've fixed their attention firmly to the front." A quick check of sword and pistol. "Have my back, love, I'll stay to the left o' the road."

"Gotcha," Julie said, a little distantly as she got her rifle back into battery and began picking aiming marks for iron sights. They'd paced the road in the half-light of dawn, and noted clumps of flowers, easily spotted rocks and so on. With that much preparation and over these ranges, Alex knew he was tits on a bull as a spotter, and stayed with Julie for her close protection. His wife was lethal past fifty yards. Inside that, there wasn't a man to touch a Mackay with his blood up. Ahead the foursome had turned on to the flinted forecourt to the front of Slepe Hall, and looked like they were talking to the old fellow. If there was to be trouble, it would be starting soon, so he eased himself out from under the tarp and began feeling under the hedge. It took half a minute or so, during which time he had no idea what was going on at the hall, but time enough to look again when he got up.

He was halfway to his feet when the first shot punched a shot of lightning through his veins and propelled him five yards down the road with barely a thought in his head.

"Clear my shot!" came a sharp yell from behind him and he jinked hard left. They'd picked a spot on a slow right-hand bend that gave Julie a good view of the Hall; as long as he kept to the outside of the bend he'd only be obscuring hedge.

He dropped back from the sprint, taking it at a fast walk. A second shot. Heavy pistols; dragoons? The smoke cloud about the front of the hall was thick and probably reeking. Cheap powder, at that, and Mackay had already grown used to smokeless. Swift check of pistol, left hand, ready to fire. Saber, check, even though he'd no memory of bringing the weapon to hand. As natural as breathing to fill his right hand with steel.

The drizzle washed some of the smoke away and a puff of breeze did for the rest. The old man was on his knees, clutching at his belly, or possibly one of his legs, it was hard to tell. Alex's heart sank. They'd *shot the puir bloody dug.* There were some things that just were. Just. Not. On.

Julie had seen too. One of the riders jerked upright in his stirrups, back arched and a heavy pistol—dragoon, yes—flew from his hand. The puff of blood from the front of his chest washed out almost immediately in the drizzle. Almost as an afterthought Alex was conscious of the sound of the round passing him and the muzzle report from behind. *'At's ma girl,* he thought, with a grin.

Time enough for three more brisk paces, his breathing falling into a nice, steady cadence, and another shot. A second saddle emptied, this time the shot going high and to the left, taking the side of the bastard's head clean off. Alex hoped that was the one that'd shot the dog.

Not breaking stride, he barked over his shoulder, "Prisoners!" Julie would get the idea. He'd want to take one of them no more seriously wounded than he had to be, and two-for-one odds with their morale already shot? Difficult, but he could manage the business. Besides, all he had to do was hold them while Stephen and Kit caught up from the other side. Stephen had brought a quarter-staff, really the pole of his halberd with the blade taken off, and a little singlestick practice against him had Mackay entirely happy the man knew what he was doing with it.

He was all but on them by the time they got their horses turned around. Plainly not trained warhorses, but beasts that needed careful management around the sounds and smells of gunfire and blood. To his professional's eye they were making not too bad a fist of things, but it was about to get a lot more difficult for them.

Beyond, Kit and Stephen were on their feet and charging hard. Silent, quick, no wasted breath in shouting. Mackay stepped smartly to the middle of the lane. Room enough for both horses to pass either side of him. He'd have to defend against one and stop the other. Tough, but doable. He took a deep, cleansing breath and brought his pistol to the aim.

There are a limited number of tactics for a lone man on foot against charging, mounted opponents, and most of them consist of methods to not die in the brief slice of time while the cavalryman passes. Most of them, on the record, work fairly well provided the footman isn't outnumbered and doesn't panic; all of the truly high-scoring slaughters of infantry by cavalry have been worked on fleeing soldiers. And, of course, being outnumbered is a major problem whatever the other tactical factors.

It was a given that Mackay wasn't going to panic. He knew, to a nicety, the limits a cavalryman faced in this sort of a situation, and he had the means to keep himself alive and, in theory, no worse than a little bruised. The trick was going to be hurting one of them—or his horse—badly enough that he could make no escape but not so badly that he died before he could be questioned.

To do that would take someone who was truly *good*. Alex Mackay of the Clan Mackay grinned. He need drop only one.

They'd seen Alex and Stephen coming. Where there were two armed men on watch, there were more, went the reasoning, and there were enough sharpshooters hidden about to empty two saddles already. The rate of fire of modern weapons was leading them to all manner of wrong conclusions, and Mackay was pleased to see the first knockings of panic on their faces.

A rapid gabble of Erse between them and they picked Alex's direction. The way they'd come, and only one visible enemy. With a yell of "*Fág a' Bealach!*" and a hiss of drawn steel they spurred their beasts hard at Mackay.

Daft wee laddies, he had time to think. Fifteen yards of charge was no time at all for a horse to come into a good gait for fighting. They did right with the steel, though; pissing about with pistols when it was close work was a fool's business.

Unless you had a big, solid, down-time-built 1911-pattern .45, of course. Mackay had the moves planned out in his mind as soon as he saw what the bastards were about. Time for one shot with the pistol, maybe take one of them in the guts or leg, hopefully hurt the horse enough to throw him, take high guard and be ready to drop under the blow. Had there been more room, he'd have been able to manage a sidestep and a cut at a horse's face, which would throw the beast into an utter terror and probably make it throw its rider as well.

And had ma granny baws, she'd be ma grandda, he thought as he settled his front sight neatly on the left-hand rider's nearer hip. He hoped the riders could see his grin. Even just feeling it from the inside was unnerving.

The shot came, as all good ones do, as a surprise and even so he was already twisting to get his sword into guard as the other rider closed. A flash of steel at him, and a calm quiet little voice in his mind that sounded exactly like the master-at-arms who'd taught him the cavalryman's trade said *dinnae cut at the charge, ye fool, thrust as nicely as ye may* and it was a simple roll of the wrist and sway back, so—and that was the last he knew for a moment until he was on the ground trying to cough some wind back into himself.

Distantly, two more shots, pistols, three cracks from Julie's rifle, and he heaved himself to his feet to see four horses and two filled saddles vanishing into the murk and drizzle.

Leebrick arrived just at that moment. "Loose horse knocked you on the way past, Colonel. Too busy looking at the one with a man on it. You were doing really well up to then." Leebrick was grinning. "I don't think your first shot did more than score the horse's arse, though you'd have had a good 'un on the way past if you'd not gone down. I don't think Stephen or I hit anything, but I'm pretty sure your good lady drilled a third one."

"Yep," Julie said, coming up the lane. "Alex, I need more

practice over iron sights. I've been keeping 'em properly zeroed, but I need *me* to be zeroed with them. Can't assume I won't ever get into anything this tactical again."

"Did ye not shoot at the horses?" Alex asked, without thinking, and immediately regretted it.

Of course, she'd not have shot at the horses. It was hard work to get her to shoot at deer, and about the only prey she was really happy about shooting was boar, because they were "gross" and when you got right down to it, shooting a boar wasn't just hunting but preemptive self-defense because the bastards were—very tasty—murder on four legs. He'd known that, he'd accepted that, he even cherished the softness of heart it showed as one of the many things he loved about his wife. It was, therefore, very much the case that the resulting chewing-out was his just and lawful punishment, to be endured stoically.

It was, he accepted, not the horses' fault they had assholes on their backs. True, he agreed, there was no good reason to be hurting the poor beasts for what their riders were doing. He accepted *entirely* that it would be cruel to hurt a poor beast that didn't understand why it was there and was already frightened with all the shooting. In truth, Julie had nothing to say on the matter that, from time to time, most cavalrymen would say. All of the good ones, certainly. A man who did not care greatly for horses did not long remain a cavalryman. Nevertheless, without taking the horses into harm's way, a cavalryman was nothing but a dragoon, and dragoons were a sorry lot. That didn't mean that horse-soldiers didn't quietly regret the harm the horses came to. Just not quite so *vehemently* as Julie put it.

"All clear out here," came Welch's voice over the radio. "They've gone by the Huntingdon road, too far for a good shot, sorry to say."

McCarthy and Cromwell had come out from the house by this point, accompanied by what had to be Sir Henry Steward, who'd gone immediately to see to his man, who was still clenched around a wound in his side. Mackay hadn't noticed, but two women had already come out from the house and were starting to tend to him. He couldn't see the dog anymore, so with any luck the poor beast had only been wounded and had limped off somewhere. They'd have to find him and tend to him later, but for now the people were the main thing.

"They didn't send anyone round the back, Oliver and me just

checked," Darryl said, "so I think them showing up was just an accident."

"An unhappy one," Sir Henry put in from where he was, really, doing no more than fuss over the care the two ladies were providing, "for now I am known as sheltering you."

"We might be able to do something about that," Darryl said, "if we can make it look like we came here to rob you or something?"

"Aye, I care not that my name be blackened with such as they," Cromwell said. "Give it out that I came here furious that my goods and chattels were gone from the farm I leased from you, which is truth enough. Let the king's men think I came to take them back from you, or rob you of goods to their value. 'Tis as foolish as any justification a thief gives before the bench, and plausible thereby. Give it out that the king's tyranny is turning gentlemen bandit—truth, too, for I am indeed outlawed by the king—and how long before any man is safe in his home? None of it false witness, and only the false of heart will hear it as lies."

"True, from a certain point of view," Gayle said, as she knelt by the wounded man and began unpacking an aid kit.

"From the point of view of Prince John, Robin Hood was naught but a thief," Cromwell said, with a smile, "for all he was a good Huntingdon lad."

"A Puritan Robin Hood?" Darryl was plainly amused by the idea. Especially, since in his heart of hearts, Robin Hood was and would always be a singing, animated fox.

Mackay had to put in something at this point. Robin Hood wasn't really a Scots legend—Wallace and the Bruce were real, historical figures, after all—but he'd heard the stories. "I was always told Robin Hood was a Yorkshireman," he said, "not that I've any great caring in the matter, ye ken. But I led borderers for a few years and the ones from the English side of the border would say 'Robin Hood in Barnsdale Stood' when they meant a thing was entirely plain. And Barnsdale, Gisburne and Loxley are all in Yorkshire, are they not?"

He had, over the years, wondered what the national argument of England was. They just didn't seem to feel most of the differences you could bring Scotsmen to blows over. The next ten minutes seemed to settle it in his mind; they all wanted to claim their most notorious criminal for their own. Even Leebrick had a word or two to put in for Derbyshire.

Chapter 15

"Are you hurt, Tully?" Finnegan was incredulous, and felt he had every right to be. Two horses come back without riders, and Barry slumped, gray-faced and blue-lipped in his saddle. The boys were helping him down, but if ever there was a man not long for this earth, it was Niall Barry, late of County Cork. The hole in his buffcoat wasn't a large one, but the whole of his trews were dark with blood and it was dripping from his boots. His horse, freed of her burden, stood shivering in terror, and it would be hours before the beast was fit to be ridden again, if ever she was. The lads' own mounts were stabled and being rested against need. What was supposed to be simply an early morning visit to Sir Henry Steward to remind him what was what in this locality, did he have any ideas about the burning of one of his properties, they'd taken livery nags to spare the good mounts.

Tully was off his own beast and making much of the gelding, who seemed in better color for not having had all of a man's blood poured over his back. "Not a scratch on me, nor have I, and that only by the grace of God. I saw but four of them, yet there was a hail of bullets like a winter storm from men hidden in the hedges, Finnegan. We lost Kennedy and Quinn right off the bat, two quick shots. Kennedy took a bullet to the heart of him, shot from behind by some fuckin' coward, and the head was off Quinn a moment later. They had one fellow at the gate with a musket, and three others afoot to try and take us. Barry and me, we made to cut ourselves clear, and all but made it. They shot again as we were leaving, and I think that's when Niall got shot. He put one man down, the one that got most in our way, so he's that to his credit, the poor bastard."

"Fuck," Finnegan said. He'd have to think hard on this one. Was it Cromwell, come back to search for his children, or was it the English mercenaries that Nolan had recognized, the ones the earl had offered a bounty for weeks before? Were the two connected? There was no reason to think so, but then no reason to think not either.

"Ah, will you look at what the bastard did to the poor beast?" Tully had found a graze on his mount's rump. "I *thought* I saw him get a shot off with that funny-lookin' pistol while Niall was riding him down. I was in fear I'd been shot myself, but it was the poor screw that took the shot." He went on to fuss over his horse.

"Funny-looking pistol?" Finnegan asked.

"Sure, it was a little thing. Bright metal and sort of squarish-looking. Funny the details you pick up in a fight, is it not?"

"Did it smoke?"

"I've no recollection, is it important?" Tully asked, after a pause for thought.

"It is, at that. Did you read the stuff the earl gave us about the guns they're making in the Germanies now?" Finnegan could almost smell the scent of it, now. He'd never been close enough to an up-time weapon to know if the powder in them, reputed to make not a particle of smoke, smelled different to the stuff he was used to, but a man had imagination and there was a demonic reek to the things when he thought about them. Between the lack of smoke and the rate of fire, they'd put the devil's own power in a man's hand and didn't William Finnegan want that power for his own self? Didn't he *just*.

And where those weapons and the stink of them went, there went Cromwell and the Americans who'd helped him escape. "Let's not get ourselves blathered over, here," he said. "Get a wash and some ale, and come sit with me at the Falcon and we'll have a careful think about what you saw. You've to give an affidavit to the justice of the peace, no less, and I don't want to put thoughts in your head about what I want to hear, now."

An hour and a half later, barely mid-morning, and Finnegan's mood was brightening with the weather outside. If the little short fellow wasn't Alexander Mackay, last seen in Scotland near three months before and whereabouts currently unknown, he'd eat hay with the donkeys. Which meant that that wicked sharpshooting wasn't a whole platoon of hidden bastards with rifles, but the infamous Julie Mackay, whose speed and accuracy with her future-made rifle were a legend across Europe. Over a thousand yards at the Alte Veste, went the legend, and not just Wallenstein but the two poor bastards stood behind him! Of course, you'd to mark down such stories for the embroidery they picked up, but three corpses made in a minute—for Barry had passed within the hour—was near legendary shooting.

It was a shame Kennedy had died in the first moments of the fight, for he was one of the ones who knew Leebrick, Towson and Welch by sight, he having had duty at the earl's town house the day they were brought in. There were others, one of whom Finnegan had sent to York all unknowing, but Kennedy had been on the spot. They were all sure that the three mercenaries knew nothing of Finnegan's band, as they'd been in the tender care of Captain Doncaster and his men. Finnegan had a score to settle with those three when it came right to it, as it was the Cooley brothers—old hands of Finnegan's, and less fastidious than Doncaster's gentleman soldiers—who'd taken the purse for going up there with wheel-locks to do execution, and been killed in the melee of the mercenaries' escape. Alive, none of the others had much cared for the Cooley boys, who were a bit much even by *torai* standards, but dead? There was the beginnings of a feud to be paid out when opportunity allowed. As if Finnegan had needed anything to spur his boyos to the chase!

"Is that one of the cowards?" The voice was clearly trying for booming, but was only managing querulous and sarcastic. It came from a scrawny-thin fellow in the plain black clothes affected by well-to-do Puritan gentry, who'd walked into the main taproom of the Falcon with an obvious lawyer and an obvious lawyer's clerk. "You there, Finnegan, is that you? The new justice?"

Finnegan rose. "That would be me, for a certainty. And who might you be?"

"I am Sir Henry Steward, Mister Finnegan, and I have cause for complaint regarding your so-called *constables*. And, I might add, the dilatory manner in which you are pressing your commission in the matter of Oliver Cromwell, since I was paid a visit by the fellow this morning. Whatever might have been the cause of his arrest last year, he's certainly outlaw now!"

The lawyer was standing expensively by and his clerk had found a table and was rapidly scratching notes. Finnegan got the feeling that he'd have to get some political work done to deal with this, because his commission as a justice of the peace was about to get some legal work it might have trouble with. A useful fiction, getting himself appointed such, but a fiction that would wear very thin if he had to appear in court to justify brushing this idiot off. In front of witnesses. "Now, Sir Henry," he said, putting on his most expansive manner, "If it's about the excess of zeal my fellows showed the other week—"

"It. Is. Not." Steward was plainly angry. The pantomimed efforts at self-control were more than a little hilarious coming from such a weed of a man, and him unarmed at that. "That's a matter for damages, and don't think my counsel won't be seeing to you about that, *Mister*. This is about your collection of jackanapes letting themselves be run off by the ruffians who were terrorizing my household this morning, leaving two of their number corpses on my very doorstep and a good man among my manservants sorely wounded. What good are they as constables if they'll not show fight in the presence of outlaws? What good, may I ask? They ran, Mister Finnegan, when we thought them our only hope of deliverance. I was convinced I and all my household were as good as dead, and all the good they did was convince Cromwell more would be along, so he left. A prime chance to get Cromwell in the chains His Majesty wants him in, and your men *ran*."

From the corner of his eye Finnegan could see Tully bristling. "I understand your distress, Sir Henry, truly I do. This day I've lost three good men, three! The two who you have awaiting decent burial outside your home, and it would soothe my heart so it would if you could tell me you've got them decently covered and laid out ready for the burying of them, and poor Constable Barry, who bled to death in his saddle while evading the bandits' pursuit. He, the poor creature, is laid out even now ready for the burying of him, far from home and by rites alien to him, but he was doing his duty to the last, the very last, Sir Henry! Do you care to view the corpse of him?" Finnegan wasn't sure quite where the bullshit came from on occasions such as this, but he seemed to have an inexhaustible supply. The easy part was that, yes, his boyos had indeed suffered tragedy this morning.

"That won't be necessary, I assure you. From all the shot and riot I heard I was quite convinced there were at least a dozen of your constables there, what happened to the others? And if their numbers didn't answer, why is it that I have had no return visit with more? Could not militia be turned out?"

"There was but the one man, Constable Tully as you see here, who took flight with his injured comrade, on a wounded horse, and had his heels across country to evade the very bandits you mention. Only when he was sure of no pursuit was he able to come here, with the dying Constable Barry, and make his report, such as you see writ there by him on the table, and it was as we were debating the best course of action you arrived, so you did. Do you tell me the villain has flown?"

"I do. And I am here to lay information in the proper form of the sighting. I presume you are already officially cognizant of the prison-breaking he stands accused of?"

"I saw the mined walls of the Tower with my own eyes, the very day I was commissioned by His Majesty to catch the man Cromwell and his every associate and accessory." Finnegan sighed expansively. This was a complication he hadn't been expecting. He'd have no trouble leaving the lawsuit Sir Henry was plainly planning behind when he shook the dust of this town off his feet, but the earl wouldn't be happy about the complication. Half the troubles in this blasted country were down to county gentlemen being difficult about things. Giving one of them the means to raise a scandal was certainly not going to help. On the other hand, here was also one of those local gentry raising a complaint about his quarry; if he couldn't get one problem to solve the other it was a poor look-out.

"Sir Henry, Cromwell is as cunning as the very devil and I don't doubt he has seduced several others to his aid. I know not what mischief he proposes to work as his final end, but I came here, rightly as it seems, to wait for him to try and capture him as he came for his children. If I could have found those, I might have had bait for the beast and caught him before now."

Sir Henry harrumphed. "This, Mister Finnegan, is not what any man or woman of this locality thought you were about.

There's not a one of them believes other than you proposed to throw the poor mites into the Tower in place of the father."

Finnegan gave the man his best hurt look. "I'll allow, Sir Henry, that I am a rough and plain man, with none of your gentry airs, and my boyos that I swore in as constables are an ungentle lot to a man, but I'll thank you to aver to all you have cause to tell that we're not in any way monsters. Sure we'd have used the little ones quite civilly while we held them, and returned them where we found them once we had the father in chains. A mean trick to play on the man, in all honesty, Sir Henry, but he killed a dozen men with his own hands while breaking out of the Tower and he or his ruffians have accounted for three of my men dead and several others wounded already. I'll spare no tears of sympathy for him on that account, and nor should any law-abiding man."

Sir Henry contrived to look a little mollified from the state of high dudgeon he'd come in with. "You'll hear my information, then, I take it?" The tone had become somewhat querulous.

"I will, at that, Sir Henry."

Two hours later, Finnegan was as glad as a man could be to see the back of the pedantic bastard—not that he'd been able to call him that aloud—who'd gone over every finest point of his account of the morning, pointed out every minor incorrectness of the oath Finnegan had administered to make it formal, drawn to his attention two breaches of the Profane Swearing Act within earshot in the inn's taproom, wondered aloud whether it was seemly to conduct such business in a common alehouse, inquired whether all of the boyos present were sufficiently resident not to be offending under the Act Against Common Tippling when they had beer with their luncheon and generally made a bloody nuisance of himself. To his credit, he'd pointed out that Cromwell's children were in the care of the breedlings in the fens. It seemed the oldest Cromwell boy had been in communication with England's answer to the bog-trotters. Finnegan had guessed as much already from the first trail he'd followed, but Steward had been more forthcoming. He'd even had an idea of where the breedlings were gathering to work mischief against the fen drainage and navigation works. And didn't Sir Henry have opinions about *that*, now?

Finnegan heaved a big sigh as Sir Henry, his lawyer and his

lawyer's clerk went out the door. "Thank Christ those fuckers are gone," he said, "I was sure my ears were about to fuckin' drop off. Have I profanely swore and cursed enough yet? I think it's time for some fucking tippling to top it off. Someone get that idle bastard over here with more ale."

That got a chuckle out of Tully. "We've had some use out of the *gaimbín,* for all that. If I remember aright, this Earith where they're agitating against the new river is no more than half a dozen miles past where we got to last time. Should I ask around and find why they're agitating?"

"They're agitating because a Dutchman's digging a fucking ditch, Tully, and I much doubt me that we'll ever need to know the why of either side of the tiresome business. If it comes up in conversation, make note of it, and we'll leave it at that. What we do know is that Cromwell's boy fell in with the agitators and that's where he hid himself and his little brothers and sisters. Now, it's too late in the day to get out there, but while I see poor Barry decently buried, get you a cart and take half a dozen boys and go fetch Kennedy and Quinn back here for the same. I said to Sir Profane Fucking Henry I'd see them away from his doorstep, and I'll keep the promise for their sakes. I've a notion that if we shift ourselves we can have them decently in the ground by sundown, for all the bloody Protestants won't let them have holy ground for it. There's plenty of ground we can use, and I am in no mood to hear argument on the matter."

"Nor I," Tully said, grabbing his hat. "I can be to St. Ives and back in three hours, so we'll have the evening to wake them properly. Then to Earith in the morning?"

"Earith in the morning," Finnegan affirmed. "And then we start the hunting."

Chapter 16

Earith

"So that's the Dutchman's ditch, is it?" Tully looked down from the bridge. Away in the distance, to perhaps half a mile, there was a small settlement of tents and behind that there were earthworks stretching away; from the look of the thing it was more like a pair of embankments than a ditch. "I don't envy the poor bastards digging in that boggy shite, nor do I."

"We've to talk to the poor bastards, you can ask them what the life is like," Finnegan answered. "Best way to be sure of who's causing trouble is to ask the folk who're being troubled."

"And if they'll not answer?"

"Trouble them."

In the end, there wasn't any difficulty in getting the various overseers and so on to talk. Mister Lien, the man-in-charge, wasn't around today and Finnegan could see why not. Canal-building seemed to consist of mud, and lots of it, being carted from place to place by a small horde of laborers. Everyone else had plenty to say, mostly on the subject of mud, but occasionally on the subject of the fensmen who had all manner of clever tricks to play to interfere with the works. Tools stolen, diggings filled back in, cuttings made over the preceding winter in an attempt to flood the works, cart wheels smashed and a whole series of other petty annoyances. Several of the clerks who were on site grumbled about the cost of hiring watchmen.

None of them could put a finger on precisely where the fens-men were based out of, but they were all agreed that there was a positive nest of agitation in Ely. Inasmuch as there was a definite grievance—beyond objecting to the earl of Bedford enriching himself—it was that the change in the Great Ouse navigation would cut Ely off from passing trade, and the increased drainage would turn the fens that the fensmen of that vicinity made their living from into summer-land, pasture that only flooded in winter.

Finnegan waved his commission around a little. The wording of the thing was vague enough that he could use it to elbow his way into the works, follow their line and go hunting for the fens-men and he made sure that he was heard stating he was going to do so. Let him once grab one or two of those and squeeze them a little, they'd get somewhere, and if trailing a little bait to get them to come to him worked, so much the better. The clerks of works were a little disgruntled that the earl of Bedford, whose land this was, hadn't already sent someone in to investigate the trouble they were having, and Finnegan commiserated heartily. Wasn't it always the way, that the man in charge didn't care for the poor souls doing the work? Still, he was here now, with the king's commission and all, and taking care of business.

"We'll be a while nosing around here," Tully remarked after they'd gone back for luncheon at Earith's meager alehouse. "A lot of ground to search, and plenty of it to hide in. Remember the trouble we had last time?"

"I do at that," Finnegan said, chasing the last scrap of his stirabout with a hunk of bread, "but what of it? From what Steward said yesterday, he's found his children and means to be a bandit here until he can raise a rebellion. He's got to get us off his back, and that means he'll come to us."

Tully grinned. "I get to smiling every time I think of that, so I do. The English, rebelling? Who the fuck will they find for the plantation of them when it fails? The Welsh?"

"Maybe his noble earlness will move us all over here?" Truth to tell, Finnegan thought that was pretty funny too. "We've still a tricky cross-country ride ahead of us. Plenty of daylight, good weather. We'll have our plates and helmets on, too, whatever the heat. Those slingstones hurt like the devil."

"They did at that. I'll see the lads all have their water-flasks full, they'll be sweating like pigs." That was, of course, why most cavalrymen preferred a buffcoat and a soft hat for riding, and even left the buff off if they weren't expecting trouble. The sturdy leather of a buff was at least good protection without broiling the poor bastard wearing it alive, which a horseman's cuirass was prone to do in the sunshine. The linen lining ended up drenched in sweat, which was cooling in itself. For helmets, a few of the boyos had old-fashioned morions, still popular in Munster by reason of being cheap—the Spaniards who fled after the Nine Years' War had left plenty of them behind—but most of them had picked up German zischagge-style cuirassier's helmets that provided plenty of protection and were, for helmets, fairly comfortable. Most of their armor had come from at least a short spell of service with the Imperial forces in the German wars and were munition-chest quality at best, but Finnegan had spent the money to get a good one made in London by one of the armorers who supplied the trained band companies. If ever there was a fool's bargain and a false economy, Finnegan reasoned, cheap armor was the one.

They made easy progress during the course of that afternoon, riding perhaps two or three miles beyond the beginning of the earthworks at Earith. Trotting along the paired embankments was an easy, gentle, pleasant ride with a cooling breeze and a good view of the surrounding greenery, most of which seemed to be at least chest-high if not higher. The clerk of works at Earith had told them there was another encampment at the halfway mark, but after a look at the number of watchmen they had had turning up for duty at the first one, Finnegan had decided that hanging around the camps would be a waste of time. Anyone trying anything there would be doing it by stealth, and definitely avoiding parties of armed men.

"Boyos," Finnegan said when he judged them far enough from the major work-sites to start looking for a rest spot. "We're after the shites that are trying to wreck these works, but only so's we can get after Cromwell. Now, the last thing they'll be doing is trying anything clever in broad daylight, they leave that kind of thing to ignorant paddies like us."

That got an ironic cheer. Out of the twelve men under him who weren't in York with O'Hare, eight had at least some grammar school and they were all literate. O'Hare had taken the two besides Finnegan who'd finished grammar school along with the one illiterate in the band. Which reminded Finnegan; if Mackay was, as he suspected, with Cromwell, there was no reason to leave O'Hare cooling his heels there. That royal commission would come in useful again, permitting him access to the Royal Post to get a letter to O'Hare. A task for the day after tomorrow, if they couldn't turn up any sign of the malcontents that Cromwell's son had taken up with. And, of course, there was always the possibility that the father had joined the son.

Realizing he was woolgathering, Finnegan collected himself and went on. "We'll wait here, find a spot of shelter, while the heat of the day dies down. When things get a little cooler we'll spread out and find what hiding spots there are hereabouts, and poke in them. We'll likely find nothing, but we'll know where to look when night falls. It's a full moon, or near enough, and the promise of a clear night to come. With that we'll range up and down these works, they're but ten miles, and sound a shot if we stumble across anything. Remember, I want a captive or two to question, so in with the *bata* first, if you please."

A chorus of acknowledgements and they began seeing to horses and looking for shade.

Off the embankments that were eventually going to define the new river, there was plenty of that. There weren't many bushes or trees, but the soft growth was man-height or higher in places and at least waist-height everywhere else. Worse, if anything, than they had dealt with only a couple of weeks previously out nearer the edge of the fen. Well, this time they were armed and armored for it and expecting trouble. Half the difficulty they'd had the last time was they'd started out expecting to arrest children and ended by enduring slingstones from well-hidden fensmen. This time there'd be more grit shown by all, Finnegan included.

Tully was standing at the top of the embankment on the eastern side, looking down into the fen. The ground was trying to be dry, at least, and overgrown to the height of a man with sedges and low, scrubby trees, hardly more than bushes most of them. There were tracks through it, to be sure, but they were few and narrow and twisting and, if anything, were more of an addition to the hiding places than any means of getting across the country. Anyone with half a mind to move hereabouts, Finnegan decided, would probably do best to ignore the paths and just shove his way through the greenery on horseback.

"Going to be a bastard searching that lot," he said, as Finnegan walked over.

"True, but on the bright side, if I'm right about that American bitch with her rifle, the closer the cover, the less she'll shoot at us, I'm thinking." Even in the full daylight of the evening, the long shadows made the fen a riot of patchy shadow and plentiful cover.

Tully nodded. "Probably as well to be down off this bank before long, I'm sure. Even a regular fowler would be good around here. Sure and you'd see the smoke of a regular piece, but getting there after, through that shite?"

"True enough. You watch over the lads covering the north-and-west side, there. We'll work north-and-east bit by bit, see what we don't flush out, so." Finnegan was already into a pattern of looking over the undergrowth, thinking about how he'd be best to send men into it to probe the denser patches. Whoever was out there, they and Finnegan's men would have to stumble over each other, and in that he'd have money on his own gang of brawlers any day of the week. No easy way to see where they'd be coming from, either. The embankment he was on stood maybe six or seven feet above the ground it was dug from, no more than a linear spoil-heap either side of the cut that, even without being connected to the river, was knee-deep in water already. Outside the cut, the country continued flat for miles. Somewhere a couple of miles away he could just see the smoke and church spire of a village on a slight rise of ground. There was another hamlet a little closer on the side he'd given Tully, but apart from that he and his boyos could be the only men in the whole world.

In other words, prime country for a man after being an English *tórai*. A man could vanish, here, and give the authorities the devil's own work to root him out. And so, for the next few hours, it was the devil's work for Finnegan's band, as they scouted, and hoisted themselves up as much as the trees would allow, and swore at the patches of bog that sucked at boots. Twice shots went up as a man, spooked by the shift of light and shadow in the brightly moonlit fen and the silence they were all maintaining, thought he saw something and emptied a wheel-lock into the shadows.

Twice, not a trace of human passage did they find either time.

✧   ✧   ✧

Around midnight, Darryl McCarthy was perched in the top of a willow tree where Stephen Hamilton had boosted him and scanned the distant earthworks with binoculars. "They look like they're having fun. They're going up and down from that levee and beating the bushes. They'd surely find us if we were there."

"No need to shout," Hamilton replied in a definite indoor voice. "And better not to, sound carries at night. I learned that the hard way, poaching, when I was a lad. Nearly got caught."

"Gotcha," Darryl said, lowering his voice a little. "So, are we sticking with leading them through the night?"

"I think it best. They're more likely to make stupid decisions in the dark."

"Like chasing armed men through a swamp?"

"Just like that. I'll use the radio now and get the others on our position. Sting them and fall back, and when we have them moving draw them back toward Ely and Colonel Mackay's position. Then it's into the saddle and hell-for-leather for King's Lynn, and hope someone there has managed to arrange a ship. I don't want to be stuck there when that lot catch up, I want to be able to give them two fingers from the stern of a departing ship. The aim is to show them that we've all left the area, and hopefully, the country, so they leave the locals alone. Not, and I think we're all agreed on this, get stuck in a fight with children to protect. There's precious few ways for that to end well."

"Julie and Gayle and the kids'll be there hours before us, you saw how fast that barge went." Darryl had been surprised as all hell by that. He'd seen barges towed by horses before, the things were common all over Europe. He'd been expecting that for any kind of speed you'd need a rowed boat, though, and Hamilton, Londoner born and bred, had assumed the same. It turned out that they had different ideas on the fens, and the river towpaths were also home to fast trotting horses that pulled boats at a speed that left a substantial wake, pulling the boat up onto a kind of bow wave. Once the horse got the boat moving, it was off at a smart pace quicker than it could have pulled a cart. Passage on the thing had cost far more than just riding or taking a regular barge would have, but it was a smooth ride and a quick one and there was every possibility that even if the menfolk went from Ely to King's Lynn at a dead gallop, they would still arrive hours behind the advance party.

They'd finally gotten rid of the wagon, donating it for the use of Ely's Committee of Correspondence, who didn't have any pressing need for a wagon right now—they were nearly all river bargees, for a start—but would more than likely come up with something. Nothing else, it'd make it possible to steal more tools from the earthworks for Bedford's River. Darryl was kind of in two minds about that one. He'd done some reading up on England before he came, and knew that in the future this was going to be some of the best farmland in England, where right now it was—pardon the language—nothing but a fucking swamp. He could appreciate good hunting country as well as the next man, especially if the next man was a hillbilly, but hereabouts was good for fowl and that was about it. Especially, apparently, snipe, and he'd had one pointed out to him earlier after he'd expressed suspicion. Cromwell had laughed at that and informed him that they were indeed a byword for being hard to spot, shy birds that skulked in reed beds and undergrowth.

Still and all, good hunting was a nice thing, but a lot of the folks hereabouts would be doing better with some good farmland to work.

While they waited for Cromwell, Welch, Leebrick and Towson to move up to their position, Darryl mentioned as much to Hamilton.

"Well, I'm not from around here. I was born in Kent and settled in London, but I don't think it'll be too different. A lot of that farmland will come from enclosing common land that most of these poor bleeders depend on for their living. And people get very angry about that kind of thing. There was a revolt about it up Northampton way about twenty years ago. I was a green young soldier back then, not doing much more than substitute enlistments in the Trained Bands for fat old merchants who didn't want to drill, before I took to wandering abroad to find a fight. They had trouble with some bastard of a landowner fencing off the common lands and this mad fellow as called himself Captain Pouch started a revolt. They pulled down the hedges and fences and filled in ditches, and there weren't many going to stop 'em, since the militia refused to muster for it. So the word went out they wanted hired soldiers to put down the revolt. Well, by the time I got there it was all over. Captain Pouch had been saying he had this magic pouch that would protect everyone with him from bullets and swords, and *that* worked about as well as you'd expect. When they hanged him, all he had in it was a bit of mouldy cheese."

Darryl tried to take that in, and at the same time figure out if he was having his leg pulled. "Cheese?"

"Cheese," Hamilton affirmed. "I was there for the hanging, when they finally opened it and showed it to the crowd. Didn't even look like good cheese. Can't remember the bugger's real name, now, and that's going to nag at me, it surely is."

"And you went to join in with puttin' down that revolt?" Darryl said, wondering how he was going to express this tactfully.

"Oh, I ain't proud of that," Hamilton said. "But I ain't ashamed neither. It was shovel shit for a penny a day or drill for fourpence, and I was good at the drill. Saved me a few times in the Germanies, all that training I got paid to do, as well. Way I saw it, there was going to be a fight, and I could get maybe sixpence a day and mustering bounty into the bargain if I got there fast enough. I didn't, end of story. Northamptonshire wasn't worth sticking around for, so I came home."

There was a soft hoot from the darkness. Darryl answered it, they having found out earlier that Hamilton's bird noises were comical at best. Cromwell and Welch drifted in out of the night—and hadn't Darryl smirked about that, when it turned out that pairing the Irishman with Cromwell made sense, as they paired off for raw muscle and ability to get up trees to spy out the country. Leebrick and Towson came in shortly after.

It was time to start the entertainment.

Chapter 17

"Sure I saw something. Gleam like a Dutch-glass, Chief. They're after spying on us."

Finnegan raised an eyebrow. O'Halloran was definitely in the shallows in matters of scholarship and wit, and while there were a lot of telescopes in use around Europe, they were generally not used much in military business except by artillerymen, a trade O'Halloran had almost certainly never been near.

"Don't look at me like that, Chief. There were plenty of the things about when I was with Wallenstein back in '28, at Stralsund. There were great guns going off all the time and the gunners all had them. There's a glint to them, and I just saw it again. And is it not that that woman has a Dutch-glass on her musket to see what she's shooting?"

"I've heard enough, O'Halloran, and well done with all the thinking. Go you over the cut, there, and tell Tully to bring his lads over and fall in on me. I'll be here and gather the lads ready." There might have been some sense in going over himself and leaving O'Halloran to watch out for that glint, but Finnegan decided he could recognize a glint for himself and there was no way he was going up on that bank in the plain moonlight for a legendary shooter to see. He settled in and began scanning further afield, looking in the treetops where O'Halloran said he'd caught sight of the fateful flash. *Too much to ask of the silly bastard to actually remember which stand of trees it was, of course.*

Not half an hour later the bushes around him were full of

his men, and Tully had joined him. "Be damned," Finnegan said, "if O'Halloran wasn't entirely right. I've caught sight myself, not that I'm going to point if they're watching, but I've an idea of distance and direction and give it but a moment and we're off a-skirmishing."

"Be hard to keep even open order in this shite," Tully remarked.

"You're not wrong, but we'll do what we do. Pass the word. We're to move slow and low and give a cry if we come on anyone. Pile on the bastard, get a prisoner, and we'll pull back."

"Not chase?"

"Not chase. Remember those bastards we made bones of in the Slieve Mishkish a couple of years ago? They'd a plan for it, and both times we went hooring in after them? We had to cut our way out, and this is far better country for that kind of work than a lot of bare-arsed mountains. All we got back then was some cuts and hurts, here we'll have corpses come morning if we're not careful." Finnegan still had a spot under his left shoulder that ached in wet weather from that. The throwing dart that was the traditional weapon of most cattle thieves—much of Ireland's militia levies, come to that—wasn't likely to kill a man outright if he'd any armor at all, and a buffcoat would answer that need. Getting one stuck in a man's flesh, even the inch or so that Finnegan had briefly suffered, hurt like the very devil, though.

"Not on horse, either, I take it. Bad country for it."

"Bad indeed, and fuck my arse if I'll sign a man's death warrant by putting him in front of that rifle on horseback. We've enough bush and sedge to have a chance of going unseen, which is a fighting chance. Pick three lads to mind the horses, no, better, three lads to string the horses back to Earith. They'll not expect that, and our beasts will be the safer for it. They might even have a plan to take the horses while we're chasing them into this. It's something I'd have thought to do."

Tully grinned back. "I've done the like myself. It's amazing how fast cattle thieves give up if you steal their ponies. A man is like to stay at home and abide the law if he has to walk all the way to the stealing he's after doing. I'll be back in two shakes."

With the horses sent back along the relative safety of the cut, Finnegan got the boyos moving out across the fen. For all they made as much effort as they could to go silently, not a one of them having missed out on the traditional country sports of poaching and stealing livestock, they still didn't know this country as well as they might and there were constant small splashes, the sounds of bushes being caught, and the other minor noises of a party of men on the move. If nothing else, the sedge-grass came up to the hems of their buffcoats, so off the few narrow tracks through the stuff, it was impossible to move without a hiss.

Of course, the same went for their opponents, and so neither side would be able to hear the other unless they stopped and listened. With only eight lads following him, Finnegan was able keep them close enough together that he could have them in command with hand signals. Every forty paces he was stopping and just listening, mouth wide and eyes closed to pick up every little sound. Night-birds, the sounds of insects, the faint hiss of the tiny breeze. Nothing so far, but they were more than halfway to where O'Halloran reckoned the spy had been with her glass.

Two hundred yards away, Darryl was just as stopped, just as frustrated with how hard it was to stalk in this kind of undergrowth. From the sounds of it Finnegan's men were having a harder time, since they were wearing armor and had much clumsier weapons than the modern pistols and small bags of improvised grenades Darryl had equipped everyone with. The bitch of it was going to be getting close enough to start Finnegan's men chasing, but not so close they were ever in a position to actually catch or hurt anyone.

And do it without killing or hurting more than maybe one or two of *them*—too many casualties and they'd break off pursuit. And, assuming there were still outlaws in the county, come back with a regiment and make life purest hell for the fen folk. That would leave Sir Henry no room in which to organize a proper resistance. Being as he was a local gentleman, any serious attempt at repression would be looking right over his shoulder if not outright demanding he join in.

Another bound forward as Cromwell hooted softly. *His* owl-hoot wasn't just realistic, it sounded like the local owls. Which made sense, since he grew up less than fifteen miles from here. From the sounds of it, Finnegan's mob were on the move as well. Now they were getting closer, and with the wind blowing the right way, Darryl was getting able to pick out the sounds of a dozen men moving together. With only six in their own party, and

Cromwell having shown them that a man made a lot less noise if he was walking behind another, and from the few glimpses Darryl had caught of moonlight gleaming off helmets—seriously, *helmets?* It was like they wanted to give their position away and ruin their hearing into the bargain. He'd a warm woolen cap on and that was going to have to be enough. The down-timer guys had gone for wide-brimmed felt hats, obvious ancestors of cowboy hats. Another glint up ahead, the distance was down to maybe a hundred yards. Cromwell hooted again and Darryl dropped into the sedge. They'd not be moving again, and it was going to be up to whoever made first contact to open the party.

Finnegan's nerves were stretched taut. He couldn't show it in front of the boyos, no more could he. But they were nearly a mile into the fen and nothing to show yet. Once it started he'd be a lot—

The words were out of his mouth before he'd even realized he'd seen a face amid the grass—"*fucking get him!*"—and he had his wheel-lock leveled and discharged.

"Prisoner, Chief!" Tully yelled, bounding forward, a stick he'd cut earlier out and brandished.

Whoever it was that Finnegan had shot at jumped up himself, fired a pistol twice with no smoke—*definitely* one of the Americans, by God!—and started to running away. Finnegan blew a whistle of relief—after all the ranting he'd done about the need for a prisoner, if he'd hit the fellow he'd have looked a prize *amadan*—and strode out to bring up the rear of his men. Time enough to start running when he had his pistol away. He inhaled the brimstone reek of his own powder smoke.

Time to chase! He felt so much better for the whiff of gunsmoke. No more nervous waiting for *him!*

"Two of them!" There were more shots. The *crack-crack-crack* of the American pistols, and a deep, throaty bellow as someone gave fire in return with a wheel-lock.

"Fucking PRISONERS!" Tully yelled into the ear-ringing silence after the wheel-lock shot.

Finnegan made note of who had fired, the smoke hanging ghostly in the moonlight behind him. O'Halloran, as might have been known, the softheaded fool. He'd have words with that one, after. He'd fired a signal shot, sure, but O'Halloran was just returning fire because he was too stupid to see that over fifty yards even if a man in buff and cuirass were hit, he'd not be harmed beyond perhaps a bruise.

Finnegan broke into a fast trot behind his men. Ahead he could see their quarry—two of them—leaping and hurdling over hummocks of sedge, dodging about bushes.

"'Nother!" someone yelled, breathless. Now there were three. Finnegan grinned as he loped along. They only had to catch one, after all.

More shooting. This time he saw the little flashes, nothing like the great long spout of flame and sparks you got with a wheel-lock, and certainly no flash from the priming. He broke into a dead run at where he'd seen the flashes.

"Jesus, Mary and Joseph, I'm hit!" O'Halloran again. Couldn't be serious, not at this distance. Wouldn't feel like that to *him*, though. Finnegan grinned.

"Toole! See to O'Halloran!" he yelled, vaulting over where the man was on the ground clutching at his belly. No time to see if he'd been *really* unlucky and had a ball go through his coat. Unlikely, but it happened.

Darryl pumped his arms and legs for all they were worth. He'd fired once, a fast group of three. Hopefully he'd aimed high enough to miss everyone that was chasing them. He wanted a bit more of a gap before he slowed down enough to to turn and fire again. He passed Cromwell, who was crouched ready.

Crack! Crack! Crack!

There was a scream. Cromwell hadn't aimed high enough. It was a common beginner's mistake for guys used to the old muzzle-loading pistols. They expected the things to buck right up on firing so they aimed low to compensate. Took a fair bit of practice to drill them right on the new firearms. Cromwell hadn't had it.

Darryl pumped out a dead sprint for another hundred yards and turned in the shade of a low willow tree, not much taller than he was. He spat to clear the leaves out of his mouth. The bad guys were still coming on, hampered by heavy coats and armor. They'd only fired the two shots, and someone over there had definitely yelled something something that sounded like "prisoner"—if that was what passed for an Irish accent down-time, it was going to take some getting used to after the brogues Darryl had heard on TV. He brought his pistol up as he spotted Cromwell coming, haring past him with a grin on his face. Turned out the big guy was faster over this rough country than Darryl. Not a big deal, but he could see he was going to come in for some ribbing over it later.

He realized he was in a proper shooter's stance and thought *no, damn it, always wanted to do this.* He flipped the pistol on its side and fired one handed, using the kick of the weapon to fan half a dozen shots in the general direction of the air over the bad guys' heads. A couple of them, gratifyingly, went headlong into the dirt as the rounds cracked over their heads.

As he turned to run again, he grinned to himself. *Sure, you can't hit shit that way, but if you don't* want to, *it surely is fun.* More yells from behind. None in pain, more in outrage. More shots—real shots, not wheel-lock nonsense, getting hit at this distance with one of those meant you probably shouldn't have got out of bed that morning—and the attention of the bad guys was on someone else for the moment.

He could concentrate on running, then, and this kind of ground needed it. What wasn't tussocks was hummocks, and what wasn't either was flat-out *squishy.* It was quite comfy underfoot, right up to the point where it took your ankle over or faceplanted you. Cromwell had made them spend a couple of hours earlier practicing running over the stuff. Man believed in preparing properly for things, and that was to the good. What wasn't was that he regarded a whole lot of prayer as part of proper preparation. Bearable, though.

There he was again, he'd picked a clump of something thorny this time. Darryl pounded past him, slacking off the pace enough to rummage in a back pocket for a spare mag. Clutch between teeth, check. Old mag out, check. Into back pocket, check. Fresh mag, check.

Fortunately the headlong fall was right into a nice, soft tussock of something with lovely little whitish flowers. By daylight, a sort of pinkish-white. About the same color as the stars that flashed across his vision.

He grunted. By some miracle he still had gun and mag in his hands, and applied one to the other as he rolled over onto his back. Cromwell came pounding over. "Up, lad," he grunted, stopping to extend a hand down to Darryl.

"Thanks," he gasped back, coming to his feet to see a helmeted, breastplated guy with a big stick in his hand pounding up.

Aim for the head he's got armor, something in the back of Darryl's mind shrieked and then *center of mass! No time!* Three quick shots, the first snatched, headed off to Lincolnshire somewhere, the second close enough to make the guy wince and the third producing a satisfying *tonk* as it hit metal and the guy spun over and went down in flail of limbs, roaring something foul-sounding. There was a flurry of sparks and then a dull, rupturing thud as the man's pistol discharged, but by then Darryl and Cromwell were already turning to run.

There was a second one almost on them, and Darryl put his head down for another sprint, blowing and heaving to get air back into himself as much as he could. It'd be a bastard to get a stitch right now. He'd never been unfit, track and football all through school followed by mine work, but he'd just spent more than half a year cooped up in the Tower. Exercise hadn't been on his list of priorities beyond a regular stroll along the walls and some work on building the steam laundry. They hadn't been out long enough to get back to peak condition, not hardly at all. Cromwell was just as bad; he'd maybe started out fitter, but he'd been locked in one room for a year.

More shots, more swearing, and a loud thud as whoever was behind them either dove for cover or tripped. Could be either.

Cromwell grunted. "Stitch."

"Got it," Darryl grunted back, and stuffed his pistol into its under-arm holster. He had a couple of sore spots from falling over, and he knew those were going to give him trouble tomorrow, but he was damned if he was going to say anything. Besides, they were now in the "getting away with it" phase of operations and the important part here was *getting away.* He dragged his zippo out of his pocket—a down-time one, the flint was bigger and the case prettier—and stopped.

One, two, three strikes. No flame. With the other hand he was pulling a short lump of dynamite out of his pocket. Three, four, five—and then it caught.

Turned. Close. Fuse lit.

He tossed the fizzing thing at his feet and lit off again. Maybe two or three seconds of fuse and—CRACK!

He staggered and stumbled, ooofing out all his wind momentarily, and with a hasty drag of cool night air dug deep for a faster sprint. He had to hope the others were ready for that as he was.

Not likely he'd killed anyone, unless someone was stupid enough to step right on an obviously burning fuse. No compression, no fragments, and a small charge. Not much more powerful than a Fourth-of-July firecracker—okay, a pretty big one—and you'd have to be right on top of it to get hurt. The flash and bang would have rattled everyone's teeth and—

CRACK! From the sounds someone else had thought the bad guys were getting a bit close. Good. Stuff needed using up. He'd cleared out his own stock that he had in the Tower and replaced it with a box of Harry's, but it was getting on to six months old and he'd had to be elaborately careful cutting the sticks down and fitting them with squibs.

He caught up with Cromwell. "Can. Ease. Off." He puffed out in time with the breaths he was taking.

Cromwell gasped back. "Match." He had pulled out two lengths of slow match. "Light. Bombs."

A moment's thought, and yes, that ought to work better than stopping to spark his lighter. Could he get it lit on the run?

Cromwell had thought of that, and stopped and took aim behind them. Darryl stopped too. Their pursuers had dropped back some, cautious about the explosions. Cromwell emptying his magazine in their general direction sent three guys Darryl could see dropping for cover, and in the time that bought them he got the matches lit and someone else threw another stub of dynamite.

He handed off one match to Cromwell as they turned to run and both of them got stubs out. He watched Cromwell do his first—hold the fuse to the match, blow on it, drop the stub, run like hell.

He did the same, another sprint away from the blast, and they settled in to a steady lope that would let them open the distance a little, but not too much.

Ten more minutes of running and the sounds of pursuit had faded to their rear. By now, everyone had converged on the same spot and slowed to an easy jog. Cromwell looked like he was getting a second wind. The four professional soldiers looked in better shape, but then they'd not been cooped up for a year with no good exercise.

"This. Is why. I went. For cavalry," Leebrick panted out. "Horse. Does. The work."

"Little Downham," Cromwell panted out, pointing off to their left, where a village was visible on a small rise. "Half way."

"Ambush. At the road?" Leebrick asked. They'd hoped to have more of a lead at this point. By the time they reached the road with its banks and ditches—from which they could deliver a volley of bullets and bombs before running again—and got dug in and the pursuers caught up, they'd only just have their breath back. Ready for another three miles of running.

"As planned," Darryl gasped out. Even a short break was better than no break, and they didn't want the pursuers getting... unenthusiastic.

Chapter 18

"Stop!" Finnegan realized he'd not managed more than a wheeze. Louder, "Stop!" Another series of explosions, then, and shots, and he yelled again. "STOP!"

He kept up a walking pace. The boyos that had heard him had converged on where he was, and some of them had run on a way, and besides, if he just stopped he'd never get going again. He took deep lungfuls of cool night air, trying hard to get his wind back. He positively burned to pull off the cuirass and open his coat, but it was suicide to do that if there was a single one of them hiding close enough to get a shot off, or to throw one of those grenadoes they were using. There was a miracle for you, those things going off and nobody on either side hurt. There wasn't anything to like about them, either, outside of a siege, and wasn't that a reason Finnegan was glad he'd never got into one of those? Take an iron pot and stuff it full of powder and gravel and birdshot and let it off, there wasn't really any way it was going to end well for anyone. Frequently, not even the *gealt* that was flinging the bastard thing.

One of the Cooley brothers, of infamous memory, had positively loved the infernal devices, the bigger the better, and had once thrown one in to a cottage they were trying to evict. The family within had got out in a hurry, but everything they owned, including a half-grown pig, had been wrecked by the blast and shards of metal in such a close space. For a finisher, the blast had dislodged the turves under the thatch and half the roof had slid off in a sodden heap. Comical, in its way, but Finnegan had had to dock the cost of re-roofing the place from Cooley's pay. Not least to stop him doing to people what he'd done to the pig, which wasn't even any use for bacon after the grenado was finished with it.

No, those things gave Finnegan the shivers, and facing them was like to freeze his piss. It was a definite mark against the fen people that they had even brought the things. They were planning on more, too, because the distinctive scent of slow match was still trailing around in the night air. And certainly not from his own people. None of his lads even had the slow matches to burn, what with all being armed with wheel-locks. Now that the Cooleys were dead, of course, nobody had any grenadoes at all. Finnegan had put his foot down at the suggestion of anyone else learning to use the things.

"Go steady, lads," he said, setting a brisk walking pace. "Smell that?" He took a deep whiff. "Slow match. Follow the scent of it, we'll keep them with us." Up ahead, there were occasional glimpses to be had of their fleeing quarry. Maybe three hundred yards, now he'd slowed the pace of pursuit, and gaining all the time. Gaining in a straight line and leaving plenty of sign, though, he noted. He could afford to be patient with them. He counted five, maybe six, judging from the trails and the hints of movement ahead, now he stopped to look.

Tully lumbered up, visibly laboring with some hurt or other. "Will we not be giving them time to form an ambush?" he asked.

"Perhaps, but they've to stop for an ambush and no great range for it in this country. We'll be on them when they spring it, so we've only to rush through a first volley and we're in. And if the smell of that slow match gets stronger, we'll know to be ready."

Tully nodded. "Those pistols they've brought have a power to them. I've a hole in my cuirass, now. The coat stopped it after, mind, but I'll have a bruise. And some burns, where my pistol fired when I fell. Still, I've something to remember it by. Queer-looking balls they shoot." He held up a little lump of metal that looked like it had been squeezed through a small hole.

Effect of going through the breastplate, Finnegan supposed. Not usual for a pistol-ball, which would account for the unusual shape. "Could have been worse, then," he said.

"It could, at that," Tully acknowledged, pocketing the spent ball. "When we catch them, I want one of those pistols for my own, mind."

"They've at least two," Finnegan said, shrugging away the question. "Maybe more. And I'll be after the earl for ordering the like from Germany, surely there's someone selling the things there that doesn't mind a little fast freight. We might even get a rifle or two. Failing that, we'll find a gunsmith that can copy them."

Toole jogged up then. "O'Halloran. He'll live," he gasped out. "They getting away? I heard grenadoes."

"They've got a Cooley back from the grave with them," someone growled in the darkness, to a round of laughter. The Cooleys' antics had *not* been popular.

Finnegan snorted, as much mirth as he had breath for. "They have, at that. Did anyone see of those three Englishmen were with them? The ones that killed the Cooleys?"

"Thought I saw Leebrick," someone called out.

"Haven't seen Mackay, if that was Mackay that I rode down the other day," Tully added. "But I'm pretty sure that was Cromwell with the other one, him that shot me."

Finnegan grinned. "Then we're chasing the right prey," he said. "Toole, how bad's O'Halloran?"

"Not at all. He'd a ball go through his coat, and it creased the side of his belly. Burnt out maybe a spoonful of the lard of him. Not even bleeding much, but he'll move slow for a time. I sent him back to the horses and told him to have the boys ride them down to Ely. I saw you headed this way and thought, well, better to press on and have the horses than have to walk back for the beasts."

"And that's a bottle of good brandy for you, Toole, when I get a moment. These bastards are faster on their feet than I expected." It was so *good* to have a band well-leavened with bright lads who could think for themselves. Especially the ones with the tact to cover his own mistakes without trying to make a show of him over them.

They carried on another ten minutes. From the few glimpses they could catch—of a hat bobbing over low spots in the undergrowth, puffs of slow-match smoke hovering ghostly when the breeze lulled, Cromwell's party had eased their pace as well, maintaining perhaps four or five hundred yards of gap. If the night was a whit less clear there'd be no tracking them at all, but with the moon so big and bright and right above, things weren't much worse than daylight. He'd been abroad on winter afternoons with no more light.

"Road ahead," one of the boyos up front, Toole by the sounds, called back, soft so as not to carry too far. The ground was rising slightly, the horizon that way shortening visibly, and although there wasn't anything you'd call a hedge there it was creating a fine area of dead ground behind it. And, yes, it looked like a road ran along the top of the slight rise. Perfect for an ambush, and assuming they'd been careful about skylining themselves, they could have been up there for minutes already, with a clear view. Nothing for it but to get in there and do it quick. The cover they were in was good and thick, but would thin out as soon as they started up the upward movement.

Finnegan nodded, pulled out a loaded pistol and checked the priming by feel. He had a lot more wind now, and called out, "Good spot for an ambush. Smell for slow match, boys. As soon as we catch sign, give 'em a pistol volley and in through the smoke and the flash-blinding. We've, what, eight to their five? Cudgels to put the fight out of them. I want prisoners for the earl to hang. Spread out, see if we can't find a flank while we're at it."

The smell of burning match got stronger and stronger, the banking that the road ran on closer and closer. The sweat was running down Finnegan's back, now, chilly on the base of his spine, and he relished the cool of it. The front of him was like an open oven door was pressed against his chest, the hard steel over leather trapping his body heat horribly. Pistol in his left hand, *bata* in his right, he strode quickly through the sedge, shouldering bushes aside. Let them think he and his lads were coming in stupid, let them think their ambush was working. He wanted to slow down, deep in himself, let the lads get in first, but to do that would give them leave to slow down as well, and the slower they were going the greater the temptation to drop and hide when they made—

Crack-crack-crack!

Those damnable American weapons. Winking like glowworms in the dark. Well, for this night's work he had better. *"Fág a' Bealach!"* and a flare of wheel-lock fire, ragged in the darkness and without command, but with one eye shut he kept his night vision as he charged up the bank and across the road.

BLAM! BLAM-BLAM! More fucking grenadoes and he heard screams. Oh Jesus and all the saints let that have been quick for whatever poor bastard it was. But now Finnegan, with someone at his left, was falling on a pair of the ambushers, whipping his stick forward in a simple strike that would have a slow man's teeth out and his head rung like a bell.

It was Cromwell he'd gone for, he saw as he recovered from the lightning-quick parry that knocked his blow aside. More shots. A round-strike and again parried, and the counterstrike came out of nowhere overhead and the double-handed block he fumbled up stung his hands even through his gauntlets.

"You're quick," Finnegan snarled, lashing out a belly-strike while Cromwell was recovering the bounce of his murder-stroke, feinted it back and went for the teeth again.

"Me too," came another snarl and he had to sway back as a huge knife with a wicked claw-point came in at him. A backstep, and then another, merely knocking aside the blade as it licked at him again and again like a serpent's tongue. Whoever this was he was fast, but had no great store of tricks. Toole was in on Cromwell now, his bouncing, swarming style of stick-fighting putting the bigger fellow onto his back foot, and Finnegan could put all his attention on the knife-man.

Who was growling out some truly bizarre insults as he stabbed away. What in the devil's name was a *pinkerton*? No matter. One more thrust and he had the fool's measure. A sweeping parry and the knife went out of line, the backstroke rapped the fingers that the idiot hadn't so much as put a glove on. As the knife spun away he snapped a kick up to try for the kneecap, or failing that the balls, and split the difference with a firm hit in the meat of the thigh. *Then* he could stamp in, and another snap-strike with the heavy end and—

The world flashed purple and rang loud as a bell.

"Chief?" Someone was lifting him by the elbow. How had he ended up on one knee? "Just a belt to the helmet, Chief, you'll need the dent hammered out. Toole's the same."

And then he was back. Only the space of a few heartbeats, he'd been knocked to his knees. His vision snapped back into focus and a bite of pain took his forehead in a pincer grip. "Who's down? Who's that?"

"Tully, Chief, I went on my arse from a grenado, I'm a touch sick but I'll live. Toole's on his arse with the teeth out of him, three more lads hurt, they're running again."

Rage filled Finnegan, rage like he'd not felt—no. Enough. Clear thought, that was the thing. "Any dead?"

"By the mercy of God, no. McGurk'll limp a while, he's a cut to the leg went through his coat-skirt."

"How long was I out?"

"Not long, I've just this moment come on you. Nor even have I counted all the boys in."

"They're heading for Ely!" someone yelled back.

"We'll have them there, then," Finnegan said. "Toole sent the horses ahead, we'll meet them there. For now we'll stay back from these bastards, they've too much fire to give us. And that Cromwell's a bastard with the *bata*, so he is."

"They call it singlestick over here," Tully said, "and did you spend more time in the alehouses in London you'd have seen it more. There's some grand matches to be had."

"Sure I found one," Finnegan snarled, "and he'd have had my skull broke if I'd no helmet on. Boys! With me! Wounded, follow as you can, be wary. I'll leave a man with your mounts at Ely and word of where we're gone."

Only two men dropped out, McGurk, who averred he could fight, "but not run worth a bollocks" and Toole, who was seeing double and could hardly breathe through a smashed nose. He'd not be running much either, and Finnegan told McGurk to make sure Toole didn't go to sleep, for it was well known that trying to sleep off a blow to the head was a sure way to die of it.

"Call warning if you smell another ambush," Finnegan said as he set a fast walk as their pace. "The fight's more even than I thought and they've the defender's advantage. We'll not get in among them without guile, I'm thinking."

As it was, the ground rose slowly from there on, growing drier and clearer as they came within a mile of the town now clearly visible on its slight rise, marked out starkly by the cathedral tower that stood silhouetted against the stars. There were more and more signs of human habitation, more than the few scraps that they had passed earlier, and here and there enclosures and small, tilled patches. Closer still, and they came on another road, following the line of a slight rise in the fen. Finnegan made a quick decision. "If they've stayed on the soft ground, we can get ahead of them. If they're on this, we need to keep up. Fast march, boyos, we're infantry for the next half-hour."

That bought him a groan. It wasn't as though they hadn't just run five miles or more on foot, but for all the men of Finnegan's troop were no more than glorified cattle thieves, they still rather thought of themselves as cavalrymen. They'd walk when walking was to the purpose, but calling them infantry rankled. "My arse is no higher off the ground than yours is, you pack of vagrants, and there'll be horses waiting in town."

There were indeed, as Mulligan clattered into town at the trot at the same time they had got down to the river road to look for him and the three with him. All four of the bastards looked horribly fresh and ready, having spent the last hour at the trot from Earith. Even O'Halloran, who had his buffcoat open and a bandage wound about him, seemed fairly chipper.

"Get spread out, you four, and find a livery that's open. We need these nags rested, fed and watered while we get out and quarter the country. The rest of us will take our mounts and go sit up by yonder church tower and get the feet of me rested."

Half an hour later Mulligan and O'Halloran rejoined them, grinning. "The bastards have been and they've left while we've been here," Mulligan said. "The only livery open at this hour was the one they had their mounts at, in care of a short-arsed Scotsman. Where they sold a wagon, yesterday, one I recognized the description of, having heard it so many bloody times before. They went by the road downriver, for the port of it, a town named Lynn."

"King's Lynn?" Finnegan asked.

"Liveryman said just Lynn. Might be the same place, you know how towns get their names shortened."

"That might be it. The port downriver is called King's Lynn, on the map at any rate. Come to think, it's a map I got from the king's people." A round of chuckles. "They'll be faster than us, at that. We've worked the horses tonight. Did the livery have anything worth the money to hire?"

Mulligan shrugged. "Indifferent horseflesh at best," he said, "We'll be best with our own, do we give them water and a chance to rest. Cromwell and his lads will be going slow with the bad light. Do we wait for the first light of dawn, we can take that road at the gallop, the liveryman says. It seems he's no great liking for Scotsmen, nor has he."

"That'll be Mackay, will it?"

"Sounded like." Mulligan shrugged. "But 'short, unpleasant, freckled, sandy hair' describes about every other one of the bastards. And before you say anything, no sign of his wife. I asked. No women with the party."

Finnegan nodded. Mulligan had been at Stralsund with Wallenstein as well, and the Scots regiment there had been, from the sounds of it, a pack of bastard die-hards. And Mulligan hadn't managed to get an easy job fetching and carrying for the artillery. "We'll assume it is Mackay. That's a thing to tell the earl when I next write him. If the Scots are coming back from the Germanies to make trouble, he'll want warning. Even if it's not Mackay, the warning's still a good one, from the looks of it. Who knows, we may even get paid to kill a few of the bastards."

Mulligan grinned in reply, and they set out for the livery stable to get the horses right for the ride to come.

Chapter 19

"They've got to be here somewhere," Darryl said. The sun had come up, but the streets of King's Lynn, being a warren of warehouses and chandleries, were still dark. There was already a muted hum and bustle; the bakeries were filling the air with the smell of damned tasty bread, cookshops were working on breakfast, and even the docks were busy. High tide was in less than two hours and several ships were making ready to pull out on the slack water to stand out on the ebb tide, whatever the hell that meant. Towson had come back with that story after a brief word with a dock worker, and though nobody was about to admit it nobody but him had the foggiest what he was talking about. Cromwell mentioned that if they could get a ride on it—his actual words, he didn't know anything about ships either—and there was a collier in port that would be a fast ship north in the right direction for Edinburgh. With, admittedly, a stop at Newcastle, but colliers went north from there too. It shouldn't be too hard to change ships at the coal docks.

"I still think we should have asked on the ships if one of them had passage booked," Welch said. "I mean, we're *trying* to leave a trail, are we not?"

"Aye, but if the ladies have no place in a ship for us," Cromwell said, "best not to spread word. I'd not like it to be the step we trip on, that we bring all to the docks and find we must fight to win through. Fighting with children with us—my children, I'll remind you—is something we already decided was a poor notion."

"Add to that," Towson put in, "there's all that river wharf and three docks at least, and did you see how many ships there were? Dozens, and hundreds of smaller tubs, luggers, fishing boats, all sorts. We'd get round maybe a tithe of the bastards in two hours between now and high tide and learn nothing but by purest good fortune."

"Fair enough," Welch said, "but how will we manage anything wandering about like this?"

"Man has a point," Darryl said, "any suggestions for a plan?"

"Breakfast," Leebrick said, wandering back, along with Hamilton, from a mosey down a small side street. "Think about it. It's dawn. If they're up, they're only just up, and they know the ship won't be sailing for at least two hours. There's a cookshop down here, if we all go for breakfast and take turns wandering down the road there to the river front and up and down. They'll be doing something similar, depend on it."

"It's the first thing Vicky would think about, right enough. She used to help with the cookshop the warders' wives ran for the Hamlets boys when they were coming on for the morning shift and going off the night shift."

"Hamlets boys?" Cromwell asked.

"You wouldn't have seen them, you were under orders for a warder guard only, same with the Grantville party. The tower guard is filled out with lads from the Trained Band of Tower Hamlets, they get let off half their muster for it. They get six-pence a day and all the training they can stand, which is a fair amount, credit to them. And, of course, the ladies took a farthing of that back off most of them, stuffing them with bacon and eggs and eels and pease. We'd usually have thirty or forty of them in to walk the walls most days, until Cork dumped all those bloody mercenaries on us. That won't have gone down well with the Bands, once word gets around; that guard pay was feeding more than a few families in the Hamlets. Anyway, she knows the importance of a good breakfast, and as we've wandered about I've been looking for the kind of cookshop she'd think well of. This one. And it's been weeks since I had a proper breakfast. This way, people, bacon is calling. Fat bacon, and good bread. If I can get them to fry an egg for me, I may count this day a happy one and it's barely begun."

Darryl's belly rumbled agreement. "I'm in."

Hamilton got his fried egg, and Towson and Alex lost the coin tosses for who got the first beat walking the streets. Nobody else had to go out, as Alex came in beaming with his wife on his arm and Vicky right behind him. She came straight across to Darryl, grabbed him and kissed him thoroughly. "Later, you," she said, and was straight over to the counter. "Got my order, love?"

The woman behind the counter had, and she and Vicky chatted like they'd known each other for decades as the crocks and pots and pans were pulled out from beside the massive range where they'd been warming and loaded into baskets. When all was done, Vicky passed over a handful of coins, by some complicated process negotiated a couple more plates for Alex and Towson and had the load divided among everyone but her. It seemed they were to head back to the house of a Committee of Correspondence member where they'd got a couple of rooms. Which they were repaying the use of by buying a hearty cookshop breakfast for themselves and their hosts.

Who turned out to be a pleasant family, more-or-less headed up by the oldest of three excessively large brothers and his wife, who was smoking a pipe with her feet up on a stool when they arrived. Stevedores, all three, and Darryl was a little confused that they seemed to be missing work to help out.

The biggest brother, Rob, who looked to Darryl like he'd unload a ship by lifting it out of the water, tipping it over and giving it a good shake, laughed like a small earthquake. "Bless you, no. The tides today, every ship that's making sail will be making ready for it at first light and they'll be standing out shortly. We got 'em all right stuffed by last light last night, and I've had a good night's sleep."

His wife swatted him behind the ear. "Tell the truth, you bloody goat. Here's me with the chance of a lie-in for a change, and don't 'e know it." She'd a grin on her face.

"Okay, more'n I needed to know," Darryl laughed. "Breakfast, here. Get to it. Do we have a ship to leave on?"

"Oh, we sorted that last night, even loaded all your stuff aboard her," Rob said. "Go to the collier right at the downstream end of the river wharf, the *Magpie*. She's a Newcastle collier, going back deadhead this morning. She'll have you in Newcastle by sundown tomorrow, with no more than ordinary winds, and from there it's another day to Edinburgh. Be a day faster than you can manage on a horse to Newcastle, even if you didn't so much as stop to piss. Couldn't tell you about the road from there to Edinburgh, mind."

"The ship should still aye be faster," Alex put in around a mouthful of bacon. "Border country. Bad roads o'er worse ground. And that's no' mindin' the borderers, who're no joke. Ye ken the gang o' savages I had under me when first I cam' tae Grantville? Borderers, to a man. And they were the ones we could civilize a wee bit, mind."

He grinned over that one. The Green Regiment lads—most of them now in various bits of the USE armed forces with chunks of newly acquired education under their belts—were mostly a decent enough bunch, if a little rough around the edges. Because, in the wilder bits of land on either side of the border between Scotland and England, the chances to acquire any polish at all were nil, let alone enough to pass for civilized.

"Well," he went on, "We've the horses left at yon livery, will I go and see to selling them if I can, or will the Committee here use them?"

"We'll likely just sell them. We want to buy a press from Magdeburg," Rob said. "It's time and past time we stopped leaving things to the gentry around here. Most of them do all right, I suppose, but most of them have got religion so far up their arses it's coming out their mouths the whole time."

Darryl saw Cromwell open his mouth to speak, and then, apparently, think better of it.

Rob went on, "I've heard where there's simple books for helping folk learn to read in German. I reckon if we could print a few of those in English, it'd be good. All you can mostly get around here is ballads or the Bible, and an almanac, and they're hard to learn from. I've got the beginnings of my letters, I can read nearly all the prayer book at church on Sunday, and I speak English and German handily, but I can't write to save my life. We've got all sorts of plans around that, and there's plenty of the dockers would go for it. Being as it's all stop-go-stop there, there's plenty of time for learning, see?"

Nods all round. And then Cromwell spoke up, "And if there was to be a godly element to such learning?"

"Well, most folk around here wouldn't object, I ain't what you'd call perfectly in line with the Book of Common Prayer myself, but there's always the thing about freedom of religion to remember. Which is a good thing. As one of the sailors from Germany put it to me, what if the Lutherans are wrong, the Calvinists are wrong, and the Catholics are right? Or we're all wrong and Our Lord is weeping over all our errors? What about that? Best not to force anything on any man, and each dispute with the other. Maybe we'll find out which way is the right way after all?" Rob shrugged. "I've heard plenty out of the Germanies about what the wars of religion did there. Not here, thank you very much, we've hard times enough in old England without having another Tilly and another Gustavus roaring back and forth and leaving us all to ruin and want."

"The king will surely strike at you for such a thing. An unlicensed press, for one thing?"

"Plenty of those already, Mister Cromwell. And how long does the king have, anyway? From what I hear you're set on having the head off him a few years early? Yes, we heard about you, all right, from your boys there, and then we sent word to Germany, and now we know about the civil war that was to be. Well, speaking for the common folk, Mister Cromwell, if you can see your way clear to a bit more civil and a bit less war, we'll thank you. But if it comes to war, then it's a rebellion for everyone, not just the godly. And I say that as one of the godly myself, by my best efforts at any rate."

Cromwell laughed, a deep and hearty roar. It was a minute or more before he could gather himself to say anything. "Two recording angels, is it now?" he spluttered out at last. "One for the Irish and one for the English? Colonel Mackay, will you watch me on the part of the Scots? And who will look to the Welsh?"

"All right, no need to get funny about it," Darryl said. "But Rob's got a point. Miz Mailey said one of the problems she had with you was that when you got told nine out of ten disagreed with you, you'd put a sword in the tenth man's hand. And that ain't right, not at all. If you're going to be startin' a revolution here, Oliver, then fine. Place needs it, far as I can see. But you're going to do it right or not. At. All. Ain't like there's a shortage of experts to advise you. Bet Mike Stearns'd be able to tell you a few things about getting a revolution right, since from what I hear he's doing it."

"Hate to interrupt this consciousness-raising," Julie put in, "but it's time we scouted the way down to the river. And, Alex?

I'd just leave the horses and we'll write a bill of sale to Rob here. He can use the money and we don't need it for now. I know what you're like when you get stuck in to a deal about horses, you'll be there hours. Days, probably."

Mackay shrugged. "I had planned on just taking the first price offered. And if we leave a writing with Rob here, surely that will have that Irish scunner after him for information?"

"Which he can have, for as much as I can bargain the bribe up to. What you said was you were going to Newcastle and then Hamburg on the next collier from there, since there wasn't a ship direct to anywhere in Germany today. And you stopped along of me because I offered Mistress Mason here when she was asking yesterday, why are them folks wanted outlaws? Well, I never, they looked so respectable an' all. I can keep that up all day and half the night at need, everyone expects the big fellow to be a friendly idiot. Worked for me since I was big enough to get a tun up over my head on a dare, that has."

"Well, you're fool enough to lift a tun on your own, what do you expect people to think?" That was one of Rob's younger brothers, whose name Darryl hadn't got in his head, and he wasn't much smaller than his big brother. If it came to tipping ships up and giving them a good shake, he'd probably need the help of the littlest billygoat Rob, whose name Darryl had caught as Paul. While he wasn't much bigger than a normal human being, the size of breakfast he put down showed he was serious about catching up. If civil war did come to England, Darryl could see the MOS for these guys right away. Give 'em a cannon apiece, none of them would have any trouble firing a galloper gun off the shoulder, armor 'em up and there you go. Instant tanks.

"Whatever. You going to go looking after any false constables by the wharf? Seems to me we need a clear coast for these good people and it's time you two got to it. Just the downriver end, mind, nobody'll be blabbing on purpose but you know how people gossip and don't care who's listening. Then, when everyone's safe aboard, we'll go sell the story to the false constables."

A little grumbling and the two got up and headed out to look over the neighborhood.

Mackay insisted on being the one to write the bill of sale for the horses, since he wasn't to have the fun of haggling a good price for them himself, and took time to give Rob a long list of instructions for the dickering he would be doing. When the tide of words ebbed, Rob blinked, was silent a moment, and then said: "When I said I wanted education, I didn't mean *right now!*"

"Welcome to my life, locked in the Tower for a year with Miz Mailey," Darryl said. "I swear, that woman figured any minute she didn't spend pounding facts into my poor brain was a minute wasted."

"She didn't think the time she got while you were at school was enough, did she?" Gayle asked, mischievous.

"Yeah, well, I'm gonna have me some words on that subject, next I see her. She tried to teach me a bunch of history and now I'm here livin' it, some of it turns out not quite the way she said it, now does it? You got Puritans who're revolutionaries in secret, Oliver Cromwell only got a year of college and spent most of that playing sports, and half of those are as likely to kill you as not, and don't think I didn't see what you done to that guy back in the fen, Oliver, would've been kinder to shoot him."

"His own fault. I was college champion at singlestick. Nobody forced him to take up that cudgel. Wouldn't mind another go-round with an Irishman, mind, it's an interesting style."

"My point exactly. Sport where you can put a dent the size of a damned fist in a steel helmet, played *without* helmets, and let's see if I got this right, you win by *drawing an inch of blood out of the other guy's head*? And you thought playing it at night, in a swamp, with guys who had guns, was interesting? This is why I got a problem with history. It all got made by crazy guys. Like this one."

"Who's after being a new Hereward, eh?" Rob grinned.

"I had more of a mind for Robin Hood," Cromwell said. "How can I Wake if I've been hit on the head so much?"

"Ah, true," Rob said, "You can go here-ward and there-ward in Lincoln green instead."

"And now puns," Darryl groaned. "My day is *complete.*"

Apart from the puns, and a little light chat about what life was like on King's Lynn these days—tough—and conditions for dock workers—tough, but improving with a little pressure from below—they got to where Rob's brothers came back with the news that the Irishmen had arrived in town and were asking along completely the wrong end of the river wharf. They were starting to spread out, though.

"Aye, well, let's be about it," Cromwell said, rising. "I could ask, though, how is it that the justices don't have you before them for restraint of trade? Enticement of servants?"

Rob laughed as he showed them out the door. "That's the best part. The wharves used to insist on day labor. Can't entice day labor, nor restrain trade if every man decides to refuse to work of his own accord, and who's to say what passed between him and friends over ale the day before? They can prove nothing. And then when one wharf finds he may only have workers by engaging men for regular wages on agreed terms—and always before witnesses—then suddenly another wharf finds no day labor will apply to him. They know what goes on, mind, but can prove nothing unlawful on oath. Perhaps a couple of fellows thought to have a shilling for informing falsely, but there's more still will inform on the informers. And I can be a most persuading sort of fellow, when I've a mind."

"Persuading?" Cromwell said, an eyebrow raised. Darryl privately thought it was a bit rich him wondering about whether or not this sort of thing was legal when he was dead set on turning rebel against the king. But he let it go.

"Thou shalt not bear false witness," Rob said, suddenly a lot less cheerful sounding. "A text I can preach on at very, very great length."

"Rightly so," Cromwell said, after a pause.

Half an hour later, they were aboard the *Magpie*, a tidy little ship made to carry a hundred and eighty tons of coal at a time. She was, of course, completely filthy with coal dust, despite the efforts of her crew of fifteen. Darryl couldn't really follow the nautical stuff that was getting yelled as she got under way, not least because the accent was so damned off. The dialect almost sounded like some of the northwest German guys he knew, but the accent had him wishing for subtitles.

None of the other English guys understood much of what the collier's crew were saying either, apart from Leebrick, who'd run into Tynesiders before. Mackay averred that he'd had a couple in his company, because although Newcastle was a bit outside the traditional Borders area, it was close enough that a few of them had been around when they'd been recruiting. And he'd never been able to understand a bloody word they said either, which was something coming from a man, who, when he decided to really come the Scotsman, was flat-out incomprehensible to one Darryl McCarthy, esquire.

So they all gathered at the stern rail, inhaling the pungent stink of coal—*that* took Darryl back to simpler times—and watched for Finnegan and his boys to get the message that their quarry was now at sea and beyond hope of capture. And, yes! Rob's timing had been perfect. Four of them, suddenly, in the gap at the wharf where the *Magpie* had been, just as she edged, under nothing more than a single sail, into the current of the Great Ouse and began to drift gently down to the Wash and on her way.

"Would you say that was about fifty yards?" Cromwell asked, of nobody in particular.

Mackay gave the matter a considering look. "A little over, Mister Cromwell."

"And, of course, we may not open fire, for fear of harming the innocent."

"A commendable caution on your part, Mister Cromwell," Mackay said, gravely.

"And, do we provoke them, we are too distant for them to do injury to this fine vessel, I think."

"That would be my conclusion also."

"Excellent," Cromwell said.

And, to Darryl's frank amazement, the man cupped his hands for an impromptu trumpet, and without once uttering blasphemy or obscenity, nor even violating the Profane Swearing Act all that much, let Finnegan know precisely what he thought of the man.

And he was right. None of the answering pistol fire so much as scratched the ship.

"That's a collier, right?" Finnegan blew the smoke away from his face. Cromwell was still yelling, but getting fainter all the time.

"That's what the man said," Tully answered, "and look at the dirt of her. She carries coal, all right."

"And high in the water, too. Ask around, but I think you'll find she's heading home, back to Newcastle."

"That where we're bound next?" Tully asked.

"No, there's nothing in Newcastle for them. But that was for certain sure Mackay there stood by Cromwell. And that means Edinburgh. The earl's packet on that one says he took his daughter to Edinburgh, where she fell ill. And lived, but he'll not have brought the mite with him here to do a prison break."

"Edinburgh, then."

"Aye. Even if the others take another ship from Newcastle, he and that bitch of a wife of his, her and the rifle, will go on to Edinburgh to pick up the brat. Do we lay hold of them, we'll know where Cromwell went, which will be something, and where Leebrick and his men went, which is another thing. And, pardon my pessimism, I for one want to report failure to the earl with something to offer him to soften it."

"And from a long way away?"

"Aye, from a long way away."

"Well, we got away." Darryl looked around at the others. "And don't you ever tell me about harsh language again, Mister Oliver so-called-Puritan Cromwell."

Cromwell grinned back. "Harsh language, where it is deserved, is no impropriety. It's filth and blasphemy I object to."

Darryl harrumphed. "I know Alex and Julie have to go on to Edinburgh, and I don't reckon it'd be right for me not to go along in case Finnegan and his mob recognized 'em, but what about you and the kids? Can we get you away to safety?"

"For me, no. Robert?" Cromwell called his son over from where he was watching the sailors getting a full spread of sail on.

"Father?" the younger Cromwell said, presenting himself as smartly as any soldier.

"It will fall to you to look after Oliver and the little ones while I attend to my duty."

"Aye, Father. In Newcastle, perhaps? It's our next port. The captain says we needn't worry about pirates on this journey, with the ship empty."

"We might be able to arrange better, actually," Gayle put in. "We've got all tonight to get messages back home, and these fine tall masts for an aerial. I'm pretty sure we can find somewhere for the kids in Grantville. My brother Arnold would take them in, I think. He makes a good living in mining administration. He's got three kids of his own but that's a big house he's got."

She hesitated a moment. "I'm sure my sister Susan would take them in, too, but she's Catholic since she married into"—here a nod toward Darryl—"that big McCarthy clan he belongs to. I don't know if that'd be a problem for you, Oliver."

He pursed his lips thoughtfully. "Might not be, if they don't insist on pushing their creed onto my children. What is your brother's faith?"

"He's Disciples of Christ, like me." Again, she hesitated. "That's ... ah, well, we're Protestants and congregationalists. I'm not sure if you'd consider us 'godly' the way you use the term, but ..."

He nodded. "Much closer than Catholics, certainly. Well, see if he's willing. If not, I've no great objection to your sister." He gave his son a rather sly smile. "I dare say Robert can withstand the blandishments of papistry."

His son looked quite stern, in response.

Gayle chuckled. "All right, then. I'll make the call tonight. If they can wait in Newcastle for a ship going the right way. You up to that, Robert?"

Robert nodded, now looking more solemn than stern.

Leebrick cleared his throat. "While I should like to come to Edinburgh, and I won't speak for the other two, I'm keen to get me over to Germany. I've Liz to support, and I'm not doing it here. The poor girl left all her livelihood behind when she left London, and the money she had of me won't last forever. I could go with Robert, here, help him with the guarding of the littl'uns in Grantville?"

After that, it was settling of details.

Part Four

August 1634

The English steel we could disdain,

Secure in valour's station;

But English gold has been our bane—

Such a parcel of rogues in a nation!

Chapter 20

Town house of Lord Reay,
Colonel-in-chief of the Mackay regiment in the Swedish Army
Copenhagen, Denmark

"Yeez c'n gaw un an see th'laird noo," the orderly said, none-too-discreetly scratching at an armpit that was clearly troubling him. And, apparently, unwilling to speak clearly to a superior officer. How the man did when he had to deal with anyone not brought up in Scotland was anyone's guess. Most foreigners learned English, if they learned it at all, the way it was spoken in England, and assumed the various forms of Scots speech were other languages altogether. Come to that, a fair few native English held the same opinion. Most Scotsmen, be they ever so broad in their brogue, managed to at least rub the rough edges off with a few years of foreign service. Not this one.

"Thank ye for that, soldier," Lennox said, speaking clearly to set an example and trying not to sniff. Not just because it wouldn't do to be too snotty about a soldier under someone else's command. Nor because he'd taken on board lectures about prejudice and didn't want to show the lowlander's bred-in-the-bone contempt for thieving, drunken papist highlanders. Rather, because the private soldier who was overseeing Lord Reay's anteroom clearly hadn't seen the inside of a laundry or bathhouse in far too long.

Major Lennox of the United States of Europe's Marine Corps still listened to his inner sergeant about such things. Long a stickler for keeping the men clean in barracks and in the field, he'd had his views confirmed by twentieth-century learning on hygiene and reinforced by the USE's up-time standards of military grooming.

Private McAuslan, in his view, *Would Not Do*. Doubtless there was some reason Colonel the Lord Reay kept the man around and tolerated his slovenliness, though. It wasn't for a late-starting major to question the eccentricities of a regimental colonel with several years seniority and a patent of nobility.

He still didn't draw breath to sigh until the horrible little man had shut the door to the laird's room behind him.

"He's a character, is he no'?" Lord Reay asked as he returned Lennox's salute in the modern style.

"As your lordship says," Lennox replied, picking the most diplomatic of the responses he could think of. And, to follow up on his hunch, "I've no doubt he's done your lordship fine service, at times."

"Aye. Man's a reekin' pint o' piss in barracks, but ye'll not see his like in a fight. Owe the man my life more times than I care t' count. He hides here wi' me to keep his comrades from having at him wi' a stiff brush an a bucket o' soap." Reay was grinning. There was clearly some joke he wasn't letting Lennox in on, for that surely wasn't the whole story.

Lennox decided that if his superior wanted to have the little joke with him, he wasn't going to object. Out loud, at any rate. "Your lordship summoned me," he prompted.

"Have a seat, Lennox. I sent for ye so as to talk man to man, without rank and the like getting about our ears."

"Aye?" Lennox took the chair Lord Reay had pointed to while the other sat himself in a plain carver by the window. "It's in my mind that we've both commissions in allied armies. And your lordship a peer of Scotland and the chief of the clan I took service with."

"Right enough, Major, but I'd have as little of that as may be today. What d'ye ken o' oil?"

"Yon stuff they mine at Wietze? Little enough, y'lordship. Enough I'm determined t' have a bright lad by me that understands the business should I have tae deal wi' it. Enough tae ken the stuff is vital. Need I more for this wee talk?"

Reay chuckled. "Have a bright lad by ye, ye say. Aye, there's half the art an' science' o' lordship in a nutshell, right enough.

I've the same understanding, it so happens. And a very clear understanding o' the importance of the stuff. Did ye hear from any o' the Americans about North Sea oil?"

"No' that I recall, Chief."

"Ye've heard about it now, then, frae me. We'll be many a year before we can mine it out, mind ye, but there's oil under the sea-bed, and much of it within waters Scotland can control. Scotland, mind ye. Not the United Kingdom." Reay stopped there and looked pointedly at Lennox.

"I—" Lennox stopped himself short. He'd be the first to admit he was none of the world's great or deep thinkers. Enough wit to manage his professional responsibilities. Enough learning to manage them well, and follow scriptures on the Sabbath. Each had served him well enough until that day in 1631 when he and young Alexander Mackay had happened on the first days of the Ring of Fire. Since then he had joined a new service, seen marvels he'd never have dreamed of as a wee lad in Coldstream, and, yes, taken a role on the fringes of high politics. There was that to be said for the Americans. They'd find you work for what you could do, not who you were born. If a peer of the kingdom of Scotland was taking up the same attitude there was a very real prospect of Lennox finding himself in the kind of situations that the treason laws applied to, will he or nil he.

"Aye, it's a grand big thought, right enough," Reay said, "take your time wi' it."

Lennox took a deep breath and let it out. "Ye're talkin' o' risky matters, y'lordship. We're the both of us in foreign service as it is, I mind that well enough, but if ye mean what I think ye mean, well..."

He groped for a word, for an idea he only had the merest mist of, an idea that he was fairly certain was more complicated than just the word *treason* would cover. "We'd no' be allowed home in peace again."

Reay nodded. "Aye, that. More than just lives, fortunes and sacred honor, but all that's at hazard too. If we try, and fail. And we may be sure Charles Stuart will not stay his hand against all in reach of it, should we make the least misstep."

Lennox felt the heat rising in his face. It would be this way, then? The lords and chiefs, moving the common men like chessmen. He mustered every effort to speak civilly. "I'm no' sure 'tis proper t' speak of it, Chief. Just to scheme of it would be the excuse the Stuart needs. We've all folk at home. I'll not see them ruined and killed over the minin' o' oil."

"Aye. Ye'll have no blame from me for the concern ye have. And were it just oil, I'd not fash ye with it. I'd no fash myself, come to that. But still. Take a drink with me. I'll tell ye how it seems to me, and how ye may do good for Scotland and Clan Mackay that ye've done good service for, and for the United States ye have the commission of now. I cannae see how a good fellow such as you will refuse, but I'll think no less o' ye if ye do. Nor will I bother ye for an answer this day nor the next. It'll be a hard thing I ask, when ye'd a mind to settle down in the new training establishment. We're of an age, we twa', an past the time where campaigning is a grand boys' adventure."

Lennox chuckled. The remark was true enough, and the little jest helped settle Reay's reassurances in his mind. "Ye've the right o' that, aye, m'lord. I've to kid on I'm not sore in the arse after a long ride, these days. It's hard work not t' let the wee nippers goin' for soldiers see that the auld bastard trainin' em's no' as hard as granite."

Reay grinned. "And there's the most o' the rest of being a master o' men. One o' the Americans said it, never let 'em see ye sweat, and I kept that right by me, depend on it." He paused while he poured hearty measures of brandy. "As I say, it's not just the oil, but much flows from that one little thing, so."

Lennox took the glass Reay handed him, and after a snort nodded in approval. Not that he'd expected a regimental colonel and peer of the realm to have anything but the best. "How so?"

"Did ye look at the future of Scotland, in the other time?" Reay had an intent, earnest look on his face now. Although the history that now never would be, after the Ring of Fire, had an unreal air to it, it was terrifying to look on and see the mistakes that the future would make, to know that they could be avoided, and to realize that they would be replaced with other, novel mistakes. Lennox, in his gloomier moments, found himself wondering if they wouldn't be worse ones. All that new knowledge, flooding into the world without giving anyone time to get used to it. Some of it good, like the dental work he'd finally had done, the plate of gold teeth he'd had young Alex's father-in-law make him with the reward he'd had from the pope.

Ha! There was a change, if you'd like. Bred-in-the-bone presbyterian kirk-going borderer, saving the pope's life from what turned out to be the utter stupidity of children. Children, dazzled by the prospect of a bright new future of freedom and prosperity, willing to follow the vilest of villains to get there. The scar where he'd lost most of one ear ached terribly sometimes.

"A wee bit, aye. Mair an' closer union with the Sassenach, rule from London. Cardinal Mazzare said he saw a single nation with nae troubles, nae mair than words o' discontent, an' those spake civil for the most part. Plenty o' Scots havin' place and station, fame and money."

"Aye, at the end. Did ye learn o' the suffering and dying that took us there?" Reay's tone was somber. "Our menfolk slaughtered, our way o' life gone? The Scotland Cardinal Mazzare saw, and aye, I've spoke wi' the fellow, wasnae the Scotland we twa ken. Neither highland nor lowland nor your ain borders."

"Aye, but those Scots of the future, they were aye happy, I hear?" Lennox had satisfied himself that whatever the political arrangements, up-time Scotland had been a nation that knew no great want, paid no tribute great or small and governed her own affairs as part of a greater nation. If there was no trouble, he reasoned, there was no call to be borrowing it. Sufficient unto the day was the evil thereof, as the scripture so correctly said, in a translation commissioned by a Scots king. Indeed, Lennox took a quiet pride in the fact that that translation, with some small editing, was still in wide use four hundred years later. And plenty of the machinists in Grantville, many of Scots extraction themselves, had taken their own pride in telling him how many of the marvels of their own home time were invented by Scotsmen. Case very much closed as far as Lennox was concerned, who fancied himself a practical man put on the earth to solve practical problems and let the conundrums of philosophy mind their own business.

"Happy, aye. But how much the better wi' a more equal partnership wi' the English on the way to that? Years o' squallin' an' brawlin' an' no a penny made but by our wits. Say instead, Scotsmen stood together, with oil tae give us capital? What a nation we'd have been!" Reay grinned. "And nae need for slaughter nor discord! I'm nae the only peer that sees his way clear to this, mind ye. We've a mort o' bright lads in Scotland. Led right and wi' capital, who's t' know what we may do? Here's tae us!"

"Wha's like us?" Lennox grinned back, raising his own glass in turn. "Ye'll no do this without bloodshed, mind," he added as he lowered his glass from the toast.

"We'll come to that, but d'ye like the taste o' the notion as well as ye seem t' like the taste o' the brandy? Another?"

"Aye, it's no' so early," Lennox said, "but ye ken I'm a borderer. Should it come to war wi' the Sassenach, it's ma own folk as it goes hardest for. I'll no' see the lowlands be another Germany."

Reay nodded "I'll not say it cannae come t' that. Was it no' a lallans boy said the schemes o' mice and men gang aft agley?"

"Was it?"

Reay grinned. "Rabbie Burns. Look him up."

"Oh, him. Ayrshire man. They're a' daft up that way." Lennox grinned back. "But enough wi' the distractions, how d'ye mean tae have no war on our own doorstep?"

"Good auld politicking, Major Lennox, politicking. That an' maybe the slittin' o' a few throats o' the worst troublemakers." Reay tried to pass that off as wit, but his grin was that of a man long in the business of killing. "I read o' the civil war the Stuart lost, right well I did. Since I was to be in wi' the losers for the most o' it."

He set his glass down and began counting on his fingers. "First, the covenanters. Minded tae have a presbyterian kirk for all Scotland. We've a fine example in the USE of a grand big nation with freedom o' religion, so they cannot say a nation must fall if she tolerates more than one confession. I've a sentiment that most o' the throats we slit'll be divines, mind."

Another finger. "Second, the bishops' wars. Hard t' find in the books, these, but there's enough there. Freedom o' confession again. Half my highlanders are papists, the rest are Church o' Scotland, I say leave that wee trouble to bide. And if the papists raise more men like Mazzare, aye, we'll find it's a wee trouble enough. And, mind ye, the bishops' party is all peers an' notables, such as can have their mooths stuffed wi' gold. Did ye tell me tae haud ma' noise aboot religion and see Scotland be great and ma purse full, if I'd no' seen the sense before I'd kid on I did then."

A third finger. "The Irish. Nae Black Tom Tyrant. With him out of power, nae rebellion, nae Confederation. Or, if they have their revolt, they'll win. I've no fash wi' offerin ma' hand in friendship t' 'em, do they only use the leavening o' Scots among 'em well enough."

A last finger. "Fourth. Royalist lairds. I'm no' among that number after the Stuart's follies, Leslie'd no' take a peerage for much the same reason. Montrose I've t' find out about, for all that I have guesses. Campbell, for one, will follow the money, as the Americans say, and with him go so, so many others. Politicking, Lennox, wi' that an' a wee bit o' luck we'll give the Stuart England an' bid him joy o' the place."

"Aye, but will he no' invade?" Lennox was finding it all convincing, compelling even, but still couldn't see where he fit in.

"The man's no' the sense o' a dead rabbit, but he can count coin an' soldiers both. We have more veterans here in Germany than we can use"—forgetting they were actually in Denmark, at the moment—"and we have the support o' half o' Grantville—aye, the half that's Scots! Wi' no more than a spirit o' unity we may have a standing army by the banks o' the Tweed. Glarin' o'er the border, and nae foraging, either. Scotland standin' by herself, friend to the USE, wi' all that oil, extendin' our hands t' the Irish." He paused to pick up the bottle. "Another o' these brandies and I'll give ye a United Kingdom governed frae Edinburgh!"

Lennox chuckled. "Ye dinnae dream small, m'chief. No' small at all. But why me? I've duties at the new Marine training establishment."

"Aye, well, if you're minded to take this wee task on, Admiral Simpson's minded to free ye for it. He and I, well, we talked of it. Man's a fine head on him, so he has. And it was him put me in mind of ye. A man that'll do his duty—no matter he's doin' it t' the benefit o' his religious enemy—that's a man ye can trust t' do right. And it's a mission o' great trust ye'll have. We've no' t' raise the heads o' the Stuart's men wi' envoys an' ambassadors traipsin' all over the place. An honest soldier, home from the wars, visitin' hither an' yon wi' news o' menfolk fallen or fighting still in Germany? No matter t' any man save himself. And all the while ye're our wee de'il, going up and down in the world."

Reay's smile had turned mischievous. "And if ye can see some good t' do for the cause, ye've a fair hand for such, I hear?"

"Ye mean the slittin' o' throats?"

"I mean more the savin' o' lives, the turnin' up where ye're needed and no' looked for. Cardinal Mazzare had high praise for ye in that regard, Major. I mean t' do this wi' as few throats slit as we may manage, and those only after we measure it all ways.

I want Scotland no' showing her weakness t' the world, and yon admiral advises me not t' have every man wi' an eye o'er his shoulder for the knife. I see the sense of it, soldier that I am."

"Aye. Ye'll have more precise instructions afore I go, aye? I've been tel't tae go save the bloody world and no more order than that the once, and I didnae care for it."

"Oh, aye, we'll have plenty o' mission for ye, if ye're agreed?"

"Aye, it's a good cause. And I'll make my first call on young Alex, wi' your permission, Chief. Does his father live, that's a man tae have words with, I'll say."

"Aye. And, the noo, we've made a start on this bottle?"

"Aye, just as your lordship said," Lennox said, thrusting out his glass in best military manner, "It'd be sinful to leave it spoil now it's opened."

Chapter 21

Canongate, Scotland

Gayle looked around the room. The process didn't take long, given that the room was small, perhaps twelve feet by seven feet; and had only five items of furniture in it:

A short bed a little wider—but not much—than what Americans would consider a twin bed;

A table somewhere in size between a nightstand and a writing desk;

A chair for said desk that looked to be sturdily built but was lower than an up-time chair would be;

A candle stand on the table;

And, tucked discreetly under the bed, a chamber pot.

There was no bedding of any kind. Mrs. Crawford, the widow who owned the boarding house, had offered to provide some, but Gayle had politely declined the offer. First, because she was asking too much. Secondly and more importantly, because boardinghouse bedding was notorious for harboring bedbugs. In the course of their travels since escaping from the Tower, Gayle had acquired her own bedding which was rolled up in one of the bags Oliver and she had hauled up to the room. It wasn't much and couldn't be much, given their constant moving about over the past months. But now that they'd arrived somewhere they were planning to stay for a while, she'd find something more substantial. Fortunately, summer in Edinburgh—Canongate, technically—was fairly warm despite the high latitude.

The room had one window on the wall opposite the bed, that was bigger than most such windows but still very small. It consisted of six panes of glass, none of which were either clear or undistorted. Still, it let some light in the room, although Gayle had her doubts how much light would be coming in once the sun passed over the roof of the house and they got into the afternoon. But at least their mornings wouldn't be too somber.

Speaking of somber...

She turned to face the other occupant in the room. Oliver Cromwell was looking here, there and anywhere except in her direction. He had that passive, stoical expression on his face that was Oliver's way of dealing with the world when he wasn't sure of himself. It was all she could do not to burst into laughter.

But that wouldn't be fair to the man. Oliver could be awkward at times, but she never doubted that his intentions were good. *Honorable,* as they were wont to say in the here and now.

"We're past that, Oliver," she said quietly. Then, pointing at the bed: "Why don't you sit down?"

He gave the chair a quick glance.

"Here," Gayle said, still pointing at the bed.

Cromwell hesitated a moment and then, rather gingerly, sat on the bed. Perched on the bed, it might be better to say. He didn't have more than a few inches of it under him and looked as if he was ready to spring back onto his feet at a moment's notice.

Again, she restrained a laugh. Then, after a moment's thought, let a soft, chuckling version of it come out.

"Will you *relax,* Oliver? We both agreed we had to pose as a married couple when we went looking for lodgings."

Having a single man and—especially—a single woman who traveled together but rented separate rooms would be sure to get tongues wagging. Not to mention that their finances were tight because of Cromwell's stubborn refusal to accept any money that might have derived from the coffers of the USE. Especially since she'd have to fudge the truth a bit. *She* had no qualms about accepting the USE's money, seeing as how *she* was a citizen of said foreign nation.

Granted, she handled that matter delicately, knowing how Oliver felt about it. While no tainted foreign silver might cross her palms, she let Darryl pay for all sorts of things that she and Oliver took advantage of. One of the things Harry Lefferts had brought to the Tower had been a fair amount of money which he gave those people who were planning to stay in Britain.

But—not directly. Which meant whatever lodgings she and Oliver found for themselves had to be paid for out of their none-too-full purse, which only escaped being completely empty because Gayle had borrowed money from Julie and Alex. To be repaid...

Whenever.

She sat down on the bed next to him. Closely next to him, their thighs touching. She half-expected Oliver to sidle away from her, but, to his credit, he didn't. The expression on his face got even more stoical, though.

Then, more stoical still, when she slid her arm around his waist.

"I can sleep on the floor," he said stiffly.

"Yes, you can. No, you won't. Oliver, look at me."

He turned his head toward her.

"I am willing to accommodate you in many ways," she said. "For starters, if you wish me to I will convert from my own church to yours." She shrugged. "I'm a Christian, and a Protestant, but I don't care that much about the ins-and-outs of doctrine."

"There's no need for that, Gayle. I am what we English call independent, which means we favor local congregational control of church affairs—much as your own church does, as I understand it. I don't much care for sectarian issues either."

He slid his own arm around her waist. "I do thank you for the offer, though." Then, smiling: "Yet I sense there was a 'but' coming at the end of that offer."

She smiled back. "Yes, there was—is. You will have to be willing to accommodate me in some matters." With her free hand, she patted the bed. "This is one of them. I am thirty-six years old—a year older than you are. I've been married and divorced."

She wasn't telling him anything he didn't know already, but felt the need to dot all necessary i's and cross all relevant t's. "To put it as bluntly as I can, my virginity is long gone and I can't say I miss it at all. I have fallen in love with you and I wish to pursue that as far as I can. But I'm a practical sort of girl and for today that means I want to make love. Tomorrow can take care of itself for the time being. If you want to get married, the answer is 'yes.' If you don't, for the time being, the answer is still 'yes.' I'm tired of dancing around."

He looked at her for a few seconds, his expression very serious, almost solemn. Then, he smiled, and the smile kept spreading. "I am quite willing to accommodate you in this matter, as I'm sure I will in many others."

The rest of the day passed with much in the way of accommodation. Gayle had been told by Melissa Mailey that the reputation Puritans had in American history of being sour, fun-hating prudes who were especially uptight about sex was all nonsense. Gayle had believed her, since one doubted Melissa Mailey's pronouncements on historical matters at one's own risk.

Still, it was nice to discover that the information she'd been given was accurate. Very accurate, in fact.

The only awkward moment came after they'd already made love twice. Rather diffidently, Oliver raised the issue of childbearing. He began by making clear that he would of course assume all his fatherly responsibilities—indeed, he looked ready to enumerate those at great length—but did express concern over how the arrival of a new infant might create difficulties given his political intentions.

Gayle cut him off in mid-assurance. "Relax, will you? I have an IUD, which by good fortune I had implanted just two years before the Ring of Fire. And it's one of the copper types which means it'll last for several more years. By which time we'll either be successful or dead or in prison or back on the Continent, any one of which eventualities will make having kids either a moot point or no big deal."

Silence followed, for a moment. Then Gayle explained the nature of an IUD, concluding with: "Mind you, there were some pro-life people who thought the IUD was no better than abortion. I thought they were idiots. This is one of those areas where you'll have to accommodate me."

Oliver pursed his lips, and looked at the ceiling. "I have no opinion on the matter one way or the other. So I will gladly defer to your wisdom."

"Such a smart man."

Vicky Short came by in mid-afternoon, which required a hasty termination of those activities which Gayle and Oliver would henceforth and forever more refer to as "mutual accommodation."

They did their best to straighten up the room and look as if they'd spent the previous hours discussing theology. Vicky was not fooled one bit. Her own virginity was also gone, albeit not long gone, and she didn't miss it any more than Gayle did.

But she said nothing. Until she got back to the room on the top floor she was sharing with Darryl.

Her command of American idiom was by now pretty much complete. "Gayle and Oliver just spent the day finally getting laid," she announced cheerily.

Darryl stared at her. "Are you sure?" he blurted out—and then immediately regretted it. The look Vicky was giving him was not one of admiration.

"Yeah, sure, of course you're sure. Stupid of me to ask."

He got up from their bed, where he'd been not quite taking a nap but doing a good imitation of it. Then, once on his feet, went over to the window in their own room.

It was also small, albeit not as small. It had eight panes instead of six, and two of them—would wonders never cease?—were pretty close to transparent and provided an almost undistorted view of the boarding house's tiny back yard.

Darryl tried to figure out how he felt about the new development.

"Does *everything* make you fret over the fate of Ireland?" Vicky demanded, mostly amused but a bit irritated. "Can't you just feel good for them?"

He *did* feel good for them, he realized. Then he tried to figure out how he felt about the fact that he felt good.

"You're hopeless," Vicky pronounced. "And ridiculous."

"Hey, look, I'm Irish," he said. By way of hopeless and ridiculous explanation.

Chapter 22

Government House
Magdeburg, capital of the United States of Europe

"Have a seat," said Mike Stearns, gesturing toward the large couch in what the prime minister of the USE liked to call his "chat room." He'd found that for some purposes—and he judged this to be one of them—having a conversation in a more intimate setting had better results than meeting people in his office. All the more so since he'd had his office decorated with portraits which, whatever their justification in political terms, would be viewed askance by his two current visitors.

Mike McCarthy and Mike McCarthy, Jr. had known Mike Stearns since he was born. The elder McCarthy had been a coal miner who'd retired just before the Ring of Fire and had then volunteered to come back to work to help get the town's coal mine up and running again. Born in 1935, he was old enough to remember once-obsolete ways of mining coal which were getting a new lease on life under the changed conditions.

He'd voted for Mike Stearns when he ran for president of their local United Mineworkers union. And while Mike hadn't had as much contact with McCarthy, Jr., he wasn't that much different from his father. Neither McCarthy was likely to consider a portrait depicting Mike as a seventeenth-century courtier attending on his monarch with a sword belted to his waist as anything other than ridiculous.

No, better to meet with them in the chat room, which had landscapes on the walls rather than portraits and whose couch and armchairs were down-time replicas of up-time furniture. They were more comfortable than the chairs in his office, even leaving aside the one whose front legs were cut slightly shorter so as to make sitting in it something of a strain. Mike had that one brought out whenever he had to entertain a guest he wanted to get rid of as soon as possible.

The two McCarthys looked at the couch he'd indicated, and then at the two men already in the room. One of them was sitting in one of the armchairs; the other was watering down a glass of wine at a side table. Both of them were wearing clothing which, though not precisely uniforms, clearly marked them as professional soldiers. Officers, judging from the quality of the fabric.

"This is something of a private matter, Mike," said the younger McCarthy.

"Yeah, I figured as much. But if the subject's what I think it is, you'll want both of these fellows to sit in." Stearns nodded toward the man sitting in the armchair. "He's Anthony Leebrick, formerly a captain in the English army. The Irish fellow making himself a drink is Patrick Welch, also a former officer in the English army. I might mention that since their escape from England—they were falsely accused of plotting to assassinate King Charles—they've both accepted commissions in the army of the United States of Europe."

"Oh." The two McCarthys glanced at each other. The elder of them cleared his throat. "So you would have met Darryl McCarthy, who's my son"—he hooked a thumb at McCarthy, Jr.—"and his half-brother. And the—ah—"

"Other guy," furnished McCarthy, Jr.

Patrick Welch smiled. "Cromwell, you mean."

"Yeah. Him."

Welch held up his glass. "Would you care for one? Or perhaps something stronger?"

"I've got whiskey," Stearns said. "I'm afraid none of it's Irish, though. I drank my last bottle of Jameson's a couple of years ago."

The older of the McCarthys headed for the side table. "A shot of whiskey'd probably do me good. Under the circumstances. You want one, son?"

"No, thanks," said the younger McCarthy. He sat down on the couch and looked at Welch. "Irish, are you?"

"Indeed." There followed a stream of words in what Stearns presumed to be Gaelic.

McCarthy looked discomfited. "Sorry, I don't know more than a few words in your—our—language, and I didn't really catch much of that."

Having poured himself a half-glass of whiskey, his father turned away from the side table. "What he said—I think—is that he was born and raised in Leinster near Dublin, but has lived most of his life outside of Ireland."

As he lowered himself onto the couch next to his son, he gave Welch an apologetic look. "Sorry. Your accent's not what I'm accustomed to when it comes to Gaelic."

Leebrick spoke, for the first time since they'd entered the room. "In answer to your question, we spent quite a bit of time in the company of your son Darryl and Oliver Cromwell in the course of our escape from the island. About two months. We parted company at Newcastle. We sailed to the Continent, bringing Cromwell's children with us, and your son and the rest of the party went on to Edinburgh. I presume they're still there although I can't say for sure."

McCarthy Senior took a deep breath. "Oliver Cromwell's kids. In Grantville, now, staying with the Masons. We heard."

The tone of his voice added the commentary, *what the hell is the world coming to?* Mike Stearns had to struggle not to laugh out loud. He couldn't keep from grinning, though.

Seeing the expression on his face, the elder McCarthy scowled. "Dammit, Mike, it's not funny. For Pete's sake, we're talking about *Oliver Cromwell.*"

"Actually, we were talking about Cromwell's kids. The oldest of whom—his name's Robert, by the way—is fourteen. The youngest kid's name is Henry. He's five."

His voice lost all traces of humor. "You want us to string 'em up, or will you settle for having them tossed in jail?"

"Dammit, Mike..."

"Dammit, *what?*" Stearns gave McCarthy a look that fell just short of being a glare. "Let's cut to the chase. I assume the reason you wanted this get-together is because you're twitchy as all hell over your son hanging out with—how's Cromwell reckoned by you folks? Ireland's worst devil? Second worst?"

McCarthy Jr. smiled, a bit crookedly. "It depends who you

talk to. Me, I never figured Cromwell ranked higher than third worst devil. Which is still way up there."

"You have to do something about it, Mike," said the senior McCarthy.

"And just what do you propose I do? I have no contact with any of the people in Scotland except intermittently by radio. And while you could make a case that Darryl is under my authority, since he's still officially being paid as a soldier even if he hasn't collected that pay for a year or so, I have no authority over Cromwell whatsoever."

He ran fingers through his hair in a gesture that mirrored the exasperation in his expression and his tone of voice. "Assume for the moment that I gave Darryl the order to break off all contact with Cromwell, and assume that Darryl obeyed the order. Is that really what you want?"

By now, Welch had taken a seat in an armchair. "I liked the fellow," he said. "Cromwell, I mean. For whatever this Irishman's opinion is worth."

"So did I," said Leebrick. "Granted, I'm English myself."

The older McCarthy now scowled at Leebrick and Welch. Who, for their part, bore up under the burden quite well. Leebrick shrugged. Welch satisfied himself with draining half his glass of watered-down wine.

Getting no satisfaction there, McCarthy transferred the scowl to Mike Stearns. Who scowled right back at him.

"Grow up," he said. "Unless he gets killed, Oliver Cromwell is a political fact of life. Keep in mind, though, that the Cromwell we're dealing with is a man in his mid-thirties, not the man in another universe who led the invasion of Ireland in his fifties. A man in his mid-thirties, moreover, who's probably going to marry an American woman and one of whose close associates is an American of Irish descent. Unless you've abandoned Catholicism and taken up with Calvinists, you don't hold with predestination."

He glanced at the younger McCarthy, who held up both hands in a gesture signifying *hey, don't look at me*. As Mike Stearns had suspected, this was mostly the older McCarthy's doing. Everybody in the McCarthy clan was an Irish nationalist, but only the patriarch was really obsessed with the issue.

He looked back at the father. "Mike, you have no idea where Cromwell's going to wind up, or what he'll wind up doing, in this universe. So like I said, grow up. If Darryl's got enough sense to realize he'd do better to try to shape Cromwell, why can't you? Who are supposed to be the older and wiser head, not that you're displaying any evidence of it at the moment."

There was silence in the room for about thirty seconds. Then the older McCarthy got to his feet. "I guess you're right. Not that I like it any. Thanks for giving us some of your time. I know you're busy." His son rose also, but didn't say anything.

After they left, Mike turned toward the two British officers. "And what do you think?"

Welch shrugged. "I'm not one of the godly, and I've never thought predestination made a lot of sense. But I doubt if any Calvinist in the world, except the most doctrinaire, is all that sure about predestination any longer. In their hearts, whatever they may say in public. The Ring of Fire pretty well knocked that apple cart over, I'd say."

Leebrick chuckled. "Like all Irishmen, he's ever the optimist. I am quite sure the world is still full of Calvinists who are certain that whatever is to be is foreordained. But I don't think Oliver Cromwell is in their number any longer, if he ever was. Or at least—he's a very smart man, don't think he isn't—he figures that God's plans aren't fathomable by men, including the divines."

"*Especially* the divines," said Welch.

After they returned to Grantville, the two McCarthys began the long walk from the train station to their house, which was located some distance outside the limits of Grantville—although not as much of a distance as it had been before the Ring of Fire. The town had grown a lot over the last three years.

When they reached one of the last intersections before passing into the countryside, McCarthy Senior stopped abruptly.

"Tired, Dad?" asked his son. "We can rest a bit."

The elder McCarthy didn't seem to hear him. He was peering down the street they'd reached.

After a moment, his son understood the meaning of that intent gaze.

"I'm not sure..."

"C'mon, let's go. I need to—I don't know. See it, I guess."

He began walking down the street, heading toward a green and white house some distance away. As they approached, they could hear the squealing sounds of young children playing in the back yard.

"Dad..." said Mike, Jr., sounding very uncertain.

The front door of the house opened and a woman came out. She looked to be in her late thirties or early forties and had a very determined expression on her face. She came down the steps to the house and strode over to the low gate leading into the front yard. By then, the two McCarthys were within ten feet of her.

"Is there going to be a problem?" she asked.

Mike Junior shook his head. "No, Vickie. We—ah—my dad..."

Vickie Mason looked at the elder of the pair. "For Christ's sake, Mike, they're just kids. I already checked 'em to see if there were any horns, hooves or tails. Didn't find a one."

Mike Senior grimaced. "Yeah, sure." He looked around, as if searching for something unseen. Then, sighed.

"I guess we'll be going." He started to turn away.

"Oh, no, you don't," said Vickie. "You don't get off that easy." She unlatched the gate and swung it wide open. "Come on in. I'll introduce you to the three youngest. The older boys—that'd be Robert and Oliver—are off with Arnold."

McCarthy hesitated.

"Come. In," Vickie commanded.

"This is Elizabeth. This is Bridget. And that's Henry."

Elizabeth was half-hiding behind her brother Henry, who, for his part, was half-hiding behind his older sister Bridget. None of the three Mason children were present. The youngest of them, Heather, was sixteen and presumably at school today. Neither her brother Derrick nor her sister Kelsey seemed to be around either.

The girl named Bridget was less shy than her two younger siblings. She advanced toward the McCarthys and stuck out her hand. "Pleased to meet you," she said. "I'm Bridget Cromwell. I'm eleven years old."

Mike Senior leaned over and solemnly shook her hand. "Pleased to meet you. I'm Michael McCarthy, Senior. I'm sixty-nine." He nodded to his left. "This is my son Mike McCarthy Junior. He's forty-five."

The girl's eyes widened. "Are you related to Darryl McCarthy?"

"My son," said Mike Senior. He hooked a thumb at his son. "He's his half-brother."

Bridget clapped her hands. "Oh, how delightful! I *like* Darryl. He's funny and he was always nice to us."

"Never thought I'd see the day when Darryl was the most levelheaded McCarthy around," muttered Vickie Mason, just loud enough for the two Mikes to hear her. "Goes to show we do live in an age of miracles."

Then, more loudly: "Anything else, gentlemen?"

Mike Junior shook his head. "No, no. We were just leaving. Nice meeting you, Bridget."

Once they were a couple of blocks away, Mike Senior said: "I feel like a damned idiot."

His son smiled wryly. "Well, sure, Dad. We're Irish. We just have to hope Darryl knows what he's doing."

A block later, Mike Senior said: "You do realize how crazy that sounds?"

Part Five

September 1634

O would, ere I had seen the day

That Treason thus could sell us,

My auld grey head had lien in clay,

Wi' Bruce and loyal Wallace!

Chapter 23

His return to his homeland began, for no good reason, with a chicken. Major Andrew Lennox got off the ship—the grandly-named *Fried und Freiheit*, a title that the wee tub would need several friends and a muckle o' feedin' to live up to—he'd come over from Germany on. Were it not for strict orders, he'd have had nothing whatever to do with one of the infernal contraptions ever again. He'd puked every roll and heave of his first voyage over the seas, heading out with the Mackay regiment, back then heading into the service of King Christian IV of Denmark. He'd pretty much resigned himself to settling in the Germanies, when his service was done, because the price of getting home was so damned steep.

And now he was back. True to form, he'd spewed all the way back as well. Or, rather, spewed the first day and just retched the rest of the time. Five days without more than a wee bit of *dunsuppe* to keep body and soul together. The *Fried und Freiheit* had come in on the flood tide to Leith just before dawn, and with the light coming up—and, more importantly, the porters—he'd gone ashore to grab a few stout lads to carry his baggage. There'd been a time he'd have hefted a sack of belongings and got on with it, but with a major's commission now and a lieutenant-colonelcy likely on its way, it wouldn't do to be seen carrying his own bags. Added to which, with the assorted plunder and rewards he'd gathered over the last few years—including a papal knighthood, and he'd better keep *that* quiet hereabouts—he had too much for one man anyway.

And here, off the ship, he stepped aside at the bottom of the gangplank to let the sailors bring his chests ashore after him, and was confronted with a chicken. Glaring at him. *You, sir, are standing where I was about to scratch,* her look was saying.

Standing. Swaying gently, it were better to say. Another reason to despise ships. They took the legs from under a man along with robbing the belly out of him. And now, he was being afforded disrespect by a blasted chicken. And, oh, the *stink*. Aboard ship, below decks in the wee cabin the ship's carpenter had walled off for him with thin timber panels, there were the simple scents of the ship's cooking, the hold full of assorted chemical goods—most, Lennox had noted with approval, bearing the mark of his good friend Tom Stone's Lothlorien Farbenwerke—and the smell of hard-working sailors. Feet, armpits and farting below decks, mostly. Word had gotten around about sauerkraut being good for the scurvy—at a fraction the price of fresh fruit, which was already well known as a cure—so sailors were eating the stuff every day if they could get it. Some of them, with every meal. It was a mercy there were hatches to be opened.

Now he was ashore and realizing how much he'd been spoiled by the increasing cleanliness of the cities of the USE. The difference a year's worth of sewer-digging and ferociously enforced hygiene could make was, it turned out, truly staggering when you didn't have the benefit of it. Although there was probably no amount of sewer that could suppress the reek of whale-blubber being boiled down in the try-works over the river. Even so, while there was a first breath of autumn in the air, and the nights would soon start drawing in, the summer stench of a town that shat in its own streets was still present.

And *still* that chicken was glaring at him, to the evident amusement of the sailors who'd brought his chests ashore. "An impudent bird, Major," one of them said, "best put in the pot as an example to others, hey?"

Lennox grinned at that, being as he was starving hungry of a sudden. The chicken, apparently getting the message, stalked away, contriving to give the impression that she had decided, on inspection, she didn't want to scratch that spot anyway. And, as parting comment, made her own small contribution to the general filth of the wharf. He gave the sailors a few coppers each, thanked them for what might, for all he knew, have been a smooth and trouble-free voyage if he'd been able to enjoy it, and looked around. Sure enough, there were a few fellows—scruffy creatures, in obviously poor health, and *damn* did public sanitation make a difference, just spending a year without periodic doses of the shits put meat on a low-income city-dweller and brightened his eye no end—edging closer and trying to catch his eye in a meaningful manner. Not an easy nor pleasant means of making ends meet, but Lennox didn't feel he could think the less of them for it. "You, you, you and you," he said, "one end of each o' these, and there's a shillin' apiece in it for you. I've tae find lodgings and a' before I'm aboot my business."

They stepped to it lively—he was, after all, offering rather more than a decent day's pay—and he took a leisurely pace toward Edinburgh proper. Time enough to get a horse when he'd walked some of the wobble out of his legs, and had a meal inside him that wasn't going to come up again. There'd be a better selection in Edinburgh anyway. He'd only been here the once before, but he recalled it as but a couple of miles from the town itself down to Leith. Last time he'd passed this way, it was to embark for Denmark as his first stage of a journey that led eventually to Grantville.

Away from the wharf the smell was a little more bearable—the Water o' Leith drained Edinburgh, after all—and as he got into the open country between Leith and Edinburgh the smell dropped to virtually nothing. Ahead, Edinburgh castle on its mount was easily visible, with the northern portion of the Flodden Wall just visible to the left, on the one bit of the city's northern approach that wasn't guarded by the Nor' Loch. Away to the left again, only visible at this distance over the hedges by its smudge of smoke, was the area around Holyrood, which was where he was headed. "Ony o' youse," he called back to the porters following him, "know o' guid lodgings at Canongate?"

They none of them had the faintest notion, being Leith laborers who probably didn't come up to the city proper very much. Lennox had the vague idea that the guards at the Flodden Wall, there mostly for the proper levying of tolls, would take note of anyone coming and going in the city proper, and he wanted to spend a night or two without the wall while he scouted a little.

Plus, it was where he was billeted—briefly, true—last time he was here. He stopped. Had it really been nine years? It had. He'd been marched aboard a ship at Leith. Not entirely willingly, but the Mackay recruiters had found him in the gaol at Berwick-upon-Tweed. They weren't, according to their warrant, supposed to recruit out of Scotland, but Berwick was also not quite England, and the magistrates of that burgh had been only too happy to save the cost of feeding a lot of ruffians until assize-time when they could all be decently and lawfully hanged.

More than a few of the said ruffians hadn't been entirely Scottish, when all was said and done, but since the attestation was signed by a magistrate who was pocketing the recruiting bounty, the Mackay regiment got a few lads from south of the border into the bargain.

Lennox took a slow turn to take in in the world around him, paying the puzzled looks of the porters no mind. He was the one paying, here, he could stop and woolgather as much as he damned well pleased. He'd gone from that—broken man, awaiting trial and more than likely hanging for cattle-thieving, driven there by catching the wrong end of a feud and getting the little he had burnt to the ground—to a major in the most powerful army in Europe, enough wealth to be comfortable in retirement, and likely a colonel soon into the bargain. *No' bad for a wee laddie frae Coldstream, aye?*

The chances that there was anyone minding out for him returning were slim at best. They certainly didn't have him under his right name at Berwick, for a start; he'd only started using that once he was asked to swear in to the regiment. He'd stand trial under a false name, and happy to, but hadn't been about to swear an oath under one. A few months later and after the mayhem at Boyzenburg—and didn't being outnumbered four companies to ten thousand concentrate a fellow on becoming a good soldier?—and he was a sergeant and looking for a light cavalry billet that suited his border nearly-a-reiver origins a little better than infantry grunt. Which, yes, he found and ended up, a few years later, sergeant to a wrong-side-of-the-blanket sprig o' minor nobility. *Very* minor nobility, at that—Alex Mackay had told him, once, that the barony amounted to basically four hamlets, a half-dozen decent farms, a nice mansion, a drafty ruined castle of a kind that might last as much as two hours against modern weapons—modern *before* the Ring of Fire, that is—and three miles of excellent trout stream. A pleasant place for a boy to grow up, and a reasonable living for the family that owned the estate, but otherwise a completely tedious bit of East Lothian. Even the castle was dull; last used in the Rough Wooing of Henry VIII of England, the last time Alex had been home, he said, they'd been keeping livestock in the thing.

He took a deep breath. A deep, law-abiding, settled man's breath. *Just a pity I've all yon political messages tae deliver.* Still, get that over with, a little visiting, he could be back in the USE before the winter made the North Sea truly miserable. And, indeed, if he was to put down roots in the USEMC training establishment, he might look to finding a nice, well-found little piece of Germany for his remote descendants to reckon a dull spot. For now, though, to business.

Canongate, the neighborhood around the Palace at Holyrood, put him slightly in mind of Venice where he'd been the previous year, commanding the security detail at the embassy there. Both were towns that were trying desperately to keep up appearances after the wealth had gone away. Venice was less so these days, being as it had started handling huge amounts of the USE's Mediterranean and Levant trade, along with some bits of manufacturing. Canongate, though, had never really recovered from the royal court leaving town thirty years previous; all of the sumptuary and services that the king and his hangers-on had paid for were now enriching the traders and artisans of London. Which meant there were some very nice buildings with some increasingly hard-up owners. The Mackay regiment recruiters had taken hearty advantage, billeting their catch, as far as they could, in vacant houses rented for as little as they could get away with in a market where landlords were undercutting each other to get business, any business. If one of them was taking in lodgers and making a decent fist of the business, Lennox would consider himself well found.

He took a fork in the road that would take him leftward toward Holyrood and Canongate. The last of Leith was behind him now, and it was just plain ordinary country smells hereabouts. The summer sun was starting to put a little warmth into the morning, not yet hot. A faint breeze was enough to keep the sweat of the toiling porters behind him, and he decided that task number one after the lodgings were settled and he'd got food in his belly was to find a livery and get a couple of decent nags, because if this wasn't about to be an afternoon for a very pleasant ride, he'd no idea what would.

He turned out to need visit only half a dozen lodging-houses before he found one that suited, and even the most expensive was less than he'd been expecting to pay. The price of lodgings in Magdeburg was skewing what he regarded as normal; prices were going mad in the USE, although against that, so were wages.

The place was run by a redoubtable, but handsome, widow who insisted on Mrs. MacPherson with the Mrs. very clearly emphasized. Her husband had died at Breitenfeld, and Lennox could, from the description, vaguely recall the man: a fairly senior captain in Hepburn's regiment before Colonel Hepburn himself was given command of Lennox's own former Green regiment. He'd been a friend of one of the handful of Scots officers who'd taken service in the mostly Prussian Green, and so whenever the two regiments had been close enough together for visits, the fellow had been around from time to time.

What with the numbers of Scots volunteers who came over without the formality of joining a regiment first, there were plenty of odd little connections like that throughout the old army. Curious situations like a wildly oversized Scots cavalry troop drawing its pay through a Prussian infantry regiment happened all the time. Mackay himself had managed to get through most of his service without ever formally being in a cavalry regiment at all, a situation he'd enjoyed because a small attached troop tacked on to an infantry brigade or regiment for whatever purpose answered the current need was generally considered sufficiently led with a sergeant in charge.

And they had to find plenty of places to stick wee packets of Scots cavalry, as there weren't enough of them to amount to a whole regiment by themselves of either heavy or light horse; the one Scots regiment of horse they had was Henderson's Dragoons, not proper cavalrymen at all. And, of course, Henderson and Mackay senior loathed each other so Mackay junior had ended up part of the "other" category of troops and, purely by accident, ended up commanding half a regiment's worth of light cavalry with a captain's commission and charged with watching half of Thuringia for trouble. At that, it wasn't even close to being the most irregular military management Lennox had seen. In a way, it was surprising that there were so many Scots in foreign service he *didn't* know. He'd certainly got at least a rough idea of most of the officers. Although he'd had no idea MacPherson was married.

After he'd got the room sorted, and a meal down him while the two youngsters Mrs. MacPherson employed put his things away for him, he took a moment to rest. And wasn't it peculiar that he could be away to the wars for nearly ten years and here he was back not five minutes and everything was making him go all sentimental over it? Mostly it had been riding up and down, doing next to nothing, with bits of bloody terror mixed in. Boizenburg, Oldenburgh Pass, Ekernforde, Stralsund—where he'd first met MacPherson, now he thought about it—and all manner of minor set-tos in between as the light horse fought their own private wars between the armies. After that, rear area service, two years of being a glorified constable with a pack of border ruffians under him, attached to one regiment after another and galloping about the German countryside for an assortment of reasons that must have made sense to some officer or other.

When it came to the sentimental memories, of course, it probably didn't help that he'd come straight back to the port he'd left from and immediately found lodgings with the widow of someone he'd known over there. He'd not been at Breitenfeld to know how the poor fellow fell, but it was something he could probably find out, which would likely be a kindness to the widow.

There were some veterans back already, with wounds or just resigned when the Scots regiments got paid off prior to being recruited wholesale in to the USE army. Less trouble, certainly, than waiting for months of desertion to reduce those regiments to nothing while putting up with the trouble arising from the Scots being mixed in all over. There were always some people who weren't happy about something, and rather than take the USE bounty, they'd gone away home or to other service they liked better.

A few of those who'd come home were, to the best of his knowledge, here in the Lothians, so he'd be able to ask and perhaps get some news for the widow. Who'd given him his luncheon "tae welcome him hame" and offered directions to a good stable. For now he'd assume her kindly disposition was down to him having given her three months' rent in advance—it was the amount of cash he'd brought for a month's lodging. If not, well, he'd make a decision about *that* when he had to and not before.

That afternoon, buying a horse when it was purely for his own use and enjoyment was a thorough pleasure. When Sharon Nichols, as was like to be married to the bampot Spanish bugger she'd met in Venice, had been about that town with Magda Stone arranging the commerce, she'd made jokes about shopping that Lennox hadn't understood at first. He'd asked, and she'd explained, and he'd realized he'd been doing the same thing since the day he was old enough to judge and haggle for horseflesh. And, well, if he'd been planning to get out for a ride the day, he'd missed it. There were plenty of stables with horses to sell or rent without venturing up the hill into Edinburgh proper, and a surprising number of good nags for sale. Of course things would be better here than on the Continent, where the horses had been picked over again and again for the armies that were slaughtering, or just plain working to death, everything they could lay their hands on that ate hay and farted. Finding a decent nag outside the private stud of a nobleman was a sore trial.

Here, though, there were plenty of good ordinary animals to be had, and a fair selection of Hackneys and Hackney crosses brought up from England. There were plenty of Galloway ponies as well, and some bloody good examples of the breed—and of course as a borderer, Andrew Lennox was not going to pass up a good Galloway if he could afford one; he'd grown up with and riding Fell ponies with the occasional Hobby, but he'd wanted a Galloway. There weren't that many of them to be had, when all was said and done, and every other bugger wanted one so the prices were always out of his reach.

Not. Any. More. A lot of shopping around—grinning the while as he wondered what the stablemen would think if they'd had to put up with a smart and strong-minded black lady shopping at their establishments—and he found what he was looking for and had more than an idea of how he was going to make a little money out of the thing. Of course, his grin when he'd seen the beasts was probably ten shillings on the price of every single one, but he'd settled in for a good haggle.

He'd ended up with two bought cash down and earnest money on another eight. For, it had to be said, nags that were only mostly Galloways. The black of them said there was a lot of Fell pony in there as well—no matter, that was a hard breed—and the oldest of the string was a hair over fourteen hands so there was probably something like a Hackney in there as well.

But, if Lennox was even half the judge of horseflesh he thought himself, they had every possibility of making the beginnings of a bloody good stud. So, for the next trip, he needed to find a banker and cash the letter of credit he'd brought. *Without* saying "cash it," of course. Associating with up-timers had *ruined* the way he talked.

Chapter 24

"That's not—"

Colonel Alexander Mackay had started up in such evident shock that his horse had stopped in utter confusion. It was no intellectual heavyweight among horsekind either—a cheap rental from a stable in Leith—so the beast didn't take much confusing.

"Lennox!" His wife's squeal of joy dislodged earwax for yards around. Her mount was in no wise confused, the dun gelding pony did as he was told as she urged him forward into a trot. *Get the job over with and get this madwoman off my back* seemed to be the order of the day.

Darryl had only the vaguest notion of who Lennox was. He'd seen the guy around the Thuringen Gardens a few times, and sort-of knew he was one of Mackay's old Green Regiment buddies, but he wasn't one of the ones he'd gotten to know well. He'd been coming the other way up the street, riding one horse and leading two others as they were shopping around for accommodations. Julie was already up to him, talking excitedly—too fast for Darryl to follow at this distance—while Alex got his beast back on the move to tender a more sensible greeting.

"Do you know this fellow?" Cromwell asked, halting his own mount next to Darryl's.

"One of Alex's veterans from the old wars," Darryl said. "He was with him when he came upon Grantville back in June of '31. He went off to Italy with Tom Stone and his boys later, but he seems to be home from the fighting now."

"Yup," Gayle said. "Looks like Captain Lennox is home at last. Never thought he would, he hates ships."

"You know the guy?"

"Yup. He was in the course on radio I taught for guys transferring into the modern forces from the old-style regiments. Smart guy, for all he got shorted in the education department. Won't say he took to Radio 101 like a duck to water, but he'd just grind away at stuff until he got it. He was a sergeant in the old forces, which is about like a lieutenant in an up-time force, and he'd been doing that for years. You gotta figure a guy who can do that job has got some smarts."

"Well, we'll wait long enough for tact and then remind Mrs. Mackay we want to find new lodgings before sundown," said Cromwell. "Which is not a long away, at that. I'll let Stephen and Vicky know what's happening."

He turned his horse and trotted back to where Vicky and Stephen Hamilton were sharing the cart they'd hired with the two carters that came with it. After he left, Darryl nodded. "Even as slack as this place seems to be about folk comin' an' goin', they're likely to pay attention if we're still up and about at night. Lennox doesn't have any bags with him so maybe he's found some good accommodations."

Gayle chuckled. "Hope so. Oliver's getting impatient."

Darryl looked back at Cromwell. "How can you tell?" When it came to life's assorted little frustrations, the man was cool personified. Maybe you'd see a little flick of the head if he was being *really* annoyed. He only got what you'd call lively in a fight or for a really lively ride. Even the seasickness on the way up the coast had hadn't really made him upset. Just, well, sick. The harshest thing he'd had to say about it was "tiresome."

"He's being stoical," Gayle said. "You can tell he's really suffering by how much he's not showing it."

Darryl examined that idea from all angles. Definitely chick logic. "Whatever," was all the comment he felt able to pass.

And, as it turned out, Lennox had lodgings arranged, had in fact arrived a few days prior and been settled in enough to buy horses. Given his strong recommendations of the place, the ones who'd been staying at Widow Grouch's boarding house—Darryl's name for her, not her real one—decided to investigate the possibility of shifting their residence. None of them had been happy with Mrs. Crawford and her way of running things. It sounded as if concealing themselves at MacPherson's boarding house would be easier, too, being as it was on a small side street instead of a main thoroughfare.

On the way to Mrs. MacPherson's place Lennox and Alex and Cromwell had a three-sided discussion of the beasts, the consensus being that if Andrew Lennox meant to breed horses, he'd got some damned fine mares for it, and wasn't it a shame the males were all gelded.

Which, of course, led into the ins and outs of getting a Galloway stallion—Darryl grasped enough to understand that that was a popular breed of pony hereabouts—and shipping him to Germany. And Lennox and Mackay filled Cromwell in on the excellent bloodlines that Grantville had brought back via the Ring of Fire. Darryl decided, at that point, he was going to by-damn learn a thing or two about horses. He'd picked up enough since the Ring of Fire to be able to get about on a well-trained even-tempered rental horse, to be able to tell roughly how expensive a horse was likely to be, and the basics of looking after the beast. Owning a truck after the Ring of Fire was one thing. Getting enough gas to use it for regular getting-about was trickier, outside of military work, so there really wasn't any choice but learn about horses.

What Darryl was hearing now was, basically, about half the conversations he and Harry Lefferts used to have when just whiling away the hours. Just about horses, not cars. Downside: guaranteed only one horsepower per ride. Upside: with a bit of effort and investment, your ride could make new rides. Let's see GM match *that* trick in next year's model! And, face it, Darryl McCarthy, esquire, was better than riding about on beat-up rentals if there was a possibility of owning something with a bit of pizzazz. Customization options were a bit limited, but you couldn't have everything.

That thought kept amusing him—and when he broke it to them, Gayle and Vicky too, right up until they got thoroughly welcomed and sat down to supper at Mrs. MacPherson's. By then they'd made arrangements that they'd move in the following day after settling their accounts with Widow Grouch.

"Ye cam' up by sea? Ye puir de'ils," Lennox opined, when he heard the outline of their journey.

Alex laughed. "We've not all the weak stomachs of the likes of you, Andrew," he said, "Although Mister Cromwell sets fair t' challenge ye."

"Tiresome business, sailing," Cromwell advanced, "I was looking forward to pirates to lift my spirits with a fight."

"So was our captain, I think," Julie said. "He had all kinds of guns, knives, swords, axes, and sharpened sticks on board. Pirates are a problem on that run he does, since coal's valuable, but he said it was just a matter of how you looked at it. Pirate ships are valuable too. He says he's taken two in his time."

"You could understand a word he said?" Gayle asked, laughing. "I swear, that man was nothing but static to me."

"To me also," Cromwell said. "It seems my lady the baroness has quite the ear for accents. For myself, I can understand anything from the home counties, all of Yorkshire and Lancashire, west-countrymen since they speak so slowly, but the black country and the Northumberlanders might as well be speaking Erse for all I understand. The time we spent in Newcastle, were it not for my lady as interpreter, I would have been as a stranger in a strange land."

"What's wrong with Erse?" Darryl asked, a lot more mildly than he once might.

"Nothing; the ignorance is all my own fault, apparently. Another insult I do the Irish." Cromwell grinned. "Perhaps you can teach me the tongue of your people, Mister McCarthy?"

"Pogue Mahone," Darryl replied, exhausting his entire command of the said language. And he only had that from owning a couple of Pogues albums. He grinned back. "If we're going there at any point, I guess we'll both have to learn it."

"Most of the Scots Erse can at least get by in English or lallans, which is near enough English once you're used to it," Lennox put in. "The ones who have no English at all are generally poorer folk, farmers who've never left the farm. I've a little Erse myself, since the Highlanders tend to forget their English in a fight, and I suppose the same applies in Ireland. I certainly never met an Irishman who couldn't speak English, but there must be some who've none."

"What's lallans?" Darryl asked.

"Scots English," Gayle said. "You ever read any Robbie Burns? He wrote in lallans."

"I only know one of his, and I only know it's his because Miz Mailey told me, and that's *Parcel of Rogues*. Which is about Scotland, not Ireland. Which she also told me. And I thought that was English?"

"So did I. Until Miz Mailey told me. She was a bit hazy on the details, but it's different enough to count as a bit more than a dialect. Could just be politics, though, finding differences to make the differences clear?" She cocked an eyebrow at the Scots around the table who demonstrated that they'd been holding back for the sake of the English around the table by letting absolute rip, with the occasional marshmallow of comprehensibility floating in the rich, rich chocolate of the Scots language.

Julie giggled. "I absolutely *love* the way that sounds. Always have."

"Don't tell me you could understand *them* too," Gayle scoffed.

"She *is* married to a Scotsman, Gayle," Cromwell rumbled, "And I think we may have some inkling of how she understood Captain Milburn. My lady has already had to learn one other flavor of English, so a second becomes the easier. Is my surmise plausible?"

"Makes sense, sure," Julie said. "Some of the stuff he came out with was kinda Scots. And some of it was kinda German, like you get from the guys over Friesland way, German that actually *sounds* like it's related to English. It all sort of fit together, if you take the trouble to really *listen* to the guy. Which, being female, I have a head start in over you mere males, of course."

"Hear hear," Mrs. MacPherson said, apparently getting over her slight stage-fright at having a real-life baroness lodging with her. "Do they not have *terrible* difficulty paying attention, the poor dears? My lady."

"You got an amen from me," Gayle said.

"Ah, *feminism*," Cromwell intoned.

"Not you too," Colonel Mackay groaned. "The lassies already run oor lives f'r us, will ye no' forbear to encourage 'em?"

"Among the godly, man and wife are accounted partners as much as anything. Gayle has been kind enough to open my eyes to the fact that what I was accustomed to think was the weakness of womankind was simply a want of education and training, and for most purposes a woman ought to be accounted a man's equal. Certainly before the law, and in matters of politics. I will say that no woman will ever be a man's equal at football." He grinned at that last.

"More sense," Gayle said, clearly announcing a point won long ago.

"Slippery word, is 'equal,' when all's said and done." Lennox put in. "Tom Stone had a lot to say on that one, that I recall. How using words that look the same as though they were *exactly* the same was the cause of a lot of bu—er, nonsense. As he said, he and I were unequal in height and fighting—he the taller, I the better fighter, but we didnae use the same word to mean how equal we were for votes or the law, even though it's said and writ the same."

Darryl laughed. "Sounds like Tom," he said. "He always had a bunch of that hippie philosophy to spout at anyone that went to him to buy weed. Some of it was interesting. Lot of it was just plain nuts, if you ask me. Sounds like you got one of the interesting bits."

Gayle was giving him a very speaking look. "Don't look at me like that," he replied. "It's legal now. But harder to get since it all gets bought for medicine. Don't feel right to be buying medicine folks need, just to get high once in a while. Besides, beer's improved over what we used to get." He raised his tankard. Mrs. MacPherson served a rather nice brew of her own with supper.

"Tom had some regrets of his own on that score," Lennox chuckled. "But no' mind that—ye're pursued by that scunner Finnegan and he's cozened himself a Royal Warrant, aye? So will we take guid care seeing your father, Colonel? For a' we know, Finnegan's got here afore ye, if ye laid over in Newcastle longer than expected."

"Aye, we will at that," said Alex, nodding. "Best for all if we collect Alexi and disappear back to Magdeburg and that right smartly. Mister Cromwell can take his party south quietly, if you can find them a good guide, Andrew, and be shot of their pursuit thereby. With only the merest good fortune, Finnegan, having failed to find us all at Newcastle, will be days yet coming to Edinburgh to try and pick up his trail. I'd recommend going west to Glasgow and taking the road south, go back to England by way of Gretna and Carlisle. There's like to be too many Catholics in Cumberland and Lancashire for you to find much support, but south of that you may be more fortunate."

"My thoughts also," Cromwell said, "but I fancy we'll do well enough by the Midlands." He looked as though he was about to say more, but then stopped. They'd agreed that keeping Cromwell's escape quiet around Mrs. MacPherson was futile, since they'd have had to remember and use a false name the whole time, and come up with some sort of explanation and stick to it. It would only be a few days, but a slip-up would look worse. Lennox had argued, quite convincingly, for letting the widow in on at least Cromwell's story, and he'd clearly taken her measure quite well, as she was all sympathy and concern when she heard about what had happened to his wife and son. Like most of the Scots officers serving with Gustavus Adolphus, the late Captain MacPherson had been a staunch Calvinist much inclined to disapprove of the machinations of the House of Stuart, and his wife was more of the same. Fortunately she didn't ask what his future plans were beyond a vague statement about fighting the injustice with his children safely out of the country. Fighting injustice was one thing; outright rebellion quite another. Lennox had also hinted, vaguely, that he was here on some business that would take him to see Mackay senior and contrived to suggest that asking about it in company would cause trouble. In short, while Mrs. MacPherson seemed like a nice lady, that didn't mean she could be told anything, and there was an awkward moment.

Darryl raised his tankard. "To fighting injustice," and got the response from around the table. So long as the pleasant widow with the nice house and the excellent beer figured that meant hiring lawyers, they were all fine.

The next morning at the Mackay town house, just off Edinburgh's high street, Darryl had to conceal his shock at how ill the old guy looked. Introductions went around. Cromwell and Gayle and Stephen Hamilton had stayed behind at the boarding house in Canongate, Darryl and Vicky posing as newlywed friends of the family to dilute the decidedly military look of two cavalrymen and a sniper riding into town. The sniper was minus her rifle today, but Julie was pretty useful with a pistol when she had to be, and even had a pair of custom-made black-powder flintlocks for when she had to blend in. Okay, so Darryl was technically a soldier, but wasn't much more than mildly military.

When it came time for Darryl to shake the old man's hand,

he could tell that the fellow had been a big and active man—his son's much leaner build must've come from his mom's side—but his hand felt somehow decayed and brittle, like dry-rotted timber.

"Dinnae fash on my account, laddie," the old guy said. "I ken richt well I'm no' long for this sinful world. A broken back will do that."

Mackay junior's tone was somber. "We've some modern medicine for my father, Darryl, and Dr. Nichols was kind enough to write with advice, but he'd no' survive the journey to get proper treatment. And it'd no' be right to have the good doctor, any doctor, leave his ain patients for one man."

Darryl swallowed. Nerves, that's all it was. He wasn't going to show his ass over the damned unfairness of it with Alex and his father right there taking it like men among men. The seventeenth century was all kinds of fucked-up, but you couldn't say it didn't breed seriously tough guys. "I'm sorry to hear it, Baron Mackay," he said. "I guess we're doing our best to improve things."

"I'll no' cry over bad fortune," Mackay said, dismissing the subject. "Meg will bring Julie and Vicky and Alexi in just so soon as the wee treasure wakes from her nap, so it's time to hear your plans. I've had a warning about ye, son."

"Aye?"

"Aye. I've no brief for or agin this Cromwell. He could be the de'il himself or God's own angel come tae earth tae show us puir sinners the promised land. And My Lord Montrose disnae care either. What he cares aboot is whether or no' you took part in felony rescue in London. Which, aye, I care about an' a'—what were ye thinking, laddie? I've nae reason t' care if I'm made hostage, the state I'm in, but wee Alexi? Ye've brothers also? Och, mind it not at all. Ye did right, and tae hell wi' the consequences, good lad. From all I hear, he's no such a bad fellow—beheaded that fool Charles Stuart, which recommends a man no end. But warn an old man first, next time?"

"Aye, I will, Father." Mackay was laughing, so there was clearly some shared joke here that Darryl wasn't getting. "But the warning?"

"My Lord Montrose wants you no' showing your face in Scotland where he might have tae see it, if I may put the business in a nutshell. Which is fair enough."

"Aye, fair enough. We were of a mind to collect Alexi and be gone as soon as we could take ship, Father. We weren't seen so far as we ken, but no sense taking needless risks, aye?"

"Aye. But no' before I have the entire story, mind! There'll be brandy poured before we're done here and I want every little detail!" Mackay senior cackled in anticipation. "Now, Major Lennox, I've been given word by Lord Reay, my chief, to expect you. His letter came like the Baptist before ye, ye ken."

"Aye, your lordship." Lennox assumed the stance Darryl had seen in movies as sergeant-reporting-to-officer, which couldn't have been easy sat down like he was. "My Lord Reay, who in a way is my chief also, charged me to convey his plans and ask you to help as far as you're able. I've brought papers with me, and—"

Lennox was interrupted by the sound of thunderous knocking. There was shouting outside, indistinct. Meg, the head housekeeper, who'd fussed around them briefly earlier, came in. "It's constables, m'lord," she said, "They say that they have a warrant for the arrest of the young colonel, and they have the house surrounded."

Chapter 25

The morning had been a soft one. No hard rain, but not dry. No more than a small breeze and occasionally cracks in the cloud. It was clearing up somewhat, but was always going to be a muggy, unpleasant day that left a man writhing with sweat in his britches. The earl of Montrose, Lord Lieutenant of Scotland, was not above such discomforts and knew he never would be. There was this to thank Campbell for, at least: this meeting wasn't indoors where it was even worse.

On the downside, he'd had to ride for three hours the night before to get here.

It was a pleasant spot, though, for all it was out in the sticks. Just short of Bathgate on the ride out of Edinburgh along the Glasgow road, and Bathgate was nobody's idea of a landmark. Although the inn Montrose had spent the night in, owned by a fast-talking MacDonald—who peppered his speech with bits of French, of all things—had been pleasant enough.

The spot Campbell had picked to meet the new Lord Lieutenant of Scotland was marked by small group of old pagan standing stone on the brow of a hill that overlooked Bathgate and the barony of Ballencrieff to its north. The country hereabouts was littered with the things. And this lot did well as a meeting-place for a king's direct representative with a powerful feudal vassal who was one error of judgment away from open, armed rebellion against his lawful monarch. There were places aplenty in the area to spend the night before, for all Montrose had cut the

Gordian knot of which local lord, laird or gentleman to favor by hiring inn-rooms.

Riding to the meeting place just before noon, Montrose had noted that with maybe six inches of concealment in the whole country around the stones neither side could easily ambush the other.

He decided he was going to take comfort in that. Argyll had had more than enough reason to be wary of royal overtures—the last one had been news to the effect that his king wanted him in a cell for a treason he'd not committed yet. So it could easily be read that the chief of the Campbells wanted to meet where he could be sure he wouldn't be taken by a ruse. Montrose was going to be very careful *not* to mention the number of times it had been the Campbells taking others by surprise or ruse. There was a reason that the other highland clans hated them.

Of course, the other side of that reason was that the Campbells made sure always to be on the side of the king of Scotland, and profited by taking land and goods from the king's enemies. A history Montrose was determined to mention as much as possible; they'd done all they had by getting and keeping royal favor. To lose it now over a single issue? By the same token, favor that was rejected could be bestowed elsewhere. The question was, did Campbell think he had enough strength in his own right to set the king at defiance? Enough to rally the critical lowland support he would need to have the throne, or at least a protectorate-and-parliament?

He left his escort behind on the road back to Bathgate and struck across the open heath to the standing stones. None of them stood particularly high; the tallest of them barely came up to his horse's withers. Campbell had left his party perhaps three hundred yards to the north and was trotting away from the road. Doubtless he'd be fuming. By simply getting on with the business at hand, Montrose had put Argyll in violation of protocol, in full sight of his own people. Montrose, theoretically the king's representative, had ceded the privilege of arriving last. His people would note that. Would have it influence their thinking. Their chief wouldn't seem quite so wronged if it looked like the king's man approached with humility. Something the actual king wouldn't ever do, as it happened.

Deciding that rubbing it in a little harder wouldn't hurt,

Montrose dismounted with Campbell still thirty yards away, and ostentatiously set to tending to his mount. Nowhere to tie him up to, but the gelding was well trained and would stand as long as required. No harm in making much of the beast, and he'd brought a couple of apples along. A little wrinkly, perhaps, but it wasn't like the horse would care. He didn't care to eat apples this late on himself; you were more likely than not to bite into a brown, rubbery, tart-tasting mass.

"Forgot your new station, Montrose," Campbell said, not dismounting.

"More that I had a sweaty arse," Montrose replied, grinning, and pretending he wasn't deliberately trying to play a different game to Campbell's own. "And it's a nice day, and I wanted the horse to enjoy it too."

He turned away, not going quite so far as to give Campbell his back, and looked out over the country. Movement caught his eye. "Is yon fellow one of yours?" If truth be told, the fellow just visible in the distance, down on the plain below the promontory where they stood, with his horse at the walk, didn't look remotely like a threat. Or like he was much to do with anyone.

"No, and I take it by your asking he's no' one of yours?" There was a wry grin on Campbell's face. "I've nae doubt we've enough lads between us to see off an inquisitive farmer. More to the point, are we here to discuss politics or the beginnings of a war?"

Montrose fed his gelding another apple. "Will ye no' dismount, Archibald? I shall have a strain in my neck if you keep your arse so high. And I find when a man's on horseback he tends to raise his voice in a vexing manner. I'd have our talk be quiet and peaceable."

Campbell took a moment to mull it over, swung out of the saddle and, like Montrose, let his beast wander. They were both rich men, schooled from an early age in horsemanship, and either could show off a good command of his mount at will. Montrose's own was staying a lot closer, in case there were more apples to be had, while Campbell's had immediately turned to sampling the ferns and heather to see if any of it was tasty. Each animal was studiously ignoring the other.

There was a moment's silence, which Campbell occupied by strolling over to the shortest of the two stones, sitting on it, and taking out his pipe and tobacco. "D'ye think, James," he asked as he filled his pipe, "that the auld pagans that put up these stones for their heathen worship, d'ye think they would have cared for bishops?"

Montrose laughed. "I imagine the pagan religions had bishops of their own, did they not? What matter, at this remove of time? I care for what is lawful in the here and now, Archibald."

"Aye, lawful. I'll allow it's lawful that you be lord lieutenant here in Scotland, James. Is it lawful that a man should be arrested for a crime that no man has yet committed?"

"If you mean Mackay—"

"I mean no such thing," Campbell said, setting aside his pipe and drawing out one of the new-fangled spirit-lighters that were coming out of Italy. Most of them seemed to have the mark of a Baron Bich on them, which led Montrose to think that the rules for the Italian nobility engaging in trade were perhaps a little looser than they were in other parts of Europe. The thing only needed a moment or two of fiddling to get a flame out of the wee wand that came with it, and Campbell had his pipe lit. Montrose had spent much of the last few years in France, where tobacco was not so widely adopted a habit, and so had not indulged more than a time or two himself. He found himself rather envying Campbell his facility in delaying conversation a little while he had his thoughts in order.

"No," Campbell went on, "I don't mean Mackay. It's for the justices to decide whether there is felony rescue of a man unlaw- fully imprisoned. Or if the man may be held here for a crime south of the Tweed. No. I mean the want of lawfulness in accept- ing fables from the future as evidence against the here-and-now."

"You're no' one of these says the Ring of Fire didn't happen?"

"No, but I am one of those who says they come from a future that's no' real. I've a fine gaggle of divines looking for God's message in the whole, and in the details. And they say that the Americans must have been created whole and new in the moment of the Ring of Fire with their whole history writ in their memories as a parable told by God to us poor sinners. Warnings against sin, gifts of knowledge, and so forth. Placed here by God for our help and warning."

"Creative," Montrose remarked, quickly sketching in the likely politics of that theology in his mind. "And do you mean to say to me, as your monarch's representative, that ye've had fair warning of the consequences of rebellion and mean to abide peaceful in the realm?"

Campbell took a deep puff on his pipe and scented the afternoon breeze with a long streamer of smoke. "Aye, that's one warning a fellow may take. I hear also that a fellow might take warning about overmuch loyalty to a monarch, and the aptness of a monarch tae discard his loyal followers, or have them stand as scapegoats for him."

Montrose nodded. Much as he'd guessed. Both he and Campbell were young men, neither having seen his thirtieth year yet, but neither were yet naifs. And with a deal of education and experience behind the both of them, they could probably manage a deal of subtlety, were it ever needed. Not today, though. "I'll remind ye we both of us ended with our heads on the topmost prick o' the Tolbooth. And here I am wi' a charge to achieve quiet north o' the Tweed. What're we to do, you and I?"

Campbell puffed on his pipe some more. "Aye, weel. Now we come tae the heart o' the matter. Charles Stuart is, one way or another, minded not to be king o' Scotland anymore. He's after a United Kingdom with one church, one parliament, one crown."

"Aye? He's not said as much. My word on that, not within my hearing." Montrose was wondering where this was going. It had been a long rumbling in the limited pamphleteering that Scotland was home to, that the House of Stuart wanted Scotland as a province, not a nation. The imposition of religious conformity was reckoned a straw in the wind of coming political conformity. Of course, the appearance of future history in which the United Kingdom was a reality was grist to their bitter, scurrilous mill. The fact that the father had forced through the first steps toward religious conformity and otherwise ruled Scotland from London was altogether evidence in aid of their case. That the son had done the same thing—not even the pretense of parliamentary government, either—could make even those at the topmost level wonder.

"No, it's what he's done," Campbell said, following through on what Montrose was thinking. "Without an Act of Union he's the problems he would have had in that other history."

"Which is now real?" Montrose put in.

"Och, ye ken what I mean. If the man will act on the warning of a civil war by imprisoning the not-yet-guilty, will he not see the single most obvious course to prevent it? I'd surely love to know what our descendants were thinking, agreeing to it, for surely there's no good call for it now." More tobacco smoke. "We gain naught but mair chains for the loss of a border."

Montrose shrugged. "Tomorrow's problem. For now what I need from you is that you bide quiet. I've no desire to see me lord lieutenant of a province governed by bishops. Clan Campbell has done well by working hard on behalf of the king of Scotland. All His Majesty the king of England requires is that you do nothing. You've my word that the charge I bear goes no further than peace."

"And the arrest of Mackay?"

"Aye, well, there's always one bloody weevil in the flour, is there not? Baron Mackay has taken it amiss, the fellow's his bastard. But, still, there's evidence, there's been an arrest, there shall be a trial. Cork wants a head over the escape of Cromwell, and he's welcome to it if he can take it. I've made it quite clear he shall have not a penny of aid from me in the matter; this Irishman he's sent was no more in hot pursuit than he was flying. It'll be for the judges to determine if he may take his man cold trod. He had the sense to swear a warrant with Edinburgh's justices, though, and—why is this relevant?"

Campbell was tapping his pipe out on the standing stone beside him. "Oh, it's no' relevant right now. Beyond that it makes your ain life hard, that is. But you've permitted a man wi' no end o' supporters among the veterans o' the Germanies tae be immured in the Tolbooth. And he's elected tae remain."

"*Elected* tae remain?"

"Aye. Elected. The Tolbooth has never been what ye might call the maist secure o' prisons tae a man wi' friends, aye? Or a man wi' money? And I've a mind that young Colonel Mackay has the both."

Montrose controlled a surge of irritation. Campbell had come out for this meeting to *tease* him? He was well aware of the ease of getting a man out of Edinburgh's Old Tolbooth. The medieval edifice that held the city's main gaol was also its principal municipal building and was hardly what you'd consider an impenetrable fortress. Montrose had made it quite clear to Mackay senior that he wanted the thing done sooner rather than later and the bastard son out of the country without delay. And now it had been four weeks. The next Assize was in two weeks yet, and the lack of movement in the case was a constant irritant. While he had to take no notice of the talk around Edinburgh, around Glasgow, around any of the streets or lanes of Scotland, it was frequently a first spatter of an oncoming political downpour.

"I'm minded to wonder how this may be relevant to the question of your own obedience to the law," Montrose said. "And aye, I ken right well what ye had to say on the subject of the proscriptions in England, and I agree with it. I speak of submission to lawful authority, not to tyranny in a panic. And before you bring Mackay up again, he's under lawful arrest, lawfully in custody. When he comes lawfully before a court lawful judgement will be upon him. He'll walk free or to the gallows and I wish the lawyers much joy of their wranglings in the matter. Never mind Mackay, Campbell, I want to hear about you."

"Aye. That depends on you. Now, I'll admit I've a deal more confidence in you since hearing how many times you said the word 'lawful' but you'll no' be the first man to say one thing and do another. My ain father had a fine record of the same, where it concerned his enemies. And, until he could stand the pretense no longer, religion."

"You seek *terms* when I ask so little?" Montrose had to admire the man's cheek, at least. "Will we now have to pay thieves to keep their hands out of the goods of others?"

"A less temperate man might be offended by that comparison, Jamie," Campbell said, grinning, "for ye ken right well that for men such as we the matter of the law contains a few more choices than for the common run of man. So, aye, *terms*."

"I'll hear them, then. And judge from them what manner of man I've to deal with, aye?"

"Aye. Well, what ye need tae know on that score is that I want Scotland a nation, no' a province. So, first, no advance for the bishops without a new National Covenant, which I fancy you'll not get. For every living you deprive a presbyterian of, I'll see an episcopalian deprived of a living also."

Montrose raised an eyebrow. "I've to find the men who may be lawfully deprived and pursue them in the Commissary court? At my ain expense? If you want that done, do it. Any man may lawfully bring a prosecution, may he not? Let me say, rather, that for every episcopalian you deprive of his living, I'll deprive a presbyterian. I fancy I'll run out before you do. For all that, there's a few that need swept out on both sides. Is it not the duty of public-spirited men to do the work of prosecuting the criminally minded?" He grinned.

Campbell chuckled. "Aye, it is at that. And aye, there's a fine collection of drunks and fornicators in livings across Scotland. Who're oft let be for want of someone to prosecute them, or because they're holding a politically important living for one party or another."

Montrose schooled his face to stillness. "And would it no' be a terrible, terrible thing if we were to disrupt the parties and factions of the Kirk?"

Campbell rocked a hand in doubtful assessment. "Maybe, maybe no'. Am I to gather you don't care overmuch for divines of either party?"

"They're men among men, some good, some bad. But, aye, I've no charge to advance the episcopalians so much as an inch unless I've to do it to settle the peace. Not that I can see any way that would be to any such purpose." Montrose shrugged. "Your first term is to ask me to do what I was minded toward anyway. The king wants his bishops kept, so keep them we must. We're no' commanded to have more, and there it lies for all I care. Your next term?"

"I've every hope it's a good word for all the auld sojers comin' hame frae the Germanies," came a third voice.

Both clan chiefs jumped, startled.

"Aye," said the third fellow, who'd appeared from what looked like nowhere. "A borderer for stealth, my lords, and permit me introduce myself. Major Andrew Lennox, formerly of the Mackay regiment, the Green Regiment and the Marine Corps of the United States of Europe."

Chapter 26

The fellow was a shortish, wide-set man, balding evident now he'd taken his hat off in greeting but with a stout set of mustachios, dressed well but sturdily. Older than either Montrose or Campbell, by perhaps as much as twenty years, he was armed with back-sword and what was unmistakably one of the future pistols that had come back in the Ring of Fire.

"Your laddies, my lords, if they saw me at all, saw a mounted man go behind trees and no' come out. And didnae stop to think that a man might dismount and seek smaller cover. Ye'd do well tae have a few veterans about ye, my lords. Is it no' a good thing I'm such a friendly fellow?"

The sound of pounding hooves showed that whatever their prior faults, both noblemens' retinues were thoroughly attentive now.

Montrose turned and waved his own people off and saw to his relief that Campbell was doing the same. The last thing anyone wanted at this point was a dozen armed retainers per side in a state of confusion with loaded weapons. It helped that Lennox had appeared as from nowhere, like one of the fair folk, and now stood straight, as tall as he could, hands clasped behind his back in token of no threat, and grinning. Montrose had not a shred of doubt that the fellow was well able to handle himself. He'd his own training in swordsmanship, and doubtless Campbell too, but all of his practical studies had been at the hands of tough old fellows like this. He'd been thrown on his arse more times than he cared to recall by men who even looked like that. There wasn't an arms-master the length or breadth of Europe who didn't have such men in his employ.

"The returning soldiers, you say, Major Lennox?" Campbell asked. "And may I ask, would you be the same as the Captain Lennox that distinguished himself so signally in Rome?"

"The very same, aye," Lennox said, "and had I known what manner of embarrassment I was storing up for myself, I'd have stayed on my arse. And, aye, returning soldiers. Thousands of guid lads of guid character, and I hear they're to be offered a choice of submission or exile? I fancy that's no' a good choice for any man."

"It's the choice your king offers, man," Montrose, said, "or would you have a bushel of burning coals tipped into the tinder that is Scotland?"

"Speaking as one of the same coals, my lord, I'm of a mind that it was no' I that made a tinderbox of my ain homeland. I went abroad, went for a soldier, all according to law, and took up arms in the Protestant cause wi' the king's blessing. I've changed not a jot of my faith in my time abroad. Why is it I must be hedged about with conditions before I come back to my home?"

"A fair question," Campbell observed.

"By royal command," Montrose said, "I am charged as I am charged. The king has cure of the nation's souls, and every concern to see that ye bring no heretical notions home with you. And what was lawfully done when you went abroad is no longer being done, if I judge aright."

Lennox put his hat back on. "Gustavus Adolphus is the emperor of the United States of Europe. I remain in his service, as permitted by my enlistment. As permitted by the enlistment of all such men as I. I've paid attention—the warrant names His Majesty Gustavus Adolphus, not the king of Sweden. Which he remains, it so happens. Does His Majesty care to give back-word on his ain warrant?"

"Do the Scots in the service of Gustavus care to levy war against their own monarch?" Montrose asked. "For such seems to be the tenor of what you say."

"If you hear that, my lord, you're no' listening. And if it's to be war, His Majesty has already struck more than enough blows. Issued warrants and charges threatening exile, demanding surety from good Protestant Scots where his father asked only for outward obedience even from papists, arrested my own former commander, charged with no crime at all, whatever gown law may say—"

Montrose held up a hand. "Enough, man. Ye talk of gown law like you're about to demand satisfaction."

Lennox snorted. "It's no' your fault, my lord, I understand that. And I've had tae carry out hard orders enough times that I'll no' think the less of you for the following of the orders you're given by your ain commander. But the best o' the case that rat Finnegan has is he says he saw the colonel fifty yards distant on a ship he thinks this man Cromwell sailed on. And there's still no guid account o' the crimes this Cromwell is said to be convict of."

Campbell cleared his throat. "I think Major Lennox is saying, in his bluff soldier's manner, that there's a great deal that disnae smell right about Colonel Mackay's remand in the Tolbooth. And he mightily suspects there's a morsel o' politics staining that arrest warrant."

"Aye. Which is why for the moment we've no taken tae prison-break ourselves," Lennox said.

"We?" Montrose asked.

Lennox grinned. "Och, did ye no' hear o' the colonel's wife? Finest rifle-shot in the world? Baroness o' some spot in Lappland I cannae even say the name o'? Lady who's watchin' us frae, it might be, three hundred yards? If either o' my lords would care for a show of her shooting, wi' smokeless powder so ye'll no see where she shoots frae, simply hold your hat up in the air and she'll shoot it. I've other signals I could give, ye mind."

Montrose didn't feel he had anything he could add to the silence that followed. He'd heard what had happened to Wallenstein at the Alte Veste. There *had* to be some exaggeration in the report of a thousand-yard shot—some accounts had it at fifteen hundred, and one at two miles, with angels wafting the bullet home in the accompanying woodcut. Three hundred yards, with a rifle, though? That was a dangerous shot to a standing man even without assuming some Ring of Fire gunsmithing. A fellow would have to be unlucky to be hit, for certain, but even levelheaded soldiers told tales of the American weapons being very accurate and long ranged. Even if the American baroness could only manage a hundred yards more than the best gun

Montrose had ever laid eyes on, they had to assume she was able to hit them.

Lennox went on. "The plain fact o' the matter is this; did we want blood shed, my lords, ye'd be bleeding. Did we simply want the colonel oot o' the Tolbooth, no' a stone would stand upon another there, for we've a muckle few fighters by us wi' all manner o' powder an' steel. We're no' even the readiest tae fight o' the German veterans, mind, but we've a muckle lot o' learnin' in the business o' war, wi' all the most modern o' arms. What I would have ye understand, gentlemen, is that if either o' ye is minded tae have the colonel hang by some bribery or subornin' o' the' judge, we'll tak' it amiss. With which, gentlemen, I'll bid ye guid day."

He was in the middle of turning away, and then paused. "Yin matter that I was like tae forget." He took a small bottle from inside his green-dyed buffcoat, and placed it gently on the taller of the two standing stones. "I'm no' happy tae be giving guid drink tae a pagan stane, ye mind, but ye've a lesson tae learn, I'm thinkin'. If ye bide here as I go, and wait while I pass from the sight o' ye, look tae this bottle tae see what the baroness would hae done wi' ye. And let the stane drink your health. Dinnae stand by it, mind, glass will fly and the losing of an eye is nae laughing matter."

The brawny cavalryman strolled away—a fairly quick stroll, it had to be said, but somehow the fellow made quick-march look casual—and both Montrose and Campbell watched him down the hill, detour slightly around a small knot of sheep, pass not so much as a blade of grass that might have hidden him on the way up, and stroll in among a small copse of trees.

It was almost an anticlimax when the wine-bottle cracked gently, the neck neatly severed and dropping into the body of the thing. Wine bled and dribbled out of a crack that ran all the way down. Looking closer Montrose could see that the ball had been barely so wide as a reed and had punched clean through the glass. The round of it was clearly visible, the crack of the gun a mere snap compared with even a pistol of the ordinary kind.

"We've a mite more to discuss, I fancy," Campbell observed, looking over Montrose's shoulder at the broken bottle.

Part Six

October 1634

But pith and power, till my last hour,

I'll mak this declaration;

We're bought and sold for English gold—

Such a parcel of rogues in a nation!

Chapter 27

"Four weeks, Alex," Julie Mackay said, "How have you not gone nuts? Also, *the smell.* Oh! Tom Stone sent some incense sticks, they should help. A bit."

Lennox could see her point. The Tolbooth was none of your fancy residences, but with the Mackay money and a daily visit from the servants, Colonel Alexander's cell was comfortable enough. He had books, and good food brought him from the kitchens, and coal and lamp-oil for the nights. None of this did much for the stench; the chamber pots were emptied into a hole at the bottom of one of the stairwells. In theory they drained. In practice, they...fermented. "You've nae stirred fra' this room?"

"Oh, I've a wander about the corridors when I've a mind," Alex said, shrugging and sinking back down on the chair he'd been brought the day he'd arrived here. Julie sank down in his lap, a heartwarming sight. "But aye, bored. Black, mortal bored, Major Andrew, old friend. What brings ye t' visit me in durance vile?"

"Well, I had a wee chat with Montrose and Campbell, as your father suggested, and as Lady Julie was minded to visit I felt I should mak' ma report in person."

"Och, well, have a seat. Is Jamie still a pompous wee arse?"

Lennox grinned. "I didn't speak to him enough to ken, mind, but yon arse is in a crack o' Charles Stuart's making, if I'm any judge. And Campbell's no help to him. The man said barely a word, but he was hardly affronted t' see me tell Montrose I'd have

229

a bone tae pick wi' him, me and a muckle o' veterans besides, and be damned tae his Episcopalian master."

Alexander whooped with laughter. "Tell me ye gave the man a ringing speech o' religious liberty, Andrew? Tell me ye did that!"

"Don't tease, Alex," Julie said, swatting her husband lightly, "what he did was heroic."

"Bloody daft, more like, hen," Lennox said, "It's no' like they couldn't have elected a new pope, and here I am, a presbyterian wi' a papal knighthood? That man Mazarini, he has a nasty sense o' humor. And aye, I ought have spoke o' freedom o' conscience, but Campbell put me off my stroke by reminding me of that bloody knighthood. But it happens I gave yon laddies all the message they needed regarding yourself. Are ye sure ye'd rather bide here?"

"I'm sure," Alex said, "the plan is a good one. Or, rather, it's the best we're like to get. Julie, did that fool of a lawyer get any further with bail for me?"

"No," she said, "he's been pestering every judge he can get his hands on and none of them want to hear in court about letting you out since you've a home in the USE and we're in the middle of sailing season. Which is the reason they're giving, that and your dad's too old to be a reliable cautioner for your bail, but there's this sense Mr. Home is getting that all of the judges are waiting to see what Montrose does, but they also don't want to piss off anyone else which is why they won't have it in court. Oh, their *excuse* is that there are, like six courts with jurisdiction in your case and they're all saying it's one of the others that's *really* supposed to handle your case. Which is why Andrew and me went to shoot at Montrose today."

Alex glared at her.

"She's twittin' ye, Colonel," Lennox said, chuckling as he spoke. "Just a wee show o' her shooting, no' a hair on anyone's head harmed. After I'd told them what was to happen, in every sense. Your father and I had words on how to do it. And we played a few tricks to make me look by far the better soldier than any other man there."

"You still were," Julie said, "One of those idiots nearly trod on me, and how they missed you up there I've still no idea. Or how they thought Oliver was Andrew, they don't even look slightly alike."

"Not everyone's got your eyes, love."

"Aye, at a mile one man in a green coat looks much like another. And for all Mister Cromwell's a head taller than me, he can ride. Darryl, bless the lad, is better than the sack o' shite he used tae be in the saddle, but nobody would take him for a horse-soldier of any kind. And wi' me startin' up like one o' the wee folk like that, I thought me they'd not be looking for the wee details o' the story we were telling them."

"Anyway, Andrew says Montrose was impressed, and Campbell too. And your dad had the full report and he's hopeful of making a big spectacle of your trial, so big they let you go rather than actually let it go ahead. And we finally got word back from Magdeburg, they're sending through a bunch of future history for us to spread around. Broadsides to print, that kind of thing. Your dad's after making a real political stink and get Montrose so busy trying to shut him up quietly there's no hope of him getting away with anything else."

"And the kirk? The bishops?"

"Montrose's problem, for now. Oliver went over the stuff we already had, and he thinks with Laud out of the country on the lam the chances of the king trying to press his luck here in Scotland are pretty thin. Your dad's got some sort of thing going on with our clan chief and some other Scots guys back home, so he's trying to spin this as the returning veterans being guardians of the covenant and Scotland's liberty. There's more details than that, but he's the expert, not me. I can sort of understand it, but I think politics around here is something you've got to grow up with to understand. It's a *leetle* more complicated than democrat and republican. Bit more like high-school politics, with all the he-said she-said bullshit."

Alex grinned at her. "Only in this version the cheerleader's got a gun?"

"And a husband with a sword, sure," she grinned back. "And a dad who convinces us all not to come out shooting, when the laws turn up to arrest him. Although I'd've taken more convincing if Alexi hadn't just gone down to sleep."

"Aye, well, let's no' be thinkin' o' getting' the wee girl shot at," Lennox put in. "The baron's a guid heid on him for that, now."

Alex and Julie both grimaced. "I get it," Julie said, "but using Alex as a pawn for this game he's playing is, well..."

She waved the hand that wasn't draped around her husband, contriving to take in the whole grim stone pile of the Tolbooth, the whole legal system it stood for, and the politics that were driving it.

"Aye, it's cold," Alex said, "but it's no' a bad move for all that. And I'm no sacrifice, mind. Boredom's the worst of it, and the worst I'll endure. The king had trouble enough with the Petition of Right in England. He'll not be after making more trouble over imprisonments here. Did I mention Finnegan came to visit yesterday? He was trying to say he'd withdraw his case if I gave up Mister Cromwell. I told him to get a warrant to arrest Cromwell and find him himself, if he cared to arrest a second man for nothing, and I'd see him in court to make a fool of him there. I don't think he was hoping for much, myself, but he brought witnesses. I think he was hoping I'd say something seditious."

"The king's got more than he had over the Petition o' Right," Lennox observed. He'd had a fair education in the matter from Cromwell, who'd not been personally involved but had known men who'd been in it up to their elbows. The change from only five years ago, when the arbitrary imprisonment of five prominent knights had ended in court proceedings, was stark. Now, a matter of imprisonment might go to court, but a visit from a troop of mercenaries made sure it never came away again. At least in England. Things seemed to be better balanced between king and subjects in Scotland.

Darryl McCarthy had joked about the English not spending near the same money on the Scots and Irish as they did on themselves, and the fact that the king was a Scotsman born in Scotland only made the jest the darker. The result was that Montrose's mission to keep Scotland quiet was both easier and harder. Easier, as the heavy hand that had the English gentry plotting wasn't laid on the Scots nobility and gentry; harder, because even without that heavy hand there was more than enough to have them plotting in any event. Lennox himself was getting involved, and while he was no experienced hand in matters political, if a king had even the sons of the peasantry scheming, he wasn't doing so well.

Colonel Mackay seemed to agree. "Aye, but there was a hope of a settlement. Since His Majesty started out with the present business by denying the Petition of Right, nobody but a fool would think this can end without bloodshed. We saw that back

in England. Without naming names where we might be overheard, we met a fellow who needed very little convincing to
begin to scheme, and I don't doubt that every fellow he's been
in touch with since was as ready for the touch as he was. Were
I a wagering fellow I'd bet that some of them were already making ready with arms and thinking of who they might muster in
their cause. As our American friends would put it, that camel
was well loaded already and His Majesty has been piling straw
after straw on the beast."

"True," Julie put in, "and your dad said to pass on that you'll
have an advocate in to see you in the next day or two. Meantime, I don't believe I shot all the bottles of liquor Andrew had
with him today?"

"Are you sure, love? You'll be exposed to a great deal of danger."
Gayle chuckled. "As if I haven't been already! Yes, Oliver,
I'm sure."

She levered herself up on one elbow and gazed down at him.
Gayle was a busty woman and, nude as she was, the motions of
the various body parts involved distracted Cromwell.

Not for long, though. First, because the matter was serious.
Second, because he was a serious man by nature. Third, because
he was also a sated man at the moment. It had been a very
pleasant afternoon.

And finally because Gayle slapped him playfully on the head.
"Pay attention, you!"

When his eyes came back to hers she smiled and said: "I've
spent hours and hours thinking about it, Oliver. I started thinking
about it while we were still in the Tower and our only contact
was by radio. I hadn't even met you in person yet."

She broke off long enough to bring herself to an upright sitting position, her back against the wall next to the bed. "I not
only had to think about it the way any woman will about a man
she's considering getting married to, but about the fact that the
man involved was Oliver Fucking Cromwell."

He made a face.

"And if you say a word about the Profane Swearing Act—"

"No, no," he said, shaking his head. "Wasn't even thinking
about it. It's just..."

He sat up himself. "I don't ever think of myself as 'Oliver

Cromwell.' I think of myself as the same man I always was. Not"—he waved his hand—"some historical figure who belongs in a painting or a book."

"Yeah, I understand. But it's not a personal thing, Oliver. I don't think of you as anything other than the man I've come to love. The real man, if you will. But even if you wanted to ignore history, history isn't going to ignore you. For better or worse, you're Oliver Cromwell."

He got a crooked little smile on his face. "And here I thought you gave predestination short shrift."

"It's got nothing to do with theology. It's just a fact that unless you change your name and go into hiding—plastic surgery would be a help too, and I'll explain what that is some other time—people will have expectations about you. Good or bad, they will. When that asshole king of yours had you thrown into the Tower, he confirmed it for everybody in Britain. *This is Oliver Cromwell.* Yeah, that's right, *the* Oliver Cromwell. He not only put a price on your head, he made you famous ahead of time, so to speak. Which means you'll be drawing admirers and would-be followers as well as bounty hunters. And you know as well as I do that you'll accept their allegiance. Because the fact is that you *are* Oliver Cromwell and you have every intention of repaying Charles Stuart in kind."

Again, he grimaced. "It's not a matter of vengeance, love. Well—a bit, I suppose. Mostly, I have simply become convinced that England needs a new political arrangement. I'm not even sure what I think it should be, yet. Perhaps a republic. Perhaps a constitutional monarchy. But if it's to be the latter, it'll have to be one without that man on the throne."

He planted his arms on his knees and laced his hands together. "I'd settle for him in prison, however. Or even in exile as long as he minds his manners. I don't insist that his head be removed, richly as he deserves it."

She laughed softly and leaned her head on his shoulder. "Like I said. Oliver Fucking Cromwell. Yes, I will marry you and share your fate, whatever it winds up being."

"And I, yours," he said.

Chapter 28

The buttresses of the church of St. Giles—due to be reconsecrated as a cathedral in the coming weeks, not that Michel Ducos or any of his followers cared about *that* all-but-papist nonsense— provided remarkably little cover. The church was not, when all was said and done, a very big building, albeit big enough for the interior to be subdivided into all manner of uses. Still, the only one of them that needed cover was Ducos himself, as none of the others could be recognized by the people they were watching.

The Edinburgh chapter of the revolutionary organization he'd been building had as yet no formal name, Ducos having considered it best to remain covert for the time being—although Party of God was coming to seem like a popular choice. The members were solid fellows, for Scotsmen, and the differences in doctrine between the local brand of Calvinism and his own Huguenot version were small enough that they were simply fodder for whiling away long winter evenings, of which Scotland had a fine supply, in debate and discussion. It had improved his grasp of English out of all recognition, as well as giving him a Scots accent he could turn on and off at will. None of them, however, had met the crypto-papist Scotsman Lennox, who had the infernal gall to claim to be a Protestant after having accepted a papal knighthood from the very hands of the Antichrist himself. For the moment, they were simply loitering, troubling nobody in the nearly empty square at the front of St. Giles. They took turns at watching the main door of the Tolbooth a few dozen paces away while Ducos stayed behind the buttress, leaning casually against the sun-warmed stone and wishing, idly, that the heathen scum in the Tolbooth would get on with it and get out here before the sun went below the houses opposite and deprived him of the pleasant warmth.

His people in Edinburgh had called him over from Glasgow when they began to suspect that the United States of Europe was getting involved in Scots politics, giving aid and comfort to the then-nascent Committees of Correspondence.

That had turned out to be nothing, or little more than nothing. The fool German had managed to get himself stabbed *and* shot in the course of preventing a local business magnate from having a greengrocer killed. Inside a month he was dead of blood poisoning. He'd not even saved the greengrocer woman; she'd taken ill in the usual round of sickness that came with summer and shat herself to death. The rump of the local Committee was currently busy with the kind of retrenchment that always followed the departure of a leader who had made himself too necessary. They would be months at least before they could do more than run a charity kitchen. Badly. It was a business of old women and street charity and no more.

No matter. Discreet inquiries—and hadn't the German made a fool of himself over *that,* his notion of subtlety being to go into a tavern and try to ask oblique questions of men he'd never met—had established the identity of the woman and that the real involvement of the USE was more in the line of offering personal help because of her acquaintance with the sole member of the local Committee of Correspondence. Of course, the woman was more useful as a dead martyr, so everywhere except Edinburgh, where people might know a contradictory truth, Jenny Geddes had been poisoned by papists for witnessing God's truth in the teeth of royal tyranny. In Edinburgh proper the story was being put about that the merely local squabble involving hired bullies had been at the orders of the king, with royal troops. The Party of God might be small, but they had printing presses and active tongues.

If there was a feature of the politics hereabouts that Ducos heartily approved of it was that the king had virtually no troops or constabulary that were directly his own. He could order the colonels of regiments and the trained bands and the noblemen with armed retainers, but not the troops themselves. And he had no practical means of compelling obedience. The clan Campbell, however, had a number of highly effective means of compelling obedience, not least of which was the power of their considerable purses; it would be a rare Scots colonel that the Campbell could not buy the debts of and ruthlessly call in in full. Which left mercenaries, and apparently the king's money had run out before he managed to send any of those north of the Tweed.

Of course, nobody needed to include inconvenient nuances of that kind in propaganda. Although this one seemed to have turned up true. Whether this Finnegan was a king's man or one of the earl of Cork's hired throat-cutters was unclear as yet. His men were a close-knit bunch who kept to Erse among themselves, and none of the Party had any of that tongue. Refused to, since apparently it was the language of papists hereabouts.

What was interesting that they had arrested the USE's man in Edinburgh, the one married to the American woman who was famous for her shooting. Apparently on a Royal Warrant of some kind. Ducos understood how such things worked in France, but the legal system here in Scotland was a closed book to him, apart from the assurance that the differences between it and the English laws made for some pretty work for lawyers. What had got the Edinburgh chapter interested enough to call Ducos in was the presence of new faces, one of whom was apparently an old acquaintance of his.

Thus, his presence here—partly to have his thoughts on the matter first hand but mostly to have him identify whether or not the Major Lennox who was suddenly making a nuisance of himself was the same Lennox that Ducos had dealt with in Venice and Rome. For his own part, Ducos had never seen Lennox close-to, as he had been careful to only meet the young, impressionable and unbelievably stupid members of the American party in Venice, but he was sure he could recognize the fellow.

The summer evenings being long in Scotland, they would not even have to be very close. Midsummer was past, but this far north the long evenings persisted well into autumn, so there would not be work for linkboys for hours yet. The market stallholders had all long since packed up and gone, but there were still plenty of idlers about the place to function as cover.

Apparently the Americans thought of a prison visit as a full day's business. It was the one place they could be sure of being found, with one of their number held pending trial. Word had been sent for Ducos mid-afternoon when they arrived, and they had not left in the hour or so it took for him to receive word and make his way there. The room that Mackay was held in had been identified, and there was light at the window. All the Party's best efforts had not gotten an agent inside. It seemed the opportunities for corruption in the place were so good the existing staff were unwilling to share. While the creation of an opening was entirely in the realm of possibility, such things required planning. Ducos decided to put such planning in train. A dead jailer more or less was of no great account if there were likely to be more jailed notables in the Tolbooth. An escape—even if the prisoner escaped no farther than a nearby lime-pit, removing the possibility of embarrassing recapture—stirred the secular authorities to tyrannical overstepping like little else.

At last! There was movement around the entrance, and the American woman emerged. Although she'd taken to wearing local clothing, there was no mistaking the differences in movement and habits of someone who'd come to such garments later in life. Ducos liked to think he was a keen observer of such things. Even when the Americans were not dressing their women with disgusting immodesty or shocking mannishness, they seemed to value ease and freedom of movement in ways that the ordinary dress of common women across Europe did not. Put an American woman in such garb and she would be months adjusting.

With her was a shorter man with the gait of a lifelong horseman. Lennox, Ducos recognized him in an instant. There was a very definite USE involvement here, then. The man was one of their serving soldiers and his actions at Rome had been as clear a statement of their disgraceful tolerance of Romish deviltry as could be sought. All that remained was to be nonchalant until they were out of sight and the next step could, with the help of the local Party men, be planned.

An hour later in the upper rooms of a common tavern—the base and drunken ways of most of the locals made a fine cover for the business of the godly, and a reminder of the worldly sin against which they strove—Ducos assessed the men he had for the task at hand. The Gordon brothers, who were at pains to assure everyone that they were in truth MacGregors, their father having changed the family name due to the Act of Proscription when they were small boys. They were as fired for revolutionary activity by that as by the desire to do God's work. No matter. McCraith, a thin and lugubrious fellow who had quit the USE in disgust over the matter of tolerance and returned home to find no work for an old soldier. Three Frasers, none related to the others, who made mild jests about the coincidence. All three—Jamie, Alexander and Rab—were at pains to point out that they were of the lowland Frasers, giving Ducos to understand that the Highland Frasers were a pack of superstitious papist savages. All six were, in essence, broken men of the kind that had been so useful in both sides of his work for the Comte d'Avaux. Some of them would work for money, but the best ones would work for the hope of vengeance against what they saw as the injustice of a world that had done them ill through no fault of their own. They could, unguided, reach some shocking misunderstandings as to the source of that injustice, but only a little persuasion to good Calvinist boys such as these brought them around to the idea that they suffered the hurts of a sinful world that had fallen from God. Ducos knew that there was no great difference between him and them save his early and burning insight that to take arms against the sin of the world was a very present remedy for the woe it brought on.

"He's oor man, then?" Jamie Fraser—far the brightest of the group—said. "For if we've tae face the full might o' the USE we've tae be richt careful. We cannae face them direct."

Ducos nodded. It was always a sore temptation to seek a bloody martyrdom. A temptation that Ducos himself wrestled with, and often, but suicide was a dire sin. "Truly," he agreed out loud. "But to summarize what we have learned, the USE is seeking to intervene in Scotland. The presence of this man Lennox confirms it. The manner of that intervention?"

"They've had a mort o' visitors at the Mackay house," McCraith said. He'd taken a potman's job at an alehouse close by, no more than a few side streets over. Close enough that he could spend quiet moments watching the street outside the residence. He didn't see everything, but enough to get a sense of the matter. "Mair around the time this Finnegan arrived. I've a fancy that there's no coincidence in that. The Mackay servants spoke aye well o' this Lennox, the Mackay bastard and his American wife is returned at the same time and there's vistors fra' England into the bargain. Put that wi' the news o' Cromwell's break frae the king's prison in England and there's a fine meal, no?"

Nods all around. It certainly helped that Finnegan's men were using the place as a rendezvous for their own watch on the Mackay house. What McCraith didn't see in person he could sometimes eavesdrop from the few things the Irishmen said in English.

"Tell me, how many of the people of this town would rise against popery?"

That got a round of chuckles. "All, tae a point," said the elder Gordon, "but they're mair agin popery than they're for the godly, if ye' tak' ma' meanin'."

More nods.

"Then we are not yet ready to provoke a rising?" Ducos asked. The future histories had shown that one would happen. Over the Romish deviation of bishops, and the Arminianism of the English king. Would the godlessness of the USE suffice?

The elder Gordon shook his head. "The divine providence may yet lead to one, if the fowk can be only persuaded to let His grace move in their hearts. Forbye, let them rage agin' popery and it may come to that. I'd no' think tae presume on it."

Ducos valued Gordon's clearheaded blend of optimism and pessimism. There was a point, though, at which consideration became inaction. "Then this motion of the great enemy is but a chance to thwart him?"

Again, nods from around the room.

The younger Gordon made one his rare contributions. "If this Lennox is as much a papist as he seems, faus knight o' th' pope as he is, can we no' make oor strife agin' the USE a strife agin' popery? Would we no' have the people wi' us in that?"

General murmurs of agreement. "If we can place the USE and the pope together in the minds of the people, certainly," Ducos allowed. Perhaps if they had begun weeks earlier, it would have been a possibility. "Fraser, Monsieurs Gordon, perhaps a broadside regarding the allegiance of the USE's man in Edinburgh?"

"Aye," Fraser said. "Be a few days, a week perhaps, before we have them writ and set and printed."

Ducos nodded. "*Bien sur,* so for the moment we need to decide. The USE have a man in the Tolbooth, their riflewoman, the crippled elder Mackay, the papist Lennox, some other persons unknown, and an Irishman come from England to take Mackay under arrest."

"Which comes tae a braw mess, aye," McCraith put in.

"A mess, certainly," said Ducos, "and I would suggest that we need not know the whys of any of it; in France, the king has his *agents provocateurs*. It is a stratagem we can use in the service of God, my brethren. Whatever might be done to cause this situation to become more of, as brother McCraith calls it, a mess, we ought to do. Whatever effusion of blood results is told to all as evidence of the USE and the popery they countenance. *Wherefore by their fruits shall ye know them.*"

"Seven Matthew," Fraser said, nodding as he capped the quotation. "If we might ensure that the American shoots only at the papist Erse, that would spare innocent bloodshed. If God wills it, o'course."

"We can but try," Ducos allowed. Fraser was at heart, a good man. It made him flinch from what had to be done in the service of God. Ducos was sure that at the moment of decision, God's grace would move the man to the fullness of service in the divine cause. In the meantime, his fervent unspoken prayers that the cup should pass from him were endearing.

That night, Michel Ducos began writing a letter to his compatriot who'd remained in Glasgow, Antoine Delerue. The process was a bit laborious, as always, because the entire missive had to be written in code—and a code that was disguised so as not to appear as such. There was not much chance that the courier who'd carry the letter would be intercepted and the letter read by what passed for authorities in Scotland. The nation—if such a riotous pack of disputants could be called such—was amazingly unregulated for someone accustomed to French rationality.

That was the reason they'd come here, of course. Still, the possibility always existed. It was best to be careful.

> *Dear Mama*

Delerue was always "Mama," as Ducos himself was always "Papa." Other members of the Party of God had other pseudonyms.

> *Aunt Marianne is doing better.*

That could be translated either as "the situation is improving" or "prospects are getting better."

*I am still concerned about her coughing, but that too
is becoming less frequent and severe. And it doesn't
seem to be coming from deep in her chest.*

Delerue would understand that to mean "the local members
of our Party are still uncertain on some matters, but are basically steady and stalwart fellows. Their errors of doctrine are not
profound and no real cause for worry."

The candle he was using for illumination began flickering.
Ducos was more concerned about that than he was the reliability
of his new Scot comrades. Most of the fortune he'd stolen from
the Comte D'Avaux earlier in the year was still intact, but he'd
left it all with Antoine in Glasgow. Here in Edinburgh, he was
operating on a very stringent budget.

If this very poor candle became more difficult to write by, a
task that was already tedious would become even more so. But
Michel Ducos was accustomed to hardships, so he paid it little
mind. The Lord's work was always a trial—and had to be, lest
it attract those unfit for His purposes.

Chapter 29

Montrose took a deep breath. He had been addressing this collection of divines—about half and half between dunderheads and lunatics, based on the last few days' performance—for over an hour now, largely reiterating His Majesty's instructions that he'd given in his opening address. He'd had daily reports that showed that most of the stern royal instructions had been ignored.

The session of the General Assembly of the Church of Scotland would continue for days yet, weeks more likely, trying to settle a final text for His Majesty's approval. Which might or might not be forthcoming. The private letters coming from the earl of Cork seemed to suggest that the king's grasp of reason was getting shakier. The king had wanted a plain compromise of governance between the presbyterians and episcopalians in the General Assembly, a *via media* such as his great-great-aunt Elizabeth had presided over in England all those years ago. It was, of course, transparent that he regarded that as a first step toward unifying the churches of England and Scotland, and the presbyterians were standing firmly on the National Covenant in opposition to any such thing.

He looked over the assembly. If he hadn't known the allegiances of the principal players there'd be no way of telling them apart. Clerical dress, of varying degrees of smartness and grooming, and while there was a general trend toward plainness among the presbyterians, some of them dressed fancy and others managed the well-tailored sleek variety of plain that managed to look richer than a braw show of gold braid and lace.

By the same token, more than one of the bishops' hangers-on was able to make the vestments of as high a church as Scotland ever got look like the weeds of a country curate. It meant gauging reactions was hard work. He had more than a few laddies watching the room, and he was keeping his eye on the key players, but it was a trial and no mistake to tally expressions to affiliations. While he ran a finger along the brief he'd laid on the lectern, he idly wondered if he couldn't prevail on this august body to vote itself conveniently-colored hats?

For all that, the next words out of his mouth were going to be unpopular with every man in the room, and he'd drawn out the rhetorical pause all he needed to.

"I will say in final summation," he said, letting out the breath, "and with the full command of His Majesty Charles, by the Grace of God, King of England, Scotland, France and Ireland, Defender of the Faith"—and it was to be hoped that the style of Defender of the Faith was not about to become as nominal as the king of France part—"that inasmuch as the divines and clerks of Scotland desire an established Kirk, it shall be a Kirk with His Majesty in command, as Christ's General of His Army on earth."

Montrose looked over the room again. He'd got the truly appalling phrase out without puking. He'd left it to the end. If the letters from Cork hadn't hinted, that instruction would have come as a shock. Telling an assembly of divines to shut up and do as they were told was strong medicine at the best of times, and with them all feeling unsettled to begin with—

He took another rhetorical pause. No heckling. That was a *very* bad sign. Shock? Probably. He'd done his best to keep all but the vaguest tenor of his remarks away from anyone likely to give a warning. Surprise? Doubtless, as this august body was used to being able to argue with its sovereign in many things. Fear? It was to be hoped. And while they were still in open-mouthed shock—

"Thus, my lords, gentlemen, clerks and divines, His Majesty's most fond and earnest hope is that he may avoid having to take such measures in Scotland as he has most regrettably taken elsewhere in his Dominions. With which I bid you a good day, and pray God's grace and wisdom guide the remainder of your deliberations."

Out. Quickly. If they were to have uproar in the chamber,

they could do it without his presence—since he was here to represent the king, letting them be emboldened by having contempt of the royal presence go unpunished would simply not do. Also, there was the faint—faint!—possibility that the theologians would learn by example the business of reaching a natural conclusion and stopping talking.

He managed a full six paces along the corridor past the closed doors of the chamber before the shouting erupted.

It was a full two hours before the first cleric arrived. Montrose nodded as the fellow was announced. About what he had expected, and if his soothsaying ran to form it would be a fellow of middling rank; enough to be sent as an envoy, low enough to be disregarded. He would, doubtless, ask for "clarification" with the clear implication that his principals would like the points in question clarified entirely out of existence.

"The Very Reverend Doctor James Hannay, Dean of St. Giles', Your Grace."

"Will ye have a seat?" Montrose invited the fellow when he had been announced.

"I will, at that, Your Grace," Hannay said, "but I should mention to begin with that I may have permitted those who despatched me here to form a slightly false impression of my purpose in coming."

Montrose schooled his face to stillness, and carefully raised an eyebrow. Hannay was, perhaps, a little young for a fellow leading a collegiate church like St. Giles, but doubtless the canons knew their own governance best. Or perhaps, with St. Giles about to become a cathedral in fact as well as name, the episcopal party had forced one of their own in to the position, with the presbyterians insisting on a younger, and hopefully more pliable candidate. And, possibly, one with sympathies they could play on. Hannay had been minister to a small-to-middling village in a parish south of Glasgow, far enough from any authority that he would have had a taste of pastoral independence. He was certainly more of the aggressively plain version of episcopalian than anything else, if that was his party, a function of his clothes not yet having caught up with the more generous benefices he would have as dean of a major church. Was that the pretense he was referring to, however obliquely? He was a presbyterian sent to bear word from episcopalians?

Montrose waited until the man was seated comfortably and the servants were ensuring he had a drink. Then he said: "Since we are doubtless to discuss the manner in which which His Majesty rendered the General Assembly speechless this afternoon, I would be concerned to find that the things I had to say were being said to the wrong man."

Hannay smiled a small, just-between-ourselves sort of smile. "Oh, set your mind at rest, Your Grace. From your point of view, I'm just the right fellow." The smile broadened. "It is simply the case that, perhaps, I'm also the fellow that goes down in history as having had a creepie-stool flung at him by some angry wee wifie that objected to episcopal prayers. Which I'm in favor of, myself, as it happens, but I rather think that some of my superiors have been away from the pastoral life a little too long to recall that a minister is, by definition, outnumbered by his congregation."

Montrose couldn't help but laugh. "Aye, I can see that that might concentrate a man's mind. That would have been you? Was you? Ye ken what I mean."

"Aye. I was tempted, the while, to write back to the Reverend Green and ask if his books had the name of the wifie, so I could perhaps ask her what she meant by it." The jocular expression vanished from Hannay's face. "But, I felt, on the whole, that taking my fellow creatures to task for wrongs they had not yet done was somehow sinful. Presuming to know how His grace would work in the hearts of men, yes? And, now I am come to Edinburgh, a chance conversation tells me that the wee wifie has vanished altogether. Right after a lot of king's men were searching high and low for her. I'd know the truth of *that* story, could I find anyone that would tell me it."

Montrose stopped short before answering. He'd been entirely ready for a few measures of political fencing. *That*, however, was a genuinely interesting question. "I'd no' thought about that," he said, not entirely addressing Hannay, but not leaving him out either. "A moment while I mull that," he went on.

Of course, it *was* political. The monarchy and the kirk were the twin axles of political power in the kingdoms of England and Scotland both, and there was simply no way in which—strangers, otherwise, so not even the possibility of friendly disputation—Montrose could address what was, in fact a *fascinating* idea without putting at least a drachm on one side of the political scale or the other. And *Oh DAMN the fellow!* He'd missed the thrust of it, what with not having been involved in the troubles south of the border. Hadn't Strafford-that-was-now-Wentworth-again got himself in to trouble with just such a business? Those fellows from the English Parliament? And hadn't the Campbell had to make rumbling noises to keep it from happening in Scotland as well? *And he, Montrose, Lord Lieutenant high-and-bloody-mighty of Scotland had just flat-footedly admitted the king might have sinned against his ain subjects.* If Hannay told a true tale, was one of those subjects—one of the small and helpless ones, yet, not as able to set proscriptions at defiance as the Campbell—so sinned against as to have disappeared.

It was only by great effort of will that the next word out of his mouth wasn't a litany of all the filthiest profanities he knew. "I'm no theologian," he said, his thoughts finally collected, "but is not evidence from that other history evidence of a man's character to resist the divine grace?"

"Do we presume to know that the Almighty will not exert His grace differently in a history he clearly intends to be different?"

That raised Montrose's eyebrows. "Is that consensus, or merely one disputant position? That He has revealed an intention by the Ring of Fire?"

"It's considered . . . suggestive. It's being forcefully advanced as perhaps expressing some measure of divine exasperation with His creatures."

"Advanced by whom?" Montrose felt his curiosity aroused. And, to certain extent, annoyance. He'd ordered full appreciations of what the theologians were thinking and saying, and this had formed no part of it.

"The Reverend Doctor Green," Hannay said, "Perhaps you've heard of him?"

"Which one?" Montrose could call to mind a number of divines by that name, none of them in the main currents of the Church of Scotland.

"The one in Grantville. Nobody wants to be seen to be corresponding with the man, but it seems Archbishop Ussher rather poked a beehive when he wrote to the fellow as the only pastor there who was a Doctor of Divinity. He's also, it seems, an indefatigable correspondent, an ardent presbyterian, and entirely willing to look up everyone in every history of modern Christianity he can find and send them a letter along with copies of the history relating to the fellow. Hence my knowing about the Prayer-Book riots and my part in their beginning. Although he addressed the letter to the dean of St. Giles' Cathedral when it was no' a cathedral and I was no' dean of it. Fortunately the letter was passed to me when it was realized I was the intended receiver, along with much jesting about the lunatic sending letters to me. Two years later, here I am dean of St. Giles' soon-to-be cathedral. It lent the man . . . credibility. Among other things that came to pass from the future history that he predicted, or would have done. Nobody's discussing his letters publicly, mind, but everyone's wondering what to make of them in private."

"And this leads you to be other than your chiefs, if I may call them that, think you are, how?" Montrose could feel a whole different series of problems and opportunities lining themselves up in front of him. The sensation was a frightening one, he could admit to himself in the silence of his own heart. Knowing how to deal in political and religious certainties he'd grown up with. Knowing how to follow a plan he'd made in careful consideration of all that was before him with the best advice he could find and take, those were things a man might face with fortitude. Being confronted, unwarned, with something entirely new from a source he'd not known existed—he schooled his face to impassivity.

Blast it all! He'd taken pains to understand what he thought was the new theology coming out of the Germanies. The Rudolstadt Colloquy had had its proceedings widely circulated. For all that the final resolution had been practical to the point of dullness, the proceedings that led up to it had given no small amount of support to the separation of church and state from the *religious* side. The Magdeburg Colloquy was rumbling on and giving out all manner of interesting material—and dangerous to circulate in England, even with Laud out of the picture. King Charles Stuart of England and Scotland really did *not* like the idea of the religious prop under his kingship being taken out from under him.

And now it turned out that as well as their governors sticking their collective oar in at the great and learned councils of religion, their small ministers were communicating with their counterparts abroad. Which was a normal occurrence, of course. Ministers argued with each other all the time about theology, it was part of what they did. And, reflecting on the last few days, the whole of how they made a bloody nuisance of themselves.

Montrose took a deep breath. First principles, then. "None of this has reached my ears. If it has reached His Majesty, he did not choose to inform me. And, perhaps, it has reached few enough ears that not everyone is aware of the arguments of the Reverend Doctor Green, do I have that right?" *Best to make sure,* he thought, *as someone is going to hear at length about me being surprised at this late stage.*

"You have the minister's name correct, yes. I shall see your secretary has the man's address before I leave. And you presume correctly, Your Grace, the good Reverend Doctor seems to have a fairly short list of correspondents. He gives me to understand that he has written to everyone mentioned by name in the various history books he has to hand as bearing on the history of religion in England, Scotland and Ireland. Once His Grace the Primate of Ireland gave him the idea, of course. He seems a pleasant enough fellow, if a trifle over-earnest in some matters. He says he doesn't presume to substitute his own advice over the guidance of the Holy Spirit to those he writes to. He simply shows us how things might have played out but for the emergence of his own home town into this time."

Montrose nodded. That last sounded like a direct quote. "You must understand," he said, "I cannot usefully say anything to you until I am familiar with this, this—" He waved a hand.

Hannay nodded. "Truth be told, Your Grace, there's not a lot to be familiar with. Green's theology is, well, prone to error here and there, let me put it no higher than that. For that, he's no worse than any of the country ministers of Scotland. And the errors all seem to me to be in the manner of having misunderstood Calvinist presbyterian theology. Again, no worse than the usual run of country ministers. I understand that that is more or less what he is. And seems likely to remain."

"So how is he relevant?" Montrose was beginning to get the feeling that Hannay didn't know either. The man was certainly taking his time about coming to anything that could be recognized as a point.

"Because he has furnished more than a few of us—myself under the misapprehension that I am entirely presbyterian in my sympathies, it would seem—with foreknowledge of the consequences of forcing English worship on the Scots church. It seems, Your Grace, I am destined to be remembered chiefly for having a stool hurled at me during divine service." Hannay smiled. "I account myself a humble man, Your Grace, but there are limits to what may be endured."

Montrose chuckled. He'd not troubled himself unduly with the future histories as they pertained to the church, only with the civil war whose imminence seemed to have loomed larger with every measure the king had taken to prevent it. "It's nothing to be proud of, aye," he said, "but may I take it you have motives larger than avoiding flying furniture?"

"Aye," Hannay said, nodding. "Have you read aught from the Rudolstadt Colloquy?"

"You brought some of it to mind now," Montrose allowed, "mentioning one of Grantville's ministers as you did. Since we've precious few Lutherans in Scotland, if any at all, what in particular do you wish to draw my attention to?"

"That part where one of the future synods made it entirely plain that they desired to be independent of the State, Your Grace. A synod I understand consists of but the one fellow, Your Grace, but who had with him a manual on how to have a church independent of the secular government."

"No." The word was out of Montrose's mouth before he had time to think. *What was this idiot trying to do?* was the thought that crossed his mind as his mouth formed the word. And for all that it was impolite to refuse outright so hastily, he realized it was all he could do. Well, damn the man for surprising him so, anyway.

To press on, then. "And I must repeat: No. Should I take such a proposal to His Majesty, that will be his answer also. He requires first the good and quiet governance of Scotland while his dominions in England are on the verge of turmoil, and second that we move toward a kingdom united under God. In which, as king, he is ruler of both the sacred and secular. His words, if I may summarize them thus, Reverend Doctor. And now I see where you differ from the bishops who think you adhere to their party, yes?"

"Aye," Hannay said, "And His Majesty has been most clear in regarding disestablishment as an anarchistic doctrine to which he is, in his royal person, opposed."

"In his private person also," Montrose put in, "let me assure you of it."

"But—and permit me to advance something for disputation between us—is it not so that establishment of the church has as its proper purpose the good governance of the realm?"

"Aye," Montrose said, "and I see where you wish to lead this argument. In my private heart, I agree: if establishment leads to discontent, it is not good governance. Stools would, if you will permit the jest, be thrown at ministers. Which is why we seek some compromise that retains establishment and governance."

"I do not see, Your Grace, nor will any presbyterian, how the compromise His Majesty seeks can be reconciled with the National Covenant. The Covenant is the basis in which the Church of Scotland has its support among the people, and deviation from it smacks of popery to the meanest of persons in our congregation. You may convince learned men, Your Grace, of the importance of outward obedience for the sake of quiet governance, but the common folk will, if you will permit me the jest in turn, throw stools at ministers. I accept that you are bound by the royal command, but I fear he has laid upon you a commission impossible to perform."

Hannay shifted uncomfortably in his seat before going on. "And in a personal matter, the common wifie that threw the stool? She has been made to disappear. Before Your Grace's time in office, but I urge on you that you discover the truth of the matter. Arbitrary arrest and secret execution, Your Grace, is the very essence of tyranny. And I should sooner be chained in the jougs and under a hail of all the creepie-stools in Edinburgh than see that come to pass."

Chapter 30

Baron Mackay didn't regard the pain as any great issue anymore. The new drugs from Grantville helped a great deal, of course, even in the limited quantities he allowed himself in the interests of keeping a clear head. He suspected he was shortening his life by keeping as active as he was, but the wheelchair that the young American McCarthy had designed for him—and doubtless some artisan in Edinburgh was looking forward to making a pretty penny from selling more of them—did much to make him feel more like he was merely crippled and less like a bedridden invalid.

And, now, Hannay. Dean of Saint Giles. Mackay had presumed, a few weeks prior, on an acquaintance with the man's cousin, who'd been a figure of middling note up until a few years ago, when he'd vanished somewhere in the Germanies, or possibly on the sea voyage over. A poet, some political noise in Ireland, a soldier in the early days of the Protestant cause in Bohemia, and a vague friend of the Mackays. The man would be remembered chiefly for his poetry, if anything, but he was part of the general group of "Scotsmen serving abroad." He wasn't the only Hannay bearing arms in the Germanies and the USE, of course, simply the only one Baron Mackay had known well enough to invite a relative of his for a social visit.

The younger Hannay had proved surprisingly amenable to being Mackay's man in the bishops' party, albeit only with a reporting brief. Mackay hoped that would, when it came time to start working on Montrose, let him obtain an entree there.

253

Montrose was, in Mackay's view, the key to the whole matter. If the histories of his conduct in the other time's civil war were to the point, he was a man loyal to his king but persuadable. He'd begun in clear adherence to the Covenanter cause for the sake of Scotland, but divided the Scots cause when he returned to his king.

Now, if the man could just be persuaded that that loyalty to Charles Stuart was a bad investment that ought be written off, they would have something. If the Campbells could be persuaded not to queer the deal by insisting on their primacy so that Scotland's strength was united, deterring military action by a man Mackay thought of, more and more, as King of England only. If, if, if.

Uniting Scotland was a doubtful proposition at best, and far and away the Bruce's greater achievement, when you looked at it, than merely liberating Scotland from English rule. At that he'd done it largely by smashing the Comyn to less than a tithe of their former power. The goal then: bring Scotland into a political unity without anyone having to be smashed. Let them bicker and snarl at each other all they wanted in private; when facing south it must needs be as a single front.

Baron Mackay felt he'd set himself to landing a muckle great fish with only a tiny hook and the slenderest of lines.

Fortunately, he had the future histories to give him an idea of how the fish would run, but they were no use in telling him how it would wriggle. He'd have to play the beast with every ounce of skill he had.

Hannay was looking uncommonly pleased with himself, preening almost. He was a shortish, thickset man with a ludicrous little mouse of a moustache that he fiddled with constantly. "Montrose was definitely uncomfortable, Laird Mackay," he said, by way of opening after the pleasantries had been dealt with. "The man knows the matter he has in charge is near to impossible, if not actually so. And as you instructed I placed the blame for all of the misgivings about the future on the Reverend Doctor Green. It's not so far from the truth as all that, as it happens. The fellow is most prolific with his letters."

"The best deceptions are done with the truth," Mackay observed. "Lead a man to place the wrong interpretation on what he sees and every new fact that comes to him leads him further astray. However, there's no great amount of deception in this matter,

Doctor Hannay. We truly are about the business of saving Scotland from civil war. If Montrose can be made to see the turmoil of civil unrest as greater than the turmoil of disestablishment, he will find it all the easier to break with the king."

"Must we?" Discomfort replaced smugness in Hannay's demeanor. "I can see, perhaps, that there is argument for His Majesty having a lighter hand in the government of the Church. Perhaps, even, for disestablishment, and His Majesty being a secular ruler on the model they are adopting in the United States. The Walther manual is most persuasive as a method of making doctrinal independence paramount over political expedience, but..."

Mackay held up a hand to stop the man in mid-whine. "It is devoutly to be hoped that His Majesty adopts that as his solution to the matter. It is certainly the case that those who encouraged him in his previous approaches are no longer counseling him."

There; let him salve his conscience with the doctrine of evil counselors. If truth be told, that had never been other than the thinnest of fig leaves to cover naked rebellion. And, if Mackay read the future histories aright, nothing short of naked rebellion would get through to Charles Stuart. By grace of God he might be king of England and Scotland, but the man seemed bent on rejecting that which the grace of God had given him. Mackay suppressed a smile. That line had just occurred to him, and it was one he'd do well to remember for the future. It was the kind of pithy aphorism that put men's discomforts into easy words.

"And if he does not?" Hannay had been willing to joke about having stools thrown at him. Not, apparently, about committing treason. Mackay had, at least, the comfort of knowing that he would be dead before he could be laid on a headsman's block, with his sons either not complicit or gone abroad with roots put down in what sounded like good lands. And, of course, the amusement of knowing that he'd met the stool-hurling Jenny Geddes before she took the bloody flux and died. One day he'd tell Hannay just for the look on his face.

Not today, though. Mackay folded his hands carefully, deliberately, before him. "In that case, Reverend Doctor, it will be just as well that we have taken good care that every man who might have supported His Majesty has as his first concern the good of Scotland."

"And if the good of Scotland be that His Majesty remains king?"

Mackay leveled his gaze hard at Hannay. "Let us pray, indeed, that that is indeed the Almighty's plan for our nation, Reverend Doctor." Not least because, even allowing for the youth of his daughter-in-law, Mr. McCarthy and Mistress Mason, the descriptions he'd had of presidential elections made them sound like a sore trial to the patience of any man of sense. "However, let us proceed on the assumption that, given no alternative, His Majesty will behave as does a man of sense, however little he may like it."

Hannay chuckled. "A touch of *lèse majesté*, Laird Mackay?"

Mackay snorted. "Perhaps. Or perhaps an honest assessment of the man under the crown? Tell me I am misguided in the matter."

"Not... entirely. He is, perhaps, not the man his father was, nor the man he was before he was injured. There are some fellows who, perhaps, do not take well to such setbacks."

Mackay nodded, acknowledging the compliment. "Charity bids me allow that, in the first days after my own injuries, I was much inclined to feel sorry for myself and be a nuisance to those around me. Which I mention as much in the spirit of confession being a tonic for the soul as anything else." He took a deep breath, as if to indicate that he was much tonicked, and went on. "Now, and I appreciate this is on the basis of one meeting, do you think Montrose took to heart that the charge he has in hand is truly impossible?"

"We spoke at length after I put it to him the first time. He has hopes of making a compromise happen, I do know that. Even if it is only in the shape of insisting, at swordpoint, that every clerk and divine in Scotland hold his tongue on the subject of church governance." Hannay shrugged. "He does not seem, I would say, much exercised by the prospect of popular revolt over the prayer book, should he try and introduce that."

"I rather suspect that that will not be an issue for the time being. Did you follow the news from London? The escapes from the Tower of London?"

"If you're referring to Laud's departure, aye, I see what you're driving at. No Laud, no great impetus for a book of prayer common to both kingdoms. The trouble is, His Majesty may yet regard it as his own project and Laud's was not the only spoon stirring that particular pot. There's not a bishop south of the border who doesn't take Hooker as his first and last in all matters of doctrine and governance. Not that Hooker isn't a fine authority in many matters, but far too many of our countrymen make an idol of the National Covenant to be readily accepting of a move to the Anglican ideal."

Mackay winced. "I hope ye're not minded to suggest the Covenant is an idol where anyone can hear you?"

Hannay chuckled again. "I've a fraction more than half my wits about me, sir, and that fraction's all I need. The Covenant is what it is, a covenant and solemn league against the errors of Rome listed in it, and those not listed, and to preserve the true religion. The argument is regarding what it permits, and what it does not permit, and which pan of the scales we place bishops in, for they are not mentioned for good or ill in the whole document. And, for that matter, what weight upon the balance His Majesty's conduct shall exert—"

Mackay held up his hand to stop what was promising to be a full theological flow. "The plain fact o' the matter is that the Kirk of Scotland will tolerate bishops, but not the prayer book, am I right?"

"Aye. The one's a matter of His Majesty exercising governance over the Kirk. The other goes to doctrine, and there's a mort o' the English common prayer's too much like popery for any Scotsman's taste. Hooker was a fine fellow, but willing to tolerate error and call it tradition and reason, when he ought to have insisted on the sufficiency of scripture and reached much of the same conclusion he did, why—"

Another warding hand. Mackay could sense that this was a man who might expound theology all the day and into the night. Keeping him attentive to the politics of the matter might prove a trial. "Can you counsel your masters and Montrose both that, perhaps, the present debate might be confined to the matter of bishops alone? We have the future histories to tell us that it was the book of common prayer that provoked the rioting and then the Bishops' Wars. His Majesty thinks least when he feels that someone is trying to force his hand. Should he feel he has had something of a victory, he might choose magnanimity in other matters and we may keep the political situation from becoming a matter of blood."

"I can counsel that, aye, my lord. I promise nothing in the

matter of success. I've read the history of the Bishops' Wars myself. The Kirk rejected everything, bishops included, when pressed by His Majesty, and sought to disestablish itself."

"Aye, and that because His Majesty was of the opinion that the Kirk was intriguing with France," Mackay said, pleased he'd got the fellow back on to more firmly political matters. "Since he is now in the pay of the king of France himself, he has not that suspicion to move him. Indeed, the fact of his paying his mercenaries with French coin is a very present scandal, Reverend Doctor, and would make a charge of popery all the more plausible to the common folk. If he'll marry a Catholic and take the pay of a Catholic king, it will not be so hard to see popery in every line of the prayer book. Bishops, on the other hand, his father introduced, and that before he took the English crown. Before, even, the final form of the Covenant, so the presbyterians can hold their noise."

Hannay nodded. "I shall try."

"No more may be asked of any man," Mackay said, knowing full well that Hannay was going to fail. The news from south of the Tweed was all of His Majesty having become even more of a holy fool than he'd ever been, and if it was the pain of his wounding that did it, Mackay knew from personal experience that they were in for months of the same yet. Probably more; he knew it was not the sin of pride telling him he had never been the petulant and wilful fool Charles Stuart had been. Mackay had been brought up to play the man and endure his hurts with dignity. That he had, temporarily, failed was a source of shame for which he hoped his actions now were adequate earthly contrition. It might be a guess, but it was a guess informed by observation and judgement, that Charles Stuart would not have that fundament to draw on when recovering from the shock of becoming a cripple.

He bid Hannay good evening, and, as he was being shown out, gently turned the crank that reclined his wheelchair. With Hannay gone, his favorite houseguest let himself into the room.

"I listened most carefully, as you bid me," Cromwell said, as Gayle Mason followed him into the room.

"Gimme a minute, here, to get this turned off." She reached under the table and took out the radio-box that had conveyed the whole conversation upstairs.

"It was admirably clear, Gayle," Cromwell said, the usually bluff country-squire tones softening as they always did when he spoke to her. Mackay felt a small cramp of annoyance that they couldn't have a proper wedding celebration for these two. He'd had an old friend, half-retired as pastor of a tiny village kirk in the wilds of West Lothian, stand witness to their marriage vows and make the necessary entries in his parish register so their marriage was lawful. Not any kind of secret, but certainly entirely without any publicity. That, and a hearty dinner and a good dig at his wine cellar, had been the limit of the hospitality he could offer without drawing attention. Hiring a few toughs was all it took to keep Finnegan's men away from the house while the lawyers wrangled over young Alex's captivity, but if the man got hold of the notion that Cromwell was a regular visitor and was staying not two miles away in Canongate, he'd be back with another warrant and no mind to back away when a houseful of baronial retainers stared him down. Alex's arrest had had to go ahead because that warrant, at least, was lawful. More resistance than limiting him to the single named party and leaving behind "other persons found therein" would have been a move too far, too soon.

Even having Oliver here now was likely asking too much of dame fortune, really.

"The Reverend Doctor"—Cromwell's Norfolk drawl could put as much contempt into that title of respect as Mackay could get into a barrage of obscenities—"seems to me to be taking counsel of his fears."

"He seemed calm enough to me," Mackay observed, and it was true. There was a certain lordly dispassion to be had with the drugs they'd sent from the United States. They did little for the pain itself, but seemed to make him uncaring, dismissive of the actual sensation. He found the coolness of regard it gave him useful in the course of political conversations, especially when it came to paying close attention to a man's eyes and expression. A little tricky for the memory at times, but that was what clerks and notes were for.

"Without the distraction of his face and eyes, Robert, I listened to what he was saying. It's a rare man who doesn't try to divert talk that makes him uncomfortable. He fled into theology more than once, and it seemed to me you noticed enough to stop him?"

"Aye, I did that," Mackay said. "Curious how dissembling face-to-face is all of a piece, and with one piece gone it becomes transparent."

"Well, Oliver's a smart guy," Gayle said, smiling from where she was coiling one of the wires that formed part of her radio. "But if you didn't grow up with the phone—which works the same as radios, when you're talking on 'em—you tend to treat the two ways of talking differently. I used to hear it from my grandma, she had a telephone voice that was a whole lot different from her speaking voice. I hear it a lot again from down-time folks when they get to using the phone and radio. Oliver spotted that it's two ways of listening as well, which I guess is down to the fact that for all those months talking to me on the radio was the only conversation he got most days."

"Aye, and naught to do but think on things. It makes a man pay attention to the smallest details, and truly consider them. Hannay is a man afraid, and of more than simply riot beneath his pulpit."

"Consider the smallest things, aye?" Mackay wondered aloud, taken with a whim of speculation. "There's a line o' Marcus Aurelius' on the matter. This, what is it in itself, and by itself, according to its proper constitution? What is the substance of it? What is the matter, or proper use? What's the man fear, and do we calm him, or spur him with it?"

Oliver grinned. "Now we sit at meat," he said.

Chapter 31

Finnegan's mood, already on the ragged edge, got the better of him when he saw O'Hare being helped in from the stables, nose bloodied, lips swollen and obviously nursing ribs that were at least bruised. "Do you fuckin' *amadan* not know to not to let yourselves get caught alone?" he roared, and followed it up with a short stream of invective.

"Go easy, Chief," Tully cautioned. From, Finnegan noticed, a safe distance. "No man can be watchful all the time."

Nevertheless, O'Halloran was looking shifty. "I had to piss, so I did," he said.

Whatever O'Hare muttered through his bloodied teeth, Finnegan didn't catch. He doubted it was words of absolution, not hardly at all. "Who's watching the Mackay house now?" he asked.

"I've sent Grady and O'Toole," Tully said, "and Mulligan to be close by. The *giambin* are watching for moments of weakness to drag a man into an alley for a thumping. Chief, it's past time to either do some more justicing and put more of the *tuilithe* in the gaol or give up on it and have at them properly."

"Don't think I'm not considering the latter strongly," Finnegan snarled, "if I can keep more than half of you from getting your fool heads bate before. Get this *cábúnach* to his bed and some cold water to that face."

O'Hare's bleeding and dazed self cleared away, Finnegan returned to his broth. It was coming to something when a man couldn't sit to eat without one of his men being battered insensible. "Tully," he said, "did you speak with that gowned fuckwit this morning?"

"I did," Tully said, "and there's no part of him that's not laboring for us, I will say that. What he tells me is that there's no judge will hear a word in open court concerning our man in the Tolbooth. They'll not try him, nor let him go. Yon fool Charles has pissed on everything for us, Chief."

"How so?"

"They've a clan chief or two here in Scotland that's worth the name. When they saw what was done with Cromwell and the other English rebels, they didn't altogether take up arms—"

"—but said to nobody in particular that their arms were all close to hand?"

"Just so, Chief," Tully nodded.

Finnegan nodded in return. If the Irish had a truly besetting sin it was that in the centuries of feud and raid and civil war, no great clans had risen to give the nation as a whole power. As it was, they were a lot of squabbling *tadgh* and easy meat for the English and Scots.

Finnegan blew through his moustaches. "There's this to be said for putting them in the Tolbooth, they're only after us with the boot and the *bata* for it. Should it come to drawn swords, Tully, I mislike our chances."

Tully rocked a hand. "Should it be a long fight? Not hardly at all. A fast in-and-out? We might manage something. If we can catch that *langer* Cromwell at home. I'd not like to just run in there with my arse on fire. Some of the lads that Mackay keeps about him are entirely too handy for my liking. And while I have my mind on the matter, it might be that some of these brawls are conveniently timed. I'll see what I can't do to have a man or two watching where he can't be seen."

Finnegan chuckled, swaying back from the table as the sour-faced streak of piss who waited the tables here cleared away his soup bowl. "Plan it, then. Don't go alone, I don't want the head of you broke. And if you're right about the brawls being distraction for somewhat, we can watch for them. And you're right, it's just the sort of tomfoolery we'd play ourselves, is it not? So, let's answer tomfoolery with head-breaking."

"We're to do this?" Tully asked, eyebrow raised.

"For now, no," Finnegan said, "but should occasion arise we'll have a plan ready."

✧   ✧   ✧

Julie Mackay kept the salt stirring into the cooling water. The stableboys were, it had to be said, not terribly hurt. But they worked with their hands in the muck of the stables, and even stables as clean and airy as the Mackays' were covered in, let's face it, horseshit. They'd all lost skin off their knuckles and the Irishman they'd given a good thumping to had got a few licks of his own in.

So there were bruises a-plenty, and grazes everywhere. Meg and the kitchen girls were ready with clean cloths while Thomas the head hostler and his four grooms sat around with their hurts ready to be tended. "Brawling in the street, Thomas," she chided, grinning to take the sting from these words. "Such a poor example to your boys."

One of the grooms was his boy in truth, a son learning his father's trade. James was all of fourteen and had inherited his father's wiry strength. "Ah'm no sure it's no' tae late, m'lady," the lad said, grinning around a loose tooth.

She handed him a cupful of strong brine. "Swill that around in there, see if it doesn't take some of the shine off."

He did, and muttered something through the pinkish bubbles that earned him an old-fashioned look from his dad. Julie kept her face straight. She was still having trouble thinking of herself as a mom—when little Lexi reminded her the awful *hugeness* of it still took her breath away at times—but was determined to get in practice. "No cussin', you," she said. "Ladies present."

Meg held a bucket up for him to spit into, mouth thinned almost to invisibility. Julie wasn't sure that that wasn't just to keep the deadpan in place; before the boys had come back she'd been full of a dark glee about the papists getting what was coming them.

The rest of the boys winced manfully as the salt water cleaned their wounds. One of the kitchen girls was, to Julie's certain knowledge, unmarried, and she was making much of the next-oldest of the stable lads after Thomas. She idly wondered if there was romance there. Or about to be.

No matter. "How many, Thomas?"

"Twa on watch, m'lady. Yin was gan f'r a pish, so we set aboot t'other. No sae hard, mind. Jist sent'm hame, t'think again." Thomas snorted. "Or tae the White Hart. Gowan's nae one t'fash if it's papist coin he takes. Master Cromwell took the chance t'be awa' t'Canongate."

"Good," Julie nodded. The skirmishing in the streets was a pleasant diversion for the Mackay retainers. Whenever they needed a moment or two for Oliver and Gayle to slip in or out, four or five young men would go out looking for a brawl. Generally it was a lot of puffed-chest bravado, insults and occasionally a chase through the streets, but that did as well as the occasional brawl to divert the watchers. One day Finnegan's men would catch wise that a walkie-talkie in a pocket with a built-in Morse key and a discreet earpiece under a bonnet—seventeenth-century women's fashion could be so *useful*—let a nondescript couple strolling up the Royal Mile carry on a conversation with someone half a mile away.

Often the boys could run the watching "constables" off for the necessary five minutes with such good timing that Oliver and Gayle barely had to break step. The way out was even easier. There was an unofficial contest running between the stable lads, the footmen and the coachmen. If Julie was any judge, this was a pretty solid point for the stable's score-sheet.

"Judging by the wincing, they had fun," Julie said a little while later in Robert Mackay's room.

"Aye?" Mackay senior graced that with one of his rare smiles. "I've more than a few memories of being a daft wee laddie myself."

"Oliver and Gayle got away clean. Gayle called a minute or two ago to say they'd reached Canongate." It still seemed odd to Julie that they treated Edinburgh and the adjoining Holyrood and Canongate as separate places. They were still in a time when city walls meant something, of course, but you had to grow up in Canongate and Holyrood to know where the one ended and the other began. It was baffling enough that none of the streets were laid out in any sensible way, but the administrative arrangements were downright medieval. She was, at best, hazy on how things had been done back in the up-time USA, but she didn't doubt that there had been some kind of system. And right angles between straight streets, too. Just straight streets would be a start in Edinburgh.

Mackay was nodding, rolling his chair over to the window. "It's a grand thing, the radio. The wee pocket radios"—Mackay had decided he didn't like the word *walkie-talkie* and refused to use it—"best of all. They've done well by us, the past few weeks."

"Finnegan and his men aren't likely to catch wise, either," Julie said. "What those boys know about radio is just about nothing."

"Aye, let's hope it stays that way. Pride goeth before destruction, lassie." Mackay had a wry smile about him as he quoted that bit of scripture. Julie had heard him reflect on his own haughty spirit before his fall, and had worried some that he was taking a depressed turn of mind. The weed that had finally come over from Thuringia was helping with that, though, and now he was sounding altogether more philosophical about things. "This Finnegan's uncommon good for the manner o' man he is. Inventive, persistent. The Irish are a sorry lot, in the main, but they've a leavening of fine fellows among 'em. 'Tis pity this one's gone to the bad."

Julie shrugged. "If he crosses the line, he's got me to answer to. And Stephen. And Andrew. And Darryl. And Oliver. I'm fairly sure he knows about most of those. If he thought he could get anywhere in a straight fight, we'd have had one by now. He went for the legal system instead."

The old baron nodded. "All true, lassie, but men grow weary and frustrated. These last weeks, oor laddies have been choosing their times and places, always having the upper hand thereby. That must surely grate at a man."

"You think he'll try a straight fight?"

"I surely believe it prudent to prepare. I saw fra' the window here how Thomas and his boys used that Irish bravo. And manly pride may only stand a little o' that before a reckoning is demanded."

Julie nodded. "I'm not exactly a fan of that macho bullsh—er, nonsense. But I understand how it works. It's even good for a man who has to go fight. I see what you mean."

"Aye, and there's the business wi' that fool Lauder afore ye' left for London."

Julie frowned. That had been a nasty little local squabble that they'd never really gotten to the bottom of. She'd not have noticed if poor Otto, God rest him, hadn't recognized the woman's name and decided that the Committee of Correspondence needed the help of the Swedish baroness. The Committee, perhaps not, but Otto himself had needed Alex to help him out of difficulty at least once. And while they'd been out of town the poor man had died, probably of blood poisoning from getting stabbed. "How's that relevant?"

"You'll recall I've a few wee birdies singing in my ear from time to time?"

Julie nodded.

"It seems that the talk is now that that was all the king's doing, in secret, with Lauder as his cat's-paw."

Julie's heart sank. "You said that everything he said about friends on the privy council was so much horse-apples."

"I did, and true it was. It's the new rumor that's the lie." Mackay drummed his fingers on the arms of his wheelchair. "It falls to one or another of us to find the root of this. Ignorance of the means and manner of royal influence in Scotland cannot be so general, surely? We are a nation that cannot even run a Poor Law establishment as the English do, and let it fall to the Kirk. And blithering fool though Charles Stuart be, he cannot have thought he could send his ain liveried men north of the Tweed and not have Campbell take note."

"Wentworth, or Strafford, or whatever his right name is, was advising the king back then." Julie knew when to drop the bubbly cheerleader act. "Met the man. Had his head screwed on right, I reckon."

"Just so," Mackay nodded. "And there's been naught to provoke rumor of royal tyranny since. Oh, Montrose has been blowing hot air at the bishops and presbyters alike, but there's naught to come of that for months yet. Years, even. I've a hope in me that it's just one of those things that happen from time to time, the mob insisting on its folly."

"Anything from the Committee that's left?"

Mackay snorted. "I've heard the tales of Germany's Committees. And a fine pack of scoundrels they sound. Major Lennox told me tales of Italy's collection of knaves and halfwits and excitable wee laddies. Here in Edinburgh, we'd a half-mad ex-soldier and a parcel o' good-hearted wifies. The soldier passed away, may the Lord give him rest, and now it's naught but the wifies. Fine charitable work they do, and pleased I am to donate. That's the limit of them, mind."

"Darryl and Vicky, then," Julie said. She was not quite sure where the idea had come from, but as she turned it over in her mind she found she liked it. Not least because the not-so-tiny ember of feminism Julie nurtured in her heart had flared into life at Mackay's dismissal of the women of the Committee. "They can come like they're just moving here, back from the wars in Germany. Sent to take over the Committee of Correspondence. New in town, asking questions, getting involved. Pretty sure they've not talked to many people here in Edinburgh proper, they'll not be recognized. Gets the Committee up and running properly, and if Vicky can't get herself plugged into the gossip network of all those wee wifies you're talking about, she ain't the girl I think I know. And if you want singing little birdies, Baron Mackay, listen to ladies gossiping."

Mackay chuckled. "All this time and it's *now* ye choose to sound like a baroness? Aye, there's merit in your plan. And I'm entirely sure Mister McCarthy can cut their way clear of trouble, if there be trouble. Young Victoria seems like no delicate wee flower, if her blood gets up."

"Oh, count on it, Robert." Victoria grinned. She'd seen Victoria let her temper rip a couple of times. There was a girl with anger she could focus and aim like a cutting torch. "Now, Alex. He's getting more comfortable in that cell than I like, and he's not happy about it either. Still no joy from our lawyers, but from what I hear, Finnegan's having the same problem. Far too many people are going to be offended no matter what the result is in court, so the entire legal profession is making excuses, all the way up to the judges. You know at least some of the people who are frightening the judges, can you not have a word?"

"I've made efforts, Julie," Mackay said, sudden weariness in his voice. "Every voice I can prevail upon to speak to Montrose comes back to say he's being strictly correct about not interfering with the bench in any legal matter. I've written to Campbell, had no answer formally, but a quiet word or two of sympathy. I see his problem. Campbell may do much, but nothing without consequence."

"He'd like to help, but he's afraid he'll light the fuse doing it?"

"Just so, we'll make a scheming noblewoman of you yet. Montrose has the same problem. Either may cut all the Gordian knots he desires, but until the time is right for force of arms— and for preference past right—may not draw sword to do so. It falls to such as us, a step or two below the top of the stair, to make things happen. The next term of court sittings will happen soon. Come the worst, Alexander will walk free then. Oliver will have begun his going up and down in the world, Finnegan will race off after him, there'll be no prosecution to trouble us. Alexander will, for all of his trouble now, be able to walk out with barely a murmur. Five minutes before the bar of the court with no prosecution, the matter is dismissed with no trouble at all."

"Wish I had your confidence," Julie said. "And your patience."

"If there's aught to be confident about in this world, young baroness, it's the sloth of the greater part of men about their duty and the conspicuous want of courage of the same in the face of even the lightest of hardship. *Especially* the lightest of hardship. Courage comes easy in the face of terrible peril. It seems to desert a man faced with mere loss of place and name." Mackay shook himself out of a gathering philosophical ramble. "Just as soon as Finnegan ceases to be a trouble—Finnegan and the earl of Cork's purse, I should rightly say—sheer idleness will do our work for us. A few weeks or so, and the last of the traveling weather will see Oliver off and away to trouble the English as he seems fated to. Finnegan will give chase, or Cork will know why not."

Julie nodded. She had to hope neither of them was being overconfident.

Chapter 32

"Oh, Montrose." Richard, earl of Cork, was starting to feel his common origins stirring as he read the letter. "Oh, Montrose."

He'd spent all day listening to Charles Stuart—a man he *prayed* he'd never refer to as King Cripple-cock out loud, and that he would never have to officially hear the servants call him by that name—prate on in the way that only a peevish idiot of that character could. Time and again he'd politely hinted at the need for dismissal to be about His Majesty's business, but the man had gone on and on and on and *fucking on.*

Richard had been born to a poor-relation branch of the Boyles, but that was measured against ownership of a large fraction of Hertfordshire. He still had the diamond ring his mother had given him as a means of making his start in life. He'd done well enough with just the money he'd gone to Ireland with. And for all the money did, he'd had to get his hands dirty more than a time or two. The urge to take the Profane Swearing Act and wipe his arse with it came from those days.

Especially when, after a long day and a tiresome one amid the stench of His Majesty's chamber pots, he'd to strain his eyes by fading summer's evening light and a couple of candles to read this latest from Montrose.

"Montrose," he murmured, weighing all that was said—and not said—between the lines of the brief, signet-sealed parchment. All the trimmings of official correspondence for a letter that was but a note of hand. "Montrose, you utter *cunt.*"

Finnegan. The man had never failed. Until now. Well. There was a first time for everything, wasn't there? And it just had to happen where it embarrassed Cork in front of Montrose. *This noise comes from south of the Tweed and disturbs the peace of Edinburgh,* coupled with *reassure me that this tumult is not of your ordering.*

Finnegan had, in his last, reported that the trail had gone cold at Edinburgh, but that they were using the Mackay bastard as a tethered goat. Lawfully, for a wonder, and they had weeks yet before the next assize, or whatever they called them in Scotland. If there was any way to use Mackay to draw out Cromwell, Finnegan had time to find it.

And now Montrose deems it time to take a piss where Cork was fishing?

He took a deep breath. Ranting fury was all very well—cleansing, in its way—but there was a time and a place for it and the planning of his next move was not that time nor place.

So. Montrose sends a subtle and coded warning that he is impatient with Cork's man. The immediate solution being, of course, to remind Finnegan that the chase was for Cromwell. Another surge of fury. The one mistake Cork hated, the one he mocked others for mercilessly, the one he loathed in his king, was that of trying to tell the man on the spot what to do when he clearly knew better than anyone else.

Therefore, tell Finnegan that his plan is having unforeseen downsides and to look for another way to the prize. *That* made more sense. And reassure the man that he'd not lost his earl's confidence. However infuriating, things like this just happened and blaming the man who they happened to was a fool's business. Even if it was Finnegan's fault, there was good cause to give the man some time to correct his error. As the earl's Irish subjects would put it, "the man who never made a mistake never made anything," and there was a wisdom in that. Finnegan's record excused much in any case.

The problem, the *real* problem, was as ever King Charles Stuart. He'd given Montrose orders to quiet Scotland while at the same time advancing policy that had Scotland, if not up in arms, at least complaining bitterly. A natural state of affairs for the Scots, true, but it meant that when they had something real to complain about, they came at it with the benefit of *practice.*

How to smooth Montrose's ruffled feathers, then? Royal command? A possibility, but the prospect of trying to get an Order In Council out of the king that wasn't hedged about with provisions and stipulations and at least one demand for religious conformity was fit to give a man a headache.

Call Finnegan off and ignore Montrose? That had the merit of being the easiest solution. But to give Montrose the cut direct—no, the cut indirect, not acknowledging his letter—would store up trouble for later. He didn't know Montrose well enough to assess whether he'd bear a grudge, but the man was a Scotsman, so that definitely slanted the betting. Better, then, to reassure the man that his concerns would be attended to. Or apologize for not doing. How, then?

"Clerk!" he bellowed. There was bound to be one still up somewhere. His load of paperwork had more than trebled since he had supplanted Wentworth. And it had been no small thing as merely the earl of Cork.

It took a short while before he had a man present with copybook and pens, time he used to gather his thoughts. "First," he said, "To My Lord Montrose, the usual greetings, and see that the fair copy of this has no flavor of officialdom about it. It must be purely a plain letter. The man sent me his last on sealed parchment, the jackanapes, and I'm not about to let him play games like that with me...."

Finnegan stamped his boots at the threshold of the White Hart. Whatever else you might say about Edinburgh, it fair rivaled Ireland for rain. The streets were a positive broth of mud when it came, and the stable yards of the White Hart no better. The coaching inn they'd found at Balgreen, west of Edinburgh proper, was a better prospect for the dirt. And for the lads making sport of the locals by calling it Ballygreen.

That little bit of fun was not going to help today. Every day, riding from Balgreen to the White Hart on Edinburgh's Grass, he stopped by the offices of the Royal Post. Usually to send a short report of his lack of progress, occasionally to receive something from his earl. Today it was a fine, fine packet of bollocks. He'd read but the first few lines and resolved to get himself to a decent breakfast before he read any more. A man could take a headache getting this angry on an empty stomach.

The White Hart was tolerably good for food and drink, but hugely convenient for the Mackay house and, helpfully, for supplies and horses. He and the rest of the *torai* were now very well-found for horseflesh indeed. Helped along by the fact that a lot of the horse-dealers were what the Scots called Erse, and their tongue was close enough cousin to Irish that they could get along. They'd not had room for the whole band the day they'd arrived, but then again, there was something to be said for not having more than a small watch-camp this far in town. The men here were at risk, had to be alert, and were surrounded by temptation. Better to give them short spells of duty at the sharp end, four men at a time, so that they should remain alert and look forward to time out of the stink of the city.

It was Mulligan's turn in charge, and a brief word that there had been no change left Finnegan a moment to order broth and bread and to read the letter from his earl. By the time the potman was clearing the dish away and bringing small beer, Finnegan was more comfortable with the whole business.

"Mulligan!" he called. "You're sure there's no change?"

"Sure, Chief," Mulligan said, "even the woman's stayed in. There was a few of the *cailleacha* from that Committee thing. From the looks his lordship's giving them food and clothes for the poor."

Finnegan chewed his lip a moment. He'd have to get a better description from one of the other boyos. Mulligan's notion of a *cailleach* was anything twenty years and over with tits smaller than his head.

"Would you say that they've settled in a ways, there? Made themselves comfortable with us at their door?"

Mulligan sat himself down. "Now you say it so, Chief, I see that they have. Every now and then there's a gang of them come out to start something, but I think Tully has the right of it that they're doing that to give themselves the liberty to move someone in or out. We've run a man to all of the ways away in turn, but we've not caught the fucker yet. Nothing yesterday, it so happens. For myself, I'm not hopeful. Too many ways out, not enough of us."

"It was Tully saying that the other day that made me think of it. You're to swear to our suspicion that Cromwell's a visitor there, by reason of the attempts to drive off the watch on the place. We'll have a warrant sworn out and then when we're good and sure the man's there, we attack."

"The few of us against a defended house?" Mulligan's voice betrayed genuine concern. "It's about even in a fair fight, not that I'd engage in such folly, but they've stout doors and narrow windows in that place."

Finnegan snorted. "Credit me with more brains than a fuckin' rabbit, Mulligan. We've a town full of folk that hate us for bein' Irish. And here and there, a few Erse who're just as hated and see us as good customers, so they do. Be having a word about which of them is good for a brawl. Tinkers into the fuckin' bargain, they'll stop a bullet with the stink of them if nothing else."

Mulligan laughed at that. "Sure and we don't mean to start a war here, Chief?"

Finnegan glared back. "See the wit of you doesn't choke the laughter, Mulligan. Be about it. And pass the word that any man that feels the need should get his leather stretched while he can, there's like to be a brawl before long."

When McCraith had finished his report, Ducos could barely suppress his laughter. "And this they said where it could be heard by all?"

McCraith nodded. "It seems to me they take no notice of servants."

"A common failing," Ducos agreed. "And they mean to recruit Erse and vagrants and the like?"

"So they said." McCraith twisted his mouth in distaste. "Like calls to like, ye might say."

"By their fruits shall ye know them," Ducos quoted, to a round of affirmations from the rest of the Party assembled. "And it is, I think, past time that the people of Edinburgh saw that."

"Aye," Jamie Fraser put in, "a few o' you laddies around the grassmarket to remark to folk on how much the Irish swine are talking to their fellow papists among the Erse, what say you, Michel?"

Ducos nodded. It was simple, subtle, drew the attention of the people to what they expected to see, and he didn't doubt... "Absolutely, and before long they will be seeing it and remarking on it amongst themselves."

The Gordons volunteered. Their family business would take

them there for the next little while, or at least there as easily as anywhere. They had a small concern in rope and cordage, with a store in Leith and a stall they moved about Edinburgh as the trade went. With summer coming to its highest, there was plenty of horse trading on the greenmarket, and where there was horse trading there would be a need for hobbles and halters and other tack. Nobody would remark on their presence, and plenty there knew their faces. With McCraith watching the Irish indoors and the Gordons without, they would know in good time if anything was to happen.

"When they act, as act they must," Ducos went on, "we must be ready. Whatever they attempt, and our brother McCraith's news is that they mean to attack the Mackay house, can we raise the crowd behind them?"

"Agin popery? Easily," Jamie said.

McCraith coughed. "Agin thievin', drunken papist teuchter horse-copers an' all. I've mair a sense of that locality, and the Erse are no' well liked, no well liked at a'."

Ducos snorted. "This is a truth wherever men gather to buy and sell horses: dealers in horseflesh are never liked. That the horse-sellers here are papists is a providence for which we should be grateful."

There were chuckles at that.

Rab Fraser was next to speak. "I'll do as I can to be in that locality for the next while. I've a wee bit put by if business there is slack." Rab was a carter, a one-man operation with a cart and two horses.

The others turned out to be able to be at least within summons distance, and undertook to be around during their non-working hours.

There were times Ducos missed working for the Comte D'Avaux most heartily, and this was one of them. He had been able to undertake all manner of operations under cover of being the comte's man, often advancing the cause of God while being about his temporal master's business. Now, he had to keep body and soul together working as a porter here, a hired bravo there, or otherwise presuming on the hospitality of the few clergy who were sympathetic to the cause.

Here and now, he, like Rab Fraser, had a store of coin put by for times like this when he simply *had* to be about the Lord's work. And the help he could find was limited to these few who had time to spare from keeping themselves and their families fed. The ungodly saw to it that the common mass of people had neither time nor resources to make their desire to serve God known. A man who found himself a single short pay-day away from starvation could do only a very little to advance God's cause on earth. Ducos was sure it was deliberate.

No matter. It took but a few men and good timing to raise a riot. That they had and more.

Chapter 33

The first thing Darryl had learned about Edinburgh's Committee of Correspondence was that it didn't have a home. Otto Artmann—nobody Darryl remembered ever meeting, but then he'd met a lot of guys—had come over with enough cash that they'd had a house for a while. He'd even made a start on turning it into a Golden Arches, but then he'd got himself into a brawl and died of what sounded like blood poisoning. Everyone he'd recruited had been, apparently, a little old lady, or so it seemed. Some of them were a little younger, and all of them seemed to have a sort of asteroid belt of nieces and stepdaughters and daughters who helped now and then.

What they were doing was basic soup-kitchen stuff. Worthy, helpful, and pretty much what every kirk in the neighborhood was doing. Mackay had been sending over regular deliveries of basic foodstuffs—oats, turnips (bigger than the ones Darryl knew from back home), whatever greens were in season and cloth and yarn to provide charity clothing for the really down-on-their-luck, but from the looks of it, some of these old ladies were Olympic-grade scroungers.

That had to change. Darryl wasn't really what you'd call politically savvy, but even he could tell that the Committee wasn't going anywhere like *that*. Half their trouble was that they'd been cut off from Germany, where the Committee was funded, resourced, and had a deep well of experienced people to draw on.

Vicky had taken one look, rolled up her sleeves and joined

in. For the first day, Darryl did nothing more than lift and move heavy objects as directed. The operation was run out of the homes of the ladies involved, and they all brought their share of the Committee supplies to wherever they were set up that day. Tarpaulins and ropes and spars, and they had an outdoor kitchen.

The second day, he had his tools and was mending and improving all day, and paying a little more attention. Whatever else the Committee in Edinburgh was achieving, they were managing a first-class information network. Some poor guy getting a bowl of soup would talk about *anything* to a motherly old lady that was feeding him. Vicky had spotted it too, and took that information back to the MacPherson house. She and Gayle spent the evening closeted with the radio, in touch with Magdeburg. They emerged with a promise of more help from the USE. A replacement for Artmann, at the very least, who they'd not known was dead, a draft of money to get things running again, and if they could find enough volunteers, a crew to capitalize on the network that was being built.

The third day, Gayle and Oliver came with them. Against advice, in Oliver's case. Darryl was not happy that after all they'd done to get him this far, he was going out and about where he could get caught. Gayle had tried to reassure him with the lack of photography and the fact that Finnegan's men were keeping to the streets around the Mackay house, but he spent the morning nervous as hell even so.

Came lunchtime and the rush over, they had a chance to sit down and talk, all but Vicky, who was in full conversational flow over the half-barrels of hot water they were washing the lunch things in.

"They need more soldiers," Oliver opened with. "One man in three that has come here is a man come back from the Germanies. They say they expected more of the Committee."

"Well, it is kinda low-rent," Darryl said, "but I hadn't noticed that there were that many veterans coming here."

Gayle snorted. "They don't wear a badge, Darryl."

"I know *that*," he said. "I just figured they'd seem more, I don't know, *soldiery*." He knew how dumb that sounded, but the laughter was good. "What I meant was, how come so many soldiers are coming home from Germany? I wasn't expecting to see any, so didn't look, I guess. And I figure there's war brewing over there, so they'd be keeping every guy they can."

Oliver took a moment with his broth. When he'd gathered his thoughts, he said, "Not every man gone abroad to fight cares to remain there. Not every man approves muchly of the USE. Not, according to one man, until he sees how the lack of it looks to him. These are men who have had a purpose and lost it—given it up, rather. To give them purpose anew would be a kindly act. A godly one, even."

Darryl knew better than to twit Oliver about the CoC's politics. The long rides, the sea voyage, there had been plenty of time to just chat. Union solidarity, the CoC's kinda sorta socialism, they'd all come up. Turned out that between the Puritanism, with its healthy portion of primitive Christianity, and the wide egalitarian streak Cromwell had, he agreed with a lot of it. Oh, he didn't approve of the Levellers, not by a long way. But then he'd been a justice of the peace, you could hardly expect him to approve of organized rioting. People looking out for their own and sticking it to the Man? He'd been hauled in front of the Privy Council for doing the same thing himself.

"You think these guys'll take to the Golden Arches thing?" Darryl asked.

"If it's that or starve, aye," Oliver said. "I bid them think on getting involved. On gathering friends. On banding together to see that these ladies can give of their charity unmolested."

Gayle tilted her head at that. "You think that's a risk?"

Oliver grinned. "Not a large one, no. But a fellow who thinks him the guardian of fair ladies doing good, that's a fellow with a good opinion of himself. Who will, as often as not, strive to live up to that good opinion."

Darryl grinned at that. While the floating pool of helpers that the Committee ladies roped in for the busy times included, yes, one or two actual lookers, they generally were only there for the busy times. The stalwarts—Otto Artmann had known what he was doing when he recruited for the soup kitchens—had left *fair* behind decades ago. These days, what was on offer was *somebody's grandma*.

"It'd be good to have more'n me around to do the lifting and the fixing," he said. "How're you going to stop them taking over? Where there's old soldiers, there's old sergeants, and they generally prefer to be giving orders over taking them."

Oliver shrugged. "For the sake of the wider world, a few

men in the front rank will surely not hurt. It is expected. And some of these ladies, I suspect, might surprise some of the old soldiers!" That last with a grin.

"There's also the crew coming over from Germany," Gayle said, "a few of whom are veterans too. It should all work out."

"Okay," Darryl said, "but are you saying the committee here should specifically recruit veterans, or just make an effort with the ones who turn up? Because if I remember what Robert Mackay was saying right, this Montrose guy is kind of afraid of the veterans getting organized. King Charles too, although he's being an assho—I mean, idiot about it."

Oliver nodded. "A good point, Darryl, a good point. One we should bring to the attention of the ladies here, and the gentlemen from Germany, when they decide how to go about it. I, for one, mean to be setting off to be about my business in England soon. This Finnegan must be convinced he has lost me, and I may be off to raise havoc in the Midlands. Did we not have reason to remain and help the Mackays, I would have been off already—assuming Gayle agrees."

"With you, honey," she said. "If I could've figured out anything to do to spring Alex that didn't involve getting Finnegan on our tail again, I'd've suggested it by now. Baron Mackay's plan to make him fizzle out seems to be working, though."

Vicky chose that moment to come over. "News," she said, rubbing her hands dry on a scrap of woolen blanket.

She sat down at a chorus of invitations. "From the sounds, them Irish lads are up to something. And there's a lot of people don't like it. Joan—"

Darryl tuned out the full details of Joan's relationship to, like, everyone else, but she was apparently the one he knew as Mrs. McAllister. He waited for Vicky to get to the actual information.

"Well, she was chatting to a girl who came in with two lovely little kids, and she was in the Grassmarket this morning, where they have the horse fairs, and they have a lot of Romish horse-copers there. Highlanders, gypsies, that sort of people. Anyway, this girl from the grassmarket was selling flowers and apples there and she overheard one of the Irishmen talking to one of the horse-copers, and it was all in Erse so she didn't know what it was about, which she thought was suspicious, and then she got talking to one of the barrow-boys there. I'm not sure from what Joan said, but it sounded like she might have been talking to him because she was a bit sweet on him, but that's not important. What is important is that there are people around the Grassmarket who actually *can* understand Erse and they say that the Irishmen *think* they're being clever when they're not. *Everyone* knows they're hiring the horse-traders to be part of a popish mob and they're going to do something *terrible*."

Vicky stopped for breath. "Of course, half that's probably bollocks, you know what a no-popery mob is like. But if Finnegan needs more men to attack somewhere, like, I don't know, a well-defended town house, it seems like these highlanders are more like Irishmen than Scotsmen. Or at least all the Scotsmen around here think so."

Oliver let out a good, old-fashioned *harrumph* at that. "There's a straw in the wind, if you like."

"Of what?" Gayle seemed to be reading more in his tone and expression than Darryl could get out of either. Although, fair's fair, he and Vicky were bit-by-bit building their own private code. Along with enough of Vicky's London accent rubbing off on him that Gayle and Julie had been making *Mary Poppins* jokes.

"You've not seen a riot against popery?" Oliver's frown was beyond the usual dour Norfolk stoicism and into Old Testament territory. "While I disapprove most strongly of clinging to the errors of Rome, the remedy is witness and reason, not arson and grievous bodily harm. And more often than not, the disorder is stirred up for reasons having nothing to do with religion."

"It happens in Germany, too," Gayle added. "Not seen one myself, but I've read the reports. Not as bad as the witch-hunts, but pretty ugly."

Darryl felt a moment of embarrassment. Mostly he didn't bother with the news if it wasn't sports or military. "So, bad, then?" he asked.

Vicky nodded. "There was a bad one when I was a little girl. Lombard street got wrecked. They'd have called out the Trained Bands, but most of them had joined in. There were hangings, after."

"Well, that was rather more about the banks than the Catholics. I seem to recall that there was a cry raised against secret Jews also. I was at Cambridge that year. It was, as these things go, not a bad one." Cromwell seemed to be lost in memory for a moment. "Be that as it may. Rumors of a popish plot might or might not be true. These fellows that claim to know Erse? It might serve us well to find the truth of that claim. 'Tis pity Mr. Welch went off from Newcastle to the Germanies."

"Sorry," Darryl said. "I learned a few more words than I already knew from Patrick, but just enough to be polite to folks. And count to, uh, four. *Aon, do, tri, ceathir.* Not sure I could spell 'em in Irish, the spelling's weird. Not helpful, I know."

Oliver waved it away. "Come now, and let us reason together, as scripture has it. At best, the rumor of the market place. Full of sound and fury, signifying nothing." He paused, snorted a brief laugh. "I seem to be talking in quotation today. To continue: there really is a plot among the Irish and the Erse."

"How's that not the worst?" Vicky asked, leaning forward.

"If it is a true plot, there is no third plotter. A third plotter we know nothing of. Hence, the worst: that the rumors of popish plot are being fomented by persons unknown. That, I confess, affrights me."

"See your point," Darryl said. "Not sure what practical things we can do to find out, since our only Irish speaker left us two months ago."

"Pay attention among the visitors tomorrow, Darryl," Oliver said. "Offer your sympathy to any that sound like they might know Erse. Or that might have heard a rumor among the horse-copers."

"You want me doing subtle and cunning intelligence work?" Darryl grinned. "You *have* met me, right?"

"Actually blunt and blatant is probably better for this, Darryl," Gayle said. "Give 'em your best Irish Republican firebrand act. If there really is a plot, they'll invite you to join in."

"And here's me with only a little dynamite left," Darryl said.

The next day, the Grassmarket turned out to be fairly short on grass, but well-provided with horseshit. There was a constant stream in and out of horses being traded, and foddered, and the animals that were pulling carts in and out and through and the ones that people were just plain riding through. There were guys with shovels and wheelbarrows, and the stuff was surely going *somewhere*, but not nearly fast enough. And there was the less, ah, solid stuff. And from the looks, the buildings around the edge of the market emptied their chamber pots right into the street. Darryl resolved *never* to get used to that. The shambles at the eastern end wasn't in use today, and Darryl was profoundly grateful. It had rained overnight, so at least the stink was fresh.

Other than the gently sloshing coating of horseshit everywhere, it was actually quite an interesting spot to have a wander about of a morning. Although if it smelled like this at seven in the morning, it'd be nothing short of a save-the-world mission that would get him back here in the warmth of mid-afternoon. And it was promising to be a fine day, too. Vicky had peeled off to check out the peddlers of what Darryl would *never* admit—to Miz Mailey, at least—as thinking of as "girl stuff"—cloth, thread, and the tools for working them. He was browsing a rope stall—can't never have too much—when the stallholder accosted him with a brief burst of lallans that he sort of understood, but not totally.

"Sorry," he said, "but I'm German. I speak English, but I don't really understand Scots. Never have, sorry." It was the cover story he and Vicky had decided on to cover the fact of their strange accents and insistence on English. Hardly anyone hereabouts would have heard a Londoner—*cockney* was something you called them only if you wanted to start a fight in this day and age—still less a hillbilly with a tinge of London.

"Ah, richt," the fellow said. "Ah said, ye're no from hereabouts. But so ye said."

The man was talking slowly and clearly, as to an idiot or foreigner. So it was like that, was it? *Hayseed hillbilly retard, comin' right up,* Darryl thought.

"*Ja!*" he said, figuring he'd play it up a bit. "I am Darl Karzigssohn. From Saxony." It was his right name, near enough.

"Whit brings ye t'em'bra?" the man asked.

Darryl sniffed. "Zu much popery in Germany. I knowed some Scotch soldiers, good Protestants, I am decided to move here. My wife, she is half-English, so we know the English. We do not want to live there." He'd heard enough German guys mangling English to be able to imitate it. The rope-seller had smiled when he'd said "too much popery." *A hit!*

"Oh, aye, too much popery. They have a cardinal, do they no'?"

Darryl nodded. "Zis Mazzare. An American. Zey tolerate. Next it is all must convert. *Achtung!*" He decided he'd better rein it in a bit before he started dropping in bits from old war movies. He'd never be able to keep his face straight.

The rope-seller sighed. "Aye, weel, we've a mort o' the filth here. Look yonder." The man gestured into the middle of the marketplace with his chin. "Teuchter horse-copers. Gypsies. Rootless, wanderin', papist thieves an' drunkards."

"*Ja?*" Darryl said, looking where he was bid. All he could see was a bunch of guys standing around talking about horses. Scruffy lot, but he wasn't generally what you'd call high-fashion himself, so he'd no cause bitching them out about it. "Zis is tolerated?"

"Aye, an' worse. There's popery comin' frae England, the Kirk o' England full o' Arminians the way it is. It's God's ain mercy the king's popish wife wa' kilt, or there'd be worse put on us."

Well, ain't you just the little fuckin' charmer, Darryl thought to himself. Charles Stuart could go piss up a rope for all of him, but wishing death on the man's wife? Darryl had heard first hand about the coaching accident that killed her and crippled the king. You'd have to be a prize shithead to wish that on anyone.

"Are zey plottink?" he asked, hoping that the angry face he was surely wearing would get read as anger against the popish plotters. Rather than as a desire to, for instance, punch this bigoted jackass in the face.

And, oh, didn't that open the whole can of worms. Friend rope-seller, proprietor, Gordon's Cordages, didn't just have an opinion on the subject. He had a whole rack of the things, and took them out and aired every single one for Darryl's appreciation and examination. In fact, once the man got into full flow, Darryl realized that this guy didn't have opinions. He had *peeves.* Whatever everyone else might make of the Protestant religion, for this guy it was the place he stashed his grievances, grudges, gripes and prejudices. And, for sure, it was just a matter of time before the Evil Catholics rose up and murdered everyone in their beds. Irish men in town! Heathen foreign jabber! Plotting! It was like the 250 Club all over again. With a touch more God and Scots and a lot less hillbilly. And, of course, the snide remarks were a bit more original, being three centuries older when this guy made them. Darryl would, at that moment, have bet a healthy pile of silver thalers that the earliest cavemen had been making the same cheap cracks about Neanderthals. He was glad to get away, in the end.

He bought some rope though. He figured he was going to need it sooner or later. Nothing else, he was taking it out of the hands of a likely supplier for the lynch mob.

He met up with Vicky after another half-hour wandering around the market. "Find anything?" he asked.

"Some nice pins, needles and thread, and and I've ordered some twill, since we'll both need winter coats. The stuff they have here is a lot sturdier than what we get in London."

"Makes sense," Darryl allowed as they passed through the Flodden Wall by Cowgate, barely acknowledged by the watchmen on the gate. They were there to collect customs charges, after all. Shoppers walking home for lunch barely rated a halfhearted greeting. "It's colder up here."

"I like it," Vicky said, "at least in the summer. The evenings are longer and, well, you've seen what London's like at the top of summer. *Gross.*"

Darryl chuckled at the up-timer word she'd chosen to adopt. "Julie's rubbing off on you. Should I buy you a rifle?"

She swatted him on the arm. "I'm a pistol sort of girl, silly. Anyway, all I got was the rumor that the drovers and horse-copers are plotting with Finnegan's Irish. Everyone murthered in their beds, the usual." Vicky's shrug managed to convey that this was what you expected of these provincials, and as a London girl she'd be far more sceptical about such rumors. Or that anyone could murder as tough a crew as native Londoners in their beds.

"I think I did a little better," Darryl said. "I bought all this rope from a guy who's probably *starting* most of those rumors. Remember me telling you about the 250 Club jackasses, and the Klan, and rednecks, and that kind of asshole? This guy was the 1634 equivalent."

There'd been a time when he'd have made jokes about pointy tartan hoods, but everyone looked blankly at him when he'd mentioned tartan the one time. There was plenty of the stuff about, but nobody called it by that name. There were lots of little details like that.

"Anyway, I kind of blew him off at the time, just another dipshit with his head up his ass, but then I was getting my knives sharpened, there was this little Irish peddler guy with a grinding wheel. Told him I wasn't really German, I just didn't want all the bullshit that came from admitting to an Irish name. He agreed with me, what with Finnegan's idiots going around stirring up trouble. They've been pretty badly behaved whenever they've come in town, apparently, especially whenever their boss isn't around. And the thing about them recruiting the drovers and horse-traders? It's *true*."

"Well, that's a relief," Vicky said, "Mister Oliver's secret plotter isn't a real thing, then."

"Oh, no," Darryl went on, "that ain't the interestin' part. The rumor about the recruiting started *before the recruiting*."

Vicky's eyes went wide as the penny—farthing or groat in this day and age, Darryl supposed—dropped.

"Ain't that something?" he said. "When Oliver and Gayle get back from helping the Committee, this is going to light 'em *up*."

Chapter 34

Montrose stood to greet his guest. The protocol perhaps called for him to remain seated. The practical politics of the matter meant that insisting on his personal representation of the king with all of the privileges of etiquette that went therewith would be unwise.

Nevertheless he took his seat before he invited Archibald Campbell, chief of Clan Campbell, to sit.

Campbell smirked as he sat, pausing while the servants laid bread and cheese and fruits on the table. "I hope you're not playing any kind of etiquette game, Jamie," he said, "because I *could* choose to take that as you acknowledging me the king's equal."

Montrose smiled back. "Now, now, Archibald. I invited a new acquaintance, and I hope a new friend, to my Edinburgh home that I might have a meal with him and discuss the interesting political issues of the day as between gentlemen of repute and influence. Without all the nonsense of court etiquette. We are not, after all, Frenchmen."

"That we're not," Campbell agreed. "And if I'm to swear on it, a seat at table with stone walls around me seems like a better prospect to meet you, since our last."

Montrose chuckled. "I don't doubt you sent for word of the Americans' rifles too. I've an order with a gunsmith at Suhl for one of my own."

"Aye?" Campbell raised an eyebrow. "Sounds like a useful article for the hunting."

"With any luck the thing will arrive in time for culling the deer. I fancy there's some good sport to be had there." Montrose watched Campbell's face carefully. "Oh, were you looking for some subtlety, Archibald?"

Campbell chuckled. "I was, rather. I wish I'd thought of getting one of those rifles for myself. I'm no great shooter, but from what I hear they're a hunting weapon of rare devising."

Montrose noted that Campbell was not saying aloud that he'd ordered a case of the blasted things for his men to train with, and that at ruinous expense. A one-off gunsmith's piece could be had readily. The products of the Americans' *machine shops* with their interchangeable parts and ammunition? Considerably more expensive to the private purchaser, since the bulk of production was being bought up by the armed forces of the USE and Sweden. Montrose had deemed it not worth the expense or effort, not least because as a great officer of the king of England his order would be treated with greater suspicion than that of a local nobleman, however powerful.

What *had* been worth the expense was the hiring of two or three smart fellows with a little experience in the art of loosening incautious tongues.

It would be some while yet before Montrose had an intelligence office up to the business of a Lord Lieutenant of Scotland—if such a thing were possible, Scots being what they were—but the obvious first target was Campbell of Argyll. Any man who could put twenty thousand men in the field, if he called everyone to his banner that would come, that man was worth watching carefully.

Of course, putting twenty thousand men in the field was all very well, but the list of Campbell enemies was long and their grudges obdurate. Montrose had already had word back from assorted MacDonalds, MacLeans and MacArthurs, to name only the three largest, that they could and would rally in the highlands if the Campbells ever marched. Not, perhaps, Campbell's twenty thousand, but they would be firmly and larcenously in his rear. Up to their thieving highlander balls, Montrose hoped.

Even some of those twenty thousand might be worked on. Lamont of the Lamonts, for one, personally loathed Campbell, and if given half the chance would enrich himself at Campbell's expense. Of course, better still would be no need for such scheming and stratagems, but it made a pleasant thought as he sat at meat with his biggest problem to know that he *could* make that problem rather smaller. Still the occasion of much effusion of blood, but by no means the ruination of the kingdom that a simple appraisal of the matter might suggest.

"Speaking o' hunting," Campbell went on, "has your man Finnegan caught this Cromwell yet?"

"He's not my man, as you know right well, Archibald," Montrose said, carefully soothing the hot flame of irritation that had sprung up in his breast at the mention of both names. Cork's letter had gone some way to assuring him that the tomfoolery unfolding in Edinburgh was not going to be laid at his door. He'd resolved to give Finnegan a week before intervening and having a lawyer appear to move that Finnegan's commission was no lawful cold trod. While it would not do to appear to be prevailing on the bench for a particular result, he could surely make it clear to the gowned laggards that the matter was vacation business and for the sake of public order the courts could sit a day out of term to send the troublesome Irishman back south of the Tweed with his tail between his legs. *Especially* if he was, as rumored, assembling a crew of vagrant ruffians to bring his business to a head. If that wasn't an abuse of *posse comitatus*, the law had no meaning whatsoever.

"Aye, aye, I know," Campbell admitted. "It seemed too ripe a jest to leave unplucked, though. Have you had words with Mackay about it?"

"Briefly," Montrose admitted, grudgingly. It might do some good to take Campbell into his confidence in the matter. Forbearance with Mackay might give the Campbell reason to talk before raising his banners if the king got himself in an uproar again. "And I told him what I tell everyone: I'm charged with peace and quiet north of the Tweed, and if that means looking the other way once in a while, that I'll do. It seems that this Finnegan has no more evidence against Mackay's bastard than one sighting at fifty yards through a cloud of smoke. A drunken pupil of a barrister could raise cause to find *that* not proven. As best we can guess he wants Mackay as his tethered goat to catch Cromwell, who may or may not be lying low about Edinburgh. For myself, I believe the man has got the idea fixed in his head that holding Mackay in the Tolbooth is the thing he must do and he's thought no further than that."

Campbell nodded. "It's not rare that a man gets himself to

folly by a lot of clever steps, aye. Forbye, there's no sighting of Cromwell anywhere but Edinburgh. I don't doubt you've had word out?"

"Aye, over and above Finnegan's," Montrose agreed. "And for all I have every sympathy with you regarding the policy of preemptive arrest that His Majesty executed in England—"

"Rankest folly, and invidious to boot," Campbell snapped.

"As you've always said." Montrose carefully omitted to disagree or agree with the plain words. "For all that there are difficulties which any reasonable man might have with the policy, Cromwell by escaping has become the danger to the king's peace that he never was before."

Campbell shrugged. "The man was turbulent before, I'm told. Required to explain himself before the English privy council. Over a matter of the rights of the common folk, I understand."

"Just so," Montrose agreed. "Such men bear watching at the best of times. After prerogative arrest in which his wife and son were killed? What the man might do in the heat of his grief I shudder to think. What he might do if pursued to a spirit of cold vengeance? Such a man might laugh to see the world burn."

Montrose could tell that that had hit home with Campbell. While the man himself had made no great store of enemies in his own person, he'd inherited *centuries* of grudges against his clan. They hadn't gotten to the position of preeminent among the clans without reducing other contenders or even mere inconvenient obstacles to penury and wretchedness. And while penury and wretchedness were oftentimes remedied by the industry of descendants, the grudges lived on. Were nurtured, nursed and fed. A man bearing such a grudge against a whole nation, especially now that he seemed to have made friends in the USE, was a man who could create the kind of chaos that unmade even the greatest.

"Did you ask me here to discuss Cromwell?" Campbell asked after a moment's thought.

"Among other matters, aye," Montrose said. "I'm sure you have people here and there that report to you. And I saw you had a fine crew of bonny lads about you when last we met. And it would be poor form of me to involve myself directly in Finnegan's misdeeds."

"Aye?" Campbell had both eyebrows raised. He'd not been expecting a recruitment, that was for sure.

"Well, it seems to me that a man who's all afire for the rights of Scotland might take offense at an Irish mercenary serving the English state holding a Scotsman prisoner while threatening a member of the Scots peerage. However felonious this Cromwell is, Finnegan's cold trod is treading all over Scots prerogatives. Would you not agree?" Montrose had come prepared to hedge the matter all about with hints and suggestions. For some reason the imp of the perverse was upon him—Campbell ought not have jested with him, really—and he was spelling it out plain.

Campbell snorted. "I'll grant ye the prize for audacity, my lord Montrose," he said. "And aye, a man in my position could count himself much happier for the likes of Finnegan gone south of the Tweed."

"Now, I'm in no case to make this a lawful command in the king's name, but a charter of suppression making it lawful for one of His Majesty's subjects to act in the name of the king's peace, would that suit you for present purposes?"

"Present purposes being?"

"I essentially want Finnegan gone. Finnegan may gather what collection of drovers, copers and vagrants he may, your pockets are the deeper when it comes to that coin. If that puts Mackay in your debt, take what advantage you may. For my part, I may say that I unleashed you to the task and thus have some favor with the Mackays and through them ease the fears of the Scots serving abroad. I want them to come home sure of the king's peace."

Campbell roared with laughter. "Oh, now here's an equivocator that swears in both scales!" he quoted when he got his voice back. "Keeping the king's peace against the king's own man—"

"He's not and we both know it," Montrose snapped.

"Oh, aye, and how many of the common folk know it? The man unfolds his royal commission more often than he unbuttons his britches."

"The worse for him. A brigand's a brigand, and him being under color of law means I have to step around the law to stop his brigandry. The man's as much an officer of the law as a Border March Warden, without even the excuse of being a born savage—"

"The man's an Irishman—" Campbell grinned.

Montrose snorted. "Aye, and there's Irishmen and Irishmen. This one's got his letters and is at least halfway to being a gentleman. Or do you think some illiterate bog-paddy could carry off the pretense of being a justice of the peace as long as he has? No, he's Cork's man, a hireling throat-cutter with education to make him dangerous. While I'll sign no man's death warrant without lawful judgment on him, should he perish in chance medley, I for one will not weep a single tear. And let Cork learn to keep his ruffians south of the Tweed."

Julie could tell that her father-in-law was agitated, although he was hiding it. She knew he was going through a lot of Tom Stone's finest, and the ease he'd had from the pain was doing him a power of good, but she'd heard that weed could make you paranoid. Did that explain the little tics that were giving his nerves away, or was this guy *really* that important? She chanced asking him.

"Oh, aye, that an' more, lassie," the old baron said, "that an' more. I cannot imagine what brings the man here—a bare quarter-hour announced, at that—and I've surely no notion how I ought to have prepared."

"Can you prepare for a meeting like this?"

A moment's sharp look. "For the mightiest clan chief in Scotland? Aye, prepare, and that right well, for the de'il take him that does not."

Julie gave him a level look. The man needed to calm the hell down, but telling him that outright was, she judged, not likely to help.

He took a deep breath. "But if you mean, as I suspect you did, can a man prepare for a meeting all unexpected such as this, no."

"So Campbell hasn't either, probably," she said, "and I reckon that that tells us something too."

Mackay raised an eyebrow. "Aye?"

"If he's willing to be this close to being rude—" Julie had taken a while to pick up all of the little customs and rules that went with not being able to call ahead before you visited. Campbell was just a hair short of being actually impolite. Which said that, whatever it was, he wanted to keep his manners but it was urgent enough that he was willing to skirt the edges of unmannerly.

"True." Baron Mackay took a deep breath and visibly settled himself. "The most we may do, I suppose, is be calm for the man. He's clearly flustered."

Julie smiled. "Yep. Poor fellow's probably got his panties in a bunch, you've got to calm him down. Get no sense out of him otherwise."

"Panties in a bunch? Och, awa' wi' ye, lassie." Mackay was openly beaming now. *Good,* Julie thought. *The last thing we need is the old boy panicking when he needs to be icy sharp. Probably the political equivalent of buck fever.*

"I'll listen in upstairs, if you turn the radio on. Since Darryl fitted that patch cable, I can get Gayle and Oliver on. Major Lennox too, if he's not out buying horses. I think Darryl and Vicky are doing helping out at the Committee charity kitchen."

"Very well," Mackay said. "All the better if Oliver can be attending. The man has an excellent ear. One of Thomas's boys came by to change the batteries this morning."

"I'll pass the word to Meg on the way out to see that there are refreshments ready for Campbell," she said, and left.

"My Lord Argyll, forgive me for not rising," Mackay said when Campbell entered.

Campbell waved it aside. "Forgive me in turn for the great fash I've put you and yours to," he said, "but my Lord Montrose seems to have the imp of the perverse upon him this day."

"Aye?" Mackay knew that Montrose was trying to carry out several sets of inconsistent orders, and that was apt to produce strange behavior, but enough to have Campbell agitated enough to be paying a call here but not raising his clan's banners...

"Aye." Campbell said, taking his seat. "I take it you're not ignorant of the Irish ruffians and their antics? The pack of *torai* Cork has sent from his lands in Ireland?"

Mackay rolled his eyes. "Alexander in the Tolbooth. Wrong side o' the blanket he may be, but my son for all that, and a bonnie youngest grandchild he's brought me. Taking her nap upstairs at the moment."

Campbell chuckled. "I've a while before I know that pleasure, I'm sure," he said, "but if you'll pardon the lateness, I'll offer my congratulations. I understand you've a fair tribe?"

"Oh, aye, my posterity is fair provided for. Alexander's my eldest, but I've three with my late wife besides him, and all grown and wed. For a wonder, all four are fast friends. I imagine it helps that Alexander did well by himself in the Germanies and so needs not be a drain on my legitimate sons' patrimony. If

I've a piece of advice for younger men, it's to see your by-blows are well-found."

"I'll take that on board, not that I've any I'm aware of," Campbell grinned. He was, especially measured against the older baron, a very young man. Twenty-seven at last birthday, and near ten years married—a loving match with four children already—there was still plenty of time for him to be indiscreet. "And perhaps it's as good a way to introduce the subject as any. Did you hear rumors that this Finnegan is recruiting vagrants as a posse to attack your house?"

"More than rumors," Mackay affirmed. "I've people who gathered it direct."

"Aye, so perchance you've begun to prepare?"

"As well I may, we being watched and all. I've stable-lads and footmen a-plenty, and coin to pay their ruffian friends and relations to stand by for a month or two. And Major Lennox, that has become a fast friend to the family, has friends in plenty among the returning veterans of the German wars. Should it come to conclusions, Finnegan and whatever trash he sweeps up will be roughly used."

"Well, there I can add some hands to make light of the work, since my Lord Montrose spoke with me this morning." Campbell shifted uneasily in his seat. "But that's the thing. I'm as keen to do right by my fellow-man as anybody. And heaven forfend I should miss a chance to have so illustrious a clan as the Mackays obliged to me—"

"—as I'm sure we would be, in mine own person at the very least," Mackay put in, with a grin. Having a care with Campbells bearing gifts was an imperative that left mere warnings about Greeks as, at best, guidelines.

Campbell snorted at the interruption, doubtless as aware of his clan's reputation as any man. More so, for it affected his every dealing outside his clan for good or ill, and in no small measure. "Aye, that's by-the-by. What brings me here hot-foot is the implication of Montrose's action in charging me with this part of the peace of this town."

"He's made it official?"

"As may be. No particular names o' no particular national character were named, but he made it clear that if he were rid o' a particular turbulent Irishman he'd not take it much amiss." Campbell's face turned gloomy as he spoke the words.

"Montrose realizes the full import o' what he's doing?"

"More than likely. I think Cork must have given him some small insult, and Jamie's a prickly wee bastard when he's a mind to be. And it's plain as day he's had no end of foolish orders to carry out from the king. I think he's setting his heels for a good run of pigheaded obdurate awkward Scotsman for the benefit of my lord Cork. Who, let us remember, is entirely English for all he holds an Irish title."

"I don't doubt there's been some correspondence between them over Finnegan's tomfoolery, not least this mummery that he's a justice in lawful cold trod. I've not met the man myself, but the history of him is littered with grievances and grudges. Ireland's the native soil of the man's spirit, if not his body, I think."

Campbell laughed out loud at that. "All of the Erse and the Scots are cousins under the skin, fondly though the lowlanders would like to forget it. And don't think that in my person as *MacCailein Mor* I don't know it in my very bones. The feuds within the Campbells are only a little less fervent than those without. And I suspect that that is how Jamie thinks that this will work. Only I'm no idiot. Did my lord Reay mention I've been in correspondence with him?"

"He did not," Mackay said, although he'd deduced as much from the general tenor of the letters his clan chief had sent.

"Aye, well, there's nothing agreed between us except for the general principle that we're all for the common wealth of Scotland. So, taking note that you're well-found for defense, I'll simply have a band of stout laddies nearby against trouble. And I ask only that you inform my lord Reay that I'm asking nothing in return. Really nothing, not some subtle, roundabout Frenchified way of asking for something in particular. It so happens that I rather fancy the notion of administering a glove across the face of my lord Cork, albeit by proxy. Whatever Jamie Montrose wants by way of silence north of the Tweed, I want more of it by way of meddling Englishmen kept out of it."

Mackay nodded.

"It is more or less only today that I can visit with you, and this briefly," Campbell said, rising to his feet again. "And I shall take my leave with only this: *I can read future histories too.*"

Chapter 35

"He said *what?*" Gayle's voice was loud enough to distort through the walkie-talkie's small speaker. "Sorry, over," she added.

"What I thought, Gayle," Julie said, deciding that proper radio discipline could, for the moment, go pee up a rope.

Baron Mackay was still looking shocked. Campbell had only left thirty minutes previously. "Can you bring the radio equipment here, Mrs. Cromwell?" he asked. "I could well do to arrange a conversation with Lord Reay if such a thing is possible."

"I suppose I can," Gayle said, "but if Finnegan's gearing up for a serious raid it's going to be difficult."

Julie smiled. Gayle had decided not to bother. And hearing herself called Mrs. Cromwell had put a note of real joy in the older woman's voice. "I reckon we can probably smuggle you in in a delivery cart. Finnegan's men don't seem to get excited about those."

"I am not sure I understand this correctly, but is this really so large a matter?" Cromwell's voice was slow and sure. Julie was glad of it. She'd maybe caught a little of Baron Mackay's excitement over Campbell's visit, and a little coolheaded Puritan stoicism was surely not going to hurt.

"Consider what you heard," Baron Mackay said, pulling the mike closer to him. "He said he could read future histories too. And he's a man whose head ended on the highest prick o' the Tolbooth. Where, I remind everyone, our Alexander is currently enduring."

"This I heard," Cromwell said, "and the prospect of a beheading does much to make a man think, this much I know from personal experience. How does it follow that there is some great matter afoot?"

"He was talking to my chief, Lord Reay, head of Clan Mackay," the baron said. "I'd not known that, although I might have guessed. And you may be sure that a man as sharp as the Campbell will have read aye more than just his own fate. I know for a fact that Reay has gone as far as the twentieth century, and drawn conclusions of his own. Conclusions regarding the proper fate of an independent Scotland, loath though the man is to say as much out loud. And then Campbell says he agrees with him regarding *the common wealth of Scotland.*"

"Oh." Cromwell's Norfolk burr drew out that single syllable, freighted it with a trainload of meaning. And Julie realized, in that moment, why Mackay senior had got so agitated over it. "Commonwealth" was an old-fashioned way of saying "state" up-time. Virginia, Massachusetts, and probably a couple of others Julie was forgetting were commonwealths rather than states, although there wasn't any practical difference that she knew about. Down-time, though, it was a word for something a whole lot more radical. A *republic.*

And Cromwell, more than anyone, would know what that term signified here in the British Isles, since in the old history he'd been the man at the head of the first one ever founded. Of course, Reay, Campbell and the rest could insist that they just meant the old meaning of the word, that of the well-being of everyone in the country. Fooling nobody, Julie thought, and probably not even a court of law conducting a treason trial. Since, as far as she could tell from her experience with the Scots legal system, Judge Lynch was on the bench every damned time. It was only the reassurance that Alexander would never face an actual trial that was keeping her from wigging out entirely.

Cromwell was speaking again. "You fancy that perhaps Campbell means to act in combination with your own chief? That Montrose might have begun the war early by unleashing him to this task?"

"Aye." Mackay's tone was grim. "I doubt it'll be some manner of nonsense like the *carte blanche* the French have, but if Montrose wants his hands clean of Campbell's interfering in Cork's work, he'll do well to be little short of it."

"Why does he need his hands clean?" Gayle asked.

"I don't imagine he'd want to be seen to be letting me get free of pursuit," Cromwell said. "for that is what this is. Are we sure that I should not simply let myself be seen elsewhere? It would draw Finnegan off."

"Only if you can contrive to be caught. A man o' Finnegan's intelligence won't give up the trail for less. He'll send a few lads to check any rumor and remain here himself to keep the pressure on us to give you up." Mackay was firm on that. "Our best stratagem to win free o' this is to send Finnegan home in failure."

"You're sure that's what he'd do?" Julie asked. She could sort of see the logic. Although she'd grown to not much care for hunting—animals, at least, and not boar, which deserved it for being so tasty and dangerous at the same time—she knew how to do it. Had done it a fair bit. And yes, once you had a good spot to wait for game, you stuck by it.

"It's how I'd do it," Mackay said, and the brief and terrible coldness of his tone reminded Julie that, twinkly old grandfather though he might be, confined to a wheelchair though he was, this was a man who was a feudal war-leader in a nation not long out of medieval darkness. Sentiment was, for such as he, strictly optional and an option not often available.

"As you think best," Cromwell answered, and Julie caught a murmur over the radio as Gayle soothed him. Underneath the prayerful self-control, there was a powerful temper that almost certainly came out as a cold, clearheaded fury. She'd seen much the same on the few occasions when her own Alex had had to fight. Small wonder that Cromwell had made such a skilled general; in the heat of battle he doubtless got icy calm.

"Darryl and Vicky just arrived," came Gayle's voice, and there were a few moments of getting the two of them up to speed.

"Sneaking the long range set into the Mackay house ain't too hard," Darryl said after a while. "Seen enough peddlers and hawkers and such-like over the last few days, I could walk straight in with the thing on my back easy as pie."

"Finnegan's men aren't looking for me, so there's no problem with me just walking up to the front door," Gayle said. "I've bought enough clothes hereabouts I can dress up as anything from a pauper on up to a prosperous clergyman's wife. And that's before I start in on the cross-dressing."

Cromwell's laughter in the background was a warm-hearted thing. "My wife, a mistress among spies!" Julie heard him say, and she was *sure* that was the James Bond theme that Darryl was humming there.

Finnegan could barely wait to open the crate with the German lettering burned on to it. He'd been savoring the arrival of this package for *weeks* and he could hardly bear it now it had finally arrived. He couldn't believe that there weren't laws preventing the Germans doing this sort of thing, but then, he reflected, there were laws against most of the things he did for a living and it hardly stopped him.

He supposed there might have been trouble if he'd ordered more ambitiously, but he'd not been entirely sure that the earl would stand for much greater expense once they'd missed Cromwell at King's Lynn. With the man caught, he didn't doubt that he'd have been able to ask for enough for everyone. As it was, he had enough for his best men to have a little advantage.

He set to with a pry bar and, with the crate open and reeking of dry straw and oil, savored the moment.

"How many did we get, Chief?" Tully asked. He was the only one he'd told. Raising the heads of the boys with the prospect of the new firearms was a recipe for disgruntlement if the commercial factor he'd gone to had been lying about having a man in Hamburg who could get these things.

"Two pistols and four long-arms. Shotguns, they're called. I'd say that's a pistol for each of us and a team of lads with the long guns. All of them repeaters of the American sort, but made by clever German boys, so."

"It'll be enough? I'm only sure of maybe fifteen of those highland shites, and none of them with guns or the knowledge of using them. Handy if it comes to cold steel, a rare lot of savages indeed, but we need more shooters, and that's a fact."

Finnegan shrugged. "It's what I could get with the spare money from what the earl sent. That lawyer's a robbing *giambin* bastard, so he is, and the lads aren't cheap to feed. I didn't dare ask for more, since we've been this many weeks failing of our charge, but if they're enough to bring success, I fancy there's more where these came from. For the present, though, and fuck my arse for saying this, but we can give the Scots laddies grenades. Culchie bastards they may be, but they can light a fuse and throw, and if there's accidents, better them than us."

Tully frowned his doubts, but didn't object. "Let's see the fancy guns," he said, obviously itching to get in among the straw in the crate.

Once they'd got it all out, there was a pair of pistols—not quite so alien-looking as the ones the Americans had, the German gunsmiths having stuck to what they knew for the most part. The revolving cylinder at the breech seemed obvious enough, and was the only unfamiliar part. The four shotguns looked more like something from the future, though, two barrels apiece and a hinge that broke the weapons open to load from the breech.

None of the weapons had wheel or flint or place for a match, so how they were fired once loaded seemed a mystery. There was a hammer-thing that snapped when the trigger was pulled on a dry chamber, but there didn't seem to be anything between it and the touch-hole that made a fire. The cartridges—big ones for the shotguns and small ones for the pistols—were a thing they had experience of, since some shooters made them up for convenience of reloading. But it was by no means a common practice. The box of little copper things was a sore bafflement, though.

"I think these papers are meant to be a manual of arms for the things," Finnegan said, once they'd been through everything and speculated about it all, and finally turned up a sheaf of printed papers amid the straw they'd discarded. "Make yourself useful and find someone that reads fuckin' German, will you?"

"This is all we have?" Jamie Fraser asked, looking over the collection of dirks and swords and cudgels and two dragoon pistols. None of it looked new. Most of it looked well cared for. Just well-cared for over the course of *decades*.

"If we need more, we have almost certainly failed in the charge God has placed on us," Ducos said. "We are few, and Satan's servants are famously legion. We cannot stand in open battle, so we must favor the indirect approach."

He was sure Jamie understood that, but it bore saying aloud for the benefit of the other men of the Party of God. While he found them congenial company and admirably dedicated to the work of God, within their limited resources, they could be a trifle belligerent at times. Still, better that than sloth and indolence.

Holding them back at need was vastly to be preferred to having to be behind them all the time.

"*Agents provocateurs* it is, then," Fraser said, mangling the French pronunciation.

McCraith chose that moment to arrive. Slightly out of breath, as it happened, and not one of the members of the Party due to assemble for that day's watch; two of the Frasers, the Gordon who wasn't at their stall on the Grassmarket. McCraith had work that day and wasn't expected until the evening's prayer vigil. "Campbells," he said, leaning on the back of a chair while he got his breath back.

Gordon lifted his head from the testament he'd been engrossed in. "Campbells?"

Ducos had rather lost the thread of how the MacGregors, with which name the Gordon brothers had been born, came to be proscribed. The tale had been convoluted in the extreme as told by two men who'd had it as small boys from a long-deceased father. A name that had featured in considerable venom, signaling a grudge that might be considered noteworthy even by Scots standards, had been that of the Campbells. Ducos knew but little of the history of the feud, but the flavor of a truly bone-deep grudge was one he knew well.

"Remember you are about God's work, brother Roy," Ducos warned, "and keep your mind on it."

"Aye, and the Campbells will be about the de'ils work," Gordon retorted with the air of a man declaring that water was, indeed, wet. "I'll have my mind on the task at hand, sure enough, but mark my words we'll have to do scant provoking where those fiends are concerned."

Ducos nodded acknowledgment. "Vengeance is the Lord's, only recall that. Come the restoration of the godly to this fallen world, all will be served as they deserve, no?"

"Oh, aye. Brother Archibald," Gordon said, addressing McCraith, who seemed to be breathing easier, if still a little shiny about the face. "What are the Campbells about?"

"A commission of justiciary," McCraith said, "against tumult and disorder in the town. Nailed up by every market cross. And talk of a braw lot o' the Campbell's own men lodging by the Royal Mile to do execution. The gossip is every which way about it, that's for sure."

"Finnegan's men?"

"Been out all mornin', away at whatever hole they're lurkin' in. If they've heard, I've no' seen sign of it. And neither Finnegan nor that throat-slitter o' his, Tully, have been by the White Hart these three days past. I could wish we had more brothers, more eyes. There's *something* afoot, for sure."

"Robbie's still at the stall?" Gordon asked, receiving a nod from McCraith. "He'll send word should there be aught new."

"Your brother is reliable," Ducos acknowledged. "Educate me, brothers, I know the Campbells are ... unpopular. What is the practical effect here and now?"

Jamie Fraser grinned. "If we're to help the first shot along, having it come from among the Campbells will help. If they're truly under a commission of justiciary, chances are they're no' allowed firearms."

"Really?" Much of the Scots legal system was a closed book to Ducos, although he had grasped that Scotland had far, far less of a state than his native France. Barring a few administrative matters in and around Edinburgh, everything done in service of the Scottish state was done by private individuals. For most practical purposes, the Scottish state had a purse and some law-courts and that was it. And most of the law-courts were simply the local chief nobleman charged with justice in his area. And the kirk ran half of the rest. It made for a refreshing degree of liberty from interference, if a man could but retain an outward appearance of respectability and religious conformity.

"Aye. The old days o' fire and the sword are supposed to be gone, and commissioners are meant to be bringing the lawless back for trial and no' stabbing them on the spot." Fraser shrugged. "Disnae always work that way, and to hear it told it *never* does in the highlands, but that's the idea."

Ducos' curiosity snatched at his attention. "Why not in the highlands?"

"*Teuchters*," Jamie said, with a sneer. "Constant feuding. And starting feuds. And robbing each other. *Papists.* A commission of justiciary is just an excuse to them."

"I see. And these Campbells, many of them are highlanders, no?"

Jamie nodded. "A highland clan. Aye. There're lowland Campbells, and a mort o' Protestant Campbells even in the highlands, but the roots of them are papist *teuchters*. And papist *teuchters* wi' no good name even for papist *teuchters*, at that."

"So nobody will be surprised if they escalate matters?"

"Nobody," Jamie confirmed.

"Then we have a little more shape to the plan we have."

"Aye, we do that," Jamie grinned. "It's pleasant when Providence is so plain in front of our faces. Fair takes the effort out!"

"Still, I dislike a plan that depends so much on reacting to what may happen," Ducos said, "especially with so many actors unknown to me. It is frustrating."

Fraser shrugged. "We've no' the means nor the men to do more. I agree it's frustratin'. But this is the task God has placed before us, we're no' such as may pray the cup passes from us. We've tae drink it tae the bitter dregs."

Ducos nodded, and there was a quiet murmur of agreement from the rest of the brothers present. "You're sure that these Campbells will be blamed for any chaos that may result?"

"Aye," Gordon said, "and we've mair than a fair chance they'll raise Cain o' their own choosing into the bargain. It might be that we've less to do than you're thinking."

"Then let us see that we are armed and ready, and fortify ourselves in prayer tonight. It cannot be long before the moment comes. We may be certain that the people will riot against popery, given only the smallest of prompting. We may hope that between the Irishman, these Campbells, and the Americans with their bloodthirsty ways there will be an effusion of blood fit to rouse the people further. We may be certain that at least one of us will find a position from which to provoke the matter. After all this, we pray that God is our guide and protector in the strife to come."

"Amen," came the chorus in reply.

Chapter 36

Whitehall Palace
London, England

Walking away from his latest meeting with King Charles—encounter would be a more accurate term—it was all Richard Boyle could do not to explode in open profanity. Doing so would probably improve the earl of Cork's disposition, to be sure. Apparently, the Americans talked of something called "high blood pressure" which was bad for you, and Boyle didn't have much doubt that if he could publicly proclaim England's monarch to be the petulant, obstinate, stupid, infuriating jackass that he was, then whatever blood pressure was, his would improve immensely.

If he'd been in private, he'd have done so. But a man in Boyle's position was rarely in private, and almost never when he was about his official business in Whitehall. At the moment he could see two guards in the corridor—no, three; there was another he'd initially missed—who'd certainly hear him. And there were bound to be at least as many courtiers and palace sycophants hanging about who'd either hear him directly or, if they couldn't make out the words, would bribe the guards to find out what Boyle had said.

Uneasy lies the head that wears a crown. That line was in one of Shakespeare's plays. One of the Henry ones, if Boyle remembered correctly, although he wasn't sure. He hadn't paid much attention to the theatre even before his elevation to the equivalent—although he'd vehemently deny it—of France's *premier ministre.*

The same uneasiness was even more true for a head that *didn't* wear the crown but was forced to implement policies and decisions made by the cretin upon whose head the crown did sit. Insofar as the terms "policies and decisions" could be applied to the king's commands in the first place. "Childish whims and temper tantrums" would be more accurate.

Find Cromwell—at whatever cost! D'ye hear me, Boyle? No matter the consequences! The regicide must be brought to justice! I'll hear no more excuses!

And never mind that King Charles had thrown Cromwell into the Tower—and killed the man's wife and one of his sons in the bargain—and kept him there for close to a year. For some three hundred days, he'd had him in a dungeon cell—on any one of which days he could have had Cromwell's head removed. Which his chief minister at the time, Wentworth, had urged him to do.

But Charles Stuart hadn't followed that simple, sage advice.

Why not? Who could say? What sane man of adult age and disposition could fathom the workings of the mind that rested in the king's skull?

No help for it. Boyle would have to send Finnegan yet another letter urging the poor bastard to do better what the man was already trying to do as best he could. Not because the instruction was of any use beyond irritating Finnegan, but because some wretched fawning courtier was bound to bribe whatever clerk Boyle used to pen the missive to find out what it said. And if it said anything other than a pompous and puerile stream of useless commands to one of the most capable and accomplished agents in the British Isles, the king was sure to hear about it.

There were times Boyle regretted his actions in having Wentworth cast down from office so he could take his place. What he found most disturbing was that those times came more and more often.

Please catch the bastard, Finnegan. Before the king forces me to force you to end the silence north of the Tweed.

Government House
Magdeburg, capital of the United States of Europe

"And what about England," asked Hermann of Hesse-Rotenburg, the USE's secretary of state, "now that we've got a cease fire with France? Did you discuss that with the emperor also, while you were in Copenhagen?"

"We spent a fair amount of time talking about it, in fact," said Mike Stearns. "Gustav Adolf thinks we'd be better off leaving the situation with England unsettled, much the way we're doing with Spain. Although his reasons are different."

The prime minister, who'd been almost slouched in his chair, sat erect and placed his forearms on the desk in front of him, with his fingers laced together. From long experience working with the man, Francisco Nasi interpreted the stance as *Mike's not sure he agrees with his sorta-boss but is willing to go along with him for the time being.*

"In the case of Spain," Mike continued, "trying to get a peace treaty would be pointless since it'd be bound to be broken quickly anyway."

"By the Spanish? Or by us?" asked Hesse-Rotenburg.

"Take your pick, Hermann," said Mike. "There are so many points and places over which we'll clash with Spain that I figure open hostilities are bound to re-emerge within a year, at the outside. The emperor shares that assessment. So why waste time and energy trying to get a treaty? Gustav Adolf says he'd rather have his hands completely untied, and while I sometimes think he's a little too bellicose, in this instance he's probably right."

By now, Hermann had become fairly familiar with the prime minister himself. "But you're less sure about the emperor's stance toward England?"

Mike's relations with the Landgrave of Hesse-Rotenburg were not as relaxed and intimate as they were with Nasi—and probably never would be, given that Herman was also the half-brother of William V of Hesse-Kassel, who was a prominent figure in the opposition Crown Loyalist party. But ever since Hesse-Rotenburg had been brought into the cabinet, partly as a measure to defuse political tensions, Mike had followed a policy of including him in all but a few of the trickiest issues. So he gave him an answer immediately and without any obvious diplomatic hedging.

"No, I'm not. There just aren't the automatic flashpoints with England that there are with Spain. The truth is, given that our interests don't really clash that much, it'd be easier for us to keep the peace with England that it will be with France. So why not just sign a formal treaty and be done with it?"

Playing the devil's advocate for a moment, Herman said: "They *did* imprison our embassy, in gross violation of diplomatic norms."

That was something of an overstatement. "Diplomatic norms" in the first half of the seventeenth century in Europe weren't the well-established procedures they would become by the next century. Still, tossing an ambassador—who was the sister of her nation's prime minister, to boot—and her entourage into the Tower of London and keeping them imprisoned for a year went far beyond normal practice except in the wooliest parts of the Balkans.

Mike shrugged. "Easy enough for all sides to place the blame for that on Wentworth. Who's now in exile in Amsterdam and in no position to contest the issue except privately. No, that's not really a sticking point."

Nasi decided to draw Mike out a little further, suspecting that was what his boss wanted. "What is the sticking point, then?"

The expression that came to Mike's face was half a grimace and half a smile. The sort of expression with which one recounts another exploit of a charming but often somewhat reckless cousin.

"You know what Gustav Adolf's like," he said. "There's a man who likes to keep his options open. No, there aren't any discernible flashpoints between us and England *now*. But who's to say what things might look like in a few months, or a year or two? What with Cromwell still loose and the way King Charles is likely to stir up trouble trying to catch him."

He broke off there, and leaned back in his chair. Nasi interpreted that motion as . . .

And let's leave it there, Francisco. Hermann's been told enough that he can't complain in the future he wasn't kept informed. There's no reason to unsettle him with minor details.

Such as the fact that Cromwell had just married an American and had another American as perhaps his closest associate. At the moment, that knowledge was very tightly held. The only person beside Mike and Nasi who knew about it yet was Gustav Adolf.

And whoever he might have told, which might be no one at all and certainly wouldn't number more than two or three.

After Hermann left, Francisco went straight to the point. "So what is it really about, Michael?"

"You know what our emperor's like, Francisco. That man does love acquiring new real estate. When I first proposed the name, Gustav Adolf understood right off that 'United States of Europe' has no inherent limits. Why he liked it."

Francisco nodded. "He wants Scotland."

"Parts of it, anyway. As an affiliated protectorate if he can't get it as an outright province."

"And what about you?"

Mike levered himself out of the chair and went over to the window in his office—the one he liked to gaze through when he was coming to a decision about something. Francisco had never been sure why Stearns found the view beyond to be a help in that process. All the window looked out over was the Elbe, which was one of the continent's more slow-moving rivers and easily its murkiest, since the massive expansion of industry in Magdeburg.

"I haven't decided yet," he said. "On the one hand—as you know—I'm no fan of empires. The human race keeps making the cruddy things and most of them aren't worth spit."

"But not all."

"But not all. The Roman Empire did a lot of good, as brutal as it often was. And I'm too honest and know too much history— now, at least, whatever the blithe innocence of my youth—not to know that the original United States—mine; the one I came from—could easily be described as an empire itself."

"Yes—but one that spread across a continent, rather than conquering it."

Mike chuckled. "Any American Indian would argue that point with you."

Nasi shook his head. "Still not the same. None of the native tribes in North America today have the population of European states or their political solidity."

"True enough, at least with regard to the first point. But nobody—not even Gustav Adolf is *that* ambitious—proposes to overrun Europe." He held up his hand, with thumb and forefinger half an inch apart. "We're just talking about one peninsula on the world's ninth largest island."

With a thin smile, he added: "I looked it up in my almanac recently. Hell, there are a couple of islands in Canada that you never heard of—Baffin and Victoria—that're bigger than Great Britain. Just a little nibble, you might say."

Nasi chuckled. "And they even speak the same language you do, which is so thoroughly corrupting German here in the USE."

Mike's smile got even thinner. "Almost makes you believe in predestination, doesn't it?"

Royal Palace
Magdeburg, capital of the United States of Europe

Not far away, just catty-corner to the Government House on Hans Richter Square, a similar conversation was being held between the emperor of the USE and the two men whom he'd told so far about Cromwell's new "American relations."

Told so far, and probably for some time to come. Gustav Adolf was no slouch himself when it came to playing his cards close to his chest, and he was a firm believer in the *need-to-know* principle. The only people he'd told were Alexander Leslie, earl of Leven and the top officer among the Scot troops serving the Swedish king—as well as the emperor of the USE, although that service was de facto and not formally acknowledged lest King Charles get his easily ruffled feathers disturbed. And a certain officer whom Leslie had introduced as Captain James Mitchell, which Gustav Adolf strongly suspected was a pseudonym. But he hadn't pressed the issue because he thought Leslie was wise to keep everything as far distant from the emperor as possible. By now, certain American idioms had been adopted by those who found them useful, two of them being *cut-outs* and *plausible deniability*.

The concepts were ancient, of course. But there was no denying the new terms were handy.

"There, you say? In the area around Manchester and Birmingham?" Gustav Adolf frowned, studying the large map of the British Isles spread out across the table in the small conference room. The palace was still unfinished, but enough had been done to enable the Swedish royals to live in the palace and to allow the emperor to use it as a functioning headquarters whenever he was resident in Magdeburg. "I would have thought he'd favor the area he came from."

"I think he'll decide it's too obvious and the main place the king's men will look for him, Your Majesty," said Captain Mitchell. "And it's too close to London. By all reports I've gotten, the king—Boyle, I should say—is having considerable difficulty keeping London under control, so he's keeping most of the mercenary troops quartered there. He really doesn't have that much to draw on in the Midlands. And there are a couple of other factors."

"Which are?" asked the emperor. As they all were, he spoke in Amideutsch even though both Leslie and Mitchell were quite fluent in Swedish. But Gustav Adolf approved of the hybrid mostly-German-but-heavily-Americanized new tongue emerging in the USE and liked to encourage it. And he'd discovered that, for whatever reason, the Scotsmen's accent in that language wasn't as bad as it was in Swedish. Speaking outright English with Scotsmen was impossible, of course.

"The first factor is the simplest, Your Majesty. That's where the English Civil War started in"—here the captain made the half-waving, half-rolling gesture that many people had adopted when referring to the bizarre other universe from which the Americans had emerged—"the up-timer history. The second factor has to do with the industry developing in the area, which is already the most concentrated in Britain."

"And this would appeal to Cromwell because...?"

"I'm not thinking so much of Cromwell, Your Majesty, as his two American companions. Whenever that folk—at least the ones who came through the Ring of Fire—set themselves in opposition to authority, the first thing they do is organize unions. And there's no better place in England for such activity than the Birmingham and Manchester area. The McCarthy fellow was himself a member of Stearns' United Mine Workers union. And I believe Cromwell's new wife was, as well."

"Do you think they'd have that much influence on Cromwell?"

Mitchell glanced at the emperor, and then around the room. Gustav Adolf chuckled.

"Stupid question, I suppose—seeing that this very palace we're standing in could be considered the product of American influence. Very far-reaching, it is."

"That's my assessment, Your Majesty." Mitchell pondered the map for a moment and then placed his finger on a site somewhat to the north of the area they'd been studying. "I think we should insert me here, to go back to our initial discussion. That area of England's west coast is full of smugglers, it's taken for granted."

Gustav Adolf nodded. "Very well, Captain. Keep us informed as best you can after you arrive."

"There'll be nothing much to report for a time, Your Majesty," the captain cautioned.

"Yes, I understand. Nothing may come of this at all, in the end. For the moment, you are simply a . . . surely there's a suitable American term?"

Leslie smiled. "Oh, there are any number of them, Your Majesty. Rabble-rouser, trouble-maker, mischief-maker—"

"I'm partial to 'promoter,' myself," said Mitchell, a bit stiffly.

"So it is, then," said Gustav Adolf. "Captain Mitchell, go ye forth and promote."

Chapter 37

There was no denying that Edinburgh was a busy town. To the south, Cowgate had spent the morning so far living up to its name. Some of the cattle had decided, of their own volition, to explore one of the side streets to the north. Cows being cows, of course. Ducos had never been a country boy, but the behavior of cattle driven into the middle of a city was entirely familiar to him. Drovers did their best, but a cow presented with an interesting side street and no swearing drover with a stick to prevent her would go and explore. With enough room to stay out of kicking range, the sight could be quite comical, with the various street vendors shrieking at the animals to stay away from stalls that had tasty greens on them. The huge and shaggy Scots cattle had entertainingly lugubrious expressions as they shied away from the brandished sticks. It was clearly, to the bovine mind, a considerable injustice that they were not permitted to eat after their long journey.

The terrain of Edinburgh being what it was, the streets either side of Cowgate were quite steep, so the cows had left a definite, well, tidemark. Ducos was glad there were no other members of the Party of God there to see him giggling like a naughty schoolboy at the sight. There was a lovely metaphor in it, too. So many people with the brains of cattle, having to be driven to God. Ducos, and such help as he could find, being the drovers.

The Gordon brothers had sent a small boy running with a note that Finnegan and all of his men were in the Grassmarket this morning, which had led to every man of the Party being in the streets. It seemed that today was to be the day. Ducos wondered whether the timing was deliberate; they would surely have known that today was a market day, the streets full of cattle. And cowshit. Had they picked the day for the large number of drovers who would be there to recruit from? Or for the chaos and tumult in the streets? Certainly, any attempt at escape from the Mackay house would be difficult. It was halfway to noon and still there were cattle arriving. And, of course, as the day wore on, there would be cows leaving with those that had purchased them, or as their owners gave up on trying to sell them. Not every cow that came to the Grassmarket ended its days in the shambles at the far end.

It did not do, of course, to assume that everything the enemy did was by fiendish design. Ducos had done well more than once—spectacularly well, earlier this year—by working with enemies who were innocent of all fiendishness and could scarcely design their way out of their own beds. So successfully that he'd had to run clear to the other end of Europe to ensure that he escaped the repercussions. It was too much to hope that he could start quite the same amount of trouble today.

Still, with three factions colliding—two with firearms for certain and the third doubtless able to get them in a hurry—a mob eager for any anti-popery riot that might start and the Party of God looking for ways to help matters along, the prospects for the undoing of Satan's work in the world looked healthy.

"Mister Brown?" Ducos started from his idle musings at the sound of today's *nom de guerre*. It was a small boy, one of the market traders' children who spent their days playing and running small errands around the stalls. Not quite a street urchin, but not far above it either.

"Aye," he nodded, trying not to think about maintaining his accent. The other men of the Party, here and in Glasgow, had teased him about his auld alliance manner of speaking if he was actively trying to sound Scots, and the smarter ones had noticed that he sounded better if he was not forcing the matter. This child was a witness who might survive. Better to say as little as possible.

"Mister Gordon says half an hour. The Irish papist is gathering men."

"Aye," Ducos replied, fishing in a pocket for a groat for the boy. Gordon had probably already paid him, but there was no harm in giving the child a little extra. On those occasions when God's work required His innocents to be sent back to him, Ducos was always regretful. Not enough to turn him from the task, though. When the Spirit was on him his resolve was always sufficient. "Run along wi' ye," he said, "and if there's trouble, hide."

Wide eyed, the youngster nodded and ran off. The child was in God's hands now.

It was but five minutes before a raucous cheer sounded from the Grassmarket. Loud indeed, to be heard over the commotion of the street. Good, Finnegan was moving. The rest of the Party would be moving about the crowd left behind, making comments, asking pointed questions. A Scots crowd that had seen known papists mobilizing their own kind was a powder keg, and it would take only a few sparks to flare them up.

"Please excuse my tardiness," Baron Mackay said to his guests, "there are times when my infirmity is more than I can stand."

"Think nothing of it," Cromwell said, one stoic to another. The baron knew that Cromwell's prayers surely included him and his welfare, and his strength of spirit. The man was, however, undemonstrative to a fault. His cool, measured sympathy was the widow's mite; small, but the more valuable for being all he would give in public.

Gayle was the summer to Cromwell's winter, the warmth of a countrywoman and her heart on her sleeve. Her face was soft and caring, the woman's strength having the heft and solidity of good sandstone masonry. "Baron, honey," she said, a form of address that never failed to raise a smile with him, "don't you fret about taking your time. Anyone that says different surely isn't worth minding."

Mackay chuckled. "Surely I'm one who says different. I'm no more fond of making excuses than I am of being slow to greet good friends. My men say that the streets are fortuitously clear today?"

"Not an Irishman to be seen," Cromwell allowed, frowning slightly. "I must admit I wonder whether this means Finnegan is up to something?"

"Doubtless," Mackay said, "since it seems he's about the

Grassmarket and has been since morning. I learned for myself only some moments ago, or I should have had you warned. I trust my daughter-in-law was well on the way to the Tolbooth last you saw her?"

"Walked her to the door ourselves. Andrew's guarding her himself, although," Gayle was grinning as she said it, "none of us are fool enough to tell her that. He's just along to see his old regimental officer."

Mackay had no trouble picturing Julie's reaction to being told she needed a guard. She might not be quite such an avenging fury with a pistol as she was with a rifle, but it'd be a brief and painful business trying to exploit the difference. "Then we know she's doubly safe. Oliver, I'm afraid you may be right. There's a mort of ruffians and villains to be found on a market day at the Grassmarket, and my lads heard a lot of Erse being spoken. I've had the boys begin preparations, but it was aye too late to warn you off."

"What might they be about?" Cromwell had risen and gone over to where his buffcoat was over a chair. There were pockets in the linen lining with American-made pistols, and his sword-belt was there too. He might not have the warlike experience of the Cromwell in the future histories, but the man had no inclination to shirk a fight.

"I'm sorry to say any answer I might give would be as rhetorical as the question. We had word yesterday that with the legal term beginning next week, young Alex is first in the list for hearing. It seems the judges have run out of reasons for delay. And I don't doubt that Finnegan has noted that, from time to time, we drive off his men. Even the biggest fool would see the pattern, for all we keep him from seeing you arrive or leave. I think he hopes to catch you here. Again, I am sorry we were unable to warn you in time."

"Think nothing of it." Cromwell had his pistols out and was checking them. Mackay watched, honestly curious. He was no stranger to firearms himself, nor to the other tools of war, and had had a chance to examine the weapons his son and daughter-in-law had. What he was curious to see was how a man with such a short time in touch with the future arms handled them. Well, it seemed, but then a man as serious and diligent as Cromwell might be expected to imbibe a manual of arms without difficulty.

"Part of the trouble was that my lads finally managed to follow Finnegan back to his lair."

"Aye?" Cromwell raised an eyebrow as he finished his drill and tucked the pistols back in his buff.

"Aye. He's taken most of an inn at Balgreen for his lodgings and for his men. I've sent a lad with a message to Campbell's men."

"They're to go straight there?"

"Here first," Mackay said. "I felt it best to be ready here first, and then take them on the riposte."

Cromwell nodded. "And if we wait for Major Lennox and my lady the baroness to return, our force becomes the stronger. Gayle?"

"Yes, honey?"

Cromwell blushed a little and smiled. "Does Mister McCarthy have his radio?"

"He does. You want him here?" She pulled out her radio and began tapping the Morse button with Darryl's call-sign.

"That I do. My lord baron, might I have the command here?"

"You expect trouble?"

"Aye. Mayhap I shall be wrong, and thereby embarrassed, but I'd sooner blush than bleed."

"You've a fair amount of sense for an Englishman," Mackay said, grinning. "Aye, take command."

At that moment, Thomas burst in without knocking. "It's yon bastard Finnegan!" he said, snarling out the words. "He's at the door, wi' all his men wi' him. And a richt braw crew o' ruffians besides!"

"Darryl's on his way," Gayle called out. "Calling Julie now."

"Stephen?" Darryl felt like everything was both far away and very close at the same time. He'd no idea how long he'd been talking on the walkie-talkie with Gayle. The connection had been a little crackly—something to do with Edinburgh being on top of big, heavy, dense rocks and if you weren't on top of the ridges, you got a crappy signal. A lot of repeating and read-backs and he finally got the message. *The Mackay house. Under attack.*

"Darryl?" Both of the Londoners spoke at once. Vicky with more concern, Stephen with sharpness. Damnedest thing, it was the sharpness made him focus.

"Mackay house. Finnegan's got himself a mob and he's attacking. They've called for Campbell's men." They'd sort of guessed something like this was going to happen, but not so goddam *soon*.

"Orders?" Stephen barked.

"No," Darryl said, realizing why he felt a bit adrift. He'd no idea what to do. Running scams and pranks with Harry, he'd been fine improvising when it dropped in the pot and the wheels came off the plan they'd made. Usually not much more of a plan than "hold my beer and watch *this*," but that counted, right? Right. Now, he had to decide. Or Stephen had to decide. Someone had to decide, and he had no idea who, or what had to be decided.

Stephen snorted. "They'll have a better idea soon. Best we can do is get near. Arms, Darryl."

"Arms? Right, arms." He patted his jacket for his pistol, grabbed his bag from behind the soup-kitchen counter and made sure of his sawed-off. He'd a rifle, but that was back at the Canongate house, no good here. Another rummage in the bag; a box of shells for each weapon. Down-time make, a good brand. Quality could be spotty, but the good makes were starting to be known.

"Check everything!" Stephen barked.

Halfway through clearing and checking his pistol, Darryl realized what the grizzled old—*man was the wrong side of thirty-five, for Pete's sake*—Warder had done to him and chuckled. He'd been doing proper care of his guns since he was in short pants. The movements, the checklist, they were all like breathing. About the only thing he was nearly as sure of was a gear check before he went underground, and he hadn't done that in the best part of four years. *Okay, panic over. There's a reason that guy's been wearing sergeant's stripes all these years.*

Stephen was doing the same. His weapons were a little more brutal. He and Darryl had done a bit of improvising and he had a partisan with a screw-on head. When the head was in its leather sheath and tucked away in a bag, Stephen was about town with a particularly heavy-duty walking stick. With which he was not much less lethal than when it was assembled. Darryl had seen him and Cromwell sparring, Cromwell's singlestick against Stephen's staff. It was a blur, and for all Cromwell's skill at the sport, he'd never landed a touch. Apparently that stuff in the Robin Hood movies about Englishmen and fighting with sticks was still the straight goods in the seventeenth century.

They could manage with guns and swords, but they surely did love their blunt instruments.

And the bill-hook Stephen carried was a gardening tool, nothing more. Albeit a gardening tool that was two pounds of forged steel with two wicked edges, a sharp point to the hook and a sturdy handle. He called it a brishing-hook and, in a pinch, he could trim hedges with it.

He'd accepted Darryl switching out the wheel-locks on his pistols for cap-locks and he was priming those. He wasn't, generally, a shooting kind of guy. Or, much, a weapons kind of guy. They'd gone for a couple of drinks in Newcastle during their stopover there. Darryl had seen the man start and end a fight with a single headbutt. Without troubling to put his drink down. He'd not spilled a drop. The pistols seemed to be mostly just in case he couldn't be bothered to walk all the way over to someone he wanted to hurt.

Vicky had her medic bag open and was checking the contents. She'd done it that morning, because there were always a few people coming to the soup kitchen with minor ailments and injuries who'd heard about what they called "Germany medicine," but she was following her uncle's lead. Go through the routine before the panic sets in. Without spilling a drop. Hopefully, Vicky's bag of tricks wouldn't be needed, nor her year following Rita around and learning. Nor, he *sincerely* hoped, the little .38 he'd talked her into tucking into the bag at long last.

"Here, let me go over that for you," he said, his own pieces checked, loaded and holstered.

"I'll be fine," she said, chewing her lip as she counted things for the second time.

"You're still a learner." He picked up the gun and flipped open the cylinder, with the barrel pointed with exaggerated care into the soup pot. No sense not demonstrating clearly for her sake, now was there? Especially since he wasn't sure about his hands not shaking. *Damn* he hated when he wasn't the one doing the acting instead of reacting.

Like a good learner, she waited until he was done—seconds, at most—before grabbing him for a kiss. "For luck," she said.

"For luck," he grinned back.

"If you two sweethearts are *quite ready?*" Stephen inquired, quirking an eyebrow at his niece and Darryl. *Yeah, Londoners and sarcasm.*

"You got a plan?" Darryl asked. It wasn't like he had one to offer. He'd spent the last couple of minutes just plain spooked.

"Go there," Stephen shrugged. "See what happens. Listen for orders."

"That'll do," Darryl said. And, after all, if it came to anyone holding his beer and watching, Stephen sure wasn't going to spill any.

It should have been a ten-minute walk to Cowgate and the side street where the Mackay town house was. It was a little less than that to the crowd around the entrance to that street. The streets of Edinburgh were narrow, crooked and overhung. Even if the crowd was only a few hundred—and there were cattle in there, just to make sure there was plenty of bullshit to go around—they were enough to mean there'd be at least hard shoving to get through. And tossing a few fireworks around would stampede the cows, damn it. People would die.

"How many did that bastard manage to recruit?" Darryl wondered aloud.

"Enough to start a riot," Stephen growled, suddenly very much Sergeant Hamilton. "Vicky, stay behind. Darryl, give her the radio."

"Don't look like a riot just yet," Darryl said, discreetly dropping the walkie-talkie into Vicky's bag and standing close to hide her sneaking the earpiece in. He wasn't hearing shooting or screams or even yells. There was some shouting up in the distance. Mostly the people who could see were doing curious-bystander stuff, craning to see over the heads of the folks in front, finding stuff to stand on. He was pretty sure he spotted a pickpocket, too. "Can we get round through the alleys and such?"

"Do you know the way?"

"Kind of hoped you did," Darryl admitted. "We going to push through?"

Stephen stopped to consider it. "I don't want to be the first to strike blows here," he said after a moment. "You're right, this isn't a riot, yet. A broken head or two and it will be. Vicky, call Mistress Cromwell and ask what's happening."

Vicky had her hand over the side of her bonnet, concentrating on the hidden earpiece. "They're calling for the baroness and Major Lennox from the Tolbooth. Finnegan says he has a warrant, and a posse to do execution. They have guns and he's threatening grenades."

"Oh, fuck," Stephen groaned.

Darryl felt his belly go for a loop. Not just because the bad guys were talking about throwing explosives—he had a few short ends of dynamite in his pockets himself, along with gunpowder squibs and a homemade smoke bomb—but because if Stephen was losing his cool, things were *really* in the shitter.

He took a deep breath and stopped to think. They needed to either take Finnegan's party in the rear, or get into the Mackay house to help the defense. There was another way to the front of the house, back up a street, but the chances of Finnegan leaving that undefended enough for two guys and one girl to actually assault were limited. If there was another way, none of them knew it.

On the other hand, there was a house behind the Mackay place, one that had a garden wall they could surely get over. It was pretty imposing from the Mackay side, but that was nothing they couldn't handle with enough rope, and he'd made sure he had a good stock only the day before.

"I got a plan," he said out loud. "House behind. Let's get up to the High Street. Vicky, see if you can raise Julie or Major Lennox. If they're still at the Tolbooth, they can join us."

Stephen nodded. He'd needed very little to work out what Darryl intended, and said nothing as he turned back to find another route up to the High Street.

Chapter 38

Tully had, notably, a dry wit, and it was making Finnegan want to find a bucket of water for him to dampen it a bit. They'd gotten a crew of ruffians from the area—men who'd been paid off from cattle-driving and thought a few more pennies to drink would be a fine thing—and marched them up toward the Mackay house.

Tully had been the first to look back.

"I think we've more Scots than we ordered, Chief," he'd said. "Do we have the money to pay them all?"

Two or three gallons over the head. "God love you and all your little jokes, Tully. If they want pay, it's coming out of your money. Get a picket out, guns and blades. Stop them down the street."

Tully had clearly been about to cap his wit with another line, but saw the look on Finnegan's face. "I'll, ah, be about it. Our boys or the Scots?"

"Half and half," Finnegan snapped. "Ours for a steady line, them for the thickening of it."

"Right." Tully turned on his heel and began yelling orders. He wasn't helped by the tendency of the drovers to mill about, cudgels over their shoulders, not troubling to pay attention until someone shoved them. Finnegan's own troop were nobody's notion of tidy soldiers, but they could look sharp when it was to the purpose.

The Mackay house was on the outside of a sharp right-hand corner in the street, leaving him with plenty of room to get the rest of the boyos dispersed, and only two avenues to picket. There were back entries on either side of the house, but no way out that didn't come to the front. Edinburgh's buildings were tight and close together; very little of the town spared space for such things as alleyways nor closes. The Mackay house shared a mews with their neighbor to the right, allowing horses and carriages in and out, but that and the small passageway to the left that led to the servants' entrance were all the ways to the rear. The back of the house was against the rear wall of the house behind, which was the residence of one of the city's doctors, and on higher ground, so there was no convenient escape that way. A daring rescuer might get in by that way, but the time it would take to climb back out meant Finnegan felt safe discounting it. He meant for this to be over within the hour, and he had a couple of lads waiting in the high street, watching for any escape attempt that way. The wall at the back wasn't quite the barrier that the old king's wall to the south was, but it'd do.

He looked and saw that Tully was taking good advantage of the narrowing of the street where the old wall had been cut through to let this street down to the Cowgate. There was a crowd building back there, as the mob that had followed from the Grassmarket caught up and began to thicken. Someone was shouting about popery, the usual Protestant blather, but the Protestant religion wasn't the one that, here and now, had guns and blades ready to hand.

And, fuck his arse for getting into a place where he needed them, grenadoes. He'd put O'Hare in charge of the handful of hired thugs who'd been fool enough to volunteer and been big enough lads to trust to throw straight. A questioning look, and O'Hare nodded. There was a slightly sickly look on the man's face, which was to the good. A man that was comfortable around bombs was an *amadan* of no small measure. Or mad entirely, like the late Cooley brothers.

Another swift look around and he was sure he had enough space to be able to work. Getting away again looked like it might be a dainty morsel of a problem, but nothing a willingness to break heads wouldn't cure. The Tolbooth was but a short walk away, and the mob would be at his heels, not in his way. And now, for the look of the thing, he'd to demand surrender. "You and you," he said, pointing at two conveniently near and burly drovers who'd not yet been tapped for any purpose. "With me.

At my shoulders, look ready to fight but not a peep without my order. Understand?"

Two nods. Clearly men who understood the business of intimidation, and doubtless had had a coin or two for standing around being large and menacing in their time. Both had stout blackthorn sticks, tools of either trade they followed.

Finnegan had his own *bata* and knocked on the door. "I have a warrant for the arrest of Oliver Cromwell, who I verily believe to be in this house!" he shouted. It'd surely be shaming if he was wrong about the Mackay servants picking fights to cover when Cromwell arrived and left, but weeks of sending his boys about town had turned up no hint about where the man might be lying low. Extravagant offers of reward had produced nothing.

The door didn't open, but a window above did. A woman's head came out. "Open the door, woman!" he shouted up.

He caught maybe one word in three; he'd got something of an ear for the way the Scots spoke, and was fairly sure he'd been told to go black his arse.

"I have grenadoes, if you don't open up!" he shouted. "Tell that your master. I'll wait his answer."

He turned to the two drovers. "About what I thought," he said, "now let's step away, she's the manner o' aiteann who'll think of chamber pots."

He was three paces away when the sound of a splattering turd confirmed his guess. He wasn't such a fool as to think that was the only one she had, so took a few more steps before turning. "A fuckin' shroud on ye, woman!" he shouted. "Grenadoes!"

"We've a child in here, ye papist de'il!" the woman shrieked, apparently out of crocks of shit to throw.

"Then open the feckin' door!" Finnegan roared back, feeling his temper rise.

All he got in answer was the window slammed shut.

"Lallans," one of the drovers growled, adding, in the dialect of Gaelic they had, that the devil's cat couldn't shit worse than any of them. At least, that's what Finnegan thought they said, as close as he could follow it. He heartily agreed with the sentiment though.

"Irish or Erse," he said, "we'll have the joy of breaking their heads before morning's out."

✧   ✧   ✧

"She's walking properly now, not just holding on to the furniture. Into *everything*. The child," Julie said, firmly, "is *curious*."

Alex grinned. "Up-time or down-time meaning?" he asked.

"Both," Lennox put in, with a grin. "The pair o' you, breedin'? A wonder the bairn hasnae kilt' a man yet."

Julie wasn't sure whether to laugh along or find something to throw. Alexi was *her* daughter, it was her exclusive right and privilege as a mother to make fun of her. "Give her time," she said when the two menfolk, father and honorary uncle alike, had stopped hooting with laughter at the lame joke. "And the day she gets her first BB gun, I'm pinning targets on both your britches. Keep up with this malarkey, I'll pin 'em on the *front*."

Lennox immediately dropped his best noncom's deadpan in place. "No' laughin', ma'am!" he barked out.

"See you don't," Julie said, suppressing the giggles she could feel bubbling up. The pair of them were doing their best stony-faced soldier, the corners of their mouths clearly fighting the oncoming grins.

"So," she said, once the pressure looked like it was getting the better of them, "Monday."

"Aye, Monday," Alex said, "Mister Home has no great worries. A deal o' talk has been in quiet corners, he tells me, but the gist is that he's confident that whatsoever judge we get, they're all determined to stick strictly to the law, which is in our favor."

Julie smiled. She'd tried to read the papers and pleadings, an honest best effort, but the mangled jumble of Scots and Latin had defeated her. In school, languages had been her weak spot. She'd never had a problem with science and math, got by with English literature and sort of muddled through with history and geography, but there seemed to be a part of her brain that just didn't want to deal with anything that wasn't plain English.

On the other hand, she'd found that learning German had been surprisingly easy when she was doing it by talking to folks, so maybe it was just a mental block on the academic side of things.

"I can't say I understand any of it," she said, "but I gathered that much. We've got everything packed up and ready to go at Mrs. MacPherson's. We make a big public production of heading down to Leith for the next ship to Hamburg. As long as Finnegan's distracted, Oliver can head out of town. He figures the Figgate Muir road is the way to go, he'll be setting off while the rest of us are in court. He has a route planned to take him down as far as Carlisle and he's going to make plans for the rest of England once he gets the lay of the land there."

Alex nodded. "Darryl still means to go with him?"

"Yup." Julie nodded. Somehow Darryl—as Irish-American as they came—had ended up friends with Oliver Cromwell. Months of traveling together would do that, even for personalities as radically different as theirs, and the pair of them had grudges against King Charles you could probably see from space. Feuding was apparently a thing English country squires did just as well as hillbillies; maybe Darryl would learn to be as classy about it as Oliver.

"Haud on," Andrew said. "Signal." It was his turn to have the earpiece in today. While down-time workshops could make the things no more than a fraction larger than their up-time equivalents, they weren't as comfortable as the few that had been brought back in time. Wearing them for any length of time was purely a chore, so they took turns. With the court hearing so close, there was a chance—Julie thought not a big one, especially with the Campbells taking an interest—that Finnegan would—

"Attack at your father's house," Lennox said, his soldier-face suddenly becoming the real thing. "We're directed to return, M'lady Baroness."

"I'm coming," Alex said, rising. There wasn't a hint of emotion on her husband's face but it was dollars-to-donuts his mind had gone to exactly the same place hers had. *Alexi.*

"Your hearing's Monday!" Julie snapped. He'd been in here most of the summer and a good chunk of the fall—and now, losing it over less than half a week? Not if she had anything to do with it. And no sooner were words and thought formed than she realized that she couldn't ask him to remain behind, not with news like that. If she was going to go all mama bear, she had to respect his right to ride to the rescue of Daddy's Little Princess.

"I'll return when it's o'er," Alex said. "There'll be a fine, at worst. Home will cluck like the auld cock he is, but there's no' a judge drawing breath would see me hang for going now."

"How are we going to get you out?" Security in this place wasn't, as far as Julie could tell, worth a damn, but there were guys on the door who'd object. She found herself feeling the weight of the pistol she'd carried. She'd taken to wearing loose vests over her dress to hide the shoulder rig; the fact that it was a great way to accessorize didn't hurt any, either. She'd even gotten pockets put in for clips and mags and loose shells. She hadn't seen any imitators, yet, but give it time.

Andrew reached inside his coat for a small cloth bag that chinked. "The guid baron bid me carry a bag o' shillins, they'll open any lock in this place. The more so when the laddies on watch mind that the colonel here is to be freed Monday." He grinned. "It's a broken man indeed that cannae leave the Tolbooth, m'lady Baroness."

Baron Mackay was never more glad that the medical products from the Lothlorien apothecary had a calming effect to them. While hearing that his own filth had been hurled into the street by way of insult to the Irishman was apt to bring the schoolboy in him back to smirking life, Meg had managed to make a bad situation worse. Cromwell had planned to send Thomas out to inform Finnegan they took no cognizance of the warrant; any delay to argue the matter would give time for the situation to go out of the man's control by his own efforts. Time, too, to prepare better defenses.

One of the maids had brought report of the business with the chamber pot, a business that would surely spur the man to be about his business. Cromwell glared icy disapproval at Meg as she reentered the back parlor. Gayle was trying to keep her mirth under control as she listened for any signal from the radio, and the rest of the house was a tumult of noise and banging as every male servant in the place—of age for a fight or not—was heaving furniture into the front and side rooms to form barricades. The furniture in the back parlor was heaped below the window that gave on to the mews, the first to be built and already with two of the stableboys posted as lookouts.

There was even the sound of hammering as the servants' entrance was nailed shut; the kitchen furniture would be dragged across it. The passage wasn't wide enough for even the strongest man to have enough room to batter the door down, not with stout timbers nailed over it and furniture behind.

If there was to be an assault, it would come from the front of the house or the side, through the mews. The side was, Cromwell had estimated, the more likely approach. To the front, Finnegan was busy holding back an angry crowd who were the merest provocation from being a riot. Cromwell planned to shoot from the upper floors as soon as the assault began to spark *that* powderkeg. Any assault from that quarter would soon be swept away in a press of angry bodies, and Finnegan would surely know that.

Assaulting from the side would permit a shrinking defense against the mob that would stop at the choked entrance to the mews that would hold the riot at bay until the fight was over.

"Do you know your neighbors to the rear?" Cromwell's voice was icy, almost eerily calm. Mackay took reassurance in that; what little soldiering he had done had taught him the value of such men.

"Dr. Scott," he said, after a moment trying to recall the fellow's name. "Quite the fellow, among physicians, or so my own man tells me. We're acquainted, little more."

"When the barricades are done," Cromwell said, "I mean to put fellows to finding ladders. That wall to the rear is fifteen feet at the least. I fancy it might be less on the uphill side?"

"It is at that. It was rebuilt perhaps twenty years ago, when my own father was still alive. He and Dr. Scott's father fell out over the matter. As I recall, it came close to lawyers, and closer still to blows. Our respective mothers persuaded the two old fools to see sense." Mackay smiled at the memory. He and his father had had no warm relationship; they'd exchanged hot words over Alex's birth that had barely cooled to the merest civility by the time the old man had begun making a show of himself over property boundaries, of all things.

"I'm afraid we may trespass on Dr. Scott's garden before the day is out," Cromwell said. "I mean to have the female servants take young Miss Mackay over the wall as soon as may be. Perhaps a couple of the younger boys, as honor guard. Gayle, perhaps you could pass word to my lady baroness? If she could come away from the Tolbooth and intercede with the good doctor, I should count myself considerably obliged."

"Sure thing, Oliver," Gayle said, taking up her instrument to pass the message.

Cromwell nodded. "Send word with one of the boys there when you know. I'll take myself upstairs where I can see better, and send the women and girls down." He pulled out his pistol and checked it again. "I shan't waste words telling you to go along,

Gayle. But know that I would think no less of you for going, if you choose. And that, if the good baron will pardon my speaking frankly to my wife in his presence, I love you."

"Love you too, you exasperating man." Mrs. Cromwell was smiling broadly, a little bright in the eye, as she raised the little radio to her lips.

Mackay gave her a moment to collect herself. To his entire approval, she did it by speaking crisply and directly to—from the sounds—Major Lennox. He wheeled his chair over to the spot she'd taken beside the window, out of sight of anyone looking in. The boys who were peering through gaps in the barricade of furniture were plainly embarrassed by the whole display, judging by the bright red their ears had gone. They had eyes fixed straight forward. They weren't going to see the grown-ups getting all maudlin, no sir. It was all Mackay could do not to laugh aloud.

"Wullie?" Gayle said, when she was done. "Upstairs and tell Mr. Cromwell that Major Lennox sends to say that his message is received and understood, and that the party at the Tolbooth have met up with the Misters McCarthy and Hamilton. They were going to break in from the rear anyway, but they'll cover the escape as they do so."

The boy dashed off, dodging around a stream of servant girls who Meg was chivvying along. The lot of them looked like they were looking for somewhere to hide, and it was no wonder. Edinburgh could be a rough old town—there wasn't a street that didn't have at least one at least slightly disorderly ale-house or inn. Men in the street with guns and grenadoes, though, was going a bit far even for Leith, let alone the streets just off the Royal Mile.

The last of the girls was carrying Alexi, who was struggling to be let down, or to come to her granddaddy, the child wasn't clear as to which. "Bring the child here a moment," Mackay said. "Meg, you can wait a while. Have the girls wait in the kitchen until the ladders are ready, and let the wee girl wait with me."

Sat on her granddaddy's knee, the girl settled, immediately resolving to have a pull of his moustaches. He blew on her nose, and sucked his lips in to make his beard bristle, and got the proper reward any grandfather wants: the child's laughter. The tumult and trouble outside could, for the moment, go hang itself for all he cared.

Chapter 39

"Right you are, Mrs. Cromwell," Andrew said, "we're on our way."

"Word?" Darryl asked.

Julie thought Darryl looked more than a bit spooked. Wasn't so surprising, at that. He and Harry Lefferts had always been up to stuff. Having to respond to other people being up to stuff probably wasn't natural for him. Even the lunacy he and the other men had got up to around Norfolk had been their plans, their initiative. Vicky was holding on to his arm, looking like she was being all girly and nervous, but Julie knew Vicky Short a whole lot better than that by now. She exchanged a significant look with the other girl.

Darryl was actually having to be brave for the first time in his life, rather than just reckless. *Do him good,* she thought. Thinking about Darryl's troubles kept her mind off the horrible little burning ball of worry that was under her heart, white hot and melting down through her insides like a red-hot musket ball through warm butter. *Alexi.*

"Same plan you had, except we ken who the householder is now," Andrew said. "A Doctor Scott. Your father's acquainted, Colonel, and your supposition about yon wall's aye richt. They're readying the servant girls and wee Alexi to come over to us."

"And here's me with plenty of rope. Let's hope it's enough," Darryl put in. "Say, Colonel Mackay, ain't you supposed to be in jail?"

Julie noticed that his voice was clear and firm, so maybe she was being oversensitive about how spooked he was. "He made bail," she said, "nearly official." Which was, after a fashion, true. The jailers were fined if their prisoner didn't show at court, and Julie entirely meant to drag him there Monday come hell or high water. The bribe was almost like paying a bondsman, and she'd be her husband's own personal bounty hunter. Fortunately, they'd gotten friendly enough with the guards that it hadn't been that hard to sell. And maybe there was a certain amount of *don't-fuck-with-me* flashing out of her eyes right now.

"I fancy that's the house," Hamilton said, nodding toward a three-story town house that looked well kept, but old even for Edinburgh. He was idly screwing a big spearhead onto his walking stick, a fancy-looking thing with points and blades all over, like the Yeoman Warders had in the tourist photos back up-time. Here and now, it didn't look like any kind of ceremonial thing. Man could probably shave with it.

"Aye, that's the Scott house," Alex said. He'd had no weapons with him, but Hamilton had lent him a vicious-looking eighteen-inch hook thing that Julie couldn't quite recall the name of. Probably not as good as the saber that was back at his father's house, but better than nothing. He was keeping it straight down by his leg. Not alarming the public or frightening any horses, but ready for use.

Julie checked her pistol was in its right place inside the coat she was wearing. Not her rifle, but it'd do until they got home and she could get to work. There were some fuckers going to *die* for putting Alexi at risk. Or, maybe not die, if things didn't get out of hand. She wasn't going to be entirely scrupulous about kneecaps, though. *Especially* not if they let her stop to think about it.

"Let's go to work," she said, striding off and not bothering to wait for the rest. She figured she'd have a head start on convincing whoever was in the house by being young and female. She'd stand behind none of the guys when it came to being dangerous, but she was well ahead of them when it came to looking unthreatening and nice. Not, it had to be said, a high bar to clear when it came to Stephen or Major Lennox, both of whom looked like they had Rottweilers in their family tree.

"With me, Vicky!" she called over her shoulder. If the situation called for cute and unthreatening, might as well double down. More than double; Vicky was smaller and politer, and more conventionally girly, and didn't look like she'd spent her early teens training up for athletic competition. Wasn't nobody going to make her back down, neither. But for just talking? Vicky was as unintimidating as a girl could get.

"You hear that?" Vicky said as she caught up.

Julie cocked her head. There were four guys stomping along behind her, and the ordinary street-noise of a busy town on a market day, but—*there.* "Crowd noise," she said, coming up short. The guys stopped with a crash of boot heels behind her, apparently having fallen into the role of heavily armed goon backup on sheer reflex. She suppressed a snicker and stopped to listen again. "Gayle said Finnegan brought help."

"There was a crowd too," Vicky said, looking worried. "You think it's gone ugly?"

"Hope not, but we better move," Julie said. Vicky's concern was valid. "You got your gun?"

"And my aid bag," Vicky said. "Rita trained me the one, Darryl the other."

"Here's hoping you don't need either," Julie said, and thumped on the door with the heel of her hand.

"Here's hoping someone's in," Vicky retorted, shuffling back to stand at Julie's elbow. *Loyal retainer position,* Julie thought, amused a little in spite of herself, as the distant sounds of someone coming to the door began to make themselves heard. Apart from Darryl, the five with her were all down-timers and understood about appearances and how someone could be made to look like they were in charge. They were following her lead naturally, like a dance they all knew even if they'd never done it together. It was a bit like a senior officer having his staff and aides with him: he was important enough to need staff, therefore the fact that he had staff made him look important. Damn fool thinking, but useful here-and-now. Bavarian Fire Drill, Tom Stone called it, although Thuringian Fire Drill was a better name for it with *this* cast of characters. And, what was more, having the retinue kind of made her *feel* important, too. She stood up straighter, and went for a haughty lift of the chin. Watching Melissa Mailey in action was paying off.

The door opened, and a shortish, round-looking guy in a dark green suit peered around it. She sized him up. No obvious professional dress nor the sort-of-academic gown doctors and lawyers wore. The clothes were good, but not obviously expensive, and well-worn. Since doctors earned good money, even compared with their twentieth-century equivalents, this guy was a servant. Senior, though. Not a big enough house to need a butler, but definitely the top manservant. Secretary, possibly?

"Yes?" the man said, quavering a bit. Not surprising. Imposing-looking woman with four goons and a maidservant. Man had been blown clear out of his comfort zone the moment the door opened.

"We need to get to your back yard," Julie said. "There's trouble at the Mackay house and we're to rescue the women and children. We're going to bring them over the back wall. Inform your master." She just had to hope she'd got that part right.

"Ah—" It was all Julie could do not to burst out laughing. Entirely out of the ordinary, but a woman being so blunt about trouble coming to his master's door? Especially since it was a woman talking about rescuing the women. Man was bound to be confused. If only she had a camera right now! Miz Mailey would be purely overjoyed at the story that led up to that expression on the poor guy's face. *Feminism, meet seventeenth-century manservant. I'm sure you'll get on famously.*

"And," she added, "by way of introduction, I am Baroness Mackay. Please, we're in a hurry." She added her best haughty glare. No idea if it was the right mannerism, but she could probably get away with it. Foreign peerage, if someone called her on it.

A long and awkward pause. "If you'd do me the honor of coming in, my lady, I'll summon the doctor—" He stepped back and held the door to one side having gabbled all that out in a rush. "First room to the left, if you would, the doctor is with a patient at the moment. If I might inquire, where are you a baroness?" He didn't sound Scots, now she listened to him. Maybe he was thinking it was a bit of Scotland he'd never heard of?

"Sweden," Julie said, striding in as briskly as she spoke. *There, that ought to cover it if I've got it wrong. Rude foreigner, that's me.* Also, worried-as-hell mother. Which covered it even more efficiently. Couldn't push too hard, though, or they'd get no help. Just plain forcing the matter would probably work, but it'd take longer. *More haste, less speed.* This was for Alexi.

A moment and they were all in a simply furnished drawing-room. "I think he might have fallen back on procedure a bit, there," Julie ventured, when the little guy had bustled off.

"Fussy wee Englishman," Alex agreed, grinning, although the smile wasn't reaching his eyes, quite. "No' sure how tae take the grand Swedish baroness."

"Hush, you," Julie said, "I was *improvising*."

"Jazz, nobility style," Darryl cracked, his smile a little less forced. Now things had moved into active shenanigans, he seemed a lot cooler, which was to the good.

"Y'did richt," Major Lennox said. "Heinzerling had a plan much like it, in Rome. Forbye I was pretending to be a Polish nobleman. Ye made a better fist than I did, my lady. Genuine article, o' course. Bound t'help." He was grinning like a loon. Clearly happy for someone else to be doing the improvising. Outside of combat, where Alex assured her the man was purely an artist, Major Lennox was the last guy you'd expect to be comfortable getting all free-and-easy. He was not, to borrow Darryl's joke, a jazz kind of guy. Lots of brass and marching in a steady two-four time.

"Well, assuming the good doctor's happy to help a bona fide baroness-in-distress, or at least a baroness in a hurry, are we all set? Major, can you radio in progress so far? Find out how things are."

"Aye." Lennox fished in his pocket for the handset, and stepped away to talk to Gayle.

There was awkward silence among the rest for a moment while they eavesdropped on Lennox's side of the conversation, before he turned back. "Mrs. Cromwell says ye'll ken what a Mexican standoff is?" he asked.

Julie and Darryl both snorted. "Sure," she said. "Everybody's armed, nobody's making the first move. No idea why it's called a Mexican standoff, I think it's a movie thing, but that's what it is."

"We've time, then," Alex observed. There was the hint of prayer in his tone. *Amen.*

"Still have to be quick," Stephen said. "Situation like that can turn ugly, quick as you like."

"What situation?" came a new voice, this one Scots-accented, but clearly cultured in tone. "Forgive my bluntness, but I understand you are in a hurry, and I have patients awaiting me."

Dr. Scott was an oldish man, short and gray-bearded, in a dark-red suit with a white ruff and a black gown with a square-cornered cap on his head. About normal for a physician in this day and age, he was dressed as the senior academic he'd qualified as. Dr. Abrabanel wore a similar outfit when treating patients, confusing the hell out of up-timers until they got used to the lack of a white lab coat. This guy, though, looked like a medieval Obi-Wan Kenobi. There was, actually, quite the resemblance with Alec Guinness.

"Doctor," Julie said, stepping forward and offering her hand, hoping to get some sort of command of the situation. *Before he tells me these aren't the droids I'm looking for, at least.*

She was briefly befuddled by him taking it and bowing low over it; up-timer handshakes had caught on fast in Germany, but this was old-fashioned even for down-time. *Old guy, right,* she thought.

"My lady Baroness," he said, straightening from the bow, "how may I be of assistance?"

"I'm related, by marriage, to the Mackays, your neighbors to the rear. I received word that there is rioting in the street to the front of the house, and Baron Mackay wishes to rescue the women and children from his house. Over your garden wall, if we can?" Julie hoped like hell she was getting the balance right between noble entitlement and polite request. She didn't want to get the guy's back up by either offending him or making him suspect she was running some kind of con. Sure, she was a gen-you-wine baroness, but not in the way of being born to it, which *counted,* damn it.

"I have, of course, heard of my lady the baroness," the doctor said, smiling pleasantly, which Julie took as a good sign. "And of your relation to the Mackays. And, indeed, of the unpleasantness that the Irish justice from England has brought to Edinburgh."

Julie nodded. These people lived without television. *Of course* the gossip was going to go around. "Whatever that Irish *person* may be up to, he's got no business raiding a house with girls and children," she said, "one of whom is *my daughter.* Do you want my word we'll not help fugitives escape?"

"Oh, far from it, my lady," the doctor said, waving the thought aside. "While I'm no lawyer, even I can see the man's not likely to get more than short shrift in a courtroom. Besides, here I am, overcome by the Swedish peerage and her large and warlike retainers..."

It was, come right to it, a good excuse. The fact that he was smiling at Vicky for the last bit about "warlike retainers" kind of took the sting out, too. The guys had noticed. There were snorts of laughter.

"You're a gentleman, and that's for sure," Julie said, trying not to exhale in relief.

"Och, I do try, my lady, I do try." The good doctor turned and shouted over his shoulder. "Spall! See the baroness and her people to the garden. And find them ladders!"

He turned back. "Forgive me if I return to my patients, my lady? I see you are well found for strong hands to help, but if you need more, Spall can turn out the rest of the servants."

"Thank you, Doctor," Julie said, choking down the urge to hug the guy.

Five minutes later they had a ladder up against the eight-foot rear garden wall, and Darryl was at the top tying it down somehow. Since it was going to be used by women in skirts, that made a lot of sense. Over the other side there were, apparently, guys fixing something up for the much higher climb on that side. Spall and another of the doctor's men were fetching another ladder, Darryl was going to use that one to give them a means to rappel down. It was a short drop, but it was bound to be easier to slide down a rope. Seventeenth-century fashion to the rescue again—Julie had gloves everywhere she went. Good strong ones, for when she had to ride. The guys all had big hefty gauntlets for the same purpose.

The sound of the crowd was much louder here, without street noise to mask it. From the sounds, things were still tense, but there wasn't much change. Waiting for the rope-work to get done was wearing on her, no matter how much she told herself it needed care and attention. Five minutes to think about things, and her thoughts kept coming back to Alexi. Sure, there were plenty of what Lennox would call *braw wee laddies*—some of them not that wee; the Mackays seemed to hire their manservants by the hundredweight—between Alexi and trouble, but she knew how messy things could get. She wasn't the brash teenager insisting on getting into the fight that she'd been three years ago. She'd seen the elephant, to borrow the old-timers' phrase. Thing was, she'd always been confident she could keep real trouble out past a hundred yards. She'd trained hard at that distance when she'd had biathlon ambitions, nearly as hard as the competition-standard fifty meters. Taking down targets rapidly at either range was second nature and when she'd started doing it against live targets it was easy enough to just see the enemy as simple round targets that would flip color when hit. *Crack-crack-crack*. She could *feel* the weight of her rifle in her arms. Alexi was in that mess. She had to get in there; nobody was getting close to her little girl.

"My lady?" Alex called out, interrupting her death-spiral.

"Colonel?" Julie had no idea why it was suddenly all formality, but it seemed right. *He'd know what works in situations like this*, she thought, *he's been a soldier for years*.

"Major Lennox has word that the girls are ready."

"McCarthy?" she called up.

"Squared away, ma'am," Darryl said, sketching a salute and swinging down for the short, arms'-length drop to the flowerbed. "I'll have the rappel rope fixed in a jiffy."

"Major? We want the girls now, youngest first. Give the radio to Vicky when you're done. Vicky, stay here to make sure nobody's hurt, come in if we call. You might want to take a moment to hitch your skirts now." Julie began working on her own attire, helped by the fact that she had up-time cut jeans on under her dress. The autumn weather was cool enough to make it worthwhile, since it even let her get away with lighter skirts. And it also meant she didn't have to ride sidesaddle, a skill she'd never learned and didn't want to learn. She'd not anticipated needing to rappel down fifteen feet of garden wall, but it was sure going to come in handy for that too.

Alex stepped close. "Julie, love?" He cleared his throat. "I don't mean this any way but the practical, but come last. If this becomes ugly, 'tis close work. Not your kind of fight."

She got a flash of rage and her first instinct was to slap him, but then the words sank in. It actually *was* the sensible way to do it. If Alexi was going to be safe, it was with a paternally enraged soldier standing in front of her, and three likewise-protective honorary uncles taking the fight to the enemy. "Sure," she choked out after a moment, "but your first job is *get Alexi out*. You ain't as good with that thing as with sword and pistol. And if it comes to crowd control, Stephen's got the right tool for the job."

He nodded.

"Rappel's ready, the girls are comin' out," Darryl called, the ensuing *Geronimo!* losing something to the thick stone wall in the way. Hamilton was next, handing his spear butt-first over the wall. Alex was close on his heels and she could see that Lennox was done passing the radio to Vicky. He'd be next, and then Julie could get in.

It was as Alex was swinging his leg over the wall that the gunfire started, the whistling, popping sound of down-time pistols, closely followed by the crack-crack of a more modern gun.

Screams.

The full, wolfish baying of an angry crowd about to surge.

And then, startling her so much she nearly fell, an *explosion*.

Oh, Jesus.

Alexi.

Chapter 40

It was only the direst of self-control that kept Ducos from hopping from foot to foot like an excited little boy—that, and the sobering weight of the pistol inside his coat that anchored him down. For all that the Party was operating without benefit of sufficient numbers or even a particularly well-settled plan, things were working out well. The crowd was swelling and thickening nicely, now the Irishman had set men to picket the street. Nobody wanted to be the first to try conclusions with armed men.

There was murmuring and muttering. *Popery. The king's men.* The earl of Cork was being mentioned—an Irishman himself, it was assumed, and Ducos wasn't about to correct anybody on that point. As far was the crowd was concerned, Irish meant Catholic as surely as sunrise meant east. And the Irish and the highland Erse were of a breed for popery, to borrow a phrase that he'd heard three times already this morning. One of the Gordon brothers was being busy with that one, if Ducos was any judge. English had never been his strongest language, and he had not yet even half a year's familiarity with the Scots dialect, but he could already tell that their turn of phrase was unique. Almost, in fact, poetic.

Jamie Fraser shouldered his way through to the spot Ducos had found where the uneven fronts of two houses had made a sort of alcove, perfect for lurking. "He's knocked a' the door, Michel," he said, "and had a pot o' pish for his trouble."

Ducos snorted. "The baron himself?" *There* was a sight that would have amused the schoolboys in the crowd, a baron in all his dignity, hurling down a chamber pot.

"No, more's the pity. Some wee wifie as does for him." Fraser grinned back. "No' that it makes any great odds to a man drenched wi' pish. Time to start?"

"It is," Ducos said, "find your place. I shall fire first."

"I ken the plan, as do the other men o' the Party," Fraser chided him, and peeled away into the crowd.

Ducos began to peer over the heads of the people in front of him for a way through. There was a natural tendency for people at the sides of the street to find things to stand or perch on for a better view, and while the crowd was not yet so thick as to make movement impossible, sneaking up the sides was definitely blocked. If nothing else, there were boys using window-sills and doorsteps to get a vantage, most of them taking advantage of the crowd to shout rude words at the men blocking the street.

And not just the naughty boys; there was plenty of barracking, and the men lined across the street—mostly drovers in their plaids, but with buffcoated soldiers here and there among them—were wooden-faced with self-control. And, doubtless, not a little fear. If they were rushed, they would go down hard under a rain of fists and boots, however many they could drop with wheel-lock and sword and cudgel. Ducos had seen such when crowds rioted; the victims were seldom beaten all the way to death, but suffered long in the dying over the following days. Those that died were the lucky ones. The ones that lived, lived crippled. It would be a rare man among the men to the front of the crowd that would not know that. They would not hesitate to shoot, to strike hard, to kill. They would have bare seconds to break the crowd, should it surge, or they would surely die.

He began to work his way forward, putting the morbid thoughts out of his mind. The sides of the street were stone-paved, at least, and the step between that and the packed gravel of the street naturally left a gap in the crowd. It was the work of a few minutes to get to the second or third rank facing the line of troops, and Ducos was glad to see that the stub of an old city wall protruded into the street and left a recess that provided good cover.

Not immediately, though. The smoke of the shot he was about to fire could not come from cover that might be investigated. It had to come from the press and now-uncomfortable jostle of the crowd. He unbuttoned his coat and worked his right arm out of the sleeve, holding his coat shut with his left. The pistol came to his hand, a reassuring weight he could now hold concealed by his right thigh.

A moment on tiptoes—one of the Frasers was a few feet to his right, another he caught a glimpse of from a little farther on. All, as he had instructed, at least two bodies back from the front. Still a position of some risk, if and when the men to their front returned fire, but they had at least a chance.

The roar of the crowd was growing louder: whistles, hoots, catcalls and bellowed insults coming thick and fast as the thickening press of bodies gave the constituent ruffians heart to hurl more abuse. It was still possible to pick out what might be going on a few yards up the street, just around the corner, though, and the shapes of men gathering against the front of the house ready to assault the narrow mews to the right were visible.

It was when he saw them move that Ducos knew that the Irishman was committed to his attack. He let his coat fall free, canted the pistol barrel forward to point between the legs of the men in front of him, and fired.

The crowd bucked and heaved around him as the pistol discharged, someone screamed, and there was a mist of blood in the air. A man in front of him began to buckle, as a pistol-ball to the leg will do to a man. More shots—men of the Party adding to the havoc—and the screams were overtaken by roars of rage.

Ducos knew what *had* to come next, and stooped as though to see to the wounded man who was toppling to the front of him. *Into thy hands,* he silently prayed, as more shots came, at least one some bizarre roaring thing that might be one of the new guns that the Americans made. The falling man collapsed outright as his head burst entirely, and Ducos felt the side of his face sting and burn as fragments of the man's skull flew apart. *Surely* one of the new guns.

Playing the part of a frightened victim to a nicety, he dived to his left and found sanctuary in the lee of the castle wall, watching the crowd recoil back from the musketry to their front.

From here, either in panicked flight or murderous assault, what the crowd would do was known only to the wisdom of God.

✧   ✧   ✧

Even through the mellow cheeriness of the medicine he'd taken, Baron Mackay could feel the tension. Every face in the room—the women servants who had not fit in the kitchen, Meg, and Mrs. Cromwell crouched in the corner listening intently to her radio—was creased with tension.

From outdoors, the sound of men running back and forth, doubtless readying an assault.

Behind that, the roar of a crowd turning ugly. Only little Alexi, sitting in her grandfather's lap, seemed oblivious to it all, alternating playing with the lace on his cuffs and the ends of his moustaches. Meg was hovering nervously, clearly anxious to be on her way with the child.

"Baron?" Mrs. Mason looked up. "They're nearly ready at the back wall. They say to send the girls out, youngest first."

Mackay nodded an acknowledgment. "That honor's yours, Alexi," he said, holding the child up for Meg to take. As he lifted his granddaughter, he called across: "Have them run one at a time, best they be as quick as may be without the shelter of the house."

Gayle nodded and rose to her feet to organize that, repeating the instruction into the radio as she did.

The movement seemed to tell the wee bairn to take note of the trouble, or at least the loss of the security of grandpa's lap made her mind it. She grabbed hold of his sleeve and protested. "'An-pa!" she shouted, and the indignation would have been, another time, comical.

"No, Alexi, go awa' w' Meg," he said, softly and with as much soothing as he could put in his voice.

"Aye, wi' y' auld Meg," Meg added, taking her cue from the baron to soothe the child.

Again, the bewilderment and indignation would have been funny to behold, were it not such a terrible business they were about.

"I'll get the girls moving," Mrs. Cromwell called out from the kitchen door. "Come through with Alexi quick as you can, Meg." With that she was gone.

"Awa' wi you, child," the baron said again. Meg had taken hold of the little girl, and he had a hand free to disengage the fistfuls of sleeve she was holding on to.

From outside, the sound of gunshots. Meg jerked and cringed

away with Alexi in her arms, and that was enough to set the child off. She was wailing for her 'an-pa and kicking her feet. Meg would have bruises, sure enough.

"Aw, hush y'greetin," Meg said, hoisting the child up on to a hip and hugging her tight. "I'll be awa', God mind ye, Baron."

"Aye," Mackay answered. "Urge the girls on, and mind ye go quick. Mister Cromwell thinks they'll try to force entry by the stables, and do they burst the garden door, well. Mind ye go quick."

The crowd had started to roar all the louder, and there were more shots. Some were sounding from inside the house, now. Cromwell had proposed not to fire unless fired upon, which meant it had begun. Nothing through the side of the house, here, though. The shooting must be at the front, to keep the defenders from sallying. That or one of Mackay's own servants had taken it on himself—aye, there was the sound of Cromwell's voice bidding someone not shoot. *Someone* would be frantically reloading with words of stern admonishment in his ears.

The business in the street with the crowd was surely turning ugly, too, and he allowed himself to hope that Finnegan's plan to assault the house would come to nothing even before Campbell's men could arrive. No man could be fool enough to think he could carry an assault with a baying mob at his heels.

That hope was dashed with the sound of a modern firearm from upstairs. Mr. Cromwell had clearly decided it was time to shoot back in his own person.

"Will ye move along in there," Meg's voice came from the kitchen door, and Mackay didn't catch the response. From the sounds of it they were having trouble getting everyone through. One at a time across the open garden, if there were bullets flying about, and some of them would be balking.

Mackay offered a silent prayer that the girls' nerves be strengthened. That was his *granddaughter* they were holding up.

Both of the boys at the barricade under the window were peering tensely through gaps. "They mean to come in!" one of them yelled, one of the younger lads from the stables as Mackay thought it.

"They'll no manage," the other said. "We've cudgels enow for this windae," and sure enough, the lad had a stout billet. There was enough furniture piled up that a man trying to climb over could be held up and knocked back with a stout blow from an active youngster.

Where are those Campbells? he wondered. It had surely been half an hour since he sent a lad running, and that before Finnegan had made his way fully up from the Grassmarket.

It could surely not be long, surely not. As if to answer the hope, the men outside showed precisely how they meant to come in.

"Grenadoes!" one of the boys yelled, looking back with fear-widened eyes to where Mackay sat.

More cracks of modern fire, and a yell from outside gave hope that one of the scum was off to his proper reward.

And then a shatter of glass and a streak of smoke from a burning fuse, and the middle of the room saw an iron sphere land, bounce, hit the hearth-stone, bounce back and spin to a stop with but an inch of fuse.

Meg and Alexi were still in the doorway to the kitchen.

Those two puir wee laddies were looking at the thing, their eyes wide and shining.

Aw, no. No' the bairns.

Mackay couldn't say where the strength of arm came from to hurl himself out of the chair, nor the grace that let him fall on the infernal device. There was a terrible, terrible moment. He *knew* what he'd done, *knew* he'd put his broken body to smother the burst of the grenade, but there was a terrible agonizing torture of hope that he'd smothered that last fraction of the fuse—

He had no notion of how long the terrible thump in his gut scrambled his wits for. Somehow he was on his back again, no breath coming but the merest gasps, the sight of his eyes filled with the cracks and crazing of a tiny patch of ceiling.

He saw his son's face rush in to the diminishing circle of his sight, felt a strong hand lift up his head.

"Oh, Father," the lad said. He dared not look at the length of him sprawled on the floor. It was starting to *hurt.*

"Aye, son," he said, "my son," and went to sleep once more.

Alex Mackay closed his father's eyes. The rest of the man was a ruin. *More* a ruin. His clothes below the waist mostly blasted away, the terrible wasting of his legs—they would waste no more—revealed. Small wonder he'd kept them hid under rugs and blankets. The middle of him was all—gone. The room a shambles with his guts. A few places where shards of the bomb he'd smothered got out. One had gone clear through the kitchen door, there were hurts among the girls in there. *They* had rushed out so soon as they'd recovered their wits, cringing from the men coming the other way.

Darryl had peeled off to help the defense in the stables. Alex had meant to go with him, but then the explosion had sounded. And he had come in to find the life's blood of his natural father splashed about like—like. No, rhetoric was a mere beggar here, and would not be admitted. His natural father's blood had been spilt under his own roof. By an infernal device that he'd given his life to smother, lest Alexi perish. There would be a *reckoning*.

"He threw himself on it," someone said, one of Thomas's boys from the stable. There was wonder in the lad's voice. "We'd surely be deid, had he no'." The tone was not wondering, but worshipful, for all it had the loudness of one recently deafened by a great report.

Hamilton and Lennox had taken over from the two lads when they'd burst into the room. By some miracle the grenado had not struck either boy with a fragment, though both had nosebleeds, and they'd risen as wee heroes to guard the window. Men had thundered down the stairs to join them repelling the assault, to drive back the party seeking to enter the front rooms of the house, likewise wrecked with grenadoes. They'd held, and when the survivors of the first defenders recovered their wits, drove back the enemy. The fools hadn't thought to drop their bombs in *front* of the barricades, to clear them.

Outside, all was chaos and yells. And shooting. None of it seemed to be coming this way.

"Julie's rifle!" Alex yelled at the lad. "Box in our bedroom. Painted green. Fetch it!" His tone was enough. The boy took off like a started hare.

It couldn't be more than moments before Julie would arrive. She'd be distracted by Alexi's hurt—hardly at all, the child wasn't but scratched, although Meg would need Dr. Scott where she'd shielded the child with her back—but after that she'd come wanting blood and Alexander Mackay would put the means in her hand with no small amount of cheer.

At the window, Hamilton and Lennox had shown the assault party that discipline and years of experience told in the face of numbers. Two corpses were now part of the barricade, both men had a fine collection of scratches and soon-to-be bruises, and neither had given so much as an inch. Both were covering the ground outside with still-smoking pistols, the attackers having retreated for the moment.

Somewhere, a crowd was roaring, and guns were firing.

Cromwell's voice: "I did not foresee the grenadoes," he said.

Alex looked up. "Who would?" he asked. The filthy things were rare enough in siege-work, when the brutal business of a defended breach called for their use. They were part of the reason the first party into the breach were called the forlorn hope. To use them against a home—there had been a child, here. But for—no. He stood up. He would not think of it.

Cromwell's face was ashen with shock. "Your father bears a martyr's crown," he said. He plainly knew it was no comfort, and Alex loved him for the honesty of his face, even if the words were as nothing.

"We'll no' see his like again," Lennox said, not looking away from the window. "Yon rabble are fightin' their way out."

Hamilton fired, once, twice. "Not that bastard," he snapped out.

"Guid shooting," Alex said, assuming as much. A pistol shot, at a brief target: it was certain to be worth a compliment. How many times he'd seen friends fall, taken refuge in such commonplaces. Never had he thought to say such over the ruin of his father. He was the oldest of his father's sons; the old man, *his* old man, was—had been—old. Not one who was supposed to see a battlefield again.

"The servants held the morning room and the parlor," Cromwell said. "We accounted for several from the upper windows before they could throw the grenadoes. I know not how many died from the ones that were dropped."

"Alex!" Julie came in. "Meg's taken Alexi out. They're helping her over the wall to Dr. Scott. I'm getting my rifle." Her face and voice were calm, serene.

"I've sent for it."

"Finnegan dies today."

"Aye." Why argue? She had the right of it.

Outside, the crowd was screaming.

Chapter 41

There was a pain in Finnegan's right ear that told him he was going to be at least hard of hearing there forever. Every part of the plan had been good, right up to the point where he just went ahead with it while there was an angry mob breathing down his neck.

It could still have worked, but apparently someone inside the house knew his business better than Finnegan did. Oh, he'd had a moment of utter rage at the inbred up-country cow-fucking collection of bollockses for not carrying the breaches, but then his own lads had been in and driving them, and done no better. How many were left?

That milk's spilt, stop crying. "Tully! O'Hare! Mulligan!" He had no idea what his voice was sounding like, those were the three he could see. Hopefully they could hear—

All three looked to him. His mind went blank. Most of the crowd had broken and run when Burke started playing with that fancy new shotgun. There were still a few brave souls ducking out of doorways, throwing stones and so forth, but the drovers were back in the mews, cowering under the windows so as not to get shot, and some bright lad had put the buffcoated and helmeted Irishmen to holding the gateway to the street. Mostly the rocks missed, stout leather and steel hats turned what hit, and a shot or two kept the *pleidhcíocht* from the townsfolk to a dull roar. It was surprising how quickly a fucked situation could turn around, if you just kept your head, and Finnegan decided he'd find out who'd kept his and see him rewarded. After all, he never told the boys he was infallible, and the trick to leading *torai* wasn't so much strength and leadership as cunning and trust. The smarter ones appreciated it, and the fools followed the smart.

And right now, a smart man would be *leaving*. "One of you, find a close that leads away. We've watched enough of these back ways someone must know a way out."

Three nods.

He looked back at the mews. Two of his own boys were crouched behind the narrow buttresses so many of the walls in this part of town had to have, with being built on hills. They were calm and steady, taking turns to fire into the stable at the end. There was someone in there who'd held, and held well. Far too much cover with stalls and horses' mangers, and more than a couple of frightened horses. He'd seen *that* for a bad bargain as soon as he arrived. No way that way, if it was defended. Into the house was out, too. The house had been warned, had defended the breaches, had organized well enough to hold in spite of grenadoes. Had even stopped one of the throwers, leaving a shambles in the mews and probably taken the fire out of the assaults with it.

They'd lose a few getting out, that was sure. There were still shots coming from the house. Nothing with modern weapons, just the occasional bullet. There was enough cover about that the main danger was flying chips of brick.

Pursuit? No, not right away. They'd gotten three grenadoes in there. There'd be wounds to lick.

"Chief?" It was O'Hare. "The next close along has but three lads in it. We can rush them, and then it's two turnings and we're on our way down the Grassmarket."

Finnegan paused before answering. He'd made one snap decision today and got heartily buggered by it. Another? *No, run away is the snap decision that always works.* "Make ready," he snapped. "We go on my shout."

He checked his gun. He'd only fired twice. Still another four. It was hard, in the press of it, to remember he didn't have to reload. He leaned back into the corner between the Mackay house and the wall that held the archway into the mews. "Make ready!" he shouted again, bracing himself to spring. "Look to the archway, we all go at once! Follow the man in front and devil take him that stands in our way! Now go! *Fág a' Bealach!*"

The next minute was a madness of running and dark closes, a Scotsman looking shocked as he fired into the man's belly, another going down to a shoulder-charge and near tripping him as he ran.

Came the Cowgate, he had eight men, fifteen of the drovers, and barely the wind to talk.

"Right," he said, after a moment whooping air into his lungs. "You lads."

It was time for hard riding and heads down. They didn't need the encumbrance. He pulled the purse he'd been carrying from inside his coat. The leather of the little pouch was damp with sweat. "Your pay," he said, throwing it to one of the bigger fellows. "The pay for them as died is in there too. On your conscience. Divide it as you will, and scatter. This day's work is done. We lost, and we're all the bastards of failure this day. Don't let yourselves be found."

Nods all round and the drovers made off.

"Still a crowd, Chief," Tully said.

Finnegan had seen that. They'd get a hundred yards, if that, before they were mired in angry Scotsmen. And he'd seen, too, the herd of cattle that some optimistic bastard was trying to drive out of town by the Cowgate. Clearly he wasn't the biggest fool in Edinburgh today; to get what looked like forty head out of town today was to take the nearest gate and go around, no matter where they were bound. He could do the same, too, but there was an easier solution, and a more satisfying one. "Grenado!" he barked, holding out his hand.

"Chief?" Tully was frowning.

Finnegan took the last bomb anyway, lit it and hurled it as far along the Cowgate as he could. The explosion cleared some of the crowd—nothing like explosions and broken iron to put flight in a bystander. What it certainly did was frighten the living daylights out of the herd of cattle who turned and ran. And where a herd, however small, of Scots highland cattle wish to run, there is no stopping the bastards. Even with his ears shocked again by the report of the grenado, the screaming and the din of hooves was terrible. There was a small satisfaction, when having a bad day, in making sure someone had it *worse*.

"Gentlemen," Finnegan said, as the ringing in his ears died down, "the way is clear. To the White Hart for our horses, and to Balgreen for our remounts. We are, in a word, *fucked*. I say we take what we have and be away, and on the ride back, be thinking. Every idea for where we go now, I will hear it. I much suspect the earl is no longer minded to be our master."

The faces of his men were torn between horror and awe. To a man, they were from cattle-farming country. Cattle run wild were at the very least a problem, and they'd all have grown up knowing someone who died that way. It was the horror closest to their childhood homes. *Yes, you pack of scoundrels, I did.* Cunning and trust, yes, but scaring the living shit out of the bastards had its place, too.

"I hear horses," Julie said. Of those in the house, she was the only one who had been far enough away not to have any ringing in her ears from the explosions. The footmen and stable hands were clearing wreckage, nailing up boards on the broken windows, making things secure again. Meg wasn't back to lay out the dead, but two of the older girls knew the business, and had sent for older women who could take proper charge. The dead would lie until tomorrow. Today, and she was not minded to hear any argument, was for *revenge*. She'd thought, all her life, that tales of old-time hillbilly feuds were tales of stupidity written in thuggery by madmen. She'd thought that the Hatfields and the McCoys had been vicious fools, answering murder with murder.

Now, though, now. *Alexi.* In the morning-room, being fitted for his shroud, his life's blood spattered across the walls, her father-in-law.

Oh, she'd played tricks with herself when she first went to war. Thinking of exes who'd made her mad. Or, when that trick started to seem childish, *just targets.* Before this day was out she'd look every last one of the bastards in the eye through her scope and watch the lights go out. No courts, no bail, no Tolbooth, no waiting for the ageing bores in their black gowns to argue it out and send them to hang. These bastards had the protection of the powerful. They would not live to run and hide behind their master. She'd think on the master another time. Today, there were some fuckers who just needed killing.

There was a fine trembling in the tips of her fingers, but not enough to get in the way of checking her rifle. She'd seen to her gun before she put it away, and that had been weeks ago. With no air-conditioning, no heating, and the damp that was never far away in Scotland, everything needed a clean and check. So far, all was well.

"I said, horses," she repeated, a little louder.

"Heard you the first time," Darryl called, from somewhere in the hallway. "Bunch of guys with weapons out in the street. They're clearing the rioters."

Julie nodded. Campbell was supposed to be sending men. And he had a commission of justiciary. So this was the cops, arriving after it was all over.

"Campbell's men," Alex said, echoing her assumption. "I'll speak with them." He rose to head out into the hallway.

"Ain't you on the lam?" Darryl asked.

"My wife gave surety for my appearance at court, Darryl," Alex said, "and since the pursuer in my case is now a wanted man himself, I doubt it will be any long hearing." The sarcasm in his voice was withering. It was the little things that told, Julie found. Gayle had noticed that Oliver got more stoical and calm when he was upset. Kind of subtle, but a good tell to those who knew him. Julie had long known that her man, one of the most direct and blunt guys she'd ever known—cheerful and good-natured and not shy about it, and straight to the point when he was angry—got sarcastic only when he was upset. His father had been the other way around. Oblique and witty most of the time, blunt when pissed off, or in quiet moments of strong emotion. She'd treasure the ones she'd seen, when Alexi was sick. It was a mercy the man hadn't lived to see his youngest granddaughter hurt. He'd doted on all his grandchildren. Alex having four half-siblings altogether and all of them married and settled, he was the elder of a fair-sized tribe. Julie meant for him to have his revenge too. She'd thought the old guy was an absolute sweetheart, and Alexi had loved him too.

No. Can't cry. Need my eyes to shoot.

Alex came back in. "Well," he said, "I've had the good fortune to meet the earl o' Argyll. The sickness in London took his father yesterday. I gave my condolences."

"He ain't worried you're on the lam?" Darryl asked.

"The matter never arose. He was at pains to assure me that wherever I chanced to take myself for the rest of today, he and his men would be busy about the Cowgate and Grassmarket and not able to concern themselves with the surrounding country."

The Cromwells came in at that moment. Gayle was the first to speak. "Well, if that ain't a promise to look the other way, I never heard one."

"Aye," Alex said. "I hinted as much that we might need it."

"Are you sure of this?" Cromwell's tone seemed a little worried. He'd had a stint in charge of law enforcement, after all, or as near as seventeenth-century England got. What little Julie had seen of the fen country, she could well imagine he'd had trouble with feuds there too. Not that she intended letting this one turn into some generations-long cycle of murder. *This ends today.*

"Aye," Alex said again. "I ken richt well that vengeance belongs tae God. And I mind Finnegan and his pack o' filthy hounds will feel the vengeance o' the Almighty. Oor part is to put doon yon rabid beasts afore they kill again."

Julie shivered. Alex's Scots burr had faded in the time they'd been together. Her friends back in Grantville teased her that she was picking it up a little. All part, she thought, of them growing together. If Alex was back to having a serious accent, he was feeling his roots, and they were the same roots as the Appalachian maniacs whose tales of feud she'd once thought so nasty.

Her scope mounted, she realized she'd not been able to zero it properly since the last time she'd had it out, for that meeting with Montrose and Campbell. She'd have to get closer than she usually did, was all. If the scope was off, she could compensate. Unless it got knocked again in the ride to Balgreen. She stopped to think about it. Sure, it was a good and durable hunting scope. She'd had years of good service out of it. She had, however, had any amount of trouble trying to shoot when it had gotten knocked. And if the bastards tried to run, she'd probably be better with iron sights anyway—*fuck it.* A moment's work to get it off and put it back in its box. Rifle. Sling. Boxes of ammo into her shoulder bag.

"Ready to go," she said, standing up and striding into the hallway.

Only Alex didn't flinch from the expression on her face. "Aye, love," he said, the barest ghost of a smile on his face.

"Oliver, can you and Gayle and Vicky stay here and mind the place while Alex and I deal with this? I want Darryl, Sergeant Hamilton and Major Lennox with us. Thomas and maybe one of his boys to hold the horses."

"You've a plan?" Alex asked.

"Yep." She nodded. "We catch up with them at Balgreen. They'll be packing and getting ready to skedaddle, back to London or off to hide somewhere. We don't catch them there, we've missed them."

"You mean to assault wherever they're staying?"

"Nope." She'd been thinking as she worked on her rifle. She didn't have all the details, but she could feel it taking shape in her head. There was a four-mile ride. They'd not be able to mount any kind of assault, not unless they could persuade Campbell to lend her his men. That would hold them up and Finnegan would get away. "We wait for them to ride out. First thing, I shoot the horses. Then we can ride 'em down at our leisure. You say you saw pistols and shotguns?" She directed the question at Oliver.

He nodded. "Not to say they might not have other arms, mind," he cautioned.

Not trying that hard to dissuade me, either, she thought. "If they had 'em, they'd've brung 'em," she said. "So we can stand off some. Alex, you and Andrew take the lead if we've got to ride any of 'em down. Darryl, you're shooting with me since I figure you're the next best with a modern rifle."

"Do my best," Darryl said. "My rifle's back at Canongate, though."

"I've a spare. I've not shot it in a while, but it should be okay. You can handle if it's out of zero or it jams. You're mostly backup anyway. Stephen, you're keeping Thomas and whoever safe with the horses."

The ex-warder nodded.

Julie nodded back, thanking him silently. His niece was looking after Alexi. She'd had a year working with Rita Simpson, and knew what she was doing. With Dr. Scott on hand, she'd have no trouble.

Outside, the stable-lads having gotten the horses calmed down enough to ride, the street was quiet. A small party of men on horseback, buffcoated but without helmets, their swords sheathed, were stood idle in the street as they emerged from the mews, apparently awaiting them. Julie supposed they'd decided to make the street outside the Mackay house their command post while their men were suppressing the last of the riot. From the little

Julie had heard before the noise retreated, mostly by whaling on the rioters with sticks.

"You're the baroness, I presume," one of them said. Julie recognized him. She'd seen the face through her scope only a few weeks prior, when she'd given him and Montrose a demonstration of just how bad an idea pissing her off could be. Shortish, balding early, a little plump, hard eyes. The Campbell. Earl of Argyll, now, apparently.

"That's me." She didn't feel like being polite. That said, she bit down hard on any kind of smart-ass remark about the cavalry coming too late. "Earl Argyll, right?" she added, after a pause.

"Aye." The man nodded. "I'll no' delay you about your business. You mean to go hunting?"

Julie snorted. There wasn't really a sensible answer to that. She supposed she ought to say something about how sorry she was about his father's death, but she was in no mood to be nice.

Campbell nodded again. "Aye, a tragedy. And sport to divert you from your sadness." Julie knew the word *sardonic* and had something of an idea of how it sounded. Like this guy.

"Move aside, you fellows," Campbell went on, waving to the other men with him. "Let the baroness at her sport. My lady, I'm sure you will find plenty of game around Balgreen. Mutual condolences can await your return." He tipped his hat. "Joy of the day, my lady."

Julie nodded, and urged her horse forward.

It was mid-afternoon before they reached Balgreen.

Chapter 42

Balgreen. Maybe a dozen buildings around a droving inn on the Glasgow road, where it detoured south of a hill with a castle on it. Coming up from the Ford, Julie noted that there was only one road out that Finnegan could have taken, the one heading west to Glasgow. The sun was definitely getting low in the sky; it was the kind of washed-out brightness that Scotland specialized in in autumn, but the light was good. It would be all the better with the sun at her back.

Fortunately, there wasn't much in the way of hedges or walls around the village, and it was easy enough to lead the boys at a canter in a wide, quarter-mile arc around to a spot about three hundred yards along from where the road left the village. The inn was on the far side, so unless Finnegan was excessively smart, any time they spent preparing would be unobserved.

If they'd been spotted cutting across country, there was enough of a track through the dotted stands of undergrowth that cutting up and over the low rise that the road went around was a known shortcut. Anyone who spotted them would, she hoped, assume they were in a hurry to make as much of the remaining daylight as they could. Edinburgh to Glasgow was, at a quick pace, a day and a half, so they weren't *entirely* obvious. It wasn't much of a shortcut, as she found on the other side of it. There was a small and grungy looking lake there that meant you either had to go at least an extra mile around to the left or cut straight back into the road on the right.

That was to the good, actually. The road was clearly going through a choke-point. Alex and his soldier buddies looked for such things without really thinking about what they were doing. Cavalrymen all, most of their job was riding about between the main bodies of the armies they were with, scouting routes and supplies and all the other stuff an army needed to pay attention to, and trying to stop the other guys from doing the same. Finding good spots to set an ambush, spotting good ambushes before they rode into them. Julie had soaked it up by being immersed in it, noticing what kind of ground made Alex tense up when they were out hunting together.

Truth be told, when they reached the road, and cantered along it for half a mile or so, it wasn't really much of a spot for ambushes. Centuries of stock being driven in to market in Edinburgh had cleared all the cover from either side of the road for a couple of dozen yards back. Trampled or eaten, made no odds, it was gone. Centuries of hoofbeats meant it was worn nice and smooth, just occasional tussocks. That meant Thomas and his kid—one day she was going to remember the boy's name, for sure—would be well out of the line of fire with the horses, when they took them to cover. And, of course, no cover went for everyone. Julie had the advantage of range and rate of fire and shooting skill.

The perfect terrain, really, would be flat as a pancake for miles and miles and miles. They could run, and die tired, or charge, and die with their wounds in front. Not that she, personally, gave a damn. So long as they were fucking *dead*. Oh, there was a little bit of a nagging thought in the back of her mind about law enforcement, but there wasn't a lot of that, hereabouts. If you murdered someone, it was friends and family and neighbors of the victim who hauled you before the courts. Finnegan had none of those. If the powers-that-be wanted someone arrested, they had to find someone with the muscle to do it and grant a commission of justiciary. By the time that was done, Julie was going to be back in the good old USE. Had they even *invented* extradition treaties yet? Not a big deal. She was still a bit hazy on the precise legal details, but she knew that as a feudal vassal of the king of Sweden she could count on Gustavus Adolphus to back her up on this one. The fact that they got on on a personal level was just the cherry on the top. And if there was anyone who was willing to understand that sometimes you just had to tell the written law to go pee up a rope while you did what was *right*, that was the man.

Darryl was already off his horse, the reins in Thomas's hand, and had taken a knee to clear the action on the rifle she'd lent him. It was the one Alex had been learning on, not that he'd made a lot of progress. It had some down-time parts in, but was an old reliable her dad had picked up secondhand back when. It was dependable and low-maintenance. Hopefully, Darryl would get a few shots she couldn't. And if anyone hereabouts could manage a quick fix if there was anything amiss with the weapon, it was him.

"All good," he said, after a moment. "Where you want to shoot from?"

She dismounted, handed off her reins, and looked around again. She'd not seen anything promising in the right area from horseback, but maybe the change in perspective would help.

"Julie, love," Alex said, "Andrew and I will go a wee way toward Corstorphine hill there. The hill will mask us, I see bushes. Do they pass you, that is the way they will go. The higher ground is a good vantage. When they take to their heels, we'll have clear sight of them."

"Corstorphine," Julie repeated, liking the sound of the name. "Is that the name of the castle, or just the hill?"

"Both," Alex said. "I presume you'll be south o' the road, outside this bend?"

"I will," Julie said. Alex knew her preferences. She decided there wasn't any natural shooting spot, so began to gauge angles and distances. *The only restriction is not having the village back-stopping the bastards, and we're a good ways away anyway, so...* "'Bout there, Darryl. Pile up some brush and such, we'll shoot from prone."

Hamilton unhooked his big billhook-thing from his belt. "I'll get to brishing," he said.

Darryl drew his bowie knife. "Stack of turf to shoot over?" he asked.

"Works," Julie said. A little something to rest elbows on never hurt. Digging in would be more than a bit muddy, if she was any judge of ground. Kind of rich, too, with this being a drovers' road. The cattle in particular would've been making contributions for generations. "Spot for me until they get close. You prefer a spotting scope or binoculars? I brought both."

"South or the water, Chief?" Tully asked, once the boyos were busy getting packed and the horses tacked.

"Water," Finnegan snarled. "Sure I am south isn't healthy, nor is it."

Tully shrugged. "We weren't to know there'd be a riot."

"Like his earlness will give a spoonful o' watery shite. And we've killed too many of the man's failures for me to care to try and explain. All the horses. We sell the remounts at Glasgow, sell the rest at Greenock, take whatever's floating to Dublin or Belfast. Think when we're back home. Steal a few cows, get a stake together and listen for rumors of war. Spain, possibly. We've modern guns and arms, such as us will always find work."

Tully nodded. "As long as the devil's not in charge of our luck for good, we'll do."

Finnegan nodded. "Get in and see they're shifting with our traps. I'll go and boot some arses in the stables. Rob the moneybox on your way out. Most of it's our coin anyway."

"Oh, I reckon we got something," Darryl said. There'd been movement for the last fifteen minutes, horses and men moving in the village. Just about visible through gaps in the houses.

Julie allowed herself to hope. They'd been here nearly half an hour, setting up a shooting position, Alex and Andrew riding off to cover. Skilled cavalrymen both, they'd demonstrated that it was entirely possible to hide two men on horses in plain sight. They'd ridden in among the stands of bushes and trees at the base of the hill and simply vanished. She'd looked over a couple of times and thought *maybe* she could tell where they were. Dead ground, greenery, and good horsemanship. As the afternoon wore on, it would get colder. She'd be able to pick out the fog from the horses' breathing, but that only because she knew where to look. The few battles Julie had fought in, there was a defense going on. Either she was on it, or shooting at the guys on the other side. She'd asked them, before they rode off, if they were sure they could hide that well. They'd both grinned, wide and toothy. Clearly, they knew *their* kind of war well enough to be confident.

"What do you see?" she asked, ducking her head and wiggling to get comfortable. *Shame Alex ain't there to enjoy the view.*

"Eight guys, mounted. Column of twos. Front guy, our left, he's yelling over his shoulder. Finnegan, I reckon. Two more guys bringing up the rear, they're leading the remounts, looks like they've got the baggage on some of the remounts. Figure those guys first?"

Julie paused to consider a moment. "Yeah. If we can spook the remounts to running, the horses they're riding might spook too." She raised her head to take in the view. The sun had dropped a little more; her targets were beautifully lit. If she'd been shooting with a camera, it would be *perfect*. Four hundred yards, give or take, and there was enough shade that she could pick out details. And it was cool and brisk, so heat haze wasn't even slightly a problem. What little breeze there was was blowing from behind, more or less. Perfect shooting conditions would include her having remembered to bring a tarp or something, this ground was cold and damp, and there being a handy shooting bench set up, but she'd take what she could get.

"Right to left or left to right?" Darryl asked.

"Right to left," Julie said. She as comfortable either way, most of the time, but the ground under her wasn't quite level. It was going to be easier to traverse the muzzle from right to left, and once she let the first round go down-range, she was going to need to get ten rounds off good and fast. And a good few more after that. She had four magazines waiting, in order of how good shape they were in, plus one in her rifle and an extra round chambered. There was a box of loose shells within arm's reach.

"Horses first," she said.

"You sure?" Darryl sounded concerned. Like he wasn't happy about shooting horses either. "Dead horses are cover, I seen enough cowboy movies to know *that*."

"If they've got cover, they're going to hold still to be shot," Julie said. It was what had occurred to her on the ride over here, when she was trying to decide how to do this. She didn't like shooting animals, never really had. But then she'd remembered that one guy she'd shot outside Sir Pedley's place, back in England. He'd died, but they only found out about it later, after he'd ridden off to do his dying well out of sight. Today, she wanted to see all of these fuckers die. She'd apologize to the horses later.

And there were plenty of poor folks hereabouts wouldn't say no to a healthy portion of horse in the pot.

"Three hundred yards," Darryl said. "I guess they're heading out for a long ride, they're still walking the horses."

"Figures," Julie said. "I went over this with Alex and Andrew. They had to come here to get their stuff. They might have gone back into town to pick up a road south or east, but west is more likely. There's roads south from Glasgow, and they can re-supply there or get a ship, not that they're going to have the chance to do either one."

The column of horsemen was getting close enough that the horses were easier to pick out details of. The horses she'd been used to had been cleaner-lined, bolder-colored. More like picture-book horses. The *actual* horses you got in the seventeenth century were shaggy, brown, and kind of small. If she wanted to put them down without causing any suffering, she needed fairly close shots. She ran her sights back and forth over the column. "... and on that farm he shot some guys," she sang to herself.

Darryl snorted. "No *way* are you old enough to have seen that. Two hundred yards."

"Nope," she agreed. "Came down-time on VHS. Kinda liked it, but it's Alex that likes movies with all clever twists and stuff. I liked the bit with the sniper, though."

Darryl was outright chuckling now. "*Not* what generally went through my mind when I seen cheerleaders, have to say. Did they change up the auditions some since I quit school?"

She reached over and poked him in the ribs. "Darryl McCarthy, you are *shallow*. Wait'll I tell Vicky."

"Hey, I was a teenager!"

"So was I, uh, bit less than three years ago. Didn't mean I had my mind in the gutter."

"Whatever, two hundred yards, they're into the first bend." He worked the action on his rifle, gently so as not to make much noise.

"Start shooting when I do," she said. "I reckon it's close enough I don't need you to spot, the light's real good. I'll start at the back, you start at the front. Stay with the main group, I'll get any runners." The desire to just open up and not stop shooting, ever, was bubbling up in her. To shoot and shoot and shoot and then run into them and smash their faces with the butt of her rifle—

"Gotcha," Darryl said. Only a few hours ago she'd been concerned about *his* nerves. Now it was him grounding her, the calm tone of his voice reminding her that she had a plan, he was part of it, and was ready to follow through.

She took a deep breath, held it, let it out. God *damn* it, she was not going to get buck fever, not now.

"That's richt, lassie, haud it aye a moment mair," Lennox crooned, standing in his stirrups to peer over the shrubs they were using as concealment. The leaves were beginning to turn, but only a few had fallen, and the wild tangle of old brambles that looped out of the mass gave them something to peer through and break up their outlines still more. With the higher ground behind them with its jumble of rock and small scrub, if anyone spotted them here, it was between him and the devil how he did it. After sneaking men into ambush by the troop and squadron, finding a spot for just the two of them had been child's play.

Mackay was sat down on his saddle. No sense putting two faces above the greenery when one would do. He chuckled. "Still the auld sergeant, Andrew?"

"Commission or no, they'll lay me tae rest wi' three stripes oan ma coffin," Lennox answered, "and yon wife o' yours has the makin's o' a fine killin' officer," he added.

"And the pair o' us ken' the inclinations o' a sergeant faced wi' a wee sprig o' an officer, aye?"

"Aye. Hae ye been a teacher tae her, or is it talent?"

"A mickle o' both," Mackay said, "And I mind she'll wait that first bend, there. We'll have runners away tae oor left."

"Aye. They cannae go far. The ground's poor, the Watter o' Leith's doon behind."

She'd planned the first three shots in her mind, but setting that front sight on the fucker's mount was still a little unsettling.
Crack.

Oh God, you poor thing, I'm sorry. The sight of the horse's front legs suddenly going to jelly under it—

She had shifted aim without even thinking about it. Hours and hours with grouped targets, it was a habit.
Crack.

Working the bolt was like the little hitch between inhale and exhale. She was doing it, but unless she specifically thought about doing it, she didn't notice.

Bigger shift, guy pulling out of the column, going for the gallop—*Crack.*

Back to the rear of the main column. *Crack.*

Looked like a miss, but the horse behind was fountaining blood from its neck and thrashing.

Try again. He'd wheeled his mount entirely out of column, shying away from the bleeding, screaming horse next to him. Or his horse had. Head on. *Crack.*

Maybe a little high. Still through the brain and spine. Horse brains all over the rider, and she'd moved on before the animal had more than begun to fall.

Reload. Magazine seated.

Crack. Off to the right, didn't lead enough. *Damn.* Through the rider's knee before it went into the chest cavity. Still, she'd done enough to that animal. It bucked once, throwing the man on its back clear except for the mangled leg in the stirrup, and went down, thrashing its legs.

Crack. Clear miss. Deep breath. Shifting to reload, she must've got her position off. A wriggle.

Crack.

Reload.

No more standing horses. One riderless, running away. Two riding clear. Darryl must've gotten the others. The remounts were off and running. Back to the escapers.

Two hundred yards already. Adjust sight. *Crack.* Miss, probably. *Crack.* Violent jerk in the saddle, leave him for Alex to run down. Shift aim. *Crack.* Puff of blood from the left shoulder. Must've jinked. *Crack.* Miss.

Reload. This magazine and one more and she was down to single shots.

Her eyes off the mound of thrashing horseflesh, she didn't see the muskets firing. A pure-white bank of smoke obscured the targets.

"Four shooters," Darryl said.

A series of pops, a winking dot of light in the smoke. One of them had a modern gun. Something cracked by, close enough to clip a few leaves out of the pile of brush Stephen had cut for their shelter. *Assume a right-handed shooter.*

Shifting her sights into a sight picture she was already focusing on was tricky, but she'd practiced it. *Crack.* A rewarding scream.

Darryl wasn't much trying to hit anything in particular, just plinking rounds into the horse carcasses the enemy were sheltering behind. *Fair enough.* He wasn't a bad shot, but he knew his limits. He was muttering "rate—of—fire" to space out his shots.

There. Dumbass was ducked down and reloading, but the feather in his hat wasn't. *Crack—Crack.* The smoke was clearing, so now she could see the red mist as the rounds went through the horsemeat into the man behind. Her .308s were doing that handily, short as the range was. The .30-06 Darryl was whacking into the horse carcasses might, maybe—probably would do a little better, in more skilled hands—but they were doing a number on the nerves of the guys behind. He just wasn't confident enough to go for shots through the top of the carcass, or pick a particular point of aim. She'd asked; he could shoot a tight group if he took it slow. If he was going to be laying down suppressive fire, he reckoned he'd be doing well to manage within a foot or so. Fair enough. At this distance, Julie could sign her name in lead and hardly slow down at all.

Reload. Last magazine.

Look for a point of aim. The smoke was thinning right out. She was vaguely aware of Alex and Andrew streaking across to head off the escapers. Andrew was peeling off to take the one that she'd definitely hit.

Then, there was a white cloth being raised. The last two were climbing to their feet, hands raised. The pair of them had horrified expressions on their faces.

For a moment, all Julie could see was Alexi, weeping, and where she'd been sliced across the thigh by a grenade fragment. Her finger began closing on the trigger.

But just as she was about to fire, Darryl's hand came down on her shoulder, startling her.

"Don't do it," he hissed. "They're surrendering. It ain't right to kill 'em now, Julie."

She started to snarl at him as she fought off his hand and brought the rifle to bear again. But then—

Darryl McCarthy. Voice of dispassion and civilized reason.

The thought was incongruous enough that she couldn't help but bark out a laugh. And, for whatever reason, that laugh seemed to shatter the dark, murderous fury that had seized her.

Carefully—she was still just *that close* to killing the bastards—she shifted the rifle to the side and up. Just a little, but enough.

"Okay, Mr. Marquis de Fucking Queensberry," she said. "You go out there and bring 'em in. Leave me a clear line of fire at all times, though. You hear me?"

Darryl heaved himself up and barked a laugh of his own. "You really think those two guys are going to try to pull some funny stuff? Not a chance, Julie. Hell, look at 'em. Yeah, sure, we Irish run to being pale. But you're looking at Casper the Ghost and his twin brother."

He started toward them, holding his rifle in the crook of his arm as if he were a gentleman hunter heading down to collect his downed pheasants.

Chapter 43

Colonel Alex Mackay, late of the armed forces of the United States of Europe, felt like he was about to grin the top of his head clean off. *Months* in the Tolbooth, not without comfort but hardly a glimpse of the outdoors. And now, clear ground, quarry running, a horse with miles of wind left in him, and a good sword in his hand. This was *living*. Oh, sure, he'd gone for a soldier to make his fortune—his father's indiscretion precluded any real inheritance and he liked his half-siblings too well to resent it. He'd stayed a soldier for moments like this. Two of the filthy bastards had shown their heels when Julie opened fire. Ten horses to drop, and two rifles between the lot of them. It would have been a surprise if they'd not had a couple of them running. Especially since for all their soldierly garb, the fuckers were naught but brigands. He'd fought against and alongside Irishmen, and underestimating them was a fool's bargain, but every nation had its trash.

Andrew had come off a pace or two behind, and rode a stone heavier than his former commander, so in the first seconds of their pursuit he was trailing by a couple of lengths. The nearer scoundrel—fifty yards, and watching Alex closing to head him off—suddenly jerked upright in the saddle, his face a perfect picture of shock. The sudden puff of the front of the man's buffcoat, the mist of red between the buttons, and the shocking burst of blood from the man's mouth told the tale.

That's my girl, he thought, and urged his mount slightly left.

A fast ride across the head of the other man's mount would make the beast shy up short, and a gesture with his sword told Andrew to take the man. Commissioned his old sergeant might be, but he still outranked him.

The second brigand was veering away. What hope of escape the man had, Alex had no idea. Downriver to Leith? Who cared. Another who rode heavy. Oh, he'd had his share of japes when a young man for his small size, but small meant quick, and him that was quick was not among the dead.

He calculated as he urged his mount to more effort. The other fellow would have the fresher horse; he could hardly have been so foolish as to set out for the long ride to Glasgow without remounting. Alex, however, had a horse that had had longer to warm. A brisk three mile canter, half an hour to get his wind back. The other fellow's horse had had a three hundred yards at the walk and was now at a flat gallop. And Alex had been leading scout cavalry for ten years while this fool had been bullying peasants and thieving cattle. He let the fellow fade into the corner of his eye and hunched down for the gallop. There was a stride or two more to be had out of the beast, if he was any judge, and a gentle curve to bring him—*there*.

Behind and to the left of his quarry. Not a *chance* the fellow could shoot, had he a pistol and the will to risk a ludicrously chancy shot. The fellow was looking frantically over his shoulder. No doubt hoping a fresher mount would see him clear over the long distance. Which it would; Alex knew he had moments only to shoot the man, and, taking the reins in with the hilt of his sword, reached for his pistol—

He winced. It'd been so long since he'd had to do this, he'd forgot that he carried his gear differently now. And not thought to put it right before taking off. His pistol was holstered to draw right-handed. Another flash of calculation. No, he'd not. On a better-trained horse, one he knew better, he might attempt some clever move. Reins back to his left hand, a whack with the flat for stride or two more, a lunge over the neck of his mount, uncoiling easily and smoothly as he reached the point forward—

Just. The tip of his blade punctured the leading horse's arse, and a savage grip of the knees recovered his seat. His mount needed no urging to swerve away as the Irishman's steed screamed and lost its stride. He winced as he heard the wreck of a bad, bad fall. He brought his horse to an easy halt, let him find his own pace, and cantered round in an easy circle to where the Irishman had been thrown clear, flat on his back. The poor horse was in a horrible jumble of legs, its neck clearly broke. It was still twitching, but there'd be no need for a bullet to end its misery.

He surely had one for the Irishman though, and was reaching across to take out his pistol until he realized.

"Finnegan," he said, reining his horse in. There was still breath in the man's body. Was it too much to hope he'd broke his back? The man's left arm was definitely broke. *Unless,* he thought as a fey mood took him, *Irishmen* naturally *have two elbows.* No bleeding, but there often wasn't, for the first moments after a fall. The right was tucked under, doubtless broke too.

Finnegan's eyes opened. His wits didn't seem to be about him. That wouldn't do, not hardly at all. Mackay re-holstered his pistol. His saber, that he'd carried all through the Germanies, had been a going-away gift from his father. It was only fitting that he use it to do execution on the man who'd killed him. And he *certainly* needed to know why, and at whose hand, he was to die.

"You should know, Finnegan," Alex said, when it looked like there was maybe someone at home behind the Irishman's eyes, "that you killed my father. Something of a mercy, if I'm to put my hand on my heart, and he's a fine lot o' grandchildren for his posterity. And, oh, he died a hero. Smothered your grenado with his ain flesh. For that I might drag you back to hang."

He took a deep breath. Flourished his saber briefly. Andrew was cantering over, his blade red in the late afternoon sun. "But it's the last of those grandchildren, Finnegan. My wee Alexi. She's hurt. No' serious, she'll mend. But she might have been killed. And that, may the Lord forgive my wrath, means I cannae leave you breathing."

Finnegan hissed. Probably still winded from his fall. Or dying, from a broken back. Alex hardly cared. And, with a feeling of heavy, leaden inevitability, he let fall his sword point and followed down smoothly, arm and shoulder behind the thrust, and from all the height of his saddle drove eight inches of steel through Finnegan's throat and into the good earth below.

There was a *crack* and Alex felt a thump, hard in the right side of his gut. He sat up in his saddle, oddly dizzy, and saw for the first time that Finnegan had had a pistol after all.

✧   ✧   ✧

Once Darryl reached the two men surrendering, he said something to them. A moment later both had their hands clasped over their heads and were moving toward her. Slowly. Darryl stayed far enough to the side to give Julie a clear line of fire if she needed it.

But it was now obvious that she wouldn't. The pair of prisoners had as much fight left in them as funnel cakes. She rose to her feet, picking up a magazine and the box of shells and began reloading, with quick and practiced motions.

Somewhere in the distance, a pistol shot. Alex or Andrew finishing one of the runners.

Stephen Hamilton began moving through the bodies, checking to see if any of the men Julie had shot were still alive.

One was, apparently—and Hamilton didn't seem to share any of Darryl's notions of the laws of war. A quick, economical cut with his billhook spilled what was left of the man's life out on the ground.

She heard a shot and looked around. Darryl, his face twisted with upset, was shooting a wounded horse. The last of them. She'd not even noticed the cries of the wounded animals.

Julie remembered tales of those first few hours after the Ring of Fire. She'd been at home that day, not doing much of anything, had really only been vaguely aware of the flash outside, the phone going dead in her hand, and the power cut. She'd been calmly waiting it out, helping her mom organize the freezer stuff that was going to spoil, when she'd learned the world had changed for good.

Mike Stearns hadn't been quite so passive those first few hours. He and a bunch of his miner buddies—one Darryl McCarthy included—had gone out and dispensed some frontier justice. And then not too long afterward, there'd been the battle against Tilly's men outside Badenburg. Julie had been one of the shooters who tore those tercios into hash.

Julie didn't recall anything about Darryl's opinions on the matter from back then. She'd been—quietly, there were too many people saying women couldn't fight to say it out loud—upset at all the killing she' done. Had resolved to, yeah, stick to the rules if she could. Had even got a bit squeamish about hunting, after. Not enough to refuse to do it ever again. Just enough that she'd decided to think about the cost more than she'd been doing.

But that had been war. There were *rules* for that and she'd taken a sort of emotional shelter behind them. Most of the guys they'd taken prisoner at Jena and after that first raid, they were guys who'd enlisted to fight, and got given crappy orders. This? This had been different. Might've been a legal dodge, but these guys swore themselves in as constables. *Cops.* They went around murdering old men—and would have murdered infants if an old man hadn't used his body as a shield.

So . . . she'd come very close to crossing a line she'd never crossed before. And was now of two minds about it. On the one hand . . . she was deliberately not looking at the two prisoners anymore, since she wasn't sure she could keep herself from shooting the bastards. That was how much she wanted to kill them.

On the other hand . . .

Oh, hell, maybe Darryl was right. *The voice of dispassion and civilized reason.* She laughed again, and this time there was some actual humor in it.

That laugh drew the eyes of the prisoners. She glanced at them and saw that—impossibly—their faces had gotten still more pale.

That caused her to laugh again. Maybe they *could* be turned into ghosts.

Stephen came up. "Company," he said, from where he'd stayed out of the way.

"Where?"

Darryl had come over as well. "Four, on horse, from Balgreen," he said, nodding in that direction.

Julie peered. She had the best eyes of the three of them—Stephen probably needed some kind of prescription, but spectacles were a big deal, down-time—and could recognize faces at a considerable distance. "That's Campbell, in the lead."

They weren't in any kind of hurry, from the looks of it. If Campbell knew he was riding toward her, of all people, he'd know not to make any threatening moves. And he'd known she was coming here. Had made sure she'd known Finnegan's bolthole was out here. What'd made him follow her?

She looked away to her left. Alex and Andrew were closer, but not moving at any kind of quick pace. Maybe one of them was hurt? Probably just needed to rest the horses some, they'd gone for a hell of a gallop.

"He's basically a cop now," Darryl said. "I asked Thomas

about that commission of justiciary he mentioned. It's like bein' deputized."

"Huh," Julie said. This was going to be interesting. They'd just killed eight guys, one of them—the one whose throat Stephen had slit—arguably in cold blood. And Alex was technically on the lam. She dropped a round in the chamber and closed the bolt. There was a single shot left in the magazine she'd just taken out, so she put it back in. She unbuttoned her jacket to make sure she could get at her pistol.

"Stephen, watch the prisoners," she said. "Darryl, keep your eyes on Alex and Andrew, tell me where they're at." She wasn't going to take her eyes of Campbell and his men.

"Will do," he replied. "There still about five hundred yards off. They'll be here pretty soon, though."

As Campbell got closer, she figured it was the earl and three bodyguards. The earl himself was what you'd get if you took a little round dweeby guy and made him live an outdoorsman's life, obviously tough and strong, probably able to handle himself, but still little, round and dweeby. So he brought along three great big Scotsmen to stop anyone getting ideas based on the little and dweeby parts. She and Alex had something similar going on. People were polite to her because of the husband with the sword, and polite to him because of the wife with the rifle.

Out the tail of her eye she could see that Thomas and his kid—still couldn't remember his name—had come out of the bushes with the horses, but weren't coming closer. Two guys with five horses to handle, they probably didn't want to get close to anything that'd spook the animals. Not so soon after the injured horses had stopped screaming.

"Ye've had your own joy of the day, I take it, my lady?" Campbell said, when he was close enough to talk. Not, apparently, bothered by the corpses. Little and dweeby were really quite deceiving. According to Alex's dad this guy could put twenty thousand angry highlanders on a battlefield just by asking, so it made sense he'd not be troubled by the aftermath of a fight.

"Been a good day's hunting," she agreed. There was probably some subtle political stuff she'd miss, here. She couldn't find it in herself to care. It'd be a lot of trouble if she killed the guy, but she had enough rounds in her rifle that at this range, she'd have them dead before they knew it. Big guys on horses from the fringes of civilization. Croats, Scotsmen, didn't make a lot of difference. She had experience of the breed. And this time she'd handed off the thirty-aught-six and was using her own rifle.

"It so happens that I have a warrant for the arrest of this Finnegan." Campbell said. "I swore it out as soon as I learned what he'd done, and came hot-foot. I had hopes you would at least run him to earth."

"Bit late," Julie said. "Neither of the ones still alive is Finnegan. I don't know who they are, actually."

Campbell gave them a quick, dismissive glance. "So I see. He might have had some gowned fool let him live after the assault on your father-in-law's house. Under color of law, and so forth. But it seems in his flight he committed further outrages with no such figleaf to clothe his naked brigandry."

That sounded...interesting. She raised an eyebrow.

"He drove a small herd out of his way on the Cowgate," Campbell said. "The law is clear in the matter. Furious driving of cattle is a serious offense. That six are dead already makes it a culpable homicide. Five more seem sure to perish of their hurts. It may be that one of them perished from the grenado he hurled to start the cows running."

"Hold on," Darryl said, "the fucker throws grenades into a house and he ain't gonna hang, but you're gonna arrest him for *stampeding cattle*?"

Campbell's smile had no more warmth in it than a highland winter. "Mister McCarthy, if I don't miss my guess? Aye. I take it this 'stampeding' means the same as furious driving?"

"Prob'ly," Darryl admitted. "And yeah, that's who I am."

"Well, perchance you've no' lived in so great a city as Edinburgh, but startled cattle in confined streets are a great terror to the people. In the country, a man might run before such, find shelter, and still drovers die when their charges get out of hand. In city streets, *there is no escape.* So, aye, I'm here to take him under arrest for the furious driving of cattle. And I have every fear that the people will storm the Tolbooth to hang him themselves. There's the small matter of the robbery he and his men did as they left Balgreen, but I see we're likely past that at this point."

"Well, shit," Darryl said.

"So, does Finnegan live?" Campbell asked.

"No," came Alex's voice. They were finally arriving. *Thanks for the heads-up, Darryl,* Julie thought, although she could see where what Campbell had said was kind of distracting. And looked at like he'd put it, stampeding those cattle was a pretty big deal. She'd seen the aftermath on the way out of town, and assumed that it had been the riot that had done the damage.

"Colonel Mackay," Campbell said. "do you give me to understand that Finnegan resisted arrest?"

"Aye," Alex said, "and I've the hurts to prove it."

Julie took her eyes off Campbell for the first time. *So much blood.*

"Oh, Alex," she said, "we need a doctor."

"That we do, love, that we do."

Suddenly Campbell was all business. Directing his muscle—who didn't, apparently, think anything of taking orders from a guy half their size—to take charge of the two prisoners and get Alex back to the inn at Balgreen. Willie—Campbell had known the boy's name where Julie hadn't, and how that had come about she had no idea. Some kind of secret Dark Political Power, no doubt—had been sent with messages back to Edinburgh to bring a doctor. Thomas followed him shortly after, with letters to lawyers, to Campbell's men back in town and the Tolbooth to the effect that Alex was out of the Tolbooth on Campbell's own recognizance, that he would be too ill for court on Monday, and that his pursuer was now dead and he would be presenting an intervening motion to have Finnegan's prosecution dropped.

When the flurry of activity was over, with Alex being tended by Darryl and his small aid kit—the wound was a through-and-through under his right arm, no lung puncture, a probable broken rib and a lot of blood loss—Campbell drew her aside.

"I can do much to settle all this," he said, "but it were better if you returned over the seas, and that right soon."

"I'd figured on that anyhow," she said. She knew she was going to be no use to anybody tomorrow. Hell, probably not much use tonight. She just wanted to use what strength she had left to get back to Alexi. And yeah, pack. They'd planned on stopping Finnegan in the courtroom to get him away long enough that Oliver would be free and clear. They'd figured that Finnegan's assault would have enough bullshit flying about to make that possible anyway. She'd gone far enough today that Oliver could probably march out of town with a band playing and a big banner with his name on and nobody would care.

Campbell kept his silence while she thought, watching her face and all the expressions that flickered on it intently. Not even troubling to disguise what he was doing, which Julie figured was open and honest for a guy like that. "I'm under a commission to keep the peace. For the moment, I can claim to be acting in that commission, settling disputes and determining the common good in all of this. The pretense will hold a few days—a few weeks, even—but your presence beyond Monday will be more than Jamie Montrose will wink at."

Julie snorted. "Thought you guys were deadly enemies."

Campbell's grin was that of the tiger contemplating a fresh carcass. "Oh, aye. No reason not to be civil to the fellow. And I fancy we'll have common cause to make afore long. I mean to keep your Major Lennox by me. He's a Mackay man through-and-through, for all he wasnae born to it. And you're a Mackay by marriage. And there's a regiment entire of Mackays over the water. Whatever may come to pass, those men will have a part to play, and no small one. I've no settled plan, you understand, but whatever schemes and plots may arise, I'd be a pure fool to not presume on the acquaintance."

Julie was amazed to hear *and you owe me, big time*, in all that. Her grasp of political maneuvering had pretty much stopped at the high-school level. Where, anyone who'd been a cheerleader could tell you, it got pretty vicious. This guy wasn't just out of her league, he was practically playing a different game. But, as she'd remarked before, the difference between Scots clan politics and a high-school he-said-she-said hissy-fit was mostly in the level of actual as opposed to metaphorical bloodshed. And Campbell had recognized all of that on the strength of knowing her an hour, and pitched what he was saying just right to get the message across without saying anything he could be called on later.

"I reckon I'd go further than acquaintance, after today," Julie said, simply, and let him make of that what he would.

She was going to have to have a word or two—letters, probably—with her brother-in-law the new Baron Mackay. The Mackay clan chief, who was back in Germany right now, so that one was going to be face-to-face. And a whole bunch of guys in the government of the USE. It was time and past time she got up to speed on this baronessing business.

Epilogue

January 1635

Darryl had just finished paying off the carters he'd unexpectedly had to hire at Ellenfoot, when Oliver showed up. Even after all the weeks they'd spent at Carlisle, just about getting in tune with the accent there, he was having trouble with the way the boys spoke who were from, like, thirty miles down the coast, so it was a bit of a pain in the ass. Fortunately, both he and the guys he'd hired to drive the carts were having a bit of fun with it, talking loudly and slowly and mocking each other's accents. They were having as much trouble with his West Virginia as he was with their Cumberland.

Oliver was chuckling. "I've as much trouble," he said. "These northerners are all of a piece with their strange manner of talking."

Darryl snorted. "I reckon the old U.S. inherited that problem. Still, we're plenty supplied now. We're going to have to get some guys who're going to come south with us."

"The fellows you hired?" Cromwell nodded to where the carters from Ellenfoot were hurrying in out of the wind and sleet to the taproom of the inn.

"I did ask," Darryl said, "but they don't want to leave. They're doing just fine smuggling graphite out—sold me some, as it happens, bound to come in handy—and whatever comes in. With King Charles squeezing everything till it squeaks because he's got no Parliament to vote him funds, the smugglers are doing a hell of a trade."

He'd not been able to follow the figures he'd been quoted, since it wasn't just money, but a whole complicated web of barter and trade that the smugglers were feeding into the bargain. The gist was that one good smuggling run in winter would keep the crew that pulled it off comfortable for a year. Two, and they could afford to be generous to the landsmen who helped. Some ships were getting three or four cargoes each winter and spring, and spending the summer and autumn when the landsmen were busy on the farms landing cargoes at legitimate ports.

Of course, the ones that weren't getting that many runs were dying at sea.

Cromwell chuckled. "Leave it to the criminals to know the affairs of state they can profit by," he said. "and aye, the ancient customs of the ports are among the few royal incomes the Stuart needs no Parliament to levy. He has every gowned fool that passed the bar reading ancient books to find lapsed fees and fines to levy, too."

"You're getting more information now?" They'd come down from Edinburgh in November. With Finnegan dead and no sign of more men to come from either Cork or the king, they'd decided to take it easy. Alex and Julie had spent the bare minimum of time needed to attend to the old baron's affairs and get Alex fit enough to travel—he wasn't going to be entirely right for months yet, if Darryl was any judge, and Julie had been pretty forceful on the subject—before taking ship back to Hamburg. That had cost a pretty penny, the North Sea being nobody's idea of a pleasure cruise in winter. The smugglers only went for it because the profits were frankly ridiculous and justified the risk.

With Alex and Julie gone, Darryl, Vicky, Oliver, Gayle and Stephen had set out for England, cutting across to the west coast, which Oliver said would be less well watched and a better route to the parts of the country he needed. They'd made good time to Carlisle, whereupon Oliver had had them stop for the worst of the winter weather. Darryl hadn't argued. It had already been closing in—sleet, hail, rain, gales, and the tops of the surrounding hills white when they weren't covered by cloud. Oliver had then started getting in touch with every old friend he could remember the address of, to find out what was what in England these days, because making a plan without that would've been dumb. Darryl didn't even slightly envy the guys they'd paid to ride with their messages.

"Aye. I've every hope of being in Manchester by the end of

March. There are a good many of the godly among the weavers. I had thought we might be poor relations in need of shelter, especially since I declined the aid of the United States, but—" He waved a hand over the carts.

They'd been in radio contact with *Someone At The State Department Who Was Totally Not Don Francisco Honest.* They'd been offered support and funding for a good run at starting the English Civil War a few years ahead of schedule.

That had come as a bit of shock. Darryl had asked, through channels, for a bit of a resupply and some tools and gear he couldn't get locally, plus his and Gayle's year of back pay from when they were in the Tower. They were going to be helping out against an enemy of the USE, after all, and didn't want to be dependent on handouts while they did it.

Oliver had been kind of okay with that, but really didn't want to be seen to be taking foreign money—he'd been quite firm in his opposition to taking the offer that had come back. For pretty good reason. He was busy writing, it looked like, to pretty much everyone to the effect that King Charles, bought and paid for with French gold, wasn't fit to be on the throne. Therefore, he'd argued, the nation needed to skip forward a couple of hundred years to where the king was a figurehead and England was mostly a democracy.

If Charles and his henchmen could say Cromwell was a paid agent of the USE, that was not going to fly quite as well.

Not-Don-Francisco had taken that on board and said he'd not intervene, then, but he'd send through a few boxes of stuff—documents and reference books et cetera, he'd not been specific—that might prove useful, and that he'd talk to some guys in the Committees of Correspondence about an aid package.

By the time the load came ashore, it filled three carts. There were crates of books, measuring instruments, tools, and cash. All of it down-time makes, none of it obviously from the USE. Some of it was French-made, for crying out loud. A bunch of mail as well, going back over a year. Darryl had been promoted, put up a pay-grade or two, and his pay back-dated to, as it happens, the month before he'd gone into the Tower. With hazard and combat pay upgrades from the date they'd been made prisoners. There was probably something similar for Gayle in the oilskin packet with her name on it. The dates on those promotions and raises were months previous, and Darryl was willing to bet that there were records to that effect somewhere in Magdeburg. He'd even bet that there wasn't any evidence at all that the whole thing had been ginned up in the first week of December or thereabouts.

Darryl shrugged. "We got what we asked for. Turns out mine and Gayle's back pay was more'n we thought. And that last etcetera in that last message, I think that might've been an excuse. There's some pretty useful stuff though. Tools especially."

"I am sure I said I'd not be the USE's hireling—" Cromwell began, his voice giving away that he was feeling his temper coming on.

"Don't think this'll look like that," Darryl said. "I've had a chance to go through most of it, 'cept what's addressed to Gayle, and it's all down-time stuff and not all of it's from the USE. And there's papers to say we were owed a lot more back pay than I thought."

Cromwell gave him a hard and piercing stare in return.

Darryl shrugged. "I didn't ask for any of it. All I said—all we said, come right to it, you were there by the radio with us—was we didn't want no official USE help."

That got a snort of amusement. "This Don Francisco hasn't earned his name in idleness, has he? They're a famous family, and him a known man among them. Remind me to consider carefully my exact words when next I converse with the man."

Darryl was about to let it go, when some perverse notion— whim? or maybe it was the most serious thought he'd ever had—led him to speak up again.

"Look, Oliver, whether or not you accept any direct help from the USE is your business. But you may as well face the fact that in this universe nothing is going to happen with the British Isles—not Ireland and Scotland, for sure, and I don't think it'll be any different with England—without the USE being involved in it one way or another."

Cromwell gave him that level, calm, considering gaze that he did so well and was all the more intimidating that there was no overt menace in it. But Darryl had gotten used to it by now.

"And what is your point?" Cromwell asked.

Gayle chimed in. "One way or the other, is what he said, my dear husband. So the point is that you should also start thinking about *which way* you'd like the USE to get involved instead of just repeating again and again that you'll take no foreign gold and be no foreign hireling. Which I don't remember anybody asking you to do or be."

"What she said," was the only thing Darryl could think to add.

That evening, in the room he and Vicky shared, Darryl found himself looking out the window. Such as it was—small, multi-paned, the glass of inferior quality—but it hardly mattered since there was nothing to see out there anyway. Carlisle's latitude was as far north as Canada and didn't get much more than eight hours of daylight in January. The sun had gone down long since.

Through a glass, darkly. But that wasn't really true any longer, he realized. For the first time, Darryl McCarthy's life was something he possessed, not just something he was passing through while having as much fun as he could manage.

He had a wife, whom he loved. Yeah, she was great-looking but that wasn't something he thought much about anymore. And he had a goal and a purpose. Oliver Cromwell had become his best friend, something he could admit to himself if not yet say it to anyone else. He was as good a friend as Harry Lefferts had ever been; better in some ways, if not in others.

Darryl wondered how Harry was doing, these days. No way to know, of course.

But Cromwell was more than just a friend. Somehow, in some fashion he didn't really understand clearly, as time passed Darryl had stopped being Oliver Cromwell's watchdog and become his partner. He wasn't worried any longer what Cromwell might or might not do in Ireland, because that wasn't the issue any longer. What were *they* going to do in Ireland—and England, and Scotland? Because he'd have an influence on all those things; which might even, in the passing of time, become a very great influence.

His life *mattered.* He would make it matter.

"God help me," he said. "I'm growing up."

"I always knew you would," said Vicky, looking up from the book she was reading by candlelight. She was half-sitting, half-lying in bed, propped up against the headboard. "Or I wouldn't have married you in the first place."

He left the window and went to sit beside her. "What's the book?" he asked.

"I got it from Miz Mailey before she left the Tower."

Unusually, it was an up-time edition, not a down-time replica.

Up-time editions were getting very pricey. It must have been one of Ms. Mailey's own books that she'd brought with her to England.

Vicky held it up so Darryl could read the title on the spine.

The Century of Revolution, 1603–1714, by some guy named Christopher Hill.

There was a time when Darryl would have wondered why the Schoolmarm From Hell would have given one of her precious books to a twenty-one year old English girl betrothed to one Darryl McCarthy, a once-respectable West Virginia hillbilly.

But no longer. He knew the answer.

"God help us all," Darryl said.

The Mason residence
Grantville, State of Thuringia-Franconia
January 20, 1635

"Relax, Arnold," said Mike McCarthy, Jr. "We're just here to wish the kid happy birthday."

Arnold Mason's concentration was mostly on Mike McCarthy Senior, however. Who, for his part, smiled and held up the gift-wrapped package in his hands.

"It's not a bomb, Arnold. You can inspect it if you want."

Mason made a little snorting sound. "I never thought you were *that* nuts, Mike." The gate to the front yard was already open, so Mason just made a little sweeping gesture. "Come on in."

Central Germany in mid-January had been cold even in the universe Grantville had come from, with average temperatures hovering around the freezing point—just about where they'd been for Grantville itself. In the seventeenth century, right in the middle of the Little Ice Age, the average temperatures were well below freezing.

It was an unusually warm day, this particular twentieth of January, but still not warm enough that anyone wanted to spend much time outside. So the birthday party was being held indoors.

The noise level was impressive. Six-year-old children are not much given to sedate and quiet conversations at any time, much less at an officially sanctioned party. And the Mason house seemed to be full of them.

Mike McCarthy Senior was a little surprised. The Cromwell

children hadn't been in Grantville for more than a couple of months or so. He wouldn't have thought they'd have made this many friends so quickly.

Something of his surprise showed in his face. His son smiled crookedly. "You haven't had school-age kids in a long time, Dad. Grantville's changed a lot, that way. Used to be a town of old farts, now it's full of kids—and the schoolteachers make a point of encouraging the kids to socialize."

A woman's voice spoke behind them. "It's a deliberate policy, which we instituted right after the Ring of Fire once we saw how many immigrants we were getting."

The McCarthys turned and saw Vickie Mason, holding a big birthday cake in her hands. They hadn't noticed her coming up.

"That's right," said Mike Junior. "You work in the school system, don't you?"

"I'm the secretary to the superintendent of schools." She peered at the package in Mike Senior's hand. "Is that for the birthday boy?"

"Uh, yeah."

"Do I need to have trained dogs sniff at it? If it's food, will I need to have it tasted first?"

McCarthy scowled at her. "Damn it, Vickie—"

"Don't you 'dammit' me, Mike McCarthy. I've seen you at the Thuringen Gardens—and at least two bars back up-time—on St. Patrick's Day. Hell, any day you have too much to drink. I'll give you this much, you've got a pretty decent singing voice. Even if that Irish brogue you put on when you sing *A Nation Once Again* is thick enough to cut with a knife."

"What I keep telling him," chipped in his son, smiling. "But it's just a birthday present, Vickie. I packed it myself, seeing as how they used to belong to me."

"What are they?"

"You'll see."

Mike Senior even joined in singing "Happy Birthday," although he might have choked a little when they got to the final refrain.

Happy birthday to you,
Happy birthday to you,
Happy birthday, Henry Cromwell,
Happy birthday to youuuuuuuuuuu....

He ate a slice of cake, too, and didn't choke at all. Perhaps his spirits were picked up when he saw that the birthday boy was delighted with the gifts he got from the McCarthys and spent the rest of the day charging around wearing the presents Mike Junior had been given on his sixth birthday, back in 1959 (up-time calendar) and which had now been passed on to Oliver Cromwell's youngest child. Perched on Henry's head, a green Irish tweed cap, with a scarf around his neck—green, of course—decorated with Celtic crosses.

"You oughta be ashamed of yourself," Vickie Mason said to him.

Mike Senior finished swallowing his slice of cake. "I am so far beyond shame it isn't funny. At this point, I'm just clutching to the hope that my son Darryl knows what the hell he's doing."

"You do realize how crazy that sounds?"

Cast of Characters

Royalty and Nobility

Charles Stuart	By the Grace of God King of England, Scotland, France and Ireland, Defender of the Faith etc. Popularly styled the Cripple King.
Richard Boyle	Earl of Cork, of the peerage of Ireland
James Graham	Earl of Montrose and Chief of Clan Graham
Archibald Campbell	Lord Lorne, heir to the earldom of Argyll and *de facto* Chief of Clan Campbell
Donald Mackay	Lord Reay, Chief of Clan Mackay and colonel-in-chief of the Mackay Regiment
Julie Mackay, née Sims	Swedish baroness and noted markswoman
Robert Mackay	Baron Mackay, nobleman without the peerage of Scotland

Knights, Gentry, Clergy and Commoners

Andrew Lennox — Papal Knight and Major of Horse, USEMC, also late of the Green Regiment

Sir Henry Steward — Justice of the Peace

Dr. James Hannay — Divine and Dean of St. Giles'

Nicholas Pedley, esq. — Justice of the Peace

Oliver Cromwell — Gentleman, together with Robert, Oliver Jr., Bridget, Henry and Elizabeth, his children

Alexander MacKay — Retired Colonel of Horse, formerly of the Green Regiment of Sweden

Darryl McCarthy — Military attaché in the diplomatic service of the United States of Europe

Stephen Hamilton — Yeoman Warder

Anthony Leebrick — Captain of Horse and Soldier of Fortune

Patrick Walsh — Lieutenant of Horse and Soldier of Fortune

Richard Towson — Lieutenant of Horse and Soldier of Fortune

Gayle Mason — Radio operator in the diplomatic service of the United States of Europe

Janet MacPherson — Widow, of Canongate, nr. Edinburgh

Victoria Walsh — East London girl of practical disposition

Meg — An auld wifie of Edinburgh, in service to the Baron Mackay

William Finnegan — Cultured *torai* in unspecified service to the Earl of Cork

Michel Ducos — Huguenot activist and leader of the Party of God